Stef Ann Holm

POCKET BOOKS

New York   London   Toronto   Sydney   Tokyo   Singapore

This book is a work of fiction. Names, characters, places and
incidents are either products of the author's imagination or are used
fictitiously. Any resemblance to actual events or locales or persons,
living or dead, is entirely coincidental.

An *Original* Publication of POCKET BOOKS

 POCKET BOOKS, a division of Simon & Schuster Inc.
1230 Avenue of the Americas, New York, NY 10020

ISBN: 0-671-74125-X

First Pocket Books printing January 1993

10 9 8 7 6 5 4 3 2 1

POCKET and colophon are registered trademarks of
Simon & Schuster Inc.

Cover art by Heide Oberheide

Printed in the U.S.A.

"ARE YOU READY FOR YOUR LESSON?" ANTHONY DRAWLED.

"M-my lesson?" Liberty replied vaguely.

"You aren't scared?"

"I am not."

Her low voice brought his head up. The desire to kiss her had been pulling at him all evening but he hadn't wanted to scare her off. He longed to be reminded of how good she felt in his arms. To explore the reasons why she fascinated him so.

"You are perfect." The gentleness in his voice startled him.

Anthony bent his head, his lips barely kissing hers. The kiss that had been suspended between them grew to a deep need within Anthony. He felt her resist, stiffen, then pull back. He saw the turmoil in her gaze as she fought to keep her distance.

"Don't kiss me. There isn't an audience to watch the performance and I'm not a good enough actress to play the part with only you."

Books by Stef Ann Holm

Liberty Rose
Seasons of Gold

Published by POCKET BOOKS

For my sister, Carrie,

*and with
special thanks to Kathy Sage, Barbara
Ankrum, Sue Rich and Caroline Tolley—three
talented writers and one editor who saw
beyond my words and helped them grow.*

*Also, a hug to Barry who gave me
the "big book" when I so desperately
needed its wisdom.*

Chapter
1

Summer 1767
Norfolk Borough
Virginia Colony

"I NEED A WOMAN, FEATHERS."

"Beg pardon, sir?"

Sitting behind the impressively carved desk in his study, Anthony Fielding crumpled the letter that he'd just read and pitched it. "My grandsire is sailing in from Antigua for a visit. I'll need a woman for the duration of his stay."

Hiram Feathers, attired in perfect servant's blue, bent at the waist and retrieved the crushed sheet from the floor. He humbly set it on the Lord and Master's disorderly desktop. "Very good, sir. Where shall I find one?"

"I'm thinking." Anthony tugged the navy ribbon free of his long hair and ran his fingers through the strands at his temple. The simple movement caused the inside of his head to smart as if it had been struck soundly by the tip of a coachman's whip. A night of all fours card gaming and sangaree in the Sign of the Mermaid with Cheswick had left him in the disagreeable dregs of alcohol aftereffects. He hadn't planned on drinking so much. Returning home with the first rays of dawn to find his grandsire's message waiting for him, freshly delivered by the post rider, snuffed out all thoughts of a lengthy sleep.

Forced to endure the pressure accumulating behind his

tired eyes, Anthony shuttered his lids in deep thought, then blinked them open again as the pain in his brain mounted. "Strike me blue, I can't think with my mind shrouded from spirits and cigars!"

"I'll have Cook make up a tonic."

"Yes, yes." Anthony barely acknowledged the suggestion as he shrugged out of his claret-colored coat. Slipping his fingers inside his silk waistcoat, he deftly unfastened the few gold buttons remaining in their holes. "But first the woman."

Hiram Feathers attentively stood at the edge of Anthony's desk, his hands neatly folded behind his ramrod straight back.

Anthony glared at his middle-aged valet and ran his thumb across his stubbled chin. "God help me, am I so wretched I can't think of one respectable woman who would tolerate me for a small length of time? Have I offended them all?"

"I wouldn't say that, sir "

"But you may think it."

"Very good, sir."

Anthony untied his cravat and let the tails hang over the front of his shoulders.

Feathers cleared his throat as if to say something, then stifled the sound.

"Yes?" Anthony looked up with expectation.

"If I may dare say, sir."

"Anything."

"Wouldn't it be wiser to admit to your grandfather you aren't interested in marriage at this time?"

"The devil, no!" Anthony brought his lace-cuffed fist down on the top of the desk. "I won't shatter his hopes for the future of the Fielding name. Better to let him think I'm entertaining the idea. Twice he has set upon me this year to see if I've found a woman to wed. I'm fond of the old man and I'm not in disagreement with the matter of an heir. But a wedding at this time . . ." Anthony paused. "My own parents' marriage—that disastrous union—is still too fresh in my mind."

"Aye," Feathers agreed slowly, as if recollecting something. He drew his fingertips across the bushy white brow that crested his gray eyes in a continuous line. "My own parents' marriage boasted no garden of Eden, either, sir."

A lapse in conversation transpired. The regular strokes of a wall clock's movements drifted through the darkened, curtain-drawn study until Anthony lifted his gaze. "Eden? Eden, you say?"

Anthony flipped back the slanted top of his writing box and began scouring the previously opened packets. Glancing at the seals, he discarded them one by one.

"Your pardon, sir?"

"Eden. Eden Bennet, the daughter of Montgomery Bennet, the man from Williamsburg whose ship I'm building."

"Aye. Of course." Feathers's steadfast face showed no expression except for a hint of dread skittering across his mouth.

"'Tis here!" Anthony held a letter; the Bennet wax seal had been broken. He unfolded the parchment and scanned the contents. "They should have arrived yesterday. I've a meeting with Montgomery the day after tomorrow to go over the final details of his snow rig. They're staying at the Blue Anchor coffeehouse. Go there and extend my home and hospitality, Feathers."

The valet's cheeks tinged a subtle shade of red. "I dare say, sir, aren't you forgetting your prior meeting with Miss Bennet?"

"What?"

"The cotillion at the Blakemore's."

Anthony sat back in his armchair and crossed his buff-breeched legs at the knee. "Ah . . . that." The night five months ago slowly came back to him with haunting shadows. Her compliant airs and sublime blond beauty—he preferred his women's crowning glories to be powdered to dull perfection—made it easy for him to initiate a year-long fling. He'd been having fun until she turned into a pretty piece of foolery by challenging him to ask her father for her hand. When he'd refused, she'd gone off in a fit of agitation, vowing she'd never grace his company again. Plague him, that little catastrophe *would* come back to him now when he direly needed a fiancée.

Unlocking the left drawer on his writing table, Anthony pulled up a false bottom and withdrew a heavy purse. "Take this to Winthrop's Jewelers. Eden had her fancy set on a pendant necklace—Winthrop will know which one. Buy it. Coax her with it if you must. Tell her I apologize for our last encounter and she can depend on me to be more . . . congenial."

Feathers took the leather pouch and weighed it in his palm. "Very good, sir."

"'Tis done then. I'll be waiting for you to return. My grandsire could arrive by the week's end if the weather is with him. There's no time for dalliance."

Concealing the money in his coat, Feathers prudently voiced, "And if the lady refuses, sir?"

"She can't." Anthony meshed his hands together, his forefinger toying with the signet ring he wore.

The idea of misleading Eden throbbed in Anthony's tired head, for it proclaimed him the blackguard all the genteel ladies of Virginia thought him to be. A misguided sot whose frame of mind was rumored to be unstable.

Damn his soul, why couldn't he be the man his grandsire wanted? As always when Anthony recalled the answer, he got The Craving.

The crystal decanter on his desk sparkled under a borrowed shine of light from the flaming taper before him. Indulgently Anthony poured himself a breakfast of sherry.

Swallowing the wine, he acknowledged that the reasons for his bitterness lay buried with his father, his death owed to the heart-piercing sword wound left in him by John Perkins.

Thwack!

Liberty Courtenay hadn't been prepared to feel the volley of hot needles shooting from her fist up and over the length of her arm. She shook out her hand, wagging her reddened fingertips in front of the fast-bruising skin around John Perkins's right eye.

"There, sir, take back your blow." Liberty refrained from cupping the slight mound of her breast where the old bag of bones had vulgarly squeezed it.

"Stab my vitals!" he cursed at her as his eye began to water profusely from her punch. "Insolent baggage! Come fair, come foul—"

Liberty didn't wait to hear more and dashed clear of Perkins's irate flood of obscenities. She quickly lifted the bands of her pocket-hoop farthingale to clear the narrow doorway and bounded free of the rooming chamber she'd just made up, before he could accost her again.

Her footfall thumped intently down the runnered-stairs that led to the welcoming lobby of the Blue Anchor coffee-house. The hazel-brown calico of her serviceable frock danced above her ankles offering a show here and there of the simply embroidered figures clocking her black stockings.

Too soon she heard Perkins at her heels, condemning her with streaks of indignant profanity Breathlessly she leaped from the final step past the open-fronted secretary desk where Mr. Cyril Lamont, the ordinary's proprietor, stood with a servant man wearing a cocked hat; both gentlemen's mouths fell agape.

At Perkins's call for her to stop, Liberty skidded short of a pedestal and snatched up a vase, dethroned it of its posies and readied it to hurl. On the hysterically stern warning of Mr. Lamont, she sobered, reconsidering what she was about to do. As much as she wanted to cuff John Perkins, her upstairs chambermaid's wages could never be stretched to cover the cost of the expensive glassware. Grudgingly, she set the vase down with exaggerated care.

Perkins panted to a halt in the vestibule, his braided white periwig askew on his sweat-beaded forehead. He took out a large square of linen from his coat pocket and sopped his brow. "I dare swear, the impertinent slut struck me! Me, a man of the Assembly, a figure of authority. Lamont, what pretext can you offer for this sort of ravaging female employee?"

Hands twitching, Cyril Lamont groped for his snuffbox. Before he spoke, he inhaled a tiny pinch of the pulverized tobacco and promptly sneezed. Sniffing, he expounded, "If you would be so good as to allow me to make amends."

The older man beside Lamont stared curiously at Liberty, but given the exhausting circumstances, she paid him no mind.

Perkins produced a silver comb and ran it through his disheveled hairpiece. "'Twould be justice for her to be put on public display. I advise lashing her to a ducking stool till she is good and soused, promising better deportment. That ought to take the vinegar out of her."

"I should say!" Liberty exclaimed incredulously. "'Tis *you*, poor sir, who should be shackled in irons till penitence touches your soul. I did not deliver the first assault."

Lamont fairly twittered at the spectacle playing before him. Already a handful of guests sifted out of the adjoining taproom to behold the scene of confusion.

Since Perkins held an esteemed position in politics, the attention made him visibly uncomfortable. He did his best to keep his swelling eye obscured, tilting his head toward the wall when he spoke. "As you are aware, I am a frequent caller here and I demand retribution."

"And you, good gentleman, shall have it," Lamont assured. He thrust back his narrow shoulders and ardently addressed Liberty. "You are no longer under the employ of the Blue Anchor. Should you take it into your head to ever cross through these doors again, I shall have no recourse but to prosecute you. Consider your week's earnings payment for damages done to Mr. Perkins."

"'Tis not fair!" Seeing her outburst had fallen on deaf ears, Liberty raised her chin. Defiant and with her nose angled toward the offending John Perkins, she warranted, "What I would say to you were I not a lady."

"To be sure, I'm cowering," he smugly huffed, then gathered his dignity and stalked from the inn, not bothering to return upstairs for the hat that had been knocked off his head by Liberty's sound smack.

Liberty's heart pulsed so sternly in her chest, she thought it would spring free of her ribs. She gave it her altogether to control the hot tears pooling on her lashes, vowing not a single droplet would fall. It was an unforgivable situation, indeed. And she had been made to suffer for it while Perkins remained blameless.

Taking her leave, Liberty departed the Blue Anchor coffeehouse in much the same manner as she'd entered it earlier that morning; with a slight swing to her shoulders and a smile on her face. But once free of the confining ordinary, she squeezed her eyelids closed and the lift to her mouth narrowed painfully. She bit her lower lip, finally tasting the tears that ran down her cheeks.

She walked with a wooden stride, not aware of where she went or why. Following the cry of the hook-beaked gulls that circled noisily over the Elizabeth River, she drifted past one public house after another. Her focus became a singular pinpoint of dread: She was unemployed.

How could she ever hope to save Aunt Ophelia from the debtor's prison now?

Inside the Blue Anchor, Hiram Feathers had recovered from the uproar he'd just witnessed. Lud! What a chirping creature she was to take on the varlet John Perkins! He knew too well the devious mind of the man, being privy to the misery he'd imposed on the Fielding family. A pity the young thing lost her employ, but who was he to interject himself in affairs with no rhyme nor reason?

And yet, Feathers couldn't cease his thoughts of her, long after Lamont had dutifully apologized for the fanfare and had begun an earnest look in the registrar books to check on the Bennets' traveling arrangements. Feathers's mind kept returning to the girl's plight. What would Fielding think of her?

Propping his cocked hat under his arm, Feathers tapped at the braided trim on its rim while staring out the window. Unbidden, he pictured Eden Bennet. Genteelly bred, the Bennet minx coveted the Lord and Master's good fortune— Feathers knew it to be truth as on occasion he overheard her speak of Anthony's exorbitant wealth to her father. When in Anthony's company, she went along with all his modes of conversation and topics, and Feathers didn't doubt her temperament would agree with anyone whose bank account was filled full of pound sterling. A cunning vixen, that's what she was.

Lamont's nasally voice penetrated Feathers's thoughts, drawing him out with a shake of his head as he faced the foppish proprietor.

"'Twould seem the Bennet party has been detained," Lamont said, looking up from his record book. "By all appearances, for at least a fortnight due to a business matter that needed Mister Bennet's urgent attention."

Hard-pressed to conceal his relief, Feathers anchored his hat on his curly wig. "'Tis of no matter now. Good tithing to you."

Feathers gleefully footed himself out the coffeehouse door to mix in with Norfolk's waterfront crowd. Naturally the Lord and Master would be perturbed, but the devil take him. He would do better to find a woman who challenged him, rather than one who pretended to crawl behind him with the wit of a turtle, all the while calculating how quickly she could go through his money.

As Feathers walked the muddy thoroughfare lined with shops packed full of foreign goods, modest residences and low-lying warehouses, he found himself heading in the opposite direction of Fielding Manor. He charted a course toward the edge of the channel where wharves were piled high with boxes and barrels; where regional timbers bound fast together by the crosspieces notched in them, jetting out into the water—the perfect docks for square-riggers. The inlet brimmed with cargo ships from as far as the British West Indies.

The leather purse weighed against his breastbone. He'd had himself a peek at the insides. A generous amount, to be sure. Eden Bennet didn't deserve a necklace this sum would fetch and perhaps God had been on his shoulder this morning seconding that very thought. Feathers recalled when he had gone to the jeweler's. Winthrop had been engaged in a heated spat with the neighboring merchant. Ignored, Feathers had waited a patient interval for service.

When none came his way, he chose to come back when the air had cleared to neutrality.

A stroke of luck that he hadn't.

Feathers came upon the chambermaid sitting on a sturdy bench that gave off a view of the active harbor. She sat there, a forlorn blush to her skin, the raven color of her hair set off against the white of her tatted mobcap. Her slender hands, ensconced in the valley of homespun red created by her apron, in no way looked lethal. Save for the scarlet mark on the knuckles of the right one, Feathers would have bet his teeth, her fingers did nothing but balance a sewing needle.

He watched a crystalline tear slip down the arch of her delicately formed cheekbone.

An idea suddenly came to him. When he thought more on it, he realized he'd been forming one ever since setting eyes on this beauty. He would get *her* for Fielding. Maybe she, with her backbone and nerve, could bring the Lord and Master out of his cups. She was an absolute contrast to Eden Bennet's pale hair and skin. And he could attest to the fact, this young thing spoke her mind.

"My dear lady," he said softly, so as to not startle her, "may I offer this?"

Darting upward, her hazel eyes mirrored suspicion and he guessed in that instant, she'd decided whether or not he was harmless. He must have gained her favor, for she nodded and accepted the muckender he held out to her. She dabbed the soft lace handkerchief under her eyes, then soundly blew her nose in it.

"I thank you. 'Tis not my nature to cry. I seem to be caught unprepared." Returning the muckender to him, Feathers wadded it back into his great, royal blue pocket.

Feathers smiled down on her face; a face that fascinated him. At the risk of sounding like a lecher, he phrased the question as best he could without being imprudent. "My dear lady, 'twould seem you are out of hire. I've a means in which you could earn a great deal of money without compromising your integrity."

She made no move, not even to blink the thick, dark

lashes framing her greenish eyes. Before he lost his courage, he recklessly blurted, "By your grace, come with me and 'tis a fair purse I'll give you for your effort."

Had he been a year older than his two score and five, Feathers may not have jumped aside as quickly as he had. He ducked his head in time to send the girl's fist whooshing in midair. "Mistress!" he cried out. "I can assure you I mean you no ill!"

"'Tis a cruel man you are! First winning my faith then beating at it as you would a dusty rug!" Liberty had risen from her bench in blind outrage. She took a swing at him, no longer thinking him a kindhearted gentleman nothing but true in character. Was this day doomed to be filled with lewd suggestions?

"Please, my dear lady, permit me to explain myself!" His stout face had soberly paled and he put his hand over the width of his coat collar, as if to still his heart. Liberty noticed the odd bulge beneath his palm and took a step backward. Did he mask a pistol, or was there indeed a valuable purse? The beseeching glint in his charcoal eyes made her ever-so-slightly sympathetic to his distress.

"What have you to say then?"

"'Tis not myself I request you entertain. 'Tis my employer, Mister Anthony Fielding." He said the name with emphasis, as if the title should cause some recognition in her. It did not. Though Norfolk stretched only a mile in length, she'd just recently settled in town, having spent her eighteen years in its country border.

Feathers straightened his cocked hat. "Fielding is in need of a woman to appear as if she's, well, er, interested in him matrimonially for the benefit of his grandfather."

"What sort of ninny do you take me for? You should be effecting your search in the illegitimate taverns."

"'Tis not a misbegotten wench he seeks, rather one with—with your attributes and resemblance. One with your spirit and character; your vivid coloring and dramatic temperament." His expression grew unreadable, as if he smothered a fib.

"What is your name?" Liberty finally asked after a lengthy deliberation.

"Feathers." The servant man bowed at the waist. "Hiram Feathers, dear lady. Valet."

Liberty slumped down on the bench again and gazed at the sandpipers milling around an oyster bucket. "If what you say is true, there must be something dreadfully wrong with the man that he has to buy a woman to feign attention toward him."

Gliding around the bench's back, Feathers plopped himself next to Liberty. "There is naught out of whack in his head, if that is what troubles you. Truth be told, the Lord and Master is arrogant, domineering, incorrigible, and damnably too handsome for his own good. But should you ever tell him my observation, I'll contradict every word of it."

"I'm not in the habit of tattling." Despite herself, Liberty smiled. What a curious man Feathers was in his sober valet garb and cauliflower-styled peruke. Surely what he proposed could be nothing more than fabrication. And yet, one look into his eager eyes said he was quite serious. Imagine! She'd heard of buying affection, but never attention.

Her glance strayed to the lump in his coat. She didn't dare ask him how much he offered—as if she would even consider it! But then she thought of Aunt Ophelia being sentenced to jail. Pressing her fingers to her lips, she shook off any notion of compliance, but wound up blurting out, "What would you have me do?"

Feathers beamed. "Honor Fielding Manor with your presence and for the well-being of his grandfather, pray act as if you cannot bear to be parted from the Lord and Master's company."

"The unprincipled man."

"Nay. Fielding can be quite principled. But 'tis best if he doesn't know of our dealings."

Liberty rubbed at her sore knuckles. "I'm afraid I don't understand."

Leaning closer, Feathers whispered in a low tone. "I was

sent to fetch Miss Eden Bennet as a houseguest"—he delayed his thought to curl his upper lip—"but, alas, the lady's arrival has been postponed. Fielding's grandfather is due to weigh anchor any day, so you can see the turmoil all this has caused. 'Tis one thing for Fielding to enlist an unsuspecting Eden Bennet, but quite another were he to know *you*, dear lady, were of my own choosing. He wouldn't be happy about it, not at all. I humbly entreat you to accept my offer; he needs a woman such as yourself."

" 'Tis a fine tale you spin, Mister Feathers, but you have overlooked one important factor. I have never been in Mister Fielding's company. Why should he receive me?"

Hesitating, Feathers pressed his fingertips together. "Well, Fielding drinks . . . a little. Quite a lot actually when he's on a binge."

"What?"

Feathers endeavored to calm her. "We'll simply tell him you were previously introduced on your last journey to Norfolk. Proud as he is, he'll never dispute his muddled memory. He'll accept our fabrication as true. And as for the matter of staying at the house, he shall be told there were no suitable accommodations available and I graciously extended Fielding Manor to you." Feathers wrung his fingers together, as if going down a list in his head, finalizing the plan he'd whisked up. "I dare speak with no intentions of insulting you, mistress, but you do know how to act like a gentlewoman," he rushed on seeing the color rise in Liberty's cheeks, "at least until he's used to you?"

"Mister Feathers, I most certainly know how to act like a gentlewoman. I may not be of wealth as your employer is, but my aunt raised me to be proper and mind my manners. Correct deportment is something taught, not born into one. 'Tis only when I'm provoked I forget myself."

"Then you will accept?"

Liberty rose. "Nay, I'm afraid you've wasted your afternoon. I could not possibly compromise myself in such a way. I thank you for the offer and wish you well in your search."

She'd executed two even strides when the vibrancy of Feathers's voice caught her.

"'Tis one hundred gold guineas plus notes worth four hundred pounds!"

The high heel to her pointed-toe shoe never touched ground for the third step; she whirled around with a quick breath of astonishment. "F-five hundred and five pounds?"

"Aye."

Liberty swallowed. Five hundred and five pounds! The implications made her feel faint. It would be enough to pay Mrs. McKeand for the damages Aunt Ophelia had caused to her boardinghouse from the explosion. With a slight amount left over to start anew. To get themselves back on their feet and start saving for their salon once again.

But Ophelia Fairweather wouldn't tolerate a man like Anthony Fielding. Her aunt was a revolutionist in her own rights, taking on those who begged to differ with her liberal ideas. Aunt Ophelia wouldn't like buying her freedom for this kind of price. And what of she, Liberty Courtenay? Could she pretend to be attracted to a drunk?

Oh, but the thought of getting her aunt free and having to suffer out a couple of weeks in this man Fielding's company would be worth it. She would abide him. The price to pay—her aunt's imprisonment—was too costly if she didn't. Her aunt's life was at stake and she'd just lost her job. She had to get money. Somehow.

Raising her lashes, Liberty's gaze met Feathers's. She nodded, breathing three words of consent. "I'll do it."

Feathers laughed. "'Tis a humanitarian deed you have done this day, dear lady!"

"'Tis no deed at all, rather a business arrangement."

"Call it what you like. I call it the smash that will spill his cup dry!"

"Before you applaud, there is a condition I must request."

Feathers halted his jubilant bounce with a ruffle of his singular brow. "And that is?"

"That my aunt be allowed to come and act as chaperon."

Relieved, Feathers granted her a wide smile. "Of course!

'Twould be all the better. How ridiculous of me for not thinking of it before. I'll have the Master's best carriage brought around to your residence, the . . ."

"Running Footman."

". . . ah, yes, the Running Footman, asking for . . ."

"Liberty Courtenay and Ophelia Fairweather . . ."

"Aye! Mistress Courtenay and Madame Fairweather in one hour."

Liberty glanced at the near noon sun and firmly shook her head. Her beehive couldn't be moved until sunset when the workers came back. "That wouldn't do. You must make it a wagon and I couldn't possibly be ready until early evening."

A little puzzled, Feathers gave her a shrug. "Then, 'tis a wagon you shall have at five o'clock."

"Thank you."

Feathers bowed once more and Liberty bade him hold his leave. "I must forewarn you about my aunt."

"Aye . . . ?"

"She's a rebel."

"Lud!" Feathers exclaimed. "Against the Crown?"

"Against arrogant, domineering and incorrigible men."

CHAPTER TWO

Chapter
2

DUST.

Ophelia Fairweather noted its accumulation on the marble chimneypiece and engraved candle stands flanking the pedestal table. It dulled the oiled hip-raised paneling and coated the fringed olive draperies—evidence they hadn't been opened in quite some time.

She shook her head at the ill-kept welcoming room, astonished by the neglect and opulence. This man Fielding disgracefully ignored his household. At least the bedrooms Mister Feathers, the valet, had shown her and Liberty earlier, had been hastily cleaned.

"I'll trumpet my sentiments again, my pet." Ophelia ran her finger across the tabletop and left a trailing imprint. "The purse, though 'twas my saving grace, may have been a grave mistake to accept. We could have managed somehow."

Ophelia clicked her tongue as Liberty stepped back from the seven-foot painted figurehead in the corner. She didn't think it suitable for her niece to examine the grandiose carving. The woman's long-haired head tilted upward; the tresses wrapped around her naked body, her shapely leg posed in a forward step.

15

"It was the only way," Liberty disagreed, her attention still focused on the Venuslike statuette.

Ophelia sighed at her niece's preoccupation. She had her doubts about this charade. She didn't know this Fielding and the little Liberty told her——and what she was seeing for herself, for she had no appreciation of his ill-placed nude model——she didn't like. If only she hadn't unintentionally blown the roof off the Running Footman!

She'd been inventing a new face ointment, experimenting with sulfur. Finding herself low on essence of roses, she set out to acquire some. Barely through the picket gate, a blast sounded behind her and the sky flowered with torn shingles. The destruction was tracked to blackened walls and the tidy hole in her room's ceiling. She admitted she'd been heating olive oil; she'd also been using carmine and liquor of ammonia, gum and spirits. She hadn't been sure which one set off the eruption. Thankfully Liberty hadn't been home and no one had been hurt, but Mrs. McKeand had threatened her with incarceration if she didn't repay the damages straightaway. Someone had to pay for the carpenters to reframe the roof and lathers to replaster the walls.

She'd been saved from prison with Anthony Fielding's money, only to risk a new sort of confinement to justify its acceptance. Even knowing there had been a small sum left to put toward her salon hadn't made her feel much better.

Somewhere in the hallway, a door clicked closed, then rhythmic footfalls sounded across the oaken floor. Hiram Feathers appeared in the welcoming room, his face flushed.

"Dear ladies, I beg you, let the introductions rest for this evening. 'Twill be much better in the morning."

Ophelia met Liberty's gaze, then looked at Feathers. Upon meeting the valet earlier in the evening, she'd rather liked the odd fellow. More to the point, he slightly reminded her of her late husband, Benjamin Hogg. Fond of him or not, the man was obviously hiding something. "Has Fielding had a change of direction?" Ophelia dared ask. "He's come to his senses and like all decent men, decided to win a woman's affection the ordinary way?"

"Madam! Discretion, please. 'Tis naught like that!" Feathers exclaimed nervously.

"We shall meet with him now, or take our presence elsewhere."

"Aunt," Liberty cautioned in an apologizing tone on Feathers's behalf. "If Mister Fielding is unable to accommodate us, maybe it would be best—"

"Pish!" In a swish of her rose brocade skirts, Ophelia exited the room and headed for the chamber from which she'd heard Feathers depart.

The valet ran ahead, the long tails to his blue coat flapping in his wake. He sprang to the paneled door, spreading himself in front of it. "Pray don't go in there!"

"What has he, another woman?" Ophelia's crystal blue eyes narrowed and she protectively looked at Liberty who had sprinted after them both.

"No!" Feathers denied.

"Rubbish!" Ophelia, though small boned and slight in stature, would never call herself too delicate to face any obstacle. On the contrary, she could be as explosive as the blunderbuss packed away up in her room and she intended to prove it to Feathers. "Aside," she commanded in a voice that demanded compliance.

Helplessly Feathers slumped his shoulders and released his hold. "He shall fleece me till there's naught but bloody bone left. Lud! I believe I hear Cook calling me." On that contrived excuse, he fled down the hallway.

Ophelia opened the door none too delicately; the hinges cried out fair warning to whatever presumed indecencies were taking place inside.

Liberty held back—in the frugal amount of time it would take to pull the weights on a clock—before deciding if there was to be any damage done. Her breathing uneven, she entered the room.

It took a few blinks before Liberty's eyes adjusted to the dimness of the study. Shadows played across the furniture and walls in varying hues of red caused by a tinted hurricane globe covering a fat candle. Liberty stood next to Ophelia and took in as many details as she could under the eerie glow of light.

The room belonged to a man. His waistcoat and outer coat had been stripped, discarded over the back of an armchair. A game of single-hand cards had been left unfinished on the desk, alongside a silver-handled pistol. The cluttered desktop was strewn with letters, quills and a knocked-over tinderbox.

Liberty ventured another step when her shoe encountered a soft lump. "Oh!" she cried out, afraid whatever she'd trod on, lived and breathed. On closer inspection she saw a crimson throw pillow that had been tossed to the floor.

Trying to calm her imaginative heartbeat, she veered her attention to the scarlet-washed walls. Shelf upon shelf of books stacked one side of an unlit hearth; a sword hung above the mantel. The other wall lay claim to a mysterious diagonal cache of heavily swagged draperies trimmed in gold.

While Ophelia poked around the writing box area, Liberty investigated the improvised alcove. She'd barely come upon it when she stopped herself short with a stifled gasp. Sprawled out on a dark velvet-upholstered settee, slumbered a man on his back. His lengthy height could not be accommodated by the slight sofa as both his left arm and left leg brushed the floor while the bulk of his weight was distributed on the solitary cushion.

Liberty moved forward, cautiously quiet, though why he hadn't awakened up to now was a riddle. They'd made enough noise to accomplish the deed. Leaning over the man, Liberty examined his features. He wore his own hair, the color indiscernible in the dim light, though appearing dark. Given the tilt of his head, the strands fell several inches beyond the expanse of his shoulder. The line from the bridge of his nose curved masculinely and straight by all standards. His eyes, closed and peaceful appearing, contrasted the brows above them; they arched in a way that could be called discontented. The entire outline of his face planed out in rigid contours; square for the jaw, angled for the cheekbones and full for the lips.

He stirred with a groan and Liberty took a quick hop backward. Anticipation sketched a path through her as she waited for him to open his eyes. He did not. His rhythmic breathing resumed, broken only by the mechanical workings of a nearby clock.

She knew she should call her aunt, but couldn't summon the voice to do so. For some unaccountable reason, she didn't want to share the moment. She was certain now, she'd stumbled onto the elusive Anthony Fielding. She felt a fluttering in her heart, its familiar winged whisper petitioned without her permission. It was not the first time she'd had these feelings.

She gazed at Anthony's shirt, the whiteness appearing pink under the hazy candlelight. The expensive cut formed a billowing cloud down his flat abdomen where the tails had been yanked free of his tight broadcloth breeches. Extraordinary long legs stretched out, his feet sheathed in soft black leather jackboots that molded his calves.

The disquiet within her came again. The air pinched from her lungs as if her stays had been laced too tightly and she grew lightheaded. She vowed not to let the sensations overcome her; she'd experienced them before, save never so strongly. Three previous times to be exact. In the company of the stocking maker's clerk, an oyster peddler and more recently, Barlary White, the lad who drove the milk dray.

To be sure, Ophelia called the fleeting spells lovesickness.

Her aunt had warned her the yearnings were nothing but the passing of her whimsical youth, her longing to have a loving and nurturing relationship like her parents had when they were living. Liberty mulled over her aunt's warnings. She knew nothing of Anthony Fielding but what Hiram Feathers told her; not a pretty picture. Could a mere look into his face give her cause for lunacy? What had Mister Feathers said . . . Fielding was too handsome for his own good. Oh, how true!

Deep in the darkness of his numbed state of mind, Anthony felt someone touching him. Not actually making contact with him, but touching him with a heat, a beguiling presence he'd never encountered before. It definitely wasn't

Feathers. Over the past ten years he'd grown accustomed to barricading his valet's voice from his sleep. Feathers could loudly recite an entire work of literature and it would have no affect on him. No, this spirit was *female*.

By the mass! Which tavern wench had he expired in front of this time? He couldn't remember a single fragment of the encounter.

He dared not move his head for fear of it lopping free of his neck and spilling to the floor. The jagged pain in it acted no better than when he'd last recalled.

With extreme will, he peeked open the lid to his right eye. He saw the world through a red blur, thinking to himself he'd gone too far this time, his eyes permanently bloodshot. After careful reflection, he ascertained himself to be in the safety of his study. Though before breathing a sigh of relief, he inhaled rather than exhaled. A feminine fragrance so bewitching came to him he nearly rolled free of his trappings. He'd never been exposed to a perfume of such enchanting allure. Who the devil was in the room?

Cocking his head to the left, he chanced opening his other eye. Before he could clearly glean the image, he attempted to right himself—and damn him, succeeded. The effort splintered open his skull, sending a shower of white cinders in his gaze.

He heard a soft scream, glass breaking in the distance, and his own moan as he flopped backward on the settee with a miserable bounce of his head.

Clamping his eyes shut, Anthony gritted his teeth against the flames in his belly. His perception had deserted him, clipped short more times than a candle's wick.

Strike him down, from where had she come? The watered caverns of his mind, or did she really exist?

"Feathers!"

"I'm afraid Mister Feathers isn't here."

Her voice carried to him; throaty, though undeniably melodic. No matter the excruciating aftermath, he had to see for himself this was no apparition.

Anthony flickered his lids and focused his gaze on the reddish ceiling before turning his head. The bruising pulse at his temples subsided to a monotonous ringing in his ears and he gave the task another try, twisting the stiff muscles in his neck.

What he saw, practically rendered him sober. His mind had gone too far; a demented hoax played upon his wits. He'd thought the creature, from sound and smell alone, to be an incomparable beauty. Judas, the middle-aged woman though not hideous, didn't match the image his senses had roused.

She boldly stared, and he returned the examination with a narrowing of his eyelids. Hair the shade of ripe apricots was dressed in a high pompadour, tufted here and there with imitation pearls. The color of her eyes, though under the red light looked lavender, had to be blue. Her complexion, powdered white, was a nigh jarring contrast to her darkly rouged lips; just below her penciled brow, a diamond-shaped patch winked at him.

Anthony promptly took in her clothing. Beribboned and bedizened, laden with knots and nosegays and silver lace. Swallowing, he asked out of a shallow sense of duty, "Are you one of my household staff? A parlor maid?"

"I think not." Her answer relieved him; then it occurred to him there was a discrepancy in her voice. It differed from the one he'd heard beforehand.

From the doorway came, "I couldn't find Mister Feathers in my brief search, Aunt."

Anthony's gaze jetted to the dulcet voice; he had *not* imagined the enchanting sound.

"I feared continue as 'tis not my place to explore the house." The huskiness of her words drifted from the hallway light spilling in through the open door of his study.

He could not see her as her outline blended into shadow. Her footfall scraped over the floor, the sound of broken glass and sand gritting beneath her shoes.

The woman at his side spoke to her. "Mind your step, Liberty. I dropped the jar of his writing sand."

"Oh."

Anthony lifted himself up on his elbow, bracing for the whirling prisms floating through his head. They gradually passed and he slouched onto the settee's camel-back, his legs straight out before him.

"Is he ill?" the voice asked.

"No. 'Tis ghastly. He's been behind the cork."

Anthony overlooked the tart commentary from the embellished matron and appraised the little bit of fluff standing next to her.

No falsities—lockets, bracelets or scent-bags—interfered with the crown of natural raven curls framing her oval face. They hung freely about her shoulders, teasing her delicate complexion that hinted the whiteness of bone china. A lush red tinted her gracefully shaped mouth, which at this moment, parted inquisitively.

"You wouldn't be a parlor maid?" he quizzed the younger woman, but knowing the odds of that were poor to none in his favor.

She shook her head.

"As I figured." Anthony drew in his legs, bringing the heel to his right boot over his left knee. "Then, who, pray tell, are you?"

The matron took control and negotiated the situation. "Upon the invitation of your valet, we're your houseguests. I am Ophelia Fairweather and this is my niece, Liberty Courtenay. And if I may speak freely, 'tis a deplorable practice to receive your guests while full as a tick."

"So freely spoken." Crossing his arms over the frothy linen of his shirtfront, Anthony frowned. "You wag a green tongue, madam."

"Never green, Anthony Fielding. True-blue to gospel."

Vaulting his brows, Anthony looked to the young woman. She trifled with a small cluster of asters tucked into a black bowknot, one of many that ran down her yellow damask stomacher. A magenta petal fell free and floated to his booted calf; he didn't brush it off. "You're a quiet piece."

" 'Tis rare I'm quiet, sir."

"Then I'm privy to a monumental moment?"

"I can assure you, not as monumental as the one you've shown us. I understand now why my aunt says you're a man to be thrown off a roof."

"Ah, when she speaks, 'tis with the same comedy as the other. Please enlighten me as to what I've done to deserve such witticism?"

"On the contrary," she returned remorsefully. "I spoke in haste and an apology is due you. 'Tis just that I've never watched a man sleeping off his cups before. You quite fascinated me into forgetting my conduct." She raised her gaze to Ophelia. "We are under Mister Fielding's hospitality and it wouldn't do to insult him unjustly. Nonetheless, I don't suggest you take back your remarks; when truth is spoken, there is no need for repentance. Merely be on your guard for further offense."

"Strike me blue, 'twas a rarity indeed." Anthony captured the petal, absently toying with it between his thumb and forefinger, then he unfolded his legs. What affliction had stormed down on Feathers to cause him to invite these two women to his home? Especially, now, with the business of his grandsire's visit.

The black-haired mistress—what was her name?—Libby?—was the likes of which he'd never encountered. Saucy in speech, yet innocent in appeal. He could fairly see the aunt's spread wing tucking her niece to the safety of her down breast. At another time, he may have been inclined to give the maid chase. In dazed exasperation, Anthony questioned his sanity. What was he thinking? His fondness had always been for women with light hair.

Confusion circled around his head like an unwanted flying pest. His muddled mind hadn't cleared enough for him to rationalize the sudden, implausible thought of the girl's charm. He needed to get up and walk off the delirium corked inside his body; to look upon the curious situation Feathers had initiated and think of a way to rectify things.

Liberty took an anxious step backward as Anthony grasped hold of the settee's arm and brought himself to his feet. His mammoth height amazed her and she tilted her chin upward to take in every inch of him. The collar of his shirt had been loosened leaving a wide slash of dark skin at his neck exposed. He swayed, only momentarily, before blowing the lengthy strands of his hair off his forehead. She almost offered her assistance, then thought better of it. He seemed to be a proud man—though what merited that pride when it came from the repercussions of a grog bottle's bottom—she couldn't fathom.

She gave him his wake and he made it to his desk, bracing his fingertips on its edge. With an unsteady hand, he worked the tinder wheel mounted on the open end of a box. His attempts to spark the flint were disastrous. Pulling smartly, he completely unwrapped the string and tipped the box over.

"Where in the nether regions is Feathers?" he bellowed with frustration.

Ophelia came forward and pushed his clumsy hand out of the way. "Stand back. You'll see us all burned up in flames." Deftly she rewound the string and gave a tug; a wheel against the flint delivered the desired sparks to the tinder. She lit the candle. Soon, the reddened study grew a notch brighter. It gave Liberty her first chance to truly view it, though more significantly, further examine Anthony Fielding.

Under the glowing light, she realized his hair to be not as dark as she'd first thought. Though a rich shade of brown, a lighter honey-tone highlighted the ends and the strands framing his face, as if bleached by the sun and wind. Smooth, tanned skin shaped his powerful profile; another indication he frequented the out-of-doors.

Anthony swung on his heels and met Liberty's gaze with golden brown eyes. The sudden movement apparently cost him as his face paled to the color of newly churned butter. He gnashed his straight white teeth together in a grimace and she was sure he also suffered from a sour stomach.

"I don't have much experience with bottle fatigue, Mister Fielding, but I would guess you should be lying down till your sickness passes."

"The devil blind me, I'm not sick."

"Mind your tongue in my niece's company," Ophelia remarked caustically, then seeing Liberty's disapproving frown, added, *"Please."*

Disregarding Ophelia's forced politeness, Anthony pinched the bridge of his nose with lean fingers. "'Tis not rest I need. 'Tis my valet." He looked over the top of his hand at Liberty, then lowered his arm in an agitated state. "Feathers!"

A single door linking the study to another room opened straightaway. A near breathless Hiram Feathers entered, immediately coming to practiced attention. His run through the main house had tilted the curling wig on his head, but he dared not right it. Instead, he fixed his hands behind his unswerving back, clasping his fingers together.

"Aye, sir?"

With long strides, Anthony made his way toward the open doorway Feathers had just come through. "A word with you, Feathers."

Feathers remained until Anthony passed under the door-sill. Fleetingly, Feathers gave Liberty a helpless smile, then disappeared into the other room.

The portal swung closed with a firm hand.

Anthony let go of the knob and backed away from the door, ignoring the suffering being hammered out in his head. He trod into the parlor room without glancing at his manservant. "Who is she?"

Feathers feigned ignorance. "Who, sir?"

Looking over his shoulder, Anthony scowled. "The woman in the other room."

"She's the woman you requested."

"What?" Anthony ceased his pacing and turned around. "I requested Eden Bennet."

Feathers maintained a perfectly calm face. "I couldn't get her. She's been detained. I came upon Miss Courtenay and her aunt, sir. Being as you were introduced last season, I extended your home to them when no accommodations could be made available."

Anthony resumed his pacing, each step pounding into his brain. For all the lifeblood in him, he couldn't remember having set eyes on her before. "Why didn't she mention we'd met?"

"'Twould be improper. She's waiting for you to make note of it."

Putting his hands on his waist, Anthony's shirt hem

25

swelled about his hips. "How can I make note of something I never took note of?"

"If I dare say, you may have been—"

"'Full as a tick?'" Anthony finished satirically.

"I wouldn't have worded it thus, sir."

"No, but you may think it thus."

"Very good, sir." Feathers's determination didn't falter. "Not to fret, sir, 'twill all come back to you. For the time being, you could use her company to your advantage."

"More to the point, an advantage over my grandsire."

Feathers didn't flutter a lash. "Aye."

In contemplation, Anthony felt the beginnings of a beard underneath his chin. It was one thing to entice a woman he knew would be receptive toward him; it was another matter entirely with a perfect stranger. Although, he did find her oddly tempting. He imagined her with asters floating all around her. Her lips would be parted, the same shade as the floral petals. And she would smell incitingly of the fragrance she wore now. Her voice, the same throaty song he'd heard upon awakening, would call to him again . . . *"I understand now why my aunt says you're a man to be thrown off a roof."*

Anthony snapped free of his musings, his studied mood eclipsed by bare facts. She spoke her mind too highly to suit him. "She's opinionated."

"Aye, sir." A muted grin transformed Feathers's unruffled face, then quickly removed itself.

"Her aunt is pretentious."

"The aunt could be outmaneuvered by one as skilled as yourself."

"Quit baiting me, Feathers, as if I were some pug dog in need of a pat on the head."

"Never, sir."

"How long has Eden been detained?"

"A good fortnight."

"A damn inconvenience." Anthony sank into an elbow chair and absently drummed his fingertips over the surface of the gaming table next to it. "'Twould seem I am left with little option."

"Very good, sir. I've already shown them to their rooms."

"Insightful of you," Anthony remarked dryly while rubbing the back of his neck.

"Since everything is settled, sir, supper will be served in one hour."

"I can't think of food with my stomach the way 'tis."

"I'll have Cook—"

"Have Cook make up a tonic for me."

"Aye." Feathers readied to leave the parlor when Anthony stopped him short.

"Feathers."

The valet faced forward. "Aye, sir?"

"Feathers, regardless of outward appearances, I'm not an imbecile who needs his thinking done for him."

"Never, sir. 'Tis no one at your thought helm, but yourself." Feathers kept a smile to himself and departed the room.

Anthony rested his head on the chair's leather back and closed his eyes. Why couldn't he be more direct with his grandsire and tell him to leave off? Because the venerable man was his father's father and that merited his respect. But to be subjected to one more raving sermon . . . Blame him, he couldn't stand it. The strident messages of his family obligation had become worse each year. Ten years now; ten years since his mother's betrayal.

Strike him blue, he hadn't thought of his mother in a long space. It must have been the residues of sangaree corrupting his body that had him envision her face at this inopportune moment. Would she still look the same to him now as she had when he was a youth of sixteen? He'd thought her the most comely woman. A pity her honor did not match it. Because of her infidelity, his father had lost his life.

The deathly scene ran through his mind. No son should ever be witness to his father's slaying. The duel had been formal, the proper seconds and witnesses in place. The ring of metal could be heard only a short time. Anthony had been suspended in limbo on that dank morning field, watching as his father lay taking his last breath. Without a single care for the grieving boy, Perkins entered his coach and gave his driver instructions to ride off.

The horror of his father's murder fogging his head, Anthony had ridden home to confront his mother. He'd found Elizabeth Fielding in the courtyard with all her belongings packed and loaded into a carriage. She'd ordered a groom to drive her to the docks.

"I will be glad to have you gone," he'd said to her.

Looking down from her seat she bore the picture of refined prettiness. Pert and cool, she'd stared at him with a sadness he'd never seen before. "I'm sorry, Anthony. So very sorry you feel the way you do."

"No sorrier than I, madam, to inform you your husband is dead."

She'd gone pale and he thought she may faint. A touching scene, indeed. She closed her eyes and braced her hand on the seat's rail. "I heard the news already. Anthony, I never meant . . ."

"No. Of course you didn't. You never meant to get caught in a liaison that would see your husband defending your honor to his death. And for what? A woman who forsakes her marriage vows to tumble with a—"

"Anthony, if you would only listen—"

"Listen to a liar." He'd felt a hatred in him at that moment that he could barely control. It mattered not that the woman had bore him, had nurtured him, had been his confidant. She'd killed his father as surely as if she'd been on the dueling field as his foe.

"I'm sailing to Antigua to be with your grandfather."

" 'Tis wise of you, madam. To stay in my company would be hell for you."

Elizabeth bit her lip and lowered her head. "If you should ever desire to write to me . . ."

"I won't." Anthony nodded for the groom to take her away. He never looked back.

The next day Anthony had gone to John Perkins's home, his wisdom crippled from being a wronged youth. Bravado lined his coat pocket: a snub-barreled pistol. He would kill Perkins in retaliation.

The pursy butler who opened the front door, denounced

his master's presence. Anthony shoved his way inside, pledging he would wait. For long hours he strode the length of the great hall, each detail embedding itself in his memory. There were twelve leather chairs, three tables, a couch, a clock, a mirror, a case of drawers, four large maps, twenty-nine pictures, fire tongs, shovel, bellows and fender.

At sundown he stopped his maniacal pacing. In the darkened segment of the house, his anguish prevailed, shattering the last threads of his courage. Consumed with exhaustion, he yielded to defeat.

As a substitution for his undelivered revenge, he'd slipped into the first ordinary wedged in his path and gotten foxed. He'd felt like a failure and a coward.

And so began his relationship with the bottle.

A white fear had consumed Anthony that he would never destroy the man who murdered his father. That the death would go unavenged. That in a fit of drunkenness, he would reach for that snub-barreled pistol and put a hole in John Perkins, then be held behind a lock and key for the duration of his years—or worse yet, be hanged. He feared he wouldn't live up to his grandsire's expectations. Though pride was his stole, underneath that cloak, he feared he'd wronged his mother for not hearing her out. For the last two years, he found alcohol dissolved his fears—for a little while.

Now he had two problems.

Fear and alcohol.

When Liberty had struck her arrangement with Hiram Feathers, she hadn't thought of appearances. A lady would have her own maid to tend to her. Good Mister Feathers had thought of this and found one for her—from where, she wasn't sure. The girl, Jane, had come into her room an hour ago to aid her in the change of her dress. Then she asked if any of Liberty's gowns needed pressing. Liberty had declined and Jane had said if she required her services, she had but to ring.

Putting her simple clothing up in her closet, Liberty knew

her wardrobe lacked the style a man like Anthony Fielding was used to. Her apparel befitted her station in life. She hadn't frocks of majestic fabric and design. No expensive jewels or headpieces. She owned only one fan made of tortoiseshell; it worked in a practical sense more than as an aid for coquettishness. She and Ophelia were country people with no airs and she would make no apologies to Mister Fielding for her gentility.

The black-ribboned yellow dress she'd worn today was her prettiest, though modest in cut. She'd done her best to enhance the bodice with the nosegay of asters. Though for all the good it did. She doubted Anthony Fielding had taken notice of her arrangement.

He hadn't been what she'd expected, but what she'd expected hadn't been altogether clear given the unusual situation. Aye, Hiram Feathers's narrative on his virile looks had been genuine, but it was his character she found peculiar. He seemed not to be concerned about etiquette and amenities associated with a man of his class. She'd at least thought while she tried to impress him, he would make likewise attempts. Evidently she'd been mistaken. She tried to rationalize his behavior coming up with no answers except he'd had a beastly wine-ache preventing him from being civil. Though silently she could not judge him at fault. Aunt Ophelia had provoked him.

Liberty couldn't help feeling as if she'd intruded on Anthony's unconventional life. She wished Mister Feathers had prepared him for their sudden arrival; to be sure, Mister Fielding had been staggered. But she had committed herself to see things through to the end and she would give him her every effort. A lady she would be.

In his company and his grandfather's, she would bring up every subject she'd ever studied. Intelligence supposedly came with breeding; thankfully Ophelia defied that ill-gotten logic, schooling her niece in all facets of enlightenment at an early age. She would do her utmost to be refined; though refined in her own rights, her dictionary of upper-class mannerisms was thin, save how they liked the testers to their beds turned down. She thought she could adopt the airs of her betters. She'd observed them often enough at the inn.

She would just have to improvise what she didn't know.

Her spirits improved, Liberty allowed herself to settle into her room. When first shown her chamber, trepidation over her introduction to Anthony Fielding had made her scarcely give the walls a glance. Now, she awarded them her full attention.

A lagging trace of river-scented air surrounded her, as if the windows had been freshly unshuttered. Whoever tidied the room had done a reckless job. Dust balls tenanted the floorboarded corners; they skipped and hopped as she churned the air with the hem of her skirts while she continued her inspection.

The bedroom's ceiling had been painted in the likeness of a summer sky; flimsy clouds and azure blue. She instantly loved it for the pattern reminded her of nature, something she cherished. The walls reflected the color-wash of blue. In the center of the chamber hung a delicate chandelier, its wrought iron loops like a fragile necklace; relics of spider's threads floated industriously between the bends. The wrought iron bedstead had the same fine lines, accented by brass fittings and covered with a small-printed yellow-flowered tester. A feather-light muslin draped over the white mantel and the bed-head.

Her smile broadened in approval and she felt a warm glow flow through her. For reasons she couldn't explain, she suspected Mister Feathers had been the one to see to her lodgings, though her assumption could very well be due to the fact she'd seen not a hint of a housekeeper. She opened the lid to her trunk and removed her journals, setting them on the writing stand near the window. She finished unpacking her clothing in a tall armoire. The personal items remaining in her chest could be organized and put to their proper places tomorrow when more time permitted. Mister Feathers had specified the evening meal would be served soon.

Liberty moved to the door connecting her bedroom with Aunt Ophelia's. The humble petticoat under her brownish gray camlet gown swished with her steps. Jane had laced her into the fresh dress and suggested adorning the neck with a tuckered band of ivory lace to favor the high edged décolletage.

Entering the room, Liberty found Ophelia at the dressing table. Her aunt looked up and they shared a smile. Ophelia patted the bench for Liberty to sit down next to her. Liberty gathered her skirts to make sufficient space for her hoops.

The table before her had been surmounted by a mirror, smothered in lace like a cradle and littered with trinkets and potions, cosmetics and creams, perfumes and patches, vermilion and rouge, ribbons, tresses and plumes.

"'Twould seem I'm settled, pet." Ophelia laughed and picked up her powder puff. She dusted the fluffy pad across her face in an evaporating cloud.

Liberty wrinkled her nose as the white particles tickled its inside. Scanning the table, she lifted a casting bottle of perfume and sniffed. *Field and Wood.* Ophelia had blended it a day before the disaster at the Running Footman. The fragrance hinted of sun and early morning dew, meadow flowers and the musky scent of earth. Liberty withdrew the stopper and sprinkled some of the oil on her wrists, rubbing it across the tops of her hands.

Ophelia chose a crescent-shaped, gummed-cloth patch and adhered it to the middle of her cheek. "I do hope Mrs. McKeand will traffic my clients to Fielding Manor."

"She said she would once I gave her an extra ten guineas for her trouble."

"Tut! The woman thought us indecorous tenants. I can't presume why." With a serious expression, Ophelia dabbed a brilliant rouge on her lips. The desired effect achieved, she broke into light laughter. "Which do you think she disliked most? My experiments or your honeybees?"

"I think 'twas both equally."

Ophelia, a naturally gifted chemist, formulated perfumes and beauty treatments, selling them to the domestic women out of their room at the Running Footman until there had been no room left. Ophelia's dream was to afford them a place of business. A salon where women could congregate to discuss the current topics of politics, gossip and be pampered under the ministrations of Ophelia's toilette secrets.

The steady trade often irritated Mrs. McKeand who ranted her inn was not a place of commerce and if they wanted to set up shopkeeping, they should find their own establishment; and, she was tired of chasing out stray bees from the kitchen and upstairs rooms. But the fussy woman could never speak out more against them, for not once, had they been late on their rent.

Appeased by the generous amount of money Liberty had given her, their departure from the Running Footman had seen Mrs. McKeand spouting good leave, though teary eyed.

"Aunt, I can't help feeling as if I'm betraying Mister Fielding's hospitality. 'Tis fraud I'm committing by pretending to have met him before."

"You mustn't rationalize in those terms. You are helping him, as he helped me. He may not be aware of his part in it, but 'tis help just the same. Were it not for you, he'd have had his valet hunt up another woman to take your place. We should be thankful Mister Feathers found you instead."

But as she verbally justified the means, Ophelia still had her doubts, but she dared not voice them to Liberty.

"We should be going down to supper," Liberty recommended, rising from the bench. "I wouldn't want to be late. An overdue entrance captures the most notice."

They departed Ophelia's bedroom and descended the three flights of stairs, broken by a half-dozen landings and decorated with woodworked balusters and balustrades. Once on the principal level, they turned toward the welcoming room and the hallway beyond.

The formal area greeted Liberty in compositions of strong gray-blue paint and decorative paper. A series of moldings formed a cornice where the woodwork met the plaster ceiling, and a projecting chair rail ran all the way around the room, acting as a frame to the long linen-covered table in its center. Thick walls made deep window recesses that were faced with small panels, the windows mullioned and leaded in diamond-shaped glass.

" 'Tis a queer judgment," Liberty felt the deep vibrations

of Anthony's voice as he breathed warmly upon the skin of her bare neck, "when a man's dining room gains more approval than the man who dines in it."

She swung her shoulders around and met his gaze. He stood irrefutably too close to her. He'd wedged his towering frame between her and Ophelia in the doorway.

His appearance had changed dramatically. No longer did he look disheveled. His hair shone from the recent grooming it had received, combed back from his bronzed face and gathered behind his head. He'd changed his clothing, too. He now sported a coat of brown twilled cotton that impeccably matched the color of his golden eyes. A snowy shirt drifted shortly over the waistband of his finely cut tan breeches.

"Or have I spoken in haste?"

Too late, Liberty understood the implication of his question. She had been staring at him with much of the same approval as she had the room. She had no fast answer

Ophelia chimed in. "Fielding, you're crimping my farthingale. Please move aside." She hung onto the wooden framework of her hoops that expanded her waistline.

"Far be it for me to crimp you, madam. I'm your servant." Anthony made a show of taking a step backward on the heel of his polished black boot. His penetrating gaze never left Liberty.

An odd unsettling melted through her insides. For a moment, she thought him playing a seduction game with her, then cast that notion afloat. If anything, he was trying to rile Aunt Ophelia. Instead, he'd riled her feelings with his mock attentiveness. She arched both her brows in a questioning air of his motives, then thrust her shoulders in a graceful line and stepped into the dining area. She could have sworn she heard Fielding chuckle at her backside.

She made it her foremost task to ignore him, putting all her concentration on the meal settings.

The table could have accommodated fifty guests, but had been dressed for three. The sideboard was loaded with dainty servers in mismatched porcelain and china; in their midst, two branch candle-lamps had been lit, the yellow flames dancing faintly by some unseen draft. On the table, a silver basket had been laden with fruit—late-in-the-season strawberries, blueberries and wafer slices of peach.

Since only the end three chairs had been made for use, Liberty assumed Anthony was to dine at the head of the table and she and her aunt on opposite sides of him. She rested her hand on the back of a tall chair, intent on seating herself when Anthony's fingers came possessively down on hers. Startled, she peered up into his face. Lines of humor bordered his wide mouth; the evidence made her irritated, though she couldn't particularly explain why. Maybe that he'd had a laugh at her expense when she had found no humor at all in being caught inspecting him.

"You needn't seat yourself," he said in a voice that rumbled deeply from his chest. "There's a man in the room."

When next Liberty made the slightest move, Anthony applied subtle pressure to her fingertips. "By the grace of God, don't look around for him. 'Tis me."

"Oh." She'd thought that mayhap he spoke of a servant whose duty it was to seat the guests. Seeing his marked aggravation, she quietly laughed.

Anthony grew curiously perplexed by her dismissal of his assistance before he'd even had a chance to properly offer it, but he did not remove himself.

The slender tapered fingers beneath his own were softer than any he'd ever held. Like the fine-grain smoothness of sandalwood and the pure whiteness of a new sail unfurled. The silky touch made his heart beat a little faster than its norm. Ophelia's pointed glower of uncensored objection to his person, made him linger a minute longer.

Anthony lightly massaged the knuckles at the base of Liberty's fingers, looking down at the frail hand. It surprised him to find the joints bruised, as if they'd been in a collision with an unyielding mass. An odd sense of purpose drove him to kneading the hurt, wishing to soothe away any discomfort it gave her.

Anthony lifted his hand, reasoning there was nothing about a female's fingers to cause a flash of bedlam in his brain. By the same account, he intended to touch her again at a later time to note if his reaction would be different.

He made quick work of holding out her chair and scooting her under the table's edge. On the heel of good manners, he traversed to Ophelia's side as well. The older woman rapped her closed ivory fan on his wrist and ended up taking her chair herself.

" 'Tis a foolish habit the seating of oneself by one supposedly superior in strength. Women are not helpless creatures."

" 'Tis quite apparent you are not, madam." Anthony took his place at the head of the table and picked up a small silver bell that had been positioned next to his plate. He flipped it upside down and examined the tiny clapper inside its bell-shaped dome. Scowling, he thumped the instrument back to the damask tablecloth without giving it a single ring.

"Feathers! We're primed to eat."

A solitary door cut in the wall behind Anthony's table position remained closed. Not a single footfall stirred on the other side of the impressively crafted door.

Anthony twisted his neck and glared at the silent facade. "Feathers!"

The portal creaked open and Feathers's hooklike nose flushed itself from the jamb. The rest of his lightly powdered face appeared. "You rang the bell, sir?"

"Where the devil did the bell come from?" Fielding returned in a loud timbre. "If I wanted to listen to music I'd trifle with it. Supper, Feathers. Supper is the song my belly wants to hear."

"Aye, sir."

Liberty could barely contain her amusement over this scene. Were all elegant households run in such a chaotic manner?

The door wedged closed with a rusty squawk. Soon, the entry swung wide open and a servant of color attired in a straight-bottomed black waistcoat and white gloves, bore a tray of hot food. Feathers came out, too, and took up residence at the paneled wall, his posture raised and proper, hands tucked at his sides.

Liberty bit down on her lip, as the footman gave her the first portions. She should have expected meat to be on the menu. Everyone ate it—everyone except her and Aunt Ophelia.

The main dish, boiled turkey with oyster sauce, made her stomach pitch in protest as the server gave her a large cut of breast meat. Folding her hands in her lap, she clamped her fingers tightly together as she waited to see what else he would put upon her plate. He gave her herbed codfish. She swallowed the saliva gathering in her mouth, forcing her rebelling stomach to settle. The last dish was turnips and she mouthed a mute thank you to no one in particular.

She would have to pretend to eat some of the fare.

None of the cutlery corresponded, as if pieces of sets had been lost or damaged throughout the years and been combined to make one. The tarnished silver was in dire need of a polishing. Liberty watched under the fringe of her eyelashes to see which utensil Anthony would use—the two-tined fork or the three.

Anthony seized his three-tined fork and began to eat. He cut his meat with the scroll-handled knife. The specifics of how he ate his turkey and fish were of no use to Liberty. She could not eat a single bite of the flesh without becoming ill. The turnips were her concern. And he seemed to be avoiding them.

Liberty raised her glance to Ophelia who stared at her plate in much of the same predicament. For once, her aunt had remained quiet on a subject of elevated delicacy and Liberty was glad. It would do no good at all to insult Anthony's cook when the meal, most likely, was tasteful to those who ate it. At last, Ophelia selected a fork of her own choosing and sampled the cod. Unlike Liberty, she didn't exclude fish from her abolishment of meats.

Liberty felt Anthony's gaze upon her and she knew if she didn't make a show of eating something, he would comment. She pinched up a few grains of salt from the silver trencher at her setting and sprinkled them across her turkey and turnips. Still sensing his attention, she felt her face coloring warmly. She chanced a glance in his direction.

Anthony casually rested his wrists on the table, his fork and knife motionless in his large fingers. Her pulse raced in an uneven rhythm as she stared into his eyes. She lowered her study to the strong lines of his nose and the full width of his mouth. He licked his lips, an action that spiraled her into lightheadedness. In all of her past infatuations, she'd never before been struck so hard by Cupid's arrow. This time, the Roman son was out for amorous warfare, propelling his aim bull's eye into the center of her heart.

Anthony set down his knife. "I cannot help wondering about our previous introduction. Perhaps 'twould refresh my memory if you told me about it." She'd been worried about his inquisition over her lack of mealtime enthusiasm, but this question by far, was worse. Had she been a good actress, she would have prepared herself better for the role, having made up some workable story. She could only stare in bewilderment at his expectant face. She looked beyond Anthony to Feathers who winked and prodded her with a confident nod.

Liberty drew courage from Ophelia who'd kicked the tip of her slipper against her ankle. The biting tap brought her to thinking. "Well," she began slowly. " 'Twas at—"

Her words cut short at the sound of a pistol's discharge. The shot echoed behind the kitchen-hall door from where the footman had entered. The boom was so loud, it rolled a blueberry from its perch in the fruit service.

"Tut!" Ophelia's slender hands rose to the necklace at her throat. Her fingers curled around the long teardrop-cast pearl suspended from the black velvet. "We're being set upon by pilferers!"

Chapter
3

"BY MY FAITH, THE BAGGAGE IS AT IT AGAIN!" ANTHONY DROPPED his fork and heatedly motioned for Feathers to come forward, though Feathers was already at his master's side. "Where the deuce did she unearth another firearm? Get it away from her, Feathers."

"I shall do that, sir " Feathers departed with a serene look on his face, as if the mishap were a common occurrence.

Liberty's broken breath caught in her throat. "Are you sure 'tis safe to send him off alone and unprotected?"

"Would you have me draw my flintlock against a senile woman?"

Her heart pounding fearfully Liberty gasped, "A senile woman?"

" 'Tis the yellowing cook whose indenture I chanced purchasing. I'd market her off were it not that she brews a blessed good healing tonic."

A shot popped again.

"The wench has two pistols!" Anthony growled.

Ophelia squeaked a scream of terror and clutched tighter to the jewel about her neck. "Fielding! What manner of diabolical servitude do you practice? She'll be upon us in a hound's breath and I for one won't be waiting to take the lead ball. Come, lambkin! Take shelter!"

Ophelia scrambled from her chair and had ducked half-way under the table. Many seconds passed, then the door opened and Feathers returned from his quest.

Liberty, seeing Mister Feathers appearing calm and composed, ignored her aunt's summon for sanctuary.

Feathers formally addressed Anthony in a low tone. " 'Twas Quashabee, as you suspected, after a hearth cricket. I believe the pest has been taken care of."

"What?" came Ophelia's muffled cry from underneath the dining table. "What is this about a cricket?"

"Madam!" Feathers spied the wide bell of Ophelia's full-skirted gown fanning above her chair's banister-back. Without delay, he drew up to her side and offered his assistance. "My dear madam, allow me to help you up!"

Holding onto Feathers's arm, Ophelia eased out of her hiding spot, backing her head from the table's edge. Her high-piled orange hair tilted to one side and she quickly remedied the slipping tresses with a coaxing push. "I dare say, I've never been driven to such humiliation."

"Are you hurt, Aunt?" Liberty tried to keep a serious face while watching as Ophelia righted herself on her chair and sank into its cushion.

"Only on the inside, my pet. I'm wounded beyond repair." With a flick of her wrist, Ophelia opened her tasseled fan and vigorously fluttered it at her reddened cheeks. She snapped out her distress, pausing here and there to murmur her disgrace to Feathers who hadn't left his gallant post by her side.

Propping his elbow on the table, Anthony cradled his chin with his hand and observed the scene between his valet and Ophelia Fairweather. Feathers humored the woman and she, in turn, permitted his coddling. The show irked Anthony. It was as if loyalty had cast itself from Feathers's blood and bones and refleshed on some fluffed up morsel of skirts who prattled on about her damaged dignity.

"Shall we get on with supper, or is it to be drawn out till signs of dawn?" Anthony's declaration held a note of impatience that was completely ignored by Ophelia. Disgruntled, he kept his gaze away from Liberty, following his own suggestion by taking up his cutlery again. One bite of the cold fish had him clicking his teeth together in a somber chew. He'd lost the little appetite he'd had and the tepid cod clogged his throat. He wished to heaven he had a goblet of Jamaican rum to smooth over his raging belly.

Eyeing the sideboard, Anthony searched for his favorite decanter. Missing. After episodes of Anthony's overindulgence, the house was emptied unexpectedly of all its liquors. Fielding knew such a coincidence was unlikely. It was more like the raid of someone in his employ. To be sure, Hiram Feathers. But he'd never been able to catch the man stretching forth his hand. The valet was the only servant who could steal and not pay for it with a sound flogging.

"Would you care for a glass of milk, Mister Fielding?"

Liberty's low voice came to him and Anthony fastened his stare on her face. He could not deny that each time he looked at her, she fascinated him more. The very blackness of her hair—a color which he should have found not to his liking—intrigued him the greatest. It shimmered in comparison to gold, yet not with a luster of brilliant white; the curls shone like polished onyx. Any other woman would have scorned such a color, dulling it with white powder; she seemed content with its uniqueness.

The contrast of dark hair and pale skin evoked a disorderly fervor inside him. The porcelain complexion cooled his blood; the black tresses heated his veins. Not to mention what it did to the sensitive region secured by the buttons of his breeches.

"I haven't had a drink of milk since I was a babe," he finally said in a slightly hoarse voice.

" 'Twould seem that's the only beverage available at the moment." Liberty rose and went to the serving board where a crystal pitcher of milk had been set out.

Anthony appraised the narrowness of her waist in the light gray-brown of her gown. He told himself it was to take his mind off his annoyance at Feathers for clucking over the aunt, but in truth, he couldn't help raking a salacious gaze

41

across her. Slender in frame, she stood delicate as a new-budded flower. Too tempting to be trusted.

Because of what he knew about women, he had opted to stay away from the legalities of them—namely marriage. He had prescribed Feathers to fetch Eden Bennet—a minx he could take for little else. He hadn't counted on her not being able to accommodate him. He needed a woman like her. A woman who neither pleased or displeased him. He needed no entanglements. No emotional involvement.

Feathers had induced a far worse fate for Anthony. He'd given him a woman who tantalized him; a woman who fascinated him. A woman who sweetened his mind.

Where that thought had come from, he didn't know. He merely wanted to look at Liberty's figure. When she turned around, he insulted her by gaping at her breasts. She'd stuffed a yard of lace about the high-cut bodice, but the size of her endowment showed through; fragile, yet tempting beyond rationality to him. He felt his uncomfortableness heighten and shifted in his seat.

Anthony tossed his serviette on his unfinished plate, blazing a glare at Feathers and accompanying it with a booming reprimand. "Feathers, quit your loitering and take up your position!"

Feathers straightened appropriately, his fingers lightly brushing the puffed sleeve of Ophelia's dress. "Aye, sir."

"Pish, Fielding." Ophelia tapped her ivory fan shut. "I was quite gone and Mister Feathers came to my aid. For that, I'm indebted."

Liberty poured Anthony's glass full of milk and resumed her seat while he issued orders to Feathers on clearing the table. It seemed now not to matter which implement she used in the eating of her turnips. Her hunger had somewhat lightened, though a bite or two would have seen her through the night.

Anthony Fielding took no notice of her untouched plate as the footman removed it and she stared silently down at its vacated spot. Anthony barked several commands that sent Feathers and the servant from the dining room. When she looked up, Anthony held onto his milk glass. With a toss of his head, he downed the contents and set the empty goblet on the table. After wiping his mouth with his napkin, he crossed his arms over the width of his chest. "You were about to tell me where we'd met."

A rush of apprehension jolted through Liberty and she hoped for another distraction to hold off her reply. Alas, when only silence met her, she heard her voice, stiff and unnatural. "'Twas at a party last November."

"Whose?"

She thought of a conceivable name; a name she'd heard once or twice at the Blue Anchor coffeehouse. Under such duress, she could think of no one. Her palms grew moist in her lap and she rubbed at the creases between her fingers. She could not lie. What difference would it make if he knew the truth? He still needed a woman to show his grandfather and she was willing to be the one on display.

"Actually, we've never before been—"

Feathers banged the door open and came in with a tray of sugar cakes and curdled cream. "Here we are, sir." He deposited the desert in front of Anthony and discreetly arched his brow at Liberty to hush her.

For Mister Feathers's sake, she remained quiet. But it was a troubled suppression of words that swirled inside her head. It would seem at the moment, Mister Feathers had the key and he didn't want things unlocked.

Feathers took the duty of passing out cake-laden plates, liberally dolloping each sweet with a scoop of cream. This time, Anthony chose a filigreed spoon. Liberty did the same, putting her energies into relishing the taste of the airy desert. If the cook indeed was a fiend, she had stirred devilish character into the flavor of her sweet cakes.

Anthony barely noticed the taste of his desert. Ophelia kept droning on about the cricket incident between nibbles of her cake. It rankled him to a dangerous level, inflaming him to silence her. He'd fight off her chatter with a heavy dose of what he knew would do the trick.

He'd trifle with her niece.

Spearing a plump strawberry with his fork, he held the fruit out to Liberty. He knew the offer would send the girl into a quandary and the aunt into a fit of the vapors.

"Strawberry?" he drawled.

Liberty blinked. Anthony had captured a ruby berry on the end of his fork and dangled the morsel in front of her. The intimate gesture was quite foreign to her. Did he expect her to eat it from his silverware? Or pluck it free with her fingers?

"Fielding!" Ophelia's rambling came to an immediate halt, her outrage mirrored in her blue eyes. "Remind yourself you're a gentleman!"

"There are those, madam, who would beg to differ with you." Anthony didn't pull back his fork, giving Ophelia a naughty grin.

The even whiteness of Anthony's smile was dazzling to Liberty. She stared, mesmerized by the softening it gave his gilded features. His eyes reminded her of the color of clover honey pulling at her awareness much as pollen did a bee.

In that breath-catching instant, she noticed every tiny detail about him. From the way his glossy hair caught the candlelight to the small crescents of white on his fingernails.

A warm ache spread inside her, fanning itself throughout her body. She practically tingled from the feeling as it seeped across her skin. This was something altogether new; she had no power over it, nor did she want to. Anthony Fielding was captivating her silly.

Liberty tentatively reached for the berry with her fingertips and freed it despite the disapproving frown her aunt gave her.

"Thank you." She knew she blushed, feeling the heat of her face right down to the tips of her toes where they curled under in the confines of her slippers.

Anthony honored her with a smile that hit her full-force and without mercy. It was a purely sensual experience, to be sure. And he hadn't even touched her. What would she feel like if he kissed her with that sculpted mouth of his? As she tried to imagine it, she braved not giving Anthony another blush and continued on with her dessert pretending as if nothing at all happened.

"Delightful!" Ophelia brought another sample of sweet cake to her lips, but her scowl bore evidence to the chiding Liberty would receive once they were alone. " 'Tis a disgrace we have to pay for such joy. 'Twould serve the Crown damages in lost taxes if we cultivated our own sugarcane in the colonies instead of importing it from the British Caribbean."

Anthony's spoon stilled. "You would have the traders do what they've done since the Sugar Act was imposed, madam? Evade it like the plague and smuggle in false goods without paying the tariff? 'Tis a penalty we've all suffered by the intrusion of the Stamp Act and its glorious repeal." The look on his face clouded. "Smugglers are not to be bloody tolerated."

"My good heaven, but you've a mean streak." Ophelia's mouth pursed like she'd bit into a sour berry. "You are a defender of the Crown," she accused as if unable to believe anyone would be.

"To the core, as anyone on the Assembly knows." He swore a great oath under this breath. "May I forewarn you, I'm getting angry."

"Then you'd best get at it before I beat you to it," Ophelia dared.

Panic rioted within Liberty at the turn of conversation. She couldn't let her aunt bait Mister Fielding into a debate. "I read an interesting fact once that a cricket's chirp can foretell the coming of rain—"

"What do sugar and the Crown have to do with one another?" Anthony blared, ignoring Liberty's remark.

So did Ophelia. "One supports oneself by keeping to the economy of one's own country."

Liberty didn't give up. "They often gnaw holes in wet woollen stockings—"

"England is my country, madam."

Liberty worried her lip, noticing the growing prominence of veins on the back of Anthony's hand as he held fast to his spoon. "What you speak of could very well be construed as treasonous—" he ground out as Liberty cut in.

"Crickets are considered good luck by most," she rushed on without a breath, "and 'tis probably why there's disaster looming about this room since the cook killed—"

"'Tis not treason to speak a free mind," Ophelia stated hotly. "England does not own mine. By the virtue of our Lord, I thank him for that!" She cast down her spoon, clinking it against the bone china of her dish. "I do not make it my policy to pay England's debts for administration extensions. 'Tis for their own gains made in the Nine Year's Great War we are forced to abide a taxation from it!"

"Crickets are never taxed—"

"But a taxation collected for the convalescing government of our Mother country, madam," Anthony reminded through clenched teeth. His eyes darkened to molasses while a tick pulled at the corner of his squared jaw. He hurled his utensil on his half-finished plate and pushed it away. "Sweet Jesus! I'm debating political tactics with a woman!"

Ophelia's expression tightened with strain. "If I may speak freely—"

"'Tis freely you have spoken thus far madam! Why arrest yourself now?"

"I think 'twould be to your benefit to listen to a conviction other than your own. 'Tis only a blind man's eyes that see naught but blackness in a world of light. Open yours, Fielding, and you will be the better for it."

Liberty knew it was hopeless. The war had begun and ended with a single battle wounding both fighter's pride. There would be no truce. She prayed she could bandage things together for the remainder of their visit.

One look at the anger on Anthony's face made that prospect dim.

Anthony flared his nostrils against the pulse jetting through his bloodstream, threatening to consume him in a rage that was in fact blind. With a great deal of self-control, he held himself in check. He'd never before thrown a woman out of his house. This one tempted fate beyond his capacity of better judgment.

Pressing his fingers to whitening into the edge of the table, he stood. A vision of his grandsire's face flashed through his mind and he blotted it out. He'd rather contend with a disappointed old man than this insulting, meddling crone.

With as much tact as he had left, he said, "First light tomorrow, I'll see to it you and your niece can be suitably outfitted in a decent lodging near town where you won't be subjected to a man of my contrary nature. Be equipped to vacate my premises at daybreak. Until then, I would caution you, madam, to save your sermon for another time of the day. This preaching has left me scourged with an attack of bellyache."

Without looking at Liberty, Anthony stalked out of the dining hall. The brick joints of the grand mansion trembled as he slammed doors behind him. He quit the entry and took the steps outside.

He pulled in great quaffs of air to cool his temper. As he crossed through the courtyard, he noticed Mistress Liberty Courtenay's maid leaving on foot. He shook his head, as if to clear the girl's name from his mind. He couldn't afford to think about *her* now. He had more important matters to tax his thoughts.

Anthony entered the stables. "Tobias! Ready my coach and take me into town."

A short time later, his driver waiting in the distance, Anthony walked the quiet streets of Norfolk. He crept up to a stately abode and hovered in the shadows.

"Bloody bastard," Anthony mumbled under his breath and stuffed his hands in his coat pockets. Crouching in the dark behind John Perkins's picket gate, he watched the man's house. Perkins passed by the lighted window once, returning shortly with a piece of cake. He sat down and ate the dessert with gusto. Halfway through, he discarded his wig and set the hair beside his plate while he finished, licking a smudge of frosting from his finger.

"Disgusting . . ." Anthony's belly roiled.

Perkins got up, poured himself a shot of liquor, then disappeared into another part of the house. Soon, the second floor dormer grew bright with light. Perkins then drew the thin curtains, and shortly after, the lamp was extinguished.

An hour later, Anthony's hopes of following the disreputable John Perkins on a nightly prowl were snuffed—just as the man's lantern had been.

Anthony would not catch Perkins tonight.

The clock's hands had traveled well past the stroke of midnight and Liberty remained in her supper attire awaiting Anthony's return. Jane had had to leave the house on short notice to tend to a personal matter, so Liberty still wore her gown. She'd been too upset to think of retiring, instead detached the stole of lace at her collar for more comfort.

Now, Liberty sat on the edge of her mattress, elbows on her knees and chin in her hands, listening to the natural settling of the house as everyone in it slumbered.

What to do? That question had haunted her equal to the amount of grains in an hourglass.

Ophelia wanted no further association with Anthony Fielding and insisted she would rather take Mister Feathers's wrath—if he was inclined to give it—and be at his mercy to repay him, than stay in the *traitor's* house an extended amount of time. She'd gone off to bed sorely vexed, searching for her headache powders.

Liberty had to admit, much of the problem was her own fault. She should have put an end to their bickering any way how. Having liberal opinions in these times of stilted patriotism toward England was something to be guarded. Thus far, her aunt had kept her ideology among those of her station; beauty clients, her late husband and several of the patrons at the Running Footman. To speak beyond that circle of confidence, courted danger. Revealing herself to a man of Mister Fielding's social position and apparent temper had been a mistake.

There was no telling what he would do in his impassioned mood. He did say he was known in the General Assembly. Come morning, he could go directly to the mayor, or a worse fate yet, the governor.

Liberty groaned at the thought. She had to give Mister Fielding a defensive explanation before it was too late. Mayhap he'd already sent out a missive to one of the aldermen. Aunt Ophelia couldn't be taken into custody after just escaping that same fate.

Liberty stood and rested her hand on her breast, measuring the frantic beats beneath her palm as she heard the coach return. She had to confront Anthony right now, but the longer she'd waited, the more distraught with indecision she'd become. In her heart, she'd always been afraid of this. Aunt Ophelia would go too far with her sentiments. Ophelia had been the only mother she'd known. If something were to happen to her, Liberty couldn't live with herself. She could only pray her fears were premature.

Half in anticipation, half in dread, Liberty left her room.

It wasn't until she'd closed her door firmly behind her, the impropriety of her ungodly-houred visit to Anthony Fielding settled in. Oh! But if Aunt Ophelia knew what she was up to, she'd swoon.

Liberty had assured Mister Feathers she was a lady. At this very moment, she was contradicting that statement in the most offending manner. Searching out a man's bedchamber was by no means a ladylike thing to do. But there was no time to deliberate her options for protocol. She had to go now, before Ophelia was exposed.

The method she used in finding his room was weak, though accurate. Ophelia had insisted they take up occupancy in the eastern wing; that meant Anthony had to reside on the western side of the manor.

The mural-papered hall offered friendly light. Four wall sconces had remained burning. Wax dribbled down the brass holders and left fresh puddles on the long rugs. The remnants of puddles past were warmed to create large pools that fingered into the wool of the carpet. It would be a bone-wrenching chore to clean it out. Was there really no housekeeper to see to any of it? It would have been more economical on all accounts to snuff out every last candle for the term of the evening.

When Liberty came to a string of closed doors, she

noticed a flickered illumination coming from the cracks surrounding one. It had to be Anthony's for who else would be in quarters on the third floor?

She lightly knocked on the door hoping he would answer it, and at the same time, hoping he would not.

Anthony Fielding opened the door, promptly filling the frame. Liberty took a hop backward. Her heart hammered foolishly as the light of his room cast his dominating silhouette in bronze.

Perched on the bridge of his sculpted nose, a pair of golden spectacles added magnetism to his already ruggedly handsome face. He'd discarded his evening clothes for a rich-figured, blue silk banyan that molded his body in a thin drape. No imagination was required to discern the muscled form beneath. The plain lining formed a long, rolling collar folded over the breadth of his shoulders. He held his arms akimbo, the full turned-back cuffs of the ample sleeves swelling about his forearms.

"I'm sorry to disturb you so late," she whispered.

"I was not abed."

His resonant voice warmed her like sunshine and she nearly forgot the purpose of her mission. "If I may have a word with you?"

He made no reply, but stood back and extended her an entrance. As she passed him by, she smelled the spicy balm of his cologne clinging to the unribboned strands of his sun-streaked hair. His naked feet drew her attention; their size, large and well shaped and a slight sprinkling of light hair across the toes. Never before had she seen a man without his shoes.

Liberty sucked in her breath knowing there was no turning back now.

The click of the door's latch made her whirl around in alarm. She'd assumed he'd leave it open; a fragment of decency—the single one in this dilemma she'd found herself in. She dared not make an issue of it. Better for him to think her undaunted by their privacy.

"Mister Fielding, I know the hour is late, but I could not

sleep for fretting over the distress my aunt put you through."
Her eyes scanned his room rather than meet his gaze while
strengthening her fortitude.

A thick taper of yellow wax burned under a hurricane
glass on the fold-down leaf of a leaded, glass-fronted writing
desk. Books and ledgers lay open, by their side, a quill and
pot of ink. A dressing stand with looking glass mounted on
its table, faced the portiered windows; a man's brush and
hair comb, vials of scent, tooth powder and shaving devices
tooled the wooden top.

Throw rugs in brown, rust and gray padded the soles to
her shoes as she progressed deeper into the bedroom. She
was surrounded by masculine things; a frilly cravat tossed
over the back of an easy chair, knee-high boots in their jacks
leaned against the cold marble of the hearth, a coiffured
brown tie wig, and on his chest-on-chest, a collection of
books on shipbuilding.

She'd avoided the only article of furniture left for her
inspection. The bed. With a massive headboard of oak, four
grand posters and abundance of printed pillows, its comforter had not been turned down. She spun away from it, the
modest skirts of her gown and petticoats swishing against
her ankles.

Anthony had followed her toward the bedstead and she
nearly collided with him. The loosely overlapped front of
his banyan left a plentiful show of his smooth chest where
the silk fell away from his skin. Again, she was struck by the
golden brown color of it. His pulse beat rhythmically at his
neck and she grew transfixed by the hollow of his throat. She
snapped her gaze from him, much as she had the ominous
bed.

Anthony had downed a short glass of cognac from his now
empty cache—the only booze he found in his brief search,
since Feathers had depleted the household's stock of liquor
He was mildly glad for it. Looking at this woman now, he
knew she was no trumped up figure his mind put to finer
perspective under the stupored moats of drink. Her wide
eyes and full mouth spoke of innocence; her stance spoke of

valiant candor. The scrap of lace she'd jammed down her bodice for supper had been abandoned and now the slight swell of her breasts teased into view. A long, wispy tendril of jet hair spiraled over the white skin of her bare neck. It rested on her bosom as softly as the petal of her aster when it had landed on his boot. He yearned to pluck the strands between his fingers and feel its sweet silk.

"Is your aunt always this difficult, or did she reserve her behavior for me?" Anthony glanced to the open set of plans he'd been reading. The distraction helped, for if he continued his heated perusal of her, he'd end up with a reflex he had no control over.

"Oh, no, Mister Fielding," Liberty rushed out, her cheeks turning a delicate shade of rose. "She's usually much more difficult."

"Then 'tis a good thing I won't be a target on one of her better days. She grates like the teeth of a saw."

His mind was settled, Liberty thought. He truly meant to see them off on the morrow. She was assailed by a terrible sense of bitterness and vowed to make him see Ophelia's side of things. She held out faith he'd understand—a little. "My aunt's persecution should not be taken as a personal insult, sir."

"How can I not when the woman attacked me with ill-sighted contempt that can only be perceived as treason, not only to my country but to my person? No one speaks against the Crown unless they want to be quartered or unless they're fool enough to believe in freedom from the land that bore us." Anthony strode to his desk, shoved his paperwork aside and removed the eyeglasses from his nose. In reflection, he said, "No matter how hard you may want it, 'tis a wish that will never happen."

Liberty defiantly stood her ground, including herself in his persecution. If Aunt Ophelia was to be condemned, then so should she. "Then consider me to be of a treasonous nature, too. For I believe entirely in what my aunt has to say."

Anthony lifted his chin. "Strike me blue, she's corrupted

you," he whispered. "You, of youth and beauty, a woman with her life blooming ahead. Is your aunt prepared to watch you tarred and feathered if the Assembly gets wind of your ideals?"

Well-a-day, 'twas as she thought! He meant to pursue the matter with the authorities! She had to prevent him. "Mister Fielding, if I could only make you see. My aunt has had a hard life." Liberty paused; to reveal more about Ophelia's past would jeopardize the proper background Mister Feathers had painted about them. "Is it wrong to want independence for the better of our shores? I defy you, sir, to maintain the king ever made us feel noble on these lands."

Anthony wordlessly stared at her. She spoke so sincerely. She really believed in what she said. Since he'd left her at supper, his anger had cooled and he somewhat regretted his actions. The somewhat being the loss of this woman. It had nothing to do with his grandsire's visit that he'd reconsidered giving them the boot. It had more to do with his own curiosity and intrigue over the girl. She was too open with her thoughts and emotions for him to make sense of her. Traits he'd frowned upon—until now.

Liberty mistook Anthony's silence to mean the worst; he intended to make Ophelia pay for her tirade. How could she have thought him a man to sympathize?

When Liberty tried to speak, her voice wavered. "Before you do anything rash, please consider the consequences of your actions first. 'Twould break my heart if something terrible happened to my aunt."

Her vision clouded with assembling tears, their salty moisture burning her blinking eyelids. She turned on her heel to leave, afraid if she stayed any longer he'd see them. She could not mount a proper defense if her wits were shattered. She would try again in the morning.

"Wait." Anthony's mellow drawl caught her back as she'd started for the door. She froze, suspended in indecision.

Anthony came up behind her and grazed his fingers across the side of her neck, taking a lock of her hair into his grasp. Liberty's throat went dry as she focused her gaze on the doorknob. He fondled the curl leisurely, then trailed his hand down the slope of her shoulder and turned her toward him.

"Why would you think I'd do something terrible to your aunt? Granted she is infuriating, but I would not send her off to be hanged, if that's what's got you worried, sweeting."

The gilded-brown of his eyes awaited her reply.

"You would not?"

Anthony fairly snorted. "You think me that much of a blackguard? That I would aid in the termination of your aunt's life? The devil, she'll probably outlive us all." He'd gotten himself fired up again and was about to tell the wench she was lucky no one had done to the aunt precisely what she'd just accused him of.

Then, a smile lit her face and he forgot to be angry.

Anthony felt drunk. It was the first time he'd become inebriated without lifting a cup. He didn't feel the normal shroud of incoherence drowning him to a state devoid of sensation. A different kind of draught poured into his belly. Prisms of iridescent light stirred in his head and rather than blinding him, they awakened a deep part of his soul that had been shut down for more years than he could count. If he named it, which dammit he didn't want to do, he would say he'd just been lifted a little in spirit.

Anthony abruptly moved away from her. He felt winded, as if he'd just run circles around the decking of a ship. Plague him, he was not ready for this. But by the same token, he was not ready to let her go. Not yet.

Returning to her, Anthony grasped her by her upper arms and scooted her to the easy chair. He forced himself to ignore the feminine feel of her beneath his fingers. He tossed off in a float, the wrinkled cravat from the chair's back and expertly lowered her into the cushion. He could not get a proper perspective on things when she was standing. Too easy to take her into his arms and kiss her.

"There, mistress. Sit down." His tone bore the authority of a schoolmaster.

Liberty complied, staring at him. He leaned his backside haphazardly against one of the bedposts. The long length of one leg crossed in front of his other; his forearms folded. The blatant bareness of his calves made her swallow and she squirmed in her seat. His closeness was like a drug, dosing her with a case of giddiness.

"You shift as if you're sitting on a pillow of fleas," Anthony mumbled. "I won't pounce on you." Then a crooked lift caught his mouth. "Unless you want me to."

"I should say . . ." she hesitated ". . . not." Though by her sanity, in that split second of indecision, she *had* imagined him pouncing on her. And kissing her. She felt a prickling radiate her insides, and her face suffused with heat. She couldn't think clearly with him so near. With him so indecently dressed. Why didn't he tighten the fold of his robe to cover his broad chest?

"I spoke in haste; you don't have to leave tomorrow. You and your aunt may stay" It was the closest thing to an apology Anthony had ever uttered. He never admitted to wrongdoing and it disorganized his train of thought. He pushed himself away from the poster and out of habit, went to the carafe on his desk and poured a brimmerful. He didn't thirst for it; a good thing. The liquid was clear as a spring thaw Water He shoved the stopper back home and left the tepid drink untouched.

Liberty pushed herself to standing in one fluid motion. "You shall not be sorry I can assure you, I'll speak with my aunt and make every attempt not to have a repetition of the scene played out at tonight's supper."

Absently, Liberty moved to the side of his bed and adjusted a throw pillow. So relieved by the outcome of her visit, she relaxed her guard. "You'll find I'm quite a conversationalist. I'm an ardent student of nature. I'm sure you'll find my stories enough to take up most of the meal discussion . . ."

Her words were lost on Anthony. He watched her tidying his tester, thoroughly fascinated by her. He tried again to bring their first meeting to mind until his head throbbed with the onslaught of an ache. For his life, the memory would not bubble forth. Why had he not recalled such a unique creature? She seemed evasive about their past encounter each time he'd pressed her for details. He found more recognition in her maid, than her. It was as if their meeting in some way had been a horrendous episode for her. The devil knew he could be unpleasant while under his ale. He opted to put the retelling to rest.

She went on with her comments. ". . . I have several folios on the subject of .   "

Anthony traced his forefinger over the edge of his jaw. She flitted about his bed smoothing this and that. He couldn't help thinking of her under the linen covers with him. Naked.

Then an amusing thought came to him. She was permanently lodged in her gown—at least until her maid helped her out of it. Or someone with expertise on the subject such as himself. He'd seen the maid exit the manor hours ago; that left the aunt. She could hardly be roused at this time of night without casting suspicion.

Liberty's predicament nearly made him laugh out loud. Anthony had mastered the fastenings of women's clothing enough to know the impossibility of her unlacing the backing herself no matter how much effort she put into it; there must have been six dozen eyelet holes the silk cording ran through.

He thought to offer his assistance, then quickly snipped that idea. Let her figure it out herself. She seemed to be very resourceful. One look at his bed told him that.

Liberty had been so engrossed in telling Anthony how cordial she and her aunt could be, she hadn't paid any attention to what she'd been doing with her hands. Even now, she stepped away from the massive headboard, without a backward look. Exhaustion had finally taken its toll on her. She was ready to go to sleep, eager to start the next day on the right foot.

"I must bid you good rest now." Liberty pinched hold of the wide bell of her gown and demurely curtsied to Anthony "I'm certain you won't regret your decision."

Anthony leaned his buttocks onto the ledge of his writing table. "I think you'd better explain yourself before you retire."

"Explain myself?" Confusion marked her words.

"Libby, you've just turned down my bed in the most orderly fashion."

Chapter

4

ONE LOOK AT THE OPEN AMUSEMENT FLICKERING IN ANTHONY'S eyes was enough. Liberty stared at the downy comforter and sheets; a fold and a tuck. The oversize pillows; a plumping and a fluff. The routine was as reflexive as breathing to her and, goodness, she'd performed it on Anthony Fielding's bed!

"In my weariness, 'twould seem I've mistakenly turned down your bed instead of mine." She sighed melodiously with forced fatigue. "No matter, 'twill save you the trouble of calling for Mister Feathers." Though calm and sedate in voice, Liberty jumped clear of the bed as if it had scorched the hem of her gown.

Tilting his head, the lengthy locks of Anthony's hair teased his shoulder as he laughed deeply.

Liberty's mouth tightened.

Anthony bellowed louder.

"Stop that laughing! I'm sure you've had moments of lapse." Anger swiftly replaced her embarrassment. He should have had the decency to overlook her error.

"My life *is* one big lapse, Libby," he confessed, sobering slightly. "But I've never found any of it as amusing as the lapse you just showed me."

58

Still frowning, she corrected him. "My name is not Libby."

Genuine surprise arched his brows. " 'Tis not?"

"Nay. My name is Liberty."

Anthony shifted on his bare feet. The movement slackened the folds of his robe, exposing the tight contours of his ribs. "How came you by that unusual name?"

"Mayhap I'll tell you one day." Captured by the display of his nudity, Liberty's gaze settled on the wedge of forbidden skin. Whisking her stare from him, she headed toward the door with more bounce to her stride than she'd intended. "I shall bid you good rest for the second time this evening."

Without giving him a chance to deny her, she'd gone. Anthony flinched as the door latched into place behind her. By the mass! She'd dismissed him like a schoolboy. The sorry thing was, it was precisely what he felt like.

Idiot! His pulse smartly throbbed with a maddening hint of confusion. He was tangled up in the bare roots of his emotions. God help him, he hadn't tripped since his youth when he used to run through the burned cane fields of Antigua playing cricket.

A poetic sunrise glazed the dawn sky, washing the stretch of shore behind Fielding Manor in subtle colors of coral. Liberty sat in a thicket of wild highland grass that grew tall as her knees when she was standing. She was obstructed from anyone's view, yet when she pushed the spears in any direction, she would see what she wanted.

She dug the tips of her shoes deeper into the sand still cool from the evening breezes. In a few short hours, the grains would be blistering hot. Perhaps as scalding as Aunt Ophelia's disposition when she informed her they would be staying on. Liberty had decided she needed serenity while waiting for Aunt Ophelia to stir to the light of day.

Hugging her knees to her breasts, the full gathers of Liberty's green-flowered skirt fanned around her, adding to her unintended foliage disguise. She smoothed the much-laundered material, wondering how Mister Fielding would react to its severity.

Moving the grass shoots in one direction, she could see a long-hulled boat under construction at the edge of the river running behind the manor house; in the other sprawled the grandiose back veranda spanning the lower level of Anthony's home.

On a board of cypress not far from an enormous mulberry shading the southern side of the mansion, she'd situated the bee gum, a hollowed section of gum tree with a movable lid, housing her honeybees. Last evening after she'd put the hive here, she'd rearranged several blades of grass at their entrance. The foreign spears would serve as a note their hive was not where it had been yesterday.

Now Liberty waited for the first worker to hover out, inspect the new setting, and alert the others they'd have to reroute flight paths to their new home.

It had been an undertaking moving the hive at dusk the previous day, but there had been no help for it. She'd had to wait until all the bees had returned to the hive from collecting their pollen. The driver Mister Feathers sent to the Running Footman was ghostly scared of the humming gum tree stump with its encasement of gossamer netting; he had to be appeased quite strongly before he'd take up the reins under the dwindling daylight. Not only was he transporting a live hive of honeybees, he'd been persuaded to load up three trunks, six boxes of glass vials, a crate of pomanders, two leather satchels of floral herbs, a case of books including Voltaire and Rousseau, and one loaded blunderbuss.

He'd mumbled and muttered the entire journey down the pocketed road that led to the pebbled and hickory-columned drive of Anthony's home. Once there, he hopped free of the wagon and rounded the side. Ophelia offered her thanks and extended her hand, asking him his name. His dark eyes widened and he'd swiftly looked from left to right as if she'd addressed someone other than himself. Her outstretched hand waited for his acceptance and he reluctantly fit his large brown palm into her small white one. Ophelia thanked Tobias for his services and left him standing in the courtyard to stare at his hand, the palm held skyward as if waiting to catch rain.

Liberty smiled in remembrance, then unfolded the napkin at her side and picked up the fruit tart she'd wrapped in it. The berries and pastry were deliciously satisfying to her rumbling stomach. She'd intended to ask Quashabee, the cook, if she could take one. But her predawn trip into the kitchen found it vacant. A banked fire warmed the hearth, the smokejack and turn spit, cold. In one of the cracks between the oven's clay bricks, black powder left a burn mark—the demise of the offending cricket. Despite that minor flaw, Quashabee kept the cooking area impeccably clean. The floor had been heavily sanded, the copper and pewter pots on the wooden island gleamed from cleaning.

Liberty sighed contentedly though the winded breath on her lips ended in more of a wince. Her ribs still smarted where the angled bones of her undergarment had cut into her waist all night. She'd had to sleep in her dress, of all things! She hadn't been able to loosen the tightly cinched lacings down her back no matter how hard she tried; she'd forgotten it took another pair of hands to divest that particular frock.

A fortunate thing Jane arrived an hour ago to help her with it or she would still be caught in her stays. Jane said nary a word while she performed her duties, but her doelike eyes spoke louder than any voice. They wondered over the circumstances of Liberty's predicament and how she had come into it.

Liberty ate the last bites of tart and wiped her sticky fingers clean on the napkin. It wouldn't be long now before the worker bees readied themselves for flight. Already, she could hear the steady drone of their wings as they did their morning hive cleaning. She held the insects in very high regard; she not only gleaned honey from their labors, but a kind and spirited friendship as well. It pained her to ever have to kill a queen should it happen two hatched. In actuality, it distressed her to ever kill a living animal—even the most lowly.

A balmy breeze skimmed over her face, caressing her lashes and hair. She drew her fingertips upward to smooth back a curl from her temple. When she looked up, Anthony Fielding stood on the low-lying balcony of the first floor. He gripped the whitewashed banister and inhaled deeply, enjoyment of the fragrant morning air clearly marked on his visage. No discontentment ruffled his gilded brows, nor the vague creases at the corners of his brown eyes. The airy wind snagged his creme-colored shirt, sailing the full sleeves about his forearms. He wore no cravat; no headpiece of powdered curls falsely played over his natural brown locks. The sole piece of adornment he wore was a ruby and gold ring on his fourth finger. The stone's color matched perfectly with his broadcloth breeches. He looked resplendent. He appeared fresh and well-rested. He must have closed his eyes and carelessly gone to sleep the minute she'd left him last night.

Anthony felt as if he'd slept in irons on nails; his massive bed had turned into a prison last night. He'd panicked that his house had been emptied of liquor, but by the same token, he'd been besieged by such shakes, he'd made an impulsive decision to limit the number of his drinks. This verdict made, what little slumber graced him had been sporadic, lulling at his conscious, then kicking him awake to think about alcohol again—and *her*. Strike him down, what was it about the wench that kept him from his colorless dreams? She was but a mere woman. He'd had dozens of them. They were all the same.

Arching his back, Anthony stretched some of the tension from his muscles. Liberty's name lingered around the edges of his tired mind. *Liberty.* Indeed, an unconventional title. A cynical inner voice told him to beware of her allure, but in his fatigue-drugged reasoning, he told it to go to the devil. This morning, he had other affairs to monopolize his thoughts.

Anthony gazed at the nearly completed snow rig in dry dock at the shallow waterway of his wharf. The hardwood had worked well, bending and molding in the precise spots he'd wanted. Montgomery Bennet had said to spare no expense on the rudder stock, cleats, pin rails and frame. An outrageous venture that had set him back some eleven hundred pounds sterling. But that exorbitant amount would turn nearly twofold when he sold the ship to Bennet.

Pushing himself away from the balcony, Anthony took the steps to the beach two at a time. His shipwrights would be arriving soon and he wanted to discuss a modification in sail cuts.

His booted feet sank in the supple sand as he made a pass by the ancient mulberry in his yard. A muffled buzzing tugged at his ears and he shook his head to clear it. This was a new affliction. He'd never before been beset by an attack of humming in his brain from limiting his cups. Then he noticed a split log and dried boards at the base of the mulberry's trunk.

His brows cast down in a sharp point, etching a bleak line over the bridge of his nose. An object the likes of which he'd never before seen. A stump, a large square board and a rock atop it all. And a damn lot of noise coming from its insides.

Had he not been under the blinding spell of an offensive night's rest, he may have had the inclination to define what made the buzzing sound before he poked his business into it. Patience to think things out first failed him.

A host of hostile wings greeted him.

Pandemonium broke loose as he plummeted the top board back onto the stump. Too late. A dozen odd bees escaped and let him know they weren't pleased with his unannounced intrusion.

Anthony vaguely heard Liberty's silvery voice scream out a warning to him; his own roar of surprise thundered loud enough to divest the tree of its leaves. The shock of being set upon by a cloud of animated bees made his legs immobile. Rather than fleeing, he dueled it out, taking on the horde with balled fists. He flailed his arms at the furious bees, his sparring enraging the insects all the more. He yelled a series of expletives that would have put a blush to even the saltiest of sailors.

"What are you doing?" Liberty shouted at him in a flurry of petticoats as she sprinted toward the disturbed gum tree.

In flight, she crooked her elbow and crushed it into his ribs. "Take yourself away, you lobcock!"

Stunned, Anthony stumbled back on his heels. "Where did you come from?" Pain twisted his face as a stinging puncture harpooned the slight swell above his left nipple. "Dammit! I'm stung!" He grabbed hold of his shirtfront and with a jerk, ripped it open to let the scavenger who'd pierced him, out. Delicate oval buttons rained down to his feet.

"What would you expect? Get away!" Liberty's fingers trembled from urgency as she sparked the dried clusters of sumac fruit in her smoker. "You've set upon their house! They're protecting what is theirs." She felt a prickle on her collarbone, ignoring the smarting sting. She puffed the bellow in the smoker, waving it around the colony to stupefy the honeybees. With her free hand, she adjusted the lid carefully over the combs inside the hollow.

She quickly worked at pacifying the disgruntled winged army. She received two more stings before she felt a tickle crawling up her thinly knit stockings. Normally, she'd laugh and dancingly lift her skirts to let the wayward bee out; now she could not pause in her labors. She knew the worker would become disoriented and frustrated, eventually stinging her. It did. The barb stuck through her hose, lancing her inner thigh. Her sensitive flesh burned for a minute, but she didn't flinch.

"Have you ever been stung before?" Liberty looked over her shoulder to stare at Anthony who'd retreated to the outside landing. His hair hung wildly about his face, his shirt limply curtaining his taut chest. He needn't answer. Already, one side of his jaw had swelled disproportionately and red welts dotted his hands. She watched him grimace as he tried to pinch hold of a stinger on top his wrist. "No! Don't do that! Leave it in! Wait for me to help you."

"The bloody hell why? The damn thing is throbbing." Anthony shuddered at the thought of all the poisons being pumped into his body. He wanted it out! He wanted it out now and the wench was telling him to let it rest. On purpose she tormented him for upsetting her blasted hive of pests.

A cold sweat traveled across Anthony's brow and he

cursed Liberty's back as she fidgeted over the stump. Since she'd apparently forgotten him, he squeezed hold of the stinger again and yanked it out. As he did, a spread of molten heat fanned under his skin where he'd removed the dart. A grip of nausea soured his belly. "Plague me   " he mumbled and grabbed hold of the banister.

Liberty stormed up the wooden steps and took hold of Anthony's silk shirtsleeve; she heard the delicate material tear at the seam. She pushed him through the double entry doors and steered him toward the flight of carpeted stairs.

"Let go of me," he howled. "I can walk. 'Tis not full of spirits I am this morning!"

"Hush up," Liberty scolded him. " 'Tis full of stupidity you are."

She piloted him toward the staircases leading to the third floor and her room where she kept her remedies. Indecision caught her, making her pause on the first step; she studied Anthony's ashen reflection in the gilded mirror that hung above the receiving table. The longer the stingers pulsed their venom into Anthony, the more apt he was to be seriously ill. But if she worked on getting them all out now, she would be wasting precious time. He desperately needed the curing medicine in him as soon as possible.

He looked at her through hooded eyes, the blacks of his pupils nearly covering the golden brown color of their rims. Her decision was made. Taking hold of his arm, she prodded him up the steep risers. He growled through the entire process as she briskly proceeded, giving him no time to catch his breath. Soon they reached her room where she kicked open the door with her heel and pushed him inside.

Anthony, though in the balance of spearing pain, quirked his mouth into a sardonic smile. " 'Tis an unusual way to go about getting a partner in your bedchamber, mistress," he slurred. "I shall have to remember this one when I'm in dire need of a ploy. Mayhap you'd loan me your bees?"

"Sit down." Liberty ignored his remark, abruptly letting go of him in front of the upholstered sitting chair that fronted the window treatments. Anthony fell into its padded cradle with no quarrel. He found he could not hold himself upright without falling. Never in all his drinking days, did he feel such a drunk as the one that filled him now. He was dying a slow death and he had not a droplet of brandy.

Anthony lolled his head on the chair's back, splayed his legs out before him, and watched Liberty through half-closed eyes. She scurried about the room in a whirl of energy, stopping here and there, picking up a vial of this from a bandbox case on her dressing table, to a spoon of that from a pot of powders sitting on her chest of drawers.

Liberty's running circles made Anthony's dizziness intensify. Slipping his gaze from her, he slowly focused on the rest of her things that spread about the chamber. Books and more books. Leather books and folios. Two trunks of them. Journals and pens. A small glass vase with her asters in it, the stems drooping and brushing the petals to the top of her washstand. Several drifted free of the stalk and sprinkled the floor. For all the clutter it beheld, there was no doubting the room belonged to a woman.

Across the slated-back of her writing chair, a pair of woolen stockings hung, freshly washed out. Despite his agonizing mood, he could smell the soap cake clinging to them; a sort of woodsy scent. Not floral.

Waves of drowsiness spilled over his body like liquid fire. He slid his lids closed.

A fluttering series of slaps buffeted him on his cheek. He growled and sprung his eyelids open. "Pray do not strike me, woman."

Liberty's hazel eyes widened. She'd kneeled in front of him, her face a whisper from his own. A fetching creature, she was. A damn shame he wasn't in the frame of mind to bring her down on his lap and kiss her senseless.

"I could not let you fall asleep." She lifted a glass to his lips and he recoiled.

"Get that brew away unless 'tis rum you're offering me."

"Don't be a willy-nilly." Her lengthy black lashes seemingly caressed her cheekbones when she blinked. "You need a curing remedy. You've had a reaction to the stings. Drink it. Quickly. Then I'll take your stingers out." She pressed the cup into his hands, wrapping his fingers around the goblet.

66

Anthony pretended helplessness, slipping his hold on the glass. Gasping, Liberty righted the potion before it could spill. Though he couldn't account for the precise reasons why, Anthony rather liked her fussing over him. Her fingertips were warm and soft, fragranted sweetly of some undefinable perfume.

He twisted his lips into a half-primed smile as she guided the glass's rim to his mouth. The elixir tasted bitter and revolting. She kept pouring it down his throat, not giving him the chance to breathe. The devil, it made the tonic the maniacal cook whipped up, a holiday treat.

When he could stand no more, Anthony choked on the remaining amount. His eyes watered and he forced Liberty's willowy hand away. "Have mercy! I've swilled down the worst of ales and never has it tainted me such as this."

"I'm sorry I didn't come out of my hiding spot sooner. And I'm even sorrier for the pain I have to put you through next. But I have to get the stingers out posthaste."

She drew up a padded footstool and sat down. In her lap were a jar of opaque liniment and a blunt blade. "I promise I'll be gentle."

"Judas . . . you cannot mean to bleed me."

"Nay! 'Tisn't sharp. I need to scrape the stingers out. You don't pull them out, that only worsens the injections of the venom from their bulbs."

"I believe you are right . . ." Anthony mumbled.

Leaning forward, Liberty placed her palm on his forehead. With diligence, she scraped the two stingers from the right side of his jaw and curve of his cheek without him wincing. Her hand trembled above the rise of his chest and he saw her indecision.

"Go on." His breathing was ragged, but by no means due to his bites; the concoction she'd fed him had outwitted any need for postmortem. It was the girl herself that had him in a fit. She was not the sort of woman he normally found himself attracted to, he reminded himself. But as she slanted in over him, her breasts coming tantalizingly close to his loins as she labored over him, he cursed his own fickleness. He wanted this woman.

A curling tendril of her ebony hair tickled his bare chest as she parted the expensive fabric and stroked the gleaming edge of her steel over his breast. By the mass! She indeed tortured him, but by no method of logic he could figure.

"I   ." Liberty began, but found her voice thick and stilted. ". .   I only have the ones on your hands left."

Liberty spared no time removing the rest, apparently sensing Anthony's discomfort.

And Anthony *was* in the throes of discomfort. But it didn't come from the smarting stings afflicting his body. It came from Liberty's nearness. Her touch, her inadvertent fondling. He'd almost risk being stung again to have her fidgeting about him once more.

Too soon, she'd finished and dabbed small dots of liniment on his stings. She straightened on her stool and smiled ruefully at him.

Liberty brought her fingertips to her cheek. Anthony looked terrible. Terribly battered. Terribly charming. His long hair fell about his face, mussed and lacking the ribbon that had restrained it in place. The line of his nose curved a little out of joint and she supposed he had a right to crook it thus; his nostrils flared upon each breath he took. The glint in his eyes hit her hardest. A tiny dash of boldness; a mixture of lazy assessment and bewilderment. She felt a large punch of lovesickness hit her.

"I'm sorry you got stung. Truly I am." The temptation too much to bear, Liberty gently pressed her lips to his bruised cheek to assure him of her sincerity.

Without warning, he turned his face and his lips met hers. Though Liberty had kissed few men—sole Barlary White— on the mouth, she knew what Anthony summoned within her could only be called passion. He lifted her off her toes when she wasn't even on them.

The coaxing pressure of his lips brought out an intensity of her own. The very shape of his lips, the touch, the feel of them on her mouth, dampened her brow and hitched her breathing. His fingers slid over the nape of her neck, stroking the fine hairs behind her earlobes. He locked her in the vise of his arms, keeping her to him, slanting his lips across hers with moist heat.

She was spinning into a gale of monumental proportions. The revolution intensified, pulling with it her every sense, reeling her over a sensual—

"Liberty! What have you to say for yourself?"

The globe came to a disjointed halt and the stool plunged right out from under Liberty's bottom. Sitting on Anthony's feet, she looked up.

At the door's threshold, a new sort of tempest was brewing.

Aunt Ophelia glared at them with the fury of pelting hail.

Chapter
5

"A-AUNT . . . YOU'RE OUT OF BED," LIBERTY STAMMERED.

"I fear I shall have to take to it again." Ophelia swooned theatrically, drawing her wrist across her penciled brow. "I'm overcome by the scandalous scene that has greeted me." Brilliant plumes fashioned in her orange hair, strands of gold beads circling her throat, and a violet on her left shoulder, Ophelia Fairweather entered the room. The vapors of her toilette clouded around her; a thin layer of white powder floured her bodice. As she heaved her meager bosom with outrage, some of the particles wafted free. "Pray get up from the floor."

Liberty bounded to her feet. In her haste, her buckle-trimmed shoe skimmed off her heel and caught on Anthony's boot. She made a dash to retrieve it, but Anthony beat her. Their fingers met and Anthony watched her turn a shade of pink. His hand lay on top of hers, trapping her. She implored him with her gaze to let go; he did.

Liberty snatched the shoe away and refit her exposed toes into the opening. Eyes wide, she collected herself and smoothed out the invisible lines of her frock.

"There was a problem—" Liberty began, but her aunt interrupted.

"I can see there is a monumental problem." Ophelia

vented one of her most pointed gazes on Anthony; a penetrating, guilt-wringing stare on his person.

Anthony neither barked nor whimpered from the bite she put into it. He coolly challenged her with an unflinching stare.

"A problem with my bees," Liberty finished at length. "Mister Fielding lifted the lid to my hive and as you can see, he got stung."

Ophelia stood her ground. "What is your explanation for this, Fielding?"

Anthony took in Ophelia's angled-down lips. She was asking him to curb the fire in him long enough to rouse a plausible excuse for his behavior. Though his passion had cooled a notch, he would not vindicate kissing her niece. He hadn't justified his actions to anyone in years—too many to tally—perhaps save Feathers if the valet goaded him soundly enough. The baggage could push him off a precipice and he'd not wage an explanation. This was *his* house.

Movement from the window's morning light snagged his gaze and he saw Liberty standing at the curtains in retreat. She toyed with the green gathers at her waist and summoned what could only be called a hasty defense.

"After he got stung, I immediately attended him. Knowing the great pain afflicting him—

Indeed, he had been in pain, but not where the blasted bees had vexed him with their poison.

"I felt sorry for him and kissed him. No more than a nurse would do for her patient."

Anthony watched as a new blush bloomed on her cheeks. Her hands crept over her face, as if to hide the telltale sign. She pretended to tame her unmanageable curls, but he knew better.

" 'Twas entirely innocent   " she trailed, not glancing at Anthony. He wished she would. He wanted to see the sparkle in her eyes. ". . . innocent and quite sisterly."

Bah! He held back a roar of laughter. Were she his sister, that kiss would have been criminal.

By the time Liberty finished her sketchy retelling of the incident, Anthony felt hot all over—this time in the tight muscles surrounding his fingers. He wanted to pound his fist through the wall.

"Pet, your story scarcely consoles my displeasure." Ophelia clicked her tongue. "I'm loath to think what would have happened if I hadn't come upon you when I did—Fielding being a man." She shot him an accusatory stare.

Anthony smiled blandly. "There's a nasty rumor to that effect."

Liberty went to her aunt's side and grasped her hands in her own. "Aunt, please be reasonable. I was terribly sorry for the entire ordeal and merely offered Mister Fielding a tiny condolence that should be taken as purely innocent."

"I shall overlook your indiscretion, lambkin, only if I never have to bear witness to the like again." Ophelia smoothed back Liberty's hair, patting the ebony tresses to order. "Since that is the end of it, I think 'tis best we pack up now and be on our way."

Liberty's lightened distress abruptly grew again. She bit her lower lip, feeling the pressure of her teeth. Any speech she'd rehearsed to change Aunt Ophelia's mind about leaving, fled her thoughts. The truth couldn't very well be blurted out in front of Anthony Fielding—they were bound and obligated to see this through until the end of his grandfather's visit because they couldn't possibly repay him the money his valet gave them.

They'd spent four hundred pounds on Mrs. McKeand's repairs, ten guineas for the landlady's inconvenience; and four pounds, sixteen shillings and two pence to recoup Aunt Ophelia's losses. There had been pots, paper, scales, a funnel, weights, a candle box and a brass mortar to replace. With all this, they had just under forty-nine pounds left. A modest sum. More than they'd ever hoped to put toward their salon in a year's span.

But Liberty's reasons to stay went beyond money. She was reluctant to give up her fragile relationship with Anthony These odd yearnings for him could not be labeled as a passing fancy or ill-blown illusions of love. No, there was definitely something wonderful happening to her. She couldn't sneeze it off as anything less.

"It isn't necessary we leave, Aunt. Mister Fielding has had a change of heart and has extended his hospitality."

"I should say!" Ophelia looked first to Anthony, then Liberty. "He no more than threw us out twelve hours past and now you say we are to stay? I won't hear of it."

Liberty didn't like having to resort to trickery, but it seemed the only way. She quickly thought of a diversion—a subtle, yet jarring jog to Ophelia's mind; the trump in a hand of cards. "I should think silver-blue will be in season this year, Aunt," she said, playing their favorite game—the decorating of the salon they'd been dreaming about. "Can you not picture it in brocade? Looped over doors. Cherubs frolicking up the archways. Medallions of women smiling into the mirror-heads whilst they while their afternoons away."

Ophelia swept her skirt about her, her face pinched tight. "I should say I can see it. But 'twill be a long time in coming."

Undaunted, Liberty pressed on. "I can see hanging from the molded ceiling, tinkling Bohemian glass shimmering with tapers. On the sideboard, pyramids of fruit towers, and of course, the plates for service are imported from France. And ladies would flock to such a resplendent place. Gossip would abound; talk of the day would be anything from politics to marital woe."

"Enough." Ophelia swayed, pressing her hand onto her forehead. She kneaded her temple and squeezed her eyes closed, as if blotting out the colorful portrait Liberty painted.

Liberty forged on mercilessly. "And in the winter, a light fire flames in the hearth, the mantel above it surmounted with a mirror and sirens who rest on a marble lion. The walls are hung with bathing nudes. But, of course, everything will be in silver-blue. That is the color of the season."

"I can picture everything, lambkin." Ophelia sweetly tucked Liberty's arm in hers. She gave her niece's slender fingertips a sound pat while addressing Anthony. "I find we'll be staying, Fielding. But I give you fair warning. From now on, I shall not let my chick stray. She'll be under the strict protection of my feathers. And might I add, they have been ruffled severely."

Anthony,
  Other things brewing tonight, can't make the meeting place. Need to sail on business, but will return in several days.

                                          Yours faithfully,
                                          T. A. Cheswick

Crumpling the note the barkeeper in the Sign of the Mermaid had just given him, Anthony staggered out of the rowdy establishment.

As the night air hit his face, he thought of the lonely vigil ahead, not looking forward to keeping watch on Perkins alone. Cheswick brought ale and humor to their evenings, making them tolerable. Spying on John Perkins wore on Anthony—especially when he had nowhere to go but the perimeters of the bastard's house.

When would Perkins make a move?

Anthony had all but come up to the fence when a voice behind him caused him to spin around.

"You drunk mongrel," Perkins spat, "quit chasing after me as if I were a bone."

"Judas." Anthony's heart had risen to his throat. His mind fuzzy from the inebriants he'd consumed at the Mermaid, he hadn't the foresight to go for his pistol. *Stupid.* "The devil, 'tis you, Perkins . . . Ha! Someone has beaten me to blackening your eye!"

"You're wearing on my patience, Fielding." John Perkins stepped back, tipping his head to obscure his bruise. "If I find you on my premises one more time, I'll have the law set upon you. Don't think I can't or won't lock you up."

"You needn't remind me," Anthony miserably returned. "You flaunt your silly laws and rules. Don't you think I'm not laughing at you for them, either."

"Get out of my sight, you're drunk."

"Not drunk enough." Anthony reeled. Having been caught and having too much to drink left him spinning.

Damn, damn, damn . . . Cheswick, you should have been here to help me clean up this mess.

"Pathetic." Perkins shoved the gate's latch open. "That's what you are. Sitting out here night after night, dropping your bottle in the gutter. That's how I knew you were here, you fool." Perkins wrinkled his nose. "I heard the glass breaking."

"Then hear this"—Anthony straightened with a sudden burst of energy—"I'll go where I want, when I want. If I desire to sit on this street, I will. If I desire to look at your damn house, I will. If it pleases me to watch you, I will."

"Then I pity you." Perkins smiled. "You'll find nothing out of the ordinary and no reward for your troubles. But set one foot on my property and I'll have you taken to the courthouse."

Perkins began walking up the cobbled path to his porch.

Anthony struggled to keep hold of his head's abating clearness. "You killed my father!" he called after Perkins. "And for that, I demand retribution! If it takes me to the gates of hell, I will see you hanged, John Perkins. Hanged, dead and buried!"

"Pish, posh." Perkins waved Anthony off, then slipped through the house's front door.

Anthony knuckled the deck of cards atop his desk, pushing them to the limits of the edge, then back in front of him again, catching them with his hand before they fell off the top. Pausing from his idle diversion, he swilled the dark red claret from the crystal goblet at his cuff. He resumed his movement of the stack of cards, nudging them to the borders of his desktop.

Tiring of his passive distraction, he whisked the stack overboard with a curse. They cascaded to the crimson rug like autumn leaves on a breeze, landing in a scattered pile at the side of his heavy desk.

He seized the pint of claret he'd smuggled into the house and refilled his glass. His limitations of drink had been poor so he'd changed his rule—he'd only drink claret.

He'd been staring at his vellum book on John Perkins,

penning in a word with his quill, then striking it out. How could he make notes on Perkins's whereabouts when the man never went anywhere? It seemed pointless to enter their recent argument, for he barely recalled the words exchanged. Only that he'd been found out. From now on, he would have to take up a different hiding spot when he watched Perkins.

Without adding anything, Anthony ended his entry with a shake of writing sand over the ink blotches.

Unbidden, Anthony thought of the years wasted tracking John Perkins. His much sought after revenge against Perkins seemed ever out of reach. But he'd had him once.

He'd seen the bastard smuggling wares into and out of Norfolk on black ships to avoid purchasing tax stamps.

Anthony called on His Majesty's Exchequer and presented him with his observances. The man had said that if indeed Perkins had violated the proper certificates, he would be guilty of a felony and suffer lifelong imprisonment without the benefit of clergy. Anthony had felt a bottomless satisfaction.

His exultation evaporated when the cocky Perkins made no qualms about opening his warehouse for the royal revenuer. The store was empty.

A year later, the Stamp Act was repealed and Perkins no longer needed to smuggle, if indeed he had resumed it after Anthony's accusations. Anthony never knew for sure. He'd begun to have lapses in memory; days vanished without him knowing what happened to them. He had periods of sobriety, yet he also had benders.

Knowing this didn't stop Anthony from tossing off his mellow claret. He thumped the fine-stemmed goblet down onto his desk. It caught on the binding of a ledger and toppled, joining the suits of destruction below. A single droplet doused the Knavery of the Rump on his head. Had Anthony been in a humorous mood, he might have seen irony on the face of the Oliver Cromwell card. But his petulant disposition of the past three days scratched out his mirth.

Unless perhaps, it had been Ophelia Fairweather's head

the unmindful drop had splotched. He could have laughed over *that*.

Before he could stop it, the memory of the morning he'd kissed Liberty found its way into his mind. Though that day had hardly strayed from him. The image of her face hovered in his head, much as one of her bees, only without the stinging bite.

The scene still rankled him. It dampened his ego to recall Liberty making light of their kiss. Damn him, he'd wanted to hear her say she'd been overcome with passion so ardent it had rattled her down to her bones.

Perhaps it was all for the better she hadn't. What did he want from abandoned desire anyway? A soul-wrenching experience to waylay all the others of his illicit past? Maybe not, but what he shared with Liberty had been close. Too close to sensibly define. The kiss left him more shaken than he wanted to confess. He who had prided himself on being the dominating one in interludes, the one who set women of all stations swooning, had become the fatality of his own craft; he'd become entrapped by one kiss.

Now he wanted to kiss her again, and again.

Pray, he could have been saved from all of this if Feathers hadn't brought her home.

Beating the end of his goose quill and blotting his hand, Anthony jabbed the recently delivered missive that had found its way to his desk. A boldly scrawled apology of detainment by a fortnight or more from Bennet. With that perfunctory news, there would be no reversing the complex situation he now found himself in by installing Eden in Liberty's place.

Perhaps he should send the women off and damn the consequences. It would seem the logical thing to do. At least, the most honorable.

One of the bee stings on top of his wrist began to itch. Absently he scratched at it while thinking of his grandsire's arrival.

Anthony held nothing against Thomas Fielding. In fact, he liked the man. Timelessly handsome at sixty-two, he could be witty and charming. Anthony generally looked forward to his grandsire's visits, but after several weeks of the elder's badgering him about taking up a wife, it plagued him to the point where he lost his temper and went on sprees of incoherency. Last time, his fury had seen him so soaked, he'd nearly married Prudence Rawlings just to keep the old man's tongue still.

Feathers had found Anthony in the Front Street Church's rectory, dead to Norfolk on the Mermaid's brandy while awaiting the reverend's morning arrival to beg him to marry him. The valet had waylaid Anthony, dragged him home and filled his stomach full of Cook's tonic to revive him enough to see the blight that match would have brought on. The chilling horror of what he'd nearly done to appease someone else had made him swear he would never be cornered again.

This time, he thought while digging his clipped fingernails deeper into the itch that bothered his hand, he'd produce a fictitious woman to thwart his grandsire's talons before they raveled the coat from his back.

To Anthony's way of thinking, he had been given no choice. He could not take another note of Thomas's whittling tongue without exploding. It would only sever the relationship completely—what fragments there were to it. He supposed Thomas Fielding still hurt over Richard Fielding's death. Anthony may have lost his father, but Thomas had lost his son.

Anthony frowned with bitterness. If Thomas had felt any compassion at all over the murder of Richard Fielding, he would have thrown that treacherous daughter-in-law of his out with the rubbish instead of harboring her on his island. It was a callous way to think of one's own mother, but he couldn't help himself. Elizabeth Fielding, though not on the dueling field, may well have been the one to put the blade into Richard's chest.

Then came Liberty Courtenay who seemed to go against the grain of his thinking. Anthony found out having emotions that warmed the soul weren't as agonizing as he'd expected.

Of course, he was no good for Liberty, but that major

point had eluded him until now when he was faced with idle time to ponder it. He'd cemented disillusionment in his head for too long; he couldn't chisel it out without chipping the walls he'd erected since his father's death. He was a man driven. Driven by revenge and retaliation. What right had he to happiness . . . and damn him . . . love? He had none of it to give. He was a man who lusted. Lusted after women, liquor and the demise of John Perkins. It had been a way of life for him for so long, he could barely see beyond the years after his ruination of Perkins.

Liberty needed someone who could compliment her; talk sweetly and find the beauty of life with her. He hadn't those traits, those attributes women found so enchanting. He was not the kind of man who walked in gardens and whispered words of love; he frequented the punch bowls and made a . . . lobcock . . . of himself, dancing with clumsiness brought on by the wine. He was not the kind of man who wrote sonnets and whimsical poetry for his lady; his words were voiced in slurs, poor excuses for rhymes and testimonies of love—expressions women wanted.

Though for all he knew to be true, he could not stop wanting Liberty.

A wincing pain shook him and he looked down at his hand, realizing he'd bloodied the bite by his constant grating. Like a cork inching its way down the mouth of a bubbling champagne bottle, Anthony Fielding's resolve catapulted through his fist as he brought it down on his desk with a loud crack.

To hell with his morals, he never had been a saint. If he so desired the girl, he would have her.

An unflinching knock disturbed his door and his thoughts. "What is it?" he barked, rifling through his vest pocket for a square of linen to clean his hand.

Feathers crossed over the threshold, his eyes immediately squinting to adjust to the red-hued light cast by the hurricane globe. "Good evening, sir. I brought you some salve for your stings and a pot of . . ." The servant's words trailed short as he spotted the claret bottle on Fielding's desk.

The valet's gray eyes faded a shade, as if they'd been

painted with disappointment. Growling, Anthony made no move to remove the evidence. The devil, he was a grown man; he needn't hide his liquor in some clever store like a naughty youth. The bottle was empty anyway.

"Set it down, Feathers." Anthony motioned toward the tray and ceramic service. "I shall drink it."

While balancing the tray in the crook of his arm, Feathers neatly shuffled the debris from Anthony's desk corner. A pencil compass, various straight rulers and the engraved disk used as the Fielding wax seal. Feathers deposited the tray, rearranging the chipped tea set in an orderly fashion on the desktop.

As he poured the brew into his master's cup, Feathers offhandedly remarked, "If I may say, sir, your eyesight would be better off if you were to study under a clear glass light. Madame Fairweather says there is no cure for ailing eyes and since you already use spectacles, I thought her observation rather pertinent."

Slighting Feathers's commentary, Anthony sat back. "Good Lord, Feathers, what happened to your wig?"

Feathers straightened and modestly adjusted the cluster of corkscrew curls at his shoulders. Though the red wash of false light enhanced the color, there was no doubting the peruke the valet wore to be a glaring orange. "'Tis called Majestic Marigold, sir. Madame Fairweather's own color."

Anthony's left brow rose a fraction. "You've had it dyed to match hers?"

"Nay, sir. Madame Fairweather dyed it. She's rather gifted with color. 'Twas her idea to match it to her own. She's been practicing the recipe."

"And you've got the daring to wear it as such?" Anthony leaned forward and snatched up his hot cup, absently curling his finger through the handle. "I think she's done more than dye your hair, Feathers. She's dyed your brain."

Hurt marked itself on Hiram Feathers's downcast face and he grew silent.

Anthony's insides suffused with guilt. Foul mood that he was in, he'd trod harshly over the most loyal servant he'd ever employed. He had never seen Feathers display any kind of gross sentiment before. "Damn. Accept my apologies, Feathers. If you like your hairpiece the way 'tis, then the devil take my opinion."

"Very good, sir." A weak smile replaced itself on Feathers's mouth.

"Pray forewarn your barber," Anthony suggested, bringing the saucer to his lips, "so he does not snip your head as a flower." Expecting the tea to warm his insides, Anthony gasped as a fragrant brew traveled across his tongue. Sputtering, he sloshed the cup to his desk. "What the—?"

"'Tis coffee, sir. From Martinique. Sweetened with fresh cream and sugar."

"I know what it is! I've seen the bean spilling from burlap sacks on the wharves."

"I thought you might like a change, sir. I have of late, been taking coffee with Mistress Courtenay and Madame Fairweather and found the drink to be most soothing. 'Tis Ophel—Madame Fairweather's—own grind." A far-off twinkle heightened the valet's eyes and he toyed with a leather-covered button on his coat cuff.

Anthony caught the dreamy expression and found himself inexplicably irritated. How was it his servant managed time with Liberty that he himself could not secure? He'd only feasted his gaze on her at mealtimes and those hours were barely tolerable when the aunt monopolized the conversation. "I'm interested in hearing more."

"The past two afternoons, I've found the ladies retired on the back porch sipping coffee." Feathers hesitated. "They asked if I would join them and I accepted. My duties to you, sir, were completed, of course. And should you have required my services, I would have been your servant." Feathers bent at the waist and fetched Anthony's abandoned forest green coat from the carpet. Smoothing it over his forearm, he walked toward the settee and laid the garment across the cushion.

Anthony gave the coffee another chance. The jolt wasn't nearly as bad as he anticipated. "Go on."

"There's no more to tell." Locking his fingers behind his back, Feathers took up his post at the head of Anthony's desk.

"How is it you manage to get close to that aunt? With me, her eyes are armed. Full of dash and fire."

"I believe . . ." Hiram tried to conceal his smile ". . . she is a mite taken with me, sir."

Anthony endured a drop more murky coffee before pushing the cup away; his pleasurable taste for tea overcame him. He'd not comment further on the romance of Madame Fairweather and Hiram Feathers.

Smearing his cotton handkerchief across the droplets of blood on his hand, Anthony's disposition blackened again. Despite the pain he'd inflicted on himself by scratching too hard, the bite still prickled him and he slapped at it to alleviate the discomfort.

"If I may say——"

"Where is the purse I gave you?" Anthony asked in agitation, bridging Feathers's pending suggestion with a far more fundamental subject.

The nostrils on Feathers's beaklike nose flared much as a rabbit's when startled. "Which purse, sir?"

"You know precisely which purse." Anthony gritted his teeth. "The gold guineas and notes I gave you to get Eden Bennet a necklace. Where is it?"

"Of course, sir. That purse." The valet unlaced his fingers from behind his back and fit them together at his waist, hooking his thumbs into his vest. "I don't have it."

Anthony's head shot up.

"I needed to pay off some household accounts. There were several market bills and a freemason had to be summoned to fix the hole Quashabee put in the kitchen hearth."

"That took up five hundred and five pounds?"

"Perhaps not that much, sir." Feathers bade the guilty look to vanish from his face, for surely it flamed upon his countenance like a bawdy flag. "I am certain I left the remaining amount in the safety of my bedchamber." Thus far, his plan had gone accordingly; Fielding accepted the white lie. Now if only he could come up with a fair amount remaining to appease his master. He hadn't wanted to, but it seemed he'd have to sell off a vintage bottle of wine from the cellar and pray God Fielding wouldn't take it to task to crave that certain spirit.

"See to it the rest of the money is in the safety of my writing box before you retire, Feathers."

"Aye, sir." Feathers swallowed the walnut-size lump in his throat, making no move to take his leave. He'd have to act fast. "Since that course of business is taken care of, I think I'd best tend to your stings now." He lifted the lid on a small crock of thick white salve.

The repugnant smell immediately fouled the room as Feathers scooped his fingertips full. The concoction could only be described as looking like squashed grubs in Anthony's mind. As the valet came at him with the glob, Anthony damned Feathers's newfound sensitive feelings. "Back down, Feathers, if you know what's good for you."

"But you need it, sir. To prevent scarring. Mistress Courtenay observed you scratching at dinner."

Anthony stilled, the suffering across the agitated red lump on skin stilling as well. "This is from Liberty?"

"Aye, sir."

Liberty was a subject that interested him. Since he'd put aside his flimsy principles, his mind began to race with possibilities. "Get on with it."

Feathers hovered over Fielding, pasting the odious ointment over the flaming welts on his hands. The valet arched his singular bushy brow in slight horror at the irritated bump above Anthony's wrist.

"'Tis been bothering me," Anthony mumbled stiffly. Though Feathers's sloppy ministrations were a sore contrast to Liberty's soft and comforting hands, Anthony accepted the gruesome dabs.

"I believe I need a ride in the country," Anthony mused while keeping his jaw straight.

"You don't like the country, sir."

"Not at all. But Liberty Courtenay does. I heard her talk of flowers . . ."

"Aye, I heard her too. She likes to watch her bees."

"I was thinking of observing something far more interesting than bees."

The manservant replaced the seal on the crock and wiped his hands clean on a towel he'd draped over his shoulder.

Anthony tucked his elbows on the table's edge and drummed his thumb across the surface. He felt a coil unspring inside him, tamping down his earlier frustration. Opening the side drawer to his desk, Anthony fished out a brass ring with three small keys and dangled them toward Feathers. "I want you to open my firearms case after breakfast tomorrow."

"Aye, sir," Feathers said without question, taking the keys and slipping them into his diagonal pocket. Only the lines at the corners of his eyes hinted at the bewilderment over the peculiar orders he was just given. Picking up the tray, he bowed his proper bow, and started to bid Anthony a good rest when the Master's voice stopped him.

"And, Feathers, make sure the cook knows the case has been left unlocked."

Chapter
6

"I DARE SAY, FIELDING IS A SLOVENLY MAN," OPHELIA SAID FROM her seat in the parlor. " 'Tisn't enough for him to have a dust and insect problem. He fortifies it by leaving refuse about."

Liberty glanced at her aunt who shook her head at a stack of newspapers rising to the chair's arm.

Fingers of warmth from early afternoon sun crept across the porch and splashed the open-windowed sill, toasting Liberty's back. She sat on a lumpy window cushion, thumbing through the pile of faded gazettes her aunt had commented on.

Ophelia kept on with her knotting, exercising her hands in a light, listless task, crooking and stretching her little finger. A pretty mother-of-pearl bobbin lay on her lap—her arsenal of charm—she called it. On the spool, she'd wound yards and yards of ribbon she'd tied together and knotted. Knotted for nothing in particular; knotted with the care of indifference, an indolence which made her seem to be doing something rather than nothing.

Liberty pointed her toes and spread her arms out to grab hold of the window molding. Balancing under the raised sash, she found her aunt's comment indisputable.

Anthony Fielding ignored his manor house to a shameful degree.

She'd witnessed the frowning walls where windows had to be shoved open to enjoy balconies overgrown with thorny vines; rooms where sooty fireplaces nestled, smelling of charred mustiness; ceilings spread to expose stout beams and the jeweled webs of spiders; where cornices, copings, double doors and gilded panels glowered under their gloves of grime. Sculpture and locksmiths' fine workmanship went dishonored beneath fringed, shawl-covered tables and heaps of almanacs and pamphlets.

The scatter and indifference marring the richly appointed chambers, the marginally maintained grounds—she had no answer for them other than Anthony cared more for his wine than his home. She'd seen him with a glass of spirits in his hand often enough to realize he drank more than socially. She had never known anyone to drink out of dependable habit. She had heard that those who did were nasty and vicious. Thus far, Anthony had been beastly only when prodded. His humor, whether mildly intoxicated or sober, put a sparkle in her day. She had found no offense in his behavior for he—mostly unconscionably—made her laugh when laughing had been the farthest thing from her mind.

Beyond that, he remained impenetrable. As if he kept up some tired facade for those who perused his enormous estate from the sandy road leading into the heart of Norfolk.

Did anyone know about his penchant for wine? He had not entertained a soul during their visit, nor, to her knowledge, had he received any invitations. She'd assumed men and women of his social standing sashayed from one soiree to the next. Had Anthony Fielding's drinking made him an outcast?

"Fielding acted rather oddly at breakfast this morning," Ophelia remarked lightly without disrupting the rhythm of her knotting. "Did you notice?"

Liberty noticed everything about Anthony Fielding, most of which she didn't find odd at all. His domineering presence commanded attention. From the gilt of his brown eyes, to the squareness of his chin and the jutting measure of his shoulders, she'd memorized him. If he had acted any different than she'd become accustomed to, she hadn't perceived it. Enraptured by his nearness, she almost forgot herself in his company.

She'd been wishing to have an afternoon alone with him. They'd not had an intimate moment together since the day she'd kissed him . . . or he kissed her, depending on how one looked at it. Though Aunt Ophelia had made it clear she would not tolerate further triflings with him, Liberty had hoped Anthony would make the effort to be with her. He seemed not to long for her company as she did his. That dismal dose of reality set a frown on her lips and she sighed.

The *pop-pop* powder explosion of two pistols being fired bounced through the serene parlor. Startled from her work, Ophelia gasped. "Tut! 'Tis his mad cook again!"

Liberty shifted in her seat on the window's ledge, tucking her feet under her thin skirts. "I do hope mister Feathers can persuade her to surrender before she does the house damage."

Within seconds, the parlor door smashed open, the hinges shuddering with the force Hiram Feathers used. He filled the entrance, his orange wig cockeyed. The untied, tatted ivory cravat around his neck hung loose at the ends and he appeared quite out of breath. With animated eyes, he petitioned Ophelia.

"Quashabee's run amok in the kitchen!" Another chorus of gunfire rattled off, emphasizing the valet's dismayed announcement. "I fear she's gotten hold of Mister Fielding's firearms collection and has set out upon a colony of ants under the butcher's block. Pray, madam, I need your help to subdue her!"

Ophelia stood, her latest knot unraveling through her fingers.

"Quickly!" Hiram Feathers beckoned.

As Feathers dashed Ophelia through the door, Liberty felt two powerful hands circle her waist from behind and snatch her out the open window. She frantically tried to get hold of the sash to foil her kidnapping, but the brawny vise held her fast.

A scream floated into her throat. She took a deep lungful

of air, readying to screech until she brought the rafters down.

"Do it, sweeting, and I fear we'll have uninvited company on our picnic."

Heated breath blazed her nape, dragging across her sensitive flesh and rousing a myriad of delicious shivers. *Anthony!* Twisting her neck, she gazed into his eyes. The spheres were filled with deviltry and limned in the deepest of browns. She relaxed in his arms. Her heartbeat tumbled out of control and she smiled, enjoying the feel of his fingers around her waist.

"This is highly irregular, Mister Fielding," she admonished, though thoroughly delighting in the eccentricity of his conduct.

He laughed as he landed her safely on her slippered feet. "Abduction becomes you."

Anthony fit her hand in his and stole her down the length of the dilapidated veranda.

The heels of his richly buffed boots tapped an impatient tattoo, as if he were timing his steps. She studied the wide span of his shoulders and close-fitting cut of his clothing. The light blue of his skirted coat with silver buttonholes and fancy stitching, furled out behind him. Stretched over his corded flanks, the snug tailoring of dove breeches made her lurch.

Anthony agilely went down a row of steps. He veered his course toward the courtyard and the circular drive that crescented the front of the manor house. Under the dappling shade of a sprawling black walnut tree, stood a decoratively painted landau with its black leather hood creased back like a fanned napkin. A team of roan horses sedately enjoyed the coolness the branches offered.

Liberty immediately recognized Tobias garbed in a colorful red plaid coat. He ran his dark hands down the points of the horse nearest him, ending with a firm pat on the animal's rump. Upon seeing Anthony, he straightened from his duties. Reaching over the side of the glossy door, he unlatched it.

Without any effort, Anthony lifted Liberty on the folded-down steps of the equipage. The four springs bobbed under her slight weight as she settled onto the seat. Anthony hoisted himself next to her while Tobias took up the coachman's box.

"Drive us to a patch of flowers." Anthony stretched out his long legs.

"Aye, sir." Tobias snapped the leather in his hands and the coach took off.

Liberty peeked over her shoulder, expecting to see Aunt Ophelia in a flurry of underskirts bounding after them. From the exterior, the large redbrick house, which rose three stories high, remained tranquil and untroubled.

Her gaze strayed a while longer on the sprawling estate. The shaggy structure which she had so recently berated, looked inviting. Its white sashed windows peered back at her, unblinking. Her heart sped up and the saluting arms of the manor's wide wings retreated and shrank. One of its two tall chimneys seemed to wave a jaunty good-bye.

A shadow on the road grayed the picture, and soon after, the house disappeared behind a row of ill-trimmed box-wood. Liberty faced forward. She settled into her abduction without apprehension; she trusted Anthony's judgment. And yet, she found his closeness very taxing on her senses. Without the distraction of the house to occupy her, she was forced to focus elsewhere.

Tobias's back proved insufficient in keeping flitting glimpses of Anthony from the corner of her eyes.

Anthony remained quiet on their journey. He appeared pleased, not offering her a single explanation for his actions. His forearms doubled confidently. The lightweight ribbon that dressed his queue-styled hair, danced on the breeze.

She dared not remain quiet, too. The silence between them made her restless, feeling as if their stolen moment would pop like a bubble. She engaged him in light conversation, noting first the subtle features of his home, then pointing out the town's landmarks.

"I have always found it interesting that the main thoroughfare cutting north and south through Norfolk has water on either side of it. 'Tis as if we are traveling on a bridge of land erected by God's touch."

Anthony's face lighted curiously and he stared off at the deep blue waves of the Elizabeth River to his right; then he looked to his left at Back Creek's tributaries which were marked by landings and houses. "I've never thought of it in such a way."

Pleased that he'd been enlightened by her geographic observation, Liberty gloried in the knowledge she'd actually shared her opinion with a man. Barlary White had never wanted to stretch their topics beyond himself and milch cows. He never wanted to hear her steadfast views of government. By the day's end, maybe she would introduce the topic of politics to Anthony.

Tobias steered the horses over a rutted street that led out of the commerce section of town. The carriage passed the deep well on Charlotte Street near Town Bridge. A group of children cranked the well's handle twisting the hemp around a solid beam to bring up buckets of water. Liberty made no comment on the children's activities, recalling too vividly the numerous times—too many to count—she'd been given the chore of fetching water to clean the rooms at the Blue Anchor. What would Anthony Fielding think of that? He'd not find that enlightening at all. Or perhaps he would, only not favorably.

The energetic sounds of city and bartering voices drifted off, supplanted by the sweet simplicity of nature's assembly. Warbling birds and the songs of their calls serenaded throughout the many fruit orchards strung along the roads.

Liberty breathed in deeply, smelling the mixed fragrances of peaches and cherries; the perfumed blossoms of apple trees. The woodsy scents reminded her of the cottage she and Ophelia lived in before her stepuncle died nearly a year ago. Thoughts of the thatched-roof dwelling with its plastered walls and simple elegance made her melancholy. She missed it terribly, though the rent on it had begun to squander nearly all of their savings for the salon. It had been necessary that they move into the city and take on a single room at the Running Footman with a cost of less than half the shillings.

Liberty hadn't discovered until now how much she genuinely missed the freedom and gentle quiet. Her duties as chambermaid didn't permit her the opportunity to enjoy outings such as this.

She closed her eyes and turned her face toward the sky.

A lazy caress touched her cheek and she abruptly blinked her eyes open to see Anthony leaning over her. His fingers seductively grazed the smooth column of her neck, as if he'd fondled her in such an intimate manner dozens of times. "You are an enchanting creature when you are not speaking of the democracies of our king."

Almost too stunned to speak, her voice rushed out in a breathless gulp. "Am I to take that as a compliment? For if 'twas spoken as one, you've just implied you like me better when my mouth is shut."

His eyes darkened, brimmed with promise. "I would like your mouth better if mine were on it. Due to the potion you fed me the last time is but a blur."

Liberty should have been shocked by his blatant suggestion; she was not. How could he have forgotten? Thoughts of the kiss they'd shared penetrated her waking hours, and even those assigned to slumber. She could not forget the way he'd commanded her lips and taken over what she'd started in tender remorse upon his hurt.

"Perhaps," he said, licking his lips, "I need to trigger my memory."

Anthony lowered his head a fraction. Anticipating his kiss, her heartbeat caught in her throat. She kept her hands firmly in her lap, suddenly uncertain where to put them, but wanting to draw him tightly to her. With a will of their own, her eyelids slipped closed and she raised her mouth to his as she swayed forward.

Her body felt like liquid, her muscles limp as a rag doll's. Before she could discover Anthony's taste once again, her shoulder butted into his and she jerked back into the seat.

Eyes snapping open, she felt the coach reel, shirking something in the road. Tobias wound the team around the center of the lane, talking to the animals in a lulling tone.

Wincing from the pain her back had taken from its slamming, Liberty steadied herself. She slumped her elbow over the door's edge, getting a brief peek at the pair of ground squirrels retreating into a farmer's pasture of yellow-blossomed sweet clover.

Tobias craned his neck to check on his passengers. "Them critters came out of nowhere, sir."

Anthony slouched into the coach's cushion, his arms at his sides. His fingers curled into distinctive fists. "Next time, run them over!"

Watching the sullen tension wash over Anthony's face, Liberty fought the urge to giggle. A black scowl marred his handsome features and he pouted, much as a young lad deprived of his due. Despite her best intentions, a small laugh seeped through and she made no effort to quell it.

Anthony glared at her, one brow cocked disarmingly. He said nothing, merely waited for her to explain her outburst of humor. Giggling, she asked, "You do not have a penchant for rodents?"

"I have no fondness for being interrupted when I'm in the middle of something." He seemed completely put off by the disruption, making no further attempts to kiss her.

"I shall remember that, Mister Fielding."

Anthony gazed forward, his mouth set in a brooding slash. "Pray don't call me Mister Fielding anymore. 'Tis aging to me."

"Very well. Anthony." She liked the sound of it over her lips when spoken aloud. Thus far, it had only graced the imaginative fancy of her daydreams.

"Good . . ." he mumbled, fixing his stare to the endless groves of walnut and hazel trees. The coach tread under the boughs of billberries and mulberries that acted as dappling umbrellas. Sunlight glittered down on them in patchy rays, brightening the landau, then plunging it into shade again.

"What is it you do, Mist—Anthony?" She caught herself, trying her best to ignore the strange aching racing through her body at his nearness. "I've seen you reading plans 'twould take me ages to decipher. And that large boat at the edge of your property is about complete. Is it yours?"

"'Tis mine." He answered back with an impersonal nod that turned to a light shrug of his shoulders. "A snow rig to be correct. Never call a ship a boat," he amended seriously. "Call her a vessel if you must. Never a boat. 'Tis insulting to her."

The raw deepness in his voice mellowed when he spoke of his snow rig; his tone softened with obvious affection and patience. His personable demeanor brought her to a new understanding about him. Anthony Fielding had a soft place in his heart about ships. "And will you sail it when 'tis finished?" she wondered aloud, though she didn't want to speculate his answer. The thought of him sailing away in his new ship saddened her.

"I don't sail."

"You won't ever sail it?"

"No. I'm selling her."

"But how can you?" She came dangerously close to resting her fingertips on the tight outline of his thigh. "You love her."

Twisting in his seat, Anthony crossed his leg over his knee. "I may love her, but I can let her go. I have let many ships before her go. I feel no remorse over it. 'Tis my business to design them, build them, then sell them."

"You make it sound so calculated."

"Liberty, business"—he rested his coated arm over the cushioned seat's back—"and life, hold no room for sentimental emotion. 'Twill do naught but botch your head."

"I should like to be very botched, then, Mister Fielding. For I should like to be truly in love. Were I, I'd not let it go for any price." Too late, she realized the significance of her declaration. How could she have been so candid with him? The implications of her words were marked as clearly as if she'd penciled them in script on parchment for him to read. She meant to have Anthony Fielding return her affections.

Tobias pulled off the country road and stopped the landau

in a meadow sprinkled with vibrant color. The servant hopped down from his box and foraged for a wicker basket that had been secured beneath his seat. Taking it out, he held on with one hand while opening the door and folding down the steps.

"Fine flowers here, Mister Fielding," he commented.

Anthony stood up, his uneven weight dipping the floor of the landau slightly to one side. He extended his hands for Liberty to take and helped her down in the brace of his arms. She lingered in his hold until Tobias shifted on his feet.

Liberty became aware of the livery servant's presence, his eyes downcast. She formally backed out of Anthony's embrace, her face warming like sunshine.

Anthony took a brusque step toward the coachman and without ado seized the basket's handles. He tossed off the large cloth that had been draped over its top, rummaged through the neatly wrapped foodstuffs and yanked out a small gingham bundle. "Wander off, man."

Tobias's black eyes stared at the offering with a bemused expression, as if that request had never been made of him. "Yes, sir   " Accepting the parcel, he saw to the horses, then disappeared into a bramble of blackberries.

"I .   " she whispered feeling herself tremble. "I find myself quite hungry

"I, too, am ravenous. Come. He smiled at her silence. "Let us find a place to sate our appetites."

Their footsteps furrowed through the meadow flushing out milky butterflies and other winged insects.

The ground was splashed with rainbows of color; flowers had been sown on the wind: mountain laurel, rhododendron and violets. Blues and yellows rose two-feet high on thistle-stalks of verdant green, while orange and crimson hugged the earth, creeping their leaves and sunning their blooms to the azure sky above.

Unfastening the single silver button that kept his coat together, Anthony shrugged free of the garment and spread it like a blanket for Liberty to sit upon. She gathered the skirts of her pattern-stamped dress and sat. Shading her gaze with her slender fingers, she took in the setting around her.

"If I could be any other creature, I would want to be a bee. For in this field, I would be happy forever."

Anthony was compelled to listen to her. Though her meditation was queer, it got him thinking. If he ever could be a creature other than himself, he would want to be a dolphin. The reason he never sailed his ships was because he became terribly afflicted with seasickness. Fish never got sick and they lived to enjoy the endless depths of blue ocean.

But he would never admit to this secret. "I'll bet you've never had a useless daydream in your life."

Liberty shrugged. "What good is a daydream if it's useless?"

Good point, he thought. "Why do you keep bees?"

"I find they are more loyal than anyone I know, excluding my aunt, of course." A gentle current of wind picked up an inky tendril from her temple and carried the tress in its fingers. "I used to sell all their honey, now Aunt Ophelia uses some in her skin recipes and I only keep a little for myself to eat, the rest stays in their stores." Raising her gaze to him, she tried to smile.

Though the subject of bees didn't particularly interest Anthony, he continued on with it. He liked the way her eyes shimmered when she spoke of them; he liked the way her lips moved when she talked, the sound of her throaty voice. "Why did you blast them with smoke when they swarmed at me?"

"It seems rather cruel, but I read in a theory paper it sedates them." Liberty plucked a clover leaf and twirled it between her fingers. "I only use the smoke when I'm moving them or tending to the hive."

Anthony leaned forward, mesmerized by her slim fingers as they toyed with the green stem. He imagined them grazing across his bare skin, tantalizing him.

"You should try some of my honey," she said, her voice wavering as if she had a hard time controlling the chords.

He indeed wanted to sample her honey, but not the fruit of her bees; he wanted the bee's mistress.

With the food hamper at his feet, forgotten by both, Anthony moved toward Liberty. He heard her breath catch as he gazed into her eyes. He took in her face; the perfect oval promised bliss. Picking up an inky tendril, he rubbed the skein between his thumb and forefinger. "You do not wear a wig. . . ." he mused aloud.

"Nay. They attract weevils and no matter how loathsome, I find I cannot kill them."

Anthony smiled as he thought of her fending off a nest of weevils with a mild shoo, rather than a strong sousing in a bucket of lye. "You are truly an amazing girl, Liberty."

Her eyelids grew heavy and her lips parted.

He slipped his hand around the curve of her waist and drew her to him. "Liberty, I cannot resist you." His mouth inched down, closing the distance between them. "I am not a saint."

Then he kissed her. Hard.

He slanted his mouth against hers as he teased her lips to submission. She melted against him and her arms tentatively came around his back and slipped across his shoulders. Anthony nipped at her lower lip, pushed his hands into the thick crown of her rich hair.

Liberty shifted.

Anthony groaned.

"Your buttons . . ." she said softly.

Only then did he realize that the buttons of his shirt had chafed the bare skin at the modest neckline of her gown. He softened his kiss before parting her lips with his tongue.

Liberty thought the kiss thoroughly enjoyable. If this was what kissing was all about, she had never been kissed until now. But somewhere in the back of her mind, a niggling little voice beckoned, advising her to confess the truth about their meeting. If they were to be this intimate, she had to tell him.

Breaking her lips free of his mouth, she settled one shy kiss on the masculine roughness of his jawbone. "Anthony," she murmured, hearing the echo of her unmanageable heartbeat in her ears. "There is something . . ."

Anthony nuzzled the column of her neck, moving upward

to trace the shell of her ear with his tongue. Liberty could not crush the shudders that tore through her limbs. "Please . . . I must tell you . . ." But the sentence trailed off of its own accord.

"Whatever it is you want to say can wait until later," he whispered, his breath tickling the sensitive area around her earlobe.

She resisted him, cupping his chiseled face in her hands. "I have a confession."

"God save me from women with confessions." Dropping his arms from her waist, he let her go. "Do you want to tell me you're not a virgin, sweeting? I'd figured you to be an innocent, but women of your station have been known to take on a lover or lovers."

"Not I!" she returned indignantly.

"Well then, what is it so we can get back to the matter at hand?"

Liberty had wanted his attention and now that she had it, she struggled with her narrative. Where to begin? As she flashed the story through her head, it sounded extremely ruthless on her part to have ever agreed to Feathers's foolish conspiracy. She looked away from Anthony, unable to think with his gaze upon her.

Now that she had a minute to consider the consequences of what their kissing was leading to, she came to her senses. Even after telling Anthony who she was, she couldn't just tumble in the meadow with him. He'd kissed her in no way she'd ever been kissed before and for that, she'd lost her head. It was time to clear it.

"Well? Enlighten me, Liberty." Anthony's resonant voice broke into her reflection.

Liberty bit her lower lip while meeting his eyes. "I should like to tell you about myself and Mister Feathers."

"Strike me blue! You and Feathers? But you'd said—"

"I beg you to tread lightly on Mister Feathers for he sought me with your well-being in mind."

Anthony massaged the taut skin that stretched across his forehead. A dubious tone marked his next question. "How can his bedding you involve my well-being?"

"W-what?" Liberty jerked her chin upward, her eyes flashing with incredulity. "Why would you think that he and I . . . that we . . . Really, sir! I could never do as you suggested with someone I didn't love!"

"Then what, mistress," he ground out impatiently, "are you talking about?"

"My being at Fielding Manor," she parried. "'Twas Mister Feathers's idea and I fear in my desperate need for coin so that Aunt Ophelia could be, well, saved from a very horrible fate, I put the purse of money he offered me before my integrity. I can only pray you'll forgive us."

Anthony brought his fingers to the knot of his cravat, releasing the frilly tie with a jerk. "You're not making sense to me. Not with my coherence fogged by passion and claret. What purse?"

Suddenly, his face dawned with understanding. "Bloody hell. Am I to guess the amount of the purse?" He arched one brow sardonically. "Let us venture, perhaps, five hundred five pounds?"

"Aye. 'Twas that amount."

Anthony whipped the white lawn stock from his neck and wadded the swath in his fist. "'Tis no wonder I did not recall our past meeting! It never took place. I may forget things, but I somehow think *you* I would have remembered." He swore under his breath. "The details—the vivid descriptions of a tawdry salon you painted for your aunt. I'd thought it sounded cheap and now I know why. From which brothel did Feathers gain your employ?"

The bitter impulse to slap him rose strongly, but Liberty contained herself. "He did not find me in a disreputable house. 'Twas at the Blue Anchor. I'd just been released from my position as chambermaid and he approached me with an offer to pose as your intended. At first, I thought him daft, and then as I heard him out, I realized that your situation and mine could benefit if we joined forces. My aunt would be free of obligations and we would have a little left over to put toward our own cosmetic salon; and you would have a woman as your fiancée for your grandfather's visit."

Anthony's eyes narrowed to slits. " 'Tis a curious explanation."

" 'Tis the truth."

Seething, Anthony vowed to see Feathers roasting on a spit over a fire till his flesh blistered off his deceitful bones. The devil! No wonder the man could not account for the guineas and pound notes; they were no longer in his possession!

"You are in the wrong occupation," Anthony ground out ruefully. "Your calling 'twould seem to be in the theater."

"My feelings for you have never been an act."

"Of all the women I've bought, none have ever hoodwinked me into feeling like a buffoon. Despite what Feathers may have told you, I am not so desperate I'd pay for false affections! When I gave that treasonous valet of mine the purse, I'd intended the money to be spent on a gift, not payment for services. If I had wanted to buy a woman outright, there are scores of ill-reputes who would have gladly volunteered!"

Liberty had known he would cut her down; she hadn't counted on bleeding from the heart. What he spoke was hurtfully true. No doubt, he could have had any number of serviceable women; he'd ended up with her. Someone not of his choosing.

Hot, blinding tears welled in her eyes and she battled to keep them from spilling. "I can only repay you close to fifty pounds. The rest has been spent. I will have to earn the balance and it may take me some time, but rest assured, you will have it." A single droplet pushed over her eye's rim, sliding down the curve of her cheek. "As I said, please do not take any of this out on Mister Feathers. He believed himself to have your best interests at heart."

"My mother pretended affection for my father. Because of her duplicity, he's now lying under a headstone in the British West Indies." Pushing himself to his booted feet, he stuffed his cravat into the cuff of his shirtsleeve. He woodenly advised, "I suggest we proceed home."

Liberty gathered her skirts and managed to get her knees

underneath her. Pressing her hands into the soft fabric of Anthony's coat to balance herself, she stood.

Feeling her cheeks suffuse with humiliating heat, she felt mussed up and bruised.

Anthony flung his coat over one side of his back. Quietly he retrieved the food basket, then left her to follow him.

The journey back to the landau progressed in silence. To Liberty, the call of the birds had been a pleasing entrance; in departure, their chirps and warbles grated endlessly on her nerves and she nearly screamed for them to suspend their chatter.

Reaching the equipage, Anthony shoved the untouched hamper beneath the front seat, but not until he'd procured a bottle. To Liberty's surprise, he offered her his hand. She took his fingers in her own; the contact was brief and cold. Seating herself, she kept her backbone unwaveringly straight.

Anthony crashed himself down next to her and searched the vining blackberry patch with a wide gaze. Not seeing Tobias, he bellowed in a thunderous tone, "Driver! Come forth, man!" He popped the cork and drank from the bottle's neck. "Judas!" he thundered, tossing the bottle into the bushes. "My claret has been purloined by Feathers! 'Tis now lemonade!"

"Aye, sir." Sleep slurred the coachman's near voice.

Liberty jumped with a start both over Tobias's immediate response and Anthony's lamentations at not having a drink.

Below her, on the opposite side of the landau on which they'd boarded, Tobias stuck his wigged head over the edge of her door. He'd apparently been napping after his meal and caught quite unawares by Anthony's shout.

"See us home," Anthony ordered, pouring the citrus punch over the side of the door.

"Aye, sir."

Tobias took up his seat and tightened the slackened reins on the team. Soon, the horses were headed back toward Norfolk.

The trip to Anthony's house seemed never ending. The stilted silence tore through Liberty as she kept her gaze fastened on the trees and scenery sidled next to the country road. When she thought she could not endure another turn of the carriage's wheels, they were rolling over the pebbled drive.

The grand house loomed ahead; a dreadful welcome.

As Tobias circled up to the front, the entry door opened and Ophelia's petite form stood under the cornice.

Liberty swallowed, knowing the impending tirade she and Anthony would be subjected to. She could not take a lecture in her state of mind. And Anthony, in his foul mood, would squash her aunt under his boot heel.

After jumping free of the coach, Anthony saw Liberty to her feet. She waited for her aunt to lash out.

The flogging never came.

Ophelia stepped aside to allow a silver-haired gentleman to pass her by. His tall and regal stature, distinctively filled out his coat and breeches of oxblood velvet.

"Anthony," came the elder man's fond greeting as he took the steps. "Madame Fairweather has told me the good news." He walked directly to Liberty and encompassed her shoulders with a steadfast embrace. "Welcome to our family, my dear."

Liberty streaked Anthony a look of alarm over the dapper man's upper arm.

Anthony gave her no freedom from the gentleman's hold. Rather he conjured an artificial smile and mumbled, "Hello, Grandsire."

Chapter
7

" 'TIS A FINE THING," THOMAS FIELDING JOVIALLY ADMONISHED, "to arrive at my grandson's house and not have him home to greet me." Releasing Liberty, he took up her hand. "No matter. The reasons for your scarcity are quite forgivable."

Liberty's nerves suspended on whether Anthony meant to denounce their romance regardless of the appearances he wanted to keep. She stared wordlessly at him, waiting for a denial that never came.

Anthony walked forward, his movements stiff. He took her fingers from his grandfather, claiming them for his own. "I am glad then, Grandsire, you remembered what it was like to be in love." He caressed her lips with his own.

Liberty shut her eyes against the humiliated, deflated feeling ripping her in two. She was helpless to stop his artificial devotions and stood woodenly until he pulled his head back. His glinting, self-satisfied eyes pinned her to the spot.

So this was how things were to be between them. She would be his puppet in this duplicitous game of courtship.

Liberty swallowed the hurt in her throat, groping for an explanation to give the elderly man who had watched the display with glowing interest. "Mister Fielding—"

"Thomas, please," he amended. "And think naught of your spectacle of love. 'Tis to be expected."

Ophelia stepped forward. Her rage over her niece's abduction apparently put on hold.

"Let us retreat inside the house, out of this heat," Thomas proposed. " 'Tis not good for these delicate ladies, and our Liberty has already had her share of sun this afternoon. I see she's without hat and parasol."

Thomas's acute perception ran through Liberty and she felt her light sunburn. She could never fool the man when his eyesight was so keen.

" 'Twas hot, this afternoon?" Thomas asked Anthony, his astute eyes flicking over the unconventional appearance of Anthony's attire; namely, the missing cravat and coat thrown over his shoulder.

"Sweltering," Anthony rhetorically confirmed, causing an enormous smile to stretch itself out on Thomas's face.

When Thomas turned his back, Liberty pulled free of Anthony's possessive arm, taking in tiny gulps of composing air Her mouth burned where he'd touched her, shamed her.

Ascending the marble steps to the manor's entryway, Liberty met Ophelia. Her aunt's rouged lips pursed with concern. Are you all right, my lambkin? I'm worried.

"I'm quite fine, Aunt," Liberty flatly answered. "The sun has merely made me dizzy

"I don't believe for a minute the sun has gotten to you, Liberty," Ophelia said in a low voice. "You love the out-of-doors and can abide it for long lengths. No, Fielding has done something to you." Her eyes snapped fire in Anthony's direction.

Liberty moved away and entered the house. The pine floorboards under her square heels moaned as she crossed into the poorly lit vestibule. Heavy curtains were drawn across the long, narrow windows flanking the main portal. The only source of gloomy illumination offered into the foyer came from the single shaft of sunlight spilling in from the front yard. Soon, that disappeared as Anthony closed the double doors behind him.

"I'm reminded once again," Thomas stated, staring at the high ceiling, dusty staircase and dense wall swags, "what a dungeon this place is. 'Tis a discredit to the builder of this home to let all of this elegance go to ruination."

"I like it thus." Anthony's wry commentary bounced through the hall.

"I find myself in agreement with your grandfather, Fielding." Ophelia wrinkled her nose, her hostility toward Anthony caused her to find flaws in anything he had to say. "The room's ambience is barely short of macabre."

"Mayhap, madam, 'tis because I am a devil. Pray you never have occasion to see me without my boots; you'll stumble upon my cloven feet." Anthony's winged brow lifted, but Ophelia didn't back down. She glared at him with icy contempt.

Thomas's buoyant laughter tumbled through the musty room. "You were always such a hellion when you were young, Anthony. I'd hoped as you aged, you would grow more serene. My wishes have been dashed." The grandfather procured a lace muckender from his vest pocket and dabbed at the humorous moisture assembled at the rims of his eyes. "My apologies, madam," Thomas bade Ophelia in a tone with forced soberness. " 'Twas heathen of me to howl at his antics. I beg your forgiveness."

Ophelia adjusted the strand of baubles encircling her powdered neck. "You may have my pardon."

"Good! Anthony, let us all sit in the drawing room and become acquainted, shall we? I've a cup of coffee Madame Fairweather gave me. Would you believe they grow the beans on Martinique and I've never tried them? I wasn't prepared for the sharp taste; mine is probably cold as a fish. Have you more?"

"I do."

"I should wonder if that would be under taxation if I take the notion to have it brought out of Antigua. Duties abound in Antigua. The less imports and exports I trade, the more sound my ledgers against the trials England imposes on me." Thomas crammed his handkerchief into the small slit pocket of his silver brocade vest. He quickly glared at the group, his mouth twisting into a bleak line. "I dare hope my political opinion has not offended you ladies."

"On the contrary," Ophelia allowed. "'Tis of the same sentiment as mine. The coffee you were drinking was *smuggled* into the country without a tariff."

"I can see you'll get on fine without me." Anthony's inhospitable announcement brooked no argument from either Ophelia or Liberty.

"Where are you going?" Thomas queried, the faint lines in his forehead creasing expectantly.

"I've some urgent business to tend to in my study. I'll send word for Cook to fashion a special meal this evening in your honor, Grandsire."

"Very well, Anthony." Thomas stepped forward and clasped the younger man's hand in his, giving it a stalwart squeeze. "'Tis good to be here."

Anthony's heart constricted at the tightening grip. Plague him, he wanted to hate Thomas Fielding for making him go through this charade. He wanted to hate everyone who made him miserable. But it was hard to dislike the amusing old gent. He had a particular knack about him that made him instantaneous friends with everyone he encountered.

Anthony allowed the warmth of the elder's handshake to skim up his arm and heat his extremities. He could not be rational when he was dying for a drink. But he did concede they were family. No matter what the past relationship, the man before him shared his blood.

Sensing Liberty's gaze on him, he looked at her. He captured her observant eyes. She was uncomfortable for him. She'd apparently read his ill at ease hold on his grandsire. Had he been as transparent as a windowpane? He wasn't used to baring himself in front of others. His expressions of indifference or blind drunkenness jacketed his thoughts. Liberty's ability to decipher his weakness shocked and troubled him.

Clearing his throat, Anthony abruptly broke free of Thomas's hold. Without another word, he left for the refuge of his dim study.

Anthony secured the solid door behind him. His breath

came in unsteady blows as he bolted to his bookcase and picked up a decorative porcelain vase. Fishing out the round decanter of his spirits, he popped the stopper with a shaking hand and took a hefty draught. The claret blanketed him against his feelings for Liberty. No one had ever been able to discern his moods, his feelings or emotions. Not even Feathers could read into him. How could this slip of a girl unravel his mind?

He took another drink. Then another.

Picking up the silver bell on the mantel, Anthony gave the clapper a strike. Not content with the solitary summons, he induced the chime once more; then added a steady ring of thirty seconds for good measure.

By the time Feathers knocked on the door, Anthony had imbibed a good portion of the half-full bottle of claret. His anxiety somewhat subdued, he'd plotted to bring the valet down on his knees for victimizing him.

Sitting behind his desk, he folded his arms over his chest. Before granting his manservant entrance, he whacked the lid to his writing box open.

"Come in." Anthony forced the vexation out of his voice, masking his fury with a graveling baritone.

Feathers peeked his marigold-wigged head inside, checking first to his left, then right, before gaining admission. "Aye, sir?" By the way Fielding had clamored the servant's bell, Feathers was certain whatever had gotten the Lord and Master's dander up would be his crucifixion.

Feathers guessed the problem the instant he set his gaze on the gaping writing box. He'd gone into the cellar as he'd planned, but when he looked for the wine, it was missing. Not only had that particular bottle been misplaced, but others of value, too. Feathers could only blame himself, for when he'd depleted the household stock, Anthony had obviously restocked the manor—secretly and who knew where—with these wines. Feathers hadn't been able to raise a decent amount and therefore had hoped Fielding would forget about it.

Lud, apparently not.

Leaning his back into the hard-cushion of his chair, Anthony propped his feet on the corner of his desk. "I'm missing an important correspondence, Feathers. I cannot find it in my letters chest. Perchance you can take a look."

"Aye . . . sir." Feathers repressed the ball of dry air blocking his throat. Fingering over the sheets of rumpled stationery, ink pots and quills, he glanced up at Anthony. "What does the correspondence in question look like, sir?"

"I cannot remember. The seal was foreign to me." Anthony knit his fingers together, running the pad of his forefinger across the smooth surface of his ruby signet ring. "By chance, it might have found its way under the false compartment. Lift the bottom."

Feathers took in a breath, the room's stuffiness cloying his chest. In one quick jerk, he hoisted the velvet-covered divider.

Emptiness greeted him; the burgundy lining was barren of any kind of letter—and any kind of purse. "There's naught in here."

Anthony's heels came crashing down on the floor and he smacked his fist on the desktop. "Precisely! Now that I think on it, 'twasn't a letter I misplaced a'tall. 'Twas my purse of five hundred five pounds!"

Though Feathers had foreseen this outburst, nevertheless, he felt his face blanch. "I meant to replace it, sir."

"Replace it?" Anthony boomed. *"Replace it?* With what? A pouch of tin slugs and cut up pieces of newsprint?" Scrubbing at his jaw, Anthony grated, "We both know exactly where that purse went, do we not?"

Feathers bunched his fingers together behind his back. Toying with the braid on his coattails, he mumbled, "Do we, sir?"

"The devil, Feathers! 'Twas given to Mistress Liberty."

"Aye . . ."

"And we both know why, do we not?"

"Aye . . . ?" Feathers felt his palms go clammy.

"Because you've gone and offered it to her to pose as my lady!" Anthony unfurled his fist, picked up his writing sand

and pitched the glass jar into the cold hearth. A shattering echo sliced through the room. For the second time that week, the container met with demise.

"Lud!" Feathers dissolved. "On my honor, Mister Fielding, 'twasn't my intention to seek her out when I left this house for the Blue Anchor as you bade me. I did indeed stop by the jeweler's shop, but Winthrop was having a row with the pewter merchant next door. I left the two gentlemen to finish it out and 'tis only that reason the purse never went toward a necklace. And 'tis a good thing, too, sir. As when I reached the Blue Anchor, Mistress Eden had been detained, as you know. 'Twas on my departure I chanced a fortunate encounter with Mistress Liberty."

"You offered her money to be fond of me!" Anthony raked through his hair with both hands. "Am I an idiot?"

"No, sir."

"But you very well think it! The devil, you hold me in such low esteem to carve my pride, man?"

"On my honor, good sir, 'twas never anything of the sort." Feathers approached the desk, his legs feeling like jelly. He leaned forward. "You were in need of a woman and there she was. You cannot deny she's beautiful—"

"I need . . ." Anthony paused. What did he need? He'd wanted a puppet, a simpering vixen with no mind of her own. A blonde. "Never mind what I need. I don't need *her* "

"Aye, but don't you find her a challenge, sir?" Feathers banked on Anthony's unswerving ego.

"How I find her, 'tis of no concern of yours."

"Aye, 'tis not."

A ghastly quiet settled over the two men, then the valet mustered the nerve to ask, "How did you find out, sir?"

"She told me!" Anthony's anger rose anew. "This afternoon. she confessed. She is but a chambermaid. Had I not feared my temper with her, I would have interrogated her on the details. She surprised me. Is this Fairweather person really her aunt?"

"Oh, aye, sir. She would not come without a chaperon. She's a very proper miss."

"Proper enough to take five hundred five pounds in an act of fraud," Anthony finished flippantly.

"I pray, do not judge her harshly. 'Tis what you wanted, after all."

"I wanted that hussy Eden Bennet."

"Precisely. If you had the choice, you never would have agreed to Liberty Courtenay. She's too bold and with an intelligent mind. If I dare say, I'd hoped she would have been the one to rid you of The Craving."

Feathers absently put the writing box to rights, knowing he'd gone too far. Even with the close relationship he and Fielding had, he'd spoken way out of turn. Closing the lid, he somberly apologized, "I'm sorry, Mister Fielding. You may ask for my termination now. I shan't give you any further trouble."

Anthony glared at the man he'd found to be a loyal and trusting servant for a decade. What had gotten into the valet to lead him astray? Perhaps it had been Anthony's own desperation that had seen the fall of the man's ethics. The possible reasons fled him. By his faith, had he started to go insane under the effects of his liquor? How could he blame Feathers? He'd been following the example set to him by his employer—calculated misrepresentations. "Nay, Feathers. I'll not end our friendship on such a sour note."

The gleam in Feathers's eyes returned.

"But I shall ask you to relate every word you exchanged with Liberty the day you found her."

Feathers did, leaving out John Perkins's involvement in Liberty's dismissal. Knowing Fielding's sore spot with the man, he glossed over that part of the tale. There was no purpose in riling Anthony further. Instead the valet described the state of grief he'd found Liberty in on the bench by the shore. He repeated the pieces of conversation he could remember, fabricating only to fill in the missing spaces.

"So you see, sir, 'tis of a great benefit for both of you to have each other." Feathers didn't add that he'd hoped the Lord and Master would soften a little in his heart around the whimsical Liberty Courtenay.

"Her lady's maid . . ." Anthony tapped his fingertips over a pile of documents, then shoved open his drawer in search of more claret. Nothing. "I couldn't figure it before, but she seems familiar to me. Where did you get her?"

"I borrowed her, sir."

Anthony's pique rose.

"From the Sign of the Mermaid. She's a sometime serving wench, but has been trained as a lady's maid. Her lady died of the influenza last month and she's looked for a fair replacement to tend to such as our Liberty. As far as Jane knows, Mistress Liberty is a woman of breeding whose own attendant ran off without a word of explanation."

"I see." Anthony shook his head, trying another niche in his desk. Nothing. " 'Tis why Liberty's clothing is so humble."

"But she does look quite nicely, don't you agree?"

"You have nailed me into a casket, Feathers."

Feathers could think of no answer to appease the Lord and Master. Placidly he creased his mouth into a wan smile, trying to pass off some of the errors of his ways. "Your grandfather is quite taken with Liberty."

Anthony did not furnish him with a reply.

"I see that Madame Fairweather and he get on splendidly."

Anthony's silence made the manservant tremble. Feathers couldn't help blurting out, "You are going to keep her sir?"

" 'Twould seem I have no choice."

"Very good, sir," Feathers replied, sighing in relief.

"Is the cook in any state of mind to prepare a meal?"

"I had a rough time of it getting your pistol from her, sir Madame Fairweather pried the firearm from her fingers. Quashabee took herself off in a fit of weeps, but I've since seen her in the kitchen hunting down a fly with a rolled-up gazette. I think she's recovered."

Anthony hunched over, his arms resting on the desk's edge. He ransacked his brain for all the spots he hid his liquor. He was averse to riding into town, but he would if he had to. "Just make sure something edible is on the table at eight."

"Very good, sir." Feathers backed from the study, an impeccable bow stooping his upper body. As he reached for the door's knob, he paused. "One more thing, sir."

"Confound it, Feathers, I'm in a great deal of pain!" Anthony arched his brow in waiting, rubbing his temple.

No doubt the Lord and Master's ego was killing him, thought Feathers. It had taken a terrible blow. "I used some of the household money to secure Jane's services, er, and had to forgo the purchase of that cask of Jamaican rum you asked me to bid on. . . ." He dared not wait for Anthony to comment on that bit of news, rushing out, "I shall take my final leave now, sir."

The door smartly moved into place, nearly catching Feathers's coat hem.

Plundering his study, Anthony tore works of fiction off the shelves, looking behind the fire screen, under his settee and behind the draperies. He could not find what he needed.

Slumping down on the arm of his chair, it came to him with woeful observance—Liberty put a fear in him. For all of her frankness and candor, her sweet smile and soft curves, she was the only woman he'd ever felt naked with—without being naked at all. As if each time she adorned his company, she chipped away at his cold heart. Piece by piece, she could crumble him. He'd be left with the barest of emotions.

Vulnerability.

Anthony reached for his claret bottle and brought it to his lips. A single droplet splashed on his tongue and he savored the taste while violently cursing the scant liquid.

She made him afraid and that was the one emotion he couldn't face while sober.

Sitting at her dressing table, Liberty rubbed sweet almond oil on her cheeks and the bridge of her nose. The permissible pink of her skin worsened in the evening hour to the color of a bright red apple.

"No amount of oil will fade the burn, Liberty," Ophelia pronounced from the doorway of their adjoining apartments. The elaborately dressed woman walked in. Upon her wrist dangled a black silk fan and in her hands, jars of face cosmetics and a rabbit's tail. "Let me tend to it, lambkin."

Liberty spoke in a weak whisper. " 'Tis kind of you, Aunt Ophelia."

Popping free the lid, Ophelia dipped the puff into the fine white powder. She whisked the chalky substance across Liberty's face in a sweeping motion, clouding the air.

Holding onto a sneeze, Liberty kept her back stiff. Generally she didn't like lead and vermilion, but she accepted her aunt's ministrations as her comeuppance. She never should have gone off with Anthony.

To be fair to Anthony, he had every right to be angry. She'd been trapped in her own lie. She should have known he'd hold her true identity in disgust. His cold and calculated kiss had erased the joy she'd previously felt in his arms. She'd withstood his gross treatment, masking her inner turmoil with deceptive calmness.

"My dear sweet lamb," Ophelia mourned. She dumped her wares on the dressing table, knocking over a vial of perfume. "I shall send Fielding to eternal damnation with a spread shot of my blunderbuss. Tell me your afternoon was innocent."

Liberty nodded. "It was."

Ophelia sat and clutched Liberty to her bosom, sobbing her relief. "Thank heavens."

Liberty sat still while her aunt praised her restraint. Guilt burned across her face. How could she tell her aunt she'd come close to surrendering to him, but he'd shoved her away once he'd known the truth?

Ophelia cradled her niece's face in her hands. "Give me an exact account of your excursion in the country."

Liberty worried her lower lip. She would not divulge the kisses she and Anthony shared. "He brought a picnic dinner for me—"

"What was the meal?"

"I believe 'twas . . ." She blushed. "I don't know."

"I thought not. If you cannot recall your dinner, then what can you recall? What did he do to you, pet? He's crushed the love from your eyes."

Fighting off her own need to cry, Liberty said with a trembling breath, "I told him I was a chambermaid and that I'd been paid by Mister Feathers to pretend affection for him."

"Oh, lamb . . ."

"He was furious, of course." Liberty could not repeat the rejection she'd suffered and the lonely drive home.

Ophelia's unhappy mouth tilted. "When I returned from the kitchen to find you missing, I bade Hiram to tell me where you'd vanished to. He sadly revealed to me his part in your abduction. I was quite gone over his story and said as much to him. He assured me you would not be harmed, that the Master had merely wanted a private afternoon with you.

"I tried to tolerate this manner of thinking, hoping perhaps I'd been mistaken about Fielding." Ophelia skimmed her hand across Liberty's glossy black hair. "But I was right in my hesitation. In this instance, it pains me to be. Fielding is unpredictable because of his penchant for spirits. Thankfully my Benjamin never overindulged, but I have seen dear friends yoked to drunkards and they have fallen to great depravation by their husbands' disorders."

Tears washed down Liberty's cheeks and she brushed them away with her knuckles. She hadn't wanted to believe he could be sick from his drinking. She'd wanted to attribute his moodiness and humor to characteristic traits born in him, not because of what he put into his belly. Had she been laughing at his farcical quips, when all the while he'd been drinking because he couldn't help himself?

She didn't understand this association Anthony had with liquor. She'd once sampled cordial water, but hadn't found the affects agreeable. It made her giddy and an hour later, nauseated.

"I don't wish to upset you further, Liberty, but you cannot draw a kind veil over his faults."

Aunt Ophelia was right, of course. He'd treated her with an aloof and forced acceptance. Under his new set of rules, her infatuation with him became pitiful at best.

Liberty wrung her hands in her lap. "Whatever shall I do, Aunt?"

"If you slow down the rush of your feelings, then judgment has a better chance of prevailing." Ophelia's voice seemed to come from a long way off. "I sympathize with your youth, lambkin. If I thought Fielding the least bit suitable for you, I would be your biggest advocate.

"Alas, not all Fielding men are so stricken. In my short introduction to Thomas while we awaited your return, I found myself liking him. He seems a devout man who desperately wants to see his grandson wed and produce an heir. I cannot help but have charity in my heart for him. I dare say, no matter how upset I was over Fielding's scandalous conduct this afternoon, I could not disclose to the old gentleman the duping he was being put through. That is for Fielding to wrestle with on his conscience—if he has one a'tall."

Looking into the silver-backed mirror with a sigh, Ophelia pressed her cheek to Liberty's so that they made a portrait. "I love you so, lambkin. You are the picture of your dear mother. You are such a virtuous girl. I shall keep close watch on you so that no further harm befalls you." She forced a smile. "Come now. We shall face him with the utmost dignity and know that our place on this earth is just as goodly as his. We will keep our heads high, you and I."

Liberty stood from the daintily cushioned toilette bench. Her cotton petticoats limply protected her thinly stockinged legs. Though her yellow dress with its run of bows down the stomacher was her best, she'd never felt the unassuming service of her station in it until now.

Her aunt's words were strong; she would respectably carry herself as was her due. But to brave Anthony without mentally preparing for the encounter lowered her resistance. She could not stop her romantic feelings for him on command. "If you please, Aunt, allow me a moment alone. I'll join you in a twinkling."

Ophelia paused, then nodded. "Don't be long, my pet." She left the door open.

Liberty moved through the opulent chamber unhurried, but hasty in purpose. Gathering her wits, she forecast what Anthony's harsh speech would be at the supper table and practiced stiff retorts. Her heart could not withstand his quiet power and barbed pride. No matter what she'd done to him, she did not deserve to be the recipient of his belittling performance.

She had hit John Perkins for daring to touch her in such an offending manner. But the coxcomb Perkins had been different. She'd never asked for his handling. With Anthony, she had relished the feel of his arms encircling her waist, his mouth discovering her lips.

While maneuvering around the wrought footboard of her bed, a clumsy hand fastened over her shoulder. She cried out in frightened alarm. Turning sharply, she knocked Anthony's fingertips from her person.

He stared at her, a wild and spiteful air about him.

In the past, she'd felt a mixture of emotions in his presence: attraction, curiosity, desire and happiness. Fear had never claimed her.

Until now.

"Hiding from me, sweeting?" His untamed hair framed his tanned visage. Wind and weather had seasoned his face; his evening binge had aged it.

Anthony swerved and groped for the black iron bedpost, his balance unsteady. Maelstrom hardened his eyes; she involuntarily curled her toes under in her shoes. He'd dressed himself in a forest green suit that informally hung open; a missing button on his silver-corded waistcoat appeared to have been torn off, as if he hadn't the capacity to fasten it. The tie of his stock hung loose and slipshod.

"My door was open," she returned, her heartbeat caged in her ribs like a butterfly.

"But had you known 'twas me on the other side, 'twould have been locked."

"I didn't say that."

"But you thought it."

His forced contradictions wore on her courage. Why had he done this to himself? To them? He had been brutal to her under the watchful eyes of others; alone, she feared he would mercilessly malign her for taking his money and falsely ensconcing herself in his home.

She tried to keep her fragile control. "I think we should go down to the dining room." She moved away and he caught her arm. She silently pleaded with him for release of his unyielding pressure. He did so.

"A word with you first." His voice, thick and reckless, had been slurred by the influence of his liquor. A swath of sunshine brown hair tumbled past his brow to tease the corner of his eye. He blinked several times, then blew the unmanageable strand out of his line of vision.

Liberty inched away from him, acutely conscious of his potential strength and the offending smell of hard liquor on him. She found herself blatantly studying him, trying to come to terms with this dark side.

The rigid outlines of his shoulders strained in the velvet he'd chosen. Beads of perspiration tarnished his browned skin as he struggled in such a heavy dress. He'd discarded his boots for hose of dark gray and black shoes with large tongue flaps and silver buckles.

As frightened as she was, she would not flee. "You wanted a word with me?"

Anthony didn't answer right away; he took no delight in her false valor. She pretended to relax, but he saw that she was strung tighter than a harp. He gave her his full attention, preferring her dark-haired beauty and ruby lips to the bitter subject he meant to raise. He appraised the close-fitted bodice of her dress—the one she'd worn when he first saw her. He missed the clump of asters at her waist, but consoled himself on knowing he hadn't forgotten that original detail.

"Aye. I wanted a word with you." A wobbly pain striped through his head, firing a blinding light on his brain. The half pint of English gin he hunted down in the base drawer of his chest-on-chest gave him the woollies. The last time he'd consumed the British distilled spirits, he'd grown violently ill from it. This eventide, in his haste to see himself soaked, he'd broken his abolition of that particular inebriant and drained the bottle dry.

Forcing the upset from his stomach at the remembrance of that occasion, Anthony declared, "Since you've seen yourself open to adopting my purse of five hundred five pounds, 'twould seem to me, you are under my employ."

Liberty tilted her chin up and calmly asked, "And my duties are to be, Mister Fielding?"

"The same as they were when you accepted Feathers's proposal. Only this time you should keep in mind I can at any time turn you and your aunt over to the authorities on the charge of theft—five hundred and five pounds." Anthony vindictively curved his mouth. "You are, mistress, to fawn over me in the most devoted manner. If we are to be in love for my grandsire's sake, we are to perform the part with great drama."

Chapter
8

FEATHERS SURVEYED HIS HANDIWORK; HE HAD TRIED TO MAKE THE long dining table look more agreeable. A dozen smoking candles burned in a tarnished silver centerpiece. He'd arranged a medley of settings. Neither bone-handled spoons nor gold knives matched their two-tined forks. Goblets stood at differing heights and shapes. The linens were of varying fabrics, yet all in the same shade of blue.

He shrugged at the empty room. There could be no help for the diverse display. The Lord and Master hadn't the slightest interest in seeing to better service settings. He could well afford them, but his entertaining days were over and he'd raved he didn't give a damn if the saucer matched its cup. Would his food taste any better if his plate were patterned after his fork? Would his brandy taste finer in new stemware?

A year ago Feathers had brought in a housekeeper, but Fielding had dismissed her by the week's end. He'd been driven to an irrational madness from the jangling of the old lawn-capped woman's circle of metal keys pinned to the bib of her apron. After her demise, every now and then Feathers had tried to remedy Fielding Manor—case in point, the newly acquired kitchen footman—but for the most part he let his employer dictate the house's ruin.

Footfalls sounded in the hallway and soon after, Thomas and Ophelia entered the eating salon. Feathers gave Madame Fairweather a devoted smile, noting the way she looked in her flattering deep red frock with smartened gorget collar of silver lace. Her spry composition and fresh ideas made him feel years younger. He'd become incurably enamored with her, but dared not hope she returned his favor.

Liberty appeared and just behind her, Anthony. Without a word and total neglect of protocol, Anthony took up his chair at the head of the table. He stared harshly down at the group, watching his grandfather seat the two ladies on opposite sides of him. Crashing his elbow on the table, he called for his manservant. "Feathers, let's get on with it, shall we?"

Feathers's good spirit fell lower than the floor. Lud . . Fielding had turned nasty, lathered to the bone. With the Master's undoing, Feathers doubted the first course would be finished before Fielding exploded.

The valet's gaze darted nervously back and forth between the guests. Thomas ignored his grandson's repugnant disposition; Ophelia shunned him, and Liberty seemed ready to weep. Lud, indeed   He made his escape to advise Quashabee to carve the roast herself. In his condition, Fielding could slip with the knife and do himself damage.

"I should like to applaud you ladies, Thomas complimented, whisking open his serviette. "You both look resplendent. I, for one, shall enjoy my meal all the more with such abounding loveliness."

"You are too kind, sir," Ophelia primly returned, cautiously examining Anthony

Overwrought, Liberty ran her fingertip along the ivy motif at the edge of her dish, upset clearly written on her face.

Anthony interrupted her action by plucking her fingers into his own, making an exaggerated show of caressing her hand. He fondled her ivory skin and the sensitive back of her wrist. "You're fidgeting, my dear "

Ophelia's blue eyes aimed a frosty dart at Anthony which warned him to mind his conduct.

Quietly, Liberty wiggled out of Anthony's hold. Her fingers trembled and she meshed them together, stilling her hands on her lap. She didn't want his touch—not this way; cold and mechanical. Not when she did not recognize him. He wasn't the vibrant man who'd challenged her aunt's political convictions with his own; nor did he resemble the curious man who'd caused tumult to her beehive and received her kiss of sympathy for his pain. And most definitely, he was *not* the man who had stolen her out of a parlor window to celebrate his conquest in a meadow of flowers where she'd delighted in his fervent kisses.

Tonight, he'd suited himself to being an ugly and unsavory monster, making her ashamed and repulsed.

"My dear Mistress Courtenay," Thomas said, smiling. "With your beauty, you could have had a charming young spark, some dapper soul sleek with manner and polish. 'Tis very glad I am that my grandson landed you. He may be rustic, but 'tis on God's teeth, I profess my great love for him."

Anthony didn't want to be praised. He didn't want love from anyone; he wanted to be left alone. If Thomas knew the details of this travesty being played out for his welfare, he would be swearing more than affection on God's teeth.

Turning his head, Anthony hunted for Feathers, trying to disconnect himself from the lauds of the elderly fellow that held him in such high esteem.

As if on cue, Feathers made himself present through the revolving door. The hinges squeaked into place, a *thump-thump* following as the aperture wagged still. Attired in his impeccable navy blue servant's garb, and wreath of fuzzy orange hair, Feathers took up his position behind Anthony's tall-backed chair. Arms crossed and stoic facade in place on his whitened face, the valet waited.

"Feathers, where is supper?" Anthony looked at the manservant who neither recognized his gaze, nor repudiated it. *"Feathers?* Damn you, answer me."

Not a single affirmation.

Mutely cursing the valet's impudence, Anthony faced forward. Spying the small gold bell before his chipped plate,

Anthony took up the dainty handle and let the striker peal in a long, drawn out ring.

"Fielding!" Ophelia screeched above the high-toned chime. "You shall have us all in need of ear trumpets! Suspend your ringing at once!"

Quirking a brow, Anthony allotted the bell one more toll to aggravate Ophelia, then trounced it back to the table.

"Supper is served," Feathers announced with stiff formality.

The newly hired footman clad in nankeen came in bearing a ceramic platter of venison which he presented to Anthony. In a fit of foul temper, Anthony waved him off. "I enjoin you, see to the others first."

Appearing undaunted, the server performed his duties in a proficient fashion, making several passes through the flapping door. The screak of the dry hinges echoed painfully in Anthony's skull. He grew jittery and bothered by the man's tried methods and systematic ways; the footman did things too perfectly. He liked Feathers to see to the serving. Feathers didn't do things orderly. Feathers didn't apparel himself in bright colors. Feathers didn't smell like bay leaves.

Holding out the platter to Anthony again, the footman subserviently waited.

Having worked himself into a fit over the servant's habits, he barked, "I haven't given you license to intrude upon me. Put it down and quit your bloody hovering. I'll help myself in good time." Anthony had no appetite, it being squelched by gin. Nausea had begun to preoccupy his thoughts. His vision lost its clarity, his muscles felt heavy and the consumption of food repulsed him.

The footman left the oval platter of roast venison and heavy brown gravy in front of Liberty.

Anthony heard her muffled shudder and slanted her a withering glance which she didn't catch. She wrinkled her nostrils, pressing her fingertips over her mouth, as if her sense of smell had been revolted by the gamey aroma. She looked to be praying for prudence not to be ill.

Narrowing down on her lack of regard for the meat, he

would have made a comment on it, save Feathers bumped his foot into the leg of his chair.

"Your pardon, sir." Feathers put a modest portion of onion pie on Anthony's plate. "But the last time you ate Cook's onion pie, you said it to be a favorite of yours."

"I did?" he suspiciously questioned.

"Aye. 'Tis why the footman—"

"Footman!" Anthony railed. "He looks a thousand times more like a gentleman than Montgomery Bennet and acts like one, aye, and smells like a tree. His head is so prettily dressed, sugared on top with powder, like a frosted cake. Those three little curls on each side annoy me. You may see his ears as plain as day. I don't like him." He went on with his censure of the servant. "I don't like his white stockings. They make him look like a fine white-legged fowl. From which fine Norfolk home did you steal him, Feathers?"

"I procured his papers from Mister Winderemere, sir."

"Winderemere?"

Thomas interceded. "Anthony, 'tis of no importance. I say, let us speak of more momentous affairs. Namely yours and Mistress Courtenay's. Tell me, my boy," he inquired, slathering butter on a roll. "How did you and your lady find each other?"

"We fell in love," Anthony answered shortly, not remembering the sordid yarn Feathers had told him why he'd brought Liberty home. "We fell in love," he repeated, staring at Thomas's eager face. "'Tis all there is to it."

"Well, I should say, that was vague." Thomas scrubbed at his chin with his napkin. He turned to Ophelia. "Have you any details on your niece and my grandson's infatuation, madam? Were it not for the fact Anthony has been so inflexible on marriage, I wouldn't be all agog for the particulars. I fear too much talk about it and he'll change his mind."

Ophelia snipped Anthony a pruning smile. "Theirs was a courtship of . . ." she let the next word hang like a rickety chandelier, "tolerance." Tracing the heart-shaped beauty patch in the middle of her rouged cheek, she continued. "My Liberty is quite patient, I might add, too forbearing, and I fear Fielding didn't see fit to bring himself 'round. She is such a beautiful girl, as you can see. Fielding didn't take the time to regard her numberless graces and untold perfections; the beauty beyond her skin. 'Twas quite a blow that hit him when he realized he would never do better than my pet."

"Splendid!" Thomas cried. "And the proposal, where did that take place?"

Ophelia frowned, a thin red pout. " 'Tis not been revealed to me."

Anthony broke in. " 'Twas at the Blue Anchor," he embellished with drunken ease. "And actually, I didn't propose myself. Feathers acted in my stead." He curved his brows in a sardonic arch at the valet who stood behind his chair. "In more ways than one, 'twas Feathers's idea. He saw the potential for mutual benefit before I." Anthony slid his gaze to Liberty. "Did he not, love?"

Liberty fiddled with her fork. Her strained voice was low. "I believe you would have proposed to me whether Mister Feathers arbitrated or not."

Laughter came from Thomas. "I should have liked to see you, Feathers," he said, glancing toward the somber valet. "I'll wager 'twas the only time you've ever professed alliance to a woman."

A sneer caught Feathers's upper lip before he could tame it. The man's drollery slapped his pride. He had declared himself to many a maiden . . . and madame. He'd just never been inclined to take his testimonies to the altar. In an unbending tone, he forced out, "Very good, sir."

Ophelia stared pensively at Hiram Feathers, gentle compassion softening her cosmetic features.

"I should think Mister Feathers would be princely at expressing affections." Ophelia raised her chin and looked directly at Thomas. "From what I have seen, he is an endearing man."

"Feathers?" Thomas chuckled. "Endearing?"

"Quite so." At Thomas's second round of merriment, she became overly flustered and forgot herself. "I know, for myself, I should be honored to pledge to such a man."

Feathers thwarted a wheeze. Did she realize what she'd spoken? A woman of refinement such as Ophelia Fairweather was posing to be would never have made a binding declaration over an ordinary servant.

Once the shock of Ophelia's announcement wore through the starched mind Feathers put on while holding his post as valet, the significance of her words shot through him to the common man. Did she mean what she said? Were he to declare himself to her, she'd have him? Lud . . . what a thought.

Then he smiled out of character.

Thomas's brows thundered down in a frown. "What did you say, madam?"

Indignantly Ophelia didn't give Thomas the courtesy of her attention while she answered him; her stare lay steadily on Hiram Feathers. "I said, I would be honored if a man such as Feathers made his intentions known to me." She gave the valet a warming smile.

Feathers went into a dither, absently fitting the dyed wig more snugly over his crown. "Madam, you flatter me with your kind words."

"They weren't meant in kindness, Mister Feathers," Ophelia projected with a bow to her mouth. "They were spoken in earnest."

"Are we to be spectators to this inopportune courtship?" Anthony rid himself of his unappetizing pie, the bone china of his dinner plate clanking against the gold bell. "Feathers, eliminate that high-flown look from your face. You're panting like an animal."

Feathers promptly recommended to his staidly self.

Liberty's shaken emotions could not stand much more. The torment of Anthony's presence as he unabashedly went on like he'd lost his sanity, tore at the last threads of her control. She began to be smothered by the smell of the roast, unable to abide its nearness anymore. She inched the oval platter toward the center of the table with subtle slowness.

Trying desperately to be casual about the affair, she didn't pay her task the proper amount of attention; she bumped the dish into the silver pedestal centerpiece and knocked a candle free of its holder. Melted wax splattered across a bowl of green grapes.

"Oh!" she sobbed.

Feathers lunged forward to right the capsized candle, ramming its waxy end back into the tarnished reserve. A thin curl of gray smoke circled upward. "'Tis a common occurrence in the household for candles to topple," he supplied in a solicitous voice. "Drafts."

"Don't spoil her, Feathers." Anthony crossly examined Liberty. "What, my dear, is this abhorrence you have for meat? You have not put one piece of it in your pretty mouth while gracing my home. You try hiding it very well. Pouring sauces over vegetables, loading up on bread. What are you about? Are my cook's recipes disgusting? Your palate is too sensitive for my table?"

"Fielding! This is—"

"Silence, madam!" Anthony yelled, pointing his finger at Ophelia. "This is *my* house and I am asking her a question and I will not be put off. I need to know. I cannot go on without knowing."

Feeling the sting of tears in her eyes, Liberty lowered her lashes. "I make it my practice not to eat living creatures."

"Living?" Anthony poked his silver fork into a portion of venison. "Living? 'Tis dead."

"Fielding, this is an outrage!" Ophelia hotly scraped her chair back, ready to set upon him.

Anthony, too, rose to his feet. He nearly lost his balance and had to brace his hands on the table's edge lest he fall down. "Nay, madam. I'm trying to grasp something here. This girl does not eat meat because she cannot stand to eat a living creature. Well, this deer is dead." Raising his fork, he sharply stabbed the meat again. "Dead." *Like me*

Liberty jumped at the brutality of his gesture, unable to contain the hot, grief-stricken tears from trickling down her cheeks.

Anthony's burning eyes held her still, then he looked away. Gasping for air, a low growl escaped his lips. In an angry move, he grabbed hold of the platter and hurled the venison at the wall behind Liberty The shattering of glass broke through the room as gravy slid down the blue wallpaper to fall into the waste below. "There! If it wasn't dead before, 'tis surely dead now!"

Falling back on his heels, Anthony's calves bumped into the seat of his chair. His belly roiled like whitecaps on the ocean and he knew he was going to be sick. Somehow he managed to get through the doorway, Liberty's soft weeps persecuting him all the way.

In the aftermath of Anthony's turbulent departure, the dining room's inhabitants grew ghostly motionless. Following a moment's hesitation, Feathers left his station to care for Fielding. His gray eyes were apologetic, while dismay mercilessly set in the lines of his narrow face. He passed Ophelia by, but said nothing to displace his allegiance to Fielding no matter how horrid his employer's moral excellence had disowned and lost him.

Thomas quietly put up his knife on the edge of his unfinished plate. " 'Twould seem my grandson isn't feeling well." His voice cracked from brittle calmness.

"I should say so!" Ophelia left her place and came around to rest her hands on her niece's quaking shoulders. "He's addicted to a baneful habit which sends him to inroads of the grossest immoralities."

" 'Tis harmless, I'm sure," Thomas denied, unable to look at Liberty whose cries had diminished to a whimper. "Quite harmless . . . he's just overindulged is all. Most men do. We've all had our share of cups. Now that he's settling down, he'll take things in moderation. He has, after all, found love."

"Love is not a cure, Mister Fielding." Cynicism lined Ophelia's words. "He needs something far stronger."

Out of great concern and much worry, Hiram Feathers had summoned a physician to attend the Lord and Master. For the first time, the cook's miracle tonic hadn't worked to rouse Fielding from his unconscious state. Feathers sent Tobias to collect a man of medicine knowing full well Fielding would object were he able.

A half hour later, the coachman returned with Isaac Spotswood. Dour in face, yet clean in a cocked hat bound by black ferret and a close-bodied dun coat, Feathers approved of him. A silver-headed cane aided his walk as he entered Fielding's bedchamber. He took one look at Anthony's pallid countenance and shook his head, muttering about the pitfalls of degrading oneself to the demoralizing appetite.

The physician set out to work immediately, taking from his case a compounded tincture of barks. With Feathers's help, they poured a half teaspoon dose down Fielding's throat. Then the physician ordered Anthony to be stripped of all clothing. Spotswood applied cold cloths to his head and vigorously rubbed his extremities to keep his blood moving.

An hour later, he left giving Feathers instructions to repeat the medicinal doses every three hours. He strongly warned Feathers to advise his master to give up his liquor if he wanted to go on living. The valet assured him he would try, then took some coins from Fielding's writing desk drawer and paid the good doctor.

The next morning and afternoon passed without Anthony regaining his awareness. In his delirium, he twisted in his bedclothes, yelling incoherent, disconnected thoughts and fears. Feathers devoted himself to Fielding, sitting by his side; he read passages aloud from the Bible. Fielding was not a religious man by any account, but Hiram Feathers thought perhaps if the room were filled with stories of a higher spirit, Fielding would improve. He did.

By evening, Anthony came to his senses. His measured improvement enabled him to stomach weak tea and a thin soup. He would doze to Feathers's faithful voice as he had complacently resumed his reading of the Good Book. Sometime into the night, Fielding's drunkenness left him entirely. He sat up in his massive bed, vaguely remembering certain episodes and wanting Feathers to fill in the blanks.

The valet's retelling buffered the worst of things, but when prompted, he did confess to Anthony's demolition of the dining room. Fielding lay his head back on his stark white pillow to stare at the ceiling; a great depression engulfed him. Feathers summoned the courage to repeat the physician's warnings.

Fielding remained silent, neither acknowledging nor rejecting the counsel.

On the eve of that second day, Fielding had recovered enough to get out of bed, take a hot bath and dress himself. He left his chamber knowing he would have to make grand restitutions to all those who had bore witness to his revolting spectacle.

The thought of that pitiable undertaking made him want a drink.

Feathers had told him he would find his houseguests in the parlor with his grandsire. He heard Liberty's low and husky speech as it drifted into the foyer. Anthony reached the landing and slowed his steps while listening to her chatter.

"Mister Fielding, are you a lover of nature?"

"To a degree. As Anthony undoubtedly told you, I live on Antigua in the Leeward Islands. Flora thrives without a single lift of man's finger. My home is populated by greenery. Quite a few palms and such. Have you ever seen them?"

"Nay, I have not."

"We should like to one day," piped Ophelia.

Anthony moved on, inconspicuously pausing outside the parlor door. His grandsire sat in a side chair enjoying a smoke and Ophelia occupied the reading chair fiddling with pieces of ribbon. She wrapped and twisted them around her fingers, then wound the knots on a mother-of-pearl bobbin. An odd pastime, but then in his opinion, Ophelia Fairweather was odd. Liberty took up the window seat.

Her pose struck a vibrant chord. Something intense flared through him. He recalled quite vividly his lifting her off that cushion and conveying her to his own private picnic. Three days ago. It seemed years.

She sat there so winsome and grand in her plain blue frock, it cheered him. Yet by the same token, seeing her unspoiled beauty, conjured up particles of his last encounter with her. He knew he'd been vile and crass, but beyond that, he could not recall the specifics.

His grandsire shifted in his chair and Anthony observed the elder man had a mild case of indigestion. A dampness sheened his face, his powdered wig looked wilted as warm lettuce. He suppressed a belch. The slight paunch that lifted his chest expanded, then fell down as he expelled a silent stream of air. He apparently felt no relief, for he puffed harder on the stem of his pipe.

"If I were a man, I should probably like to unfasten the buttons on my waistcoat at this moment," Liberty offhandedly remarked. "I often don't eat as much as I'd like to, simply because of the restrictions of a lady's stays. I read in a book once that women of the South Seas never wear corsets. Only skirts of leaves and coconuts to cover their breasts."

Anthony bit off his shocked laughter, not wanting to give himself away.

"Is that so?" Thomas's fine hand brought down his smoking devise, tapping the bowl on the heel of his pump. "I dare say, I am wearing stays so I fear 'tis too late for me."

"Pet," Ophelia mildly reprimanded with a twinkle to her blue eyes. "In mixed company, you should have said bosom."

Anthony thought neither would have been acceptable in a social circle, but who the hell cared? He found Liberty's uninhibited anecdote endearing. On that note, he strode into the parlor. "The next time I have a gardener trim my trees, I'll tell him to keep a few branches for you. The coconuts may pose a problem though. I don't have a coconut tree."

The wispy black lashes that shadowed Liberty's cheeks flew up. She blushed, but whether from embarrassment or due to his unannounced presence, Anthony wasn't sure. He could not look her square in the eyes yet.

"Anthony!" Thomas dumped his clay pipe into an ashtray on a nearby tea table. "Anthony, you've come down. Your valet said you had a case of the ague and couldn't be seen by anyone."

"Not quite so, but in any event, I've recovered." His gaze finally came to rest on Liberty and he drank in her presence. He hated to think she'd observed him in his dark and callous state. He sent her a private look of regret which she regarded speculatively, but said nothing.

Ophelia, on the other hand, glared at him with reproach and he guessed he deserved every impudent lightening bolt she soared his way. "If you please, I would like to express my apologies for the other night. I was quite gone and my conduct was unforgivable. Let me assure you, 'twill never happen again."

"Of course it won't." Thomas scoffed off his admission of error. "Join us for a nightcap. Come sit down and have a thimble of sherry with me."

Anthony felt his stomach tighten. The decanter with blown handles and faceted stopper was within his reach on that tea table. The black abyss of his drunk yawned, eager to embrace him, to seduce him.

"I'd rather not," he declined, his heartbeat harsh and uneven. "But if 'tis permissible by you, madam," he addressed Ophelia, "I should like to play a game with your niece."

"What?" Several of Ophelia's tidy knots unraveled as she raised her fist.

Tipping the corner of his mouth into a gibe smile, Anthony said, "I'm keeping you on your toes, madam, and I can see I've . . . ruffled your feathers. I meant to ask Liberty if she would join me for a game of billiards."

Ophelia wasn't given the chance to reply as Thomas embellished, "Outstanding idea! You two need to be alone and settle your future."

"I think not." Ophelia held tightly to the spindle in her lap. Knots abounded in many bright colors and she cast them aside. "I have seen what you can do with an audience. I shall not allow you to defame my niece in private. She's suffered enough."

Anthony suddenly knew what it felt like to be a criminal. He belonged in gaol, rotting in irons for what he had done to her—for not remembering precisely what it was. He could only appeal to her to accept his humility in this issue and allow him to patch things up.

"Madam, what harm would there be?" Thomas ventured to ask. "Let her decide."

Liberty flushed under the watchful gazes of all three. She could hardly think. These last two days had passed in a dazed mix of loneliness and confusion. She'd gone over and over in her mind, what she had done to Anthony to make him forget himself in such a sadistic way. Never in her life had she been so hurt by another's wounding words. Not only had he mentally abused her, he had violently given into physically attacking her beliefs.

Mayhap she should, but she could not hate him. She knew he had goodness and kindness in him. He had the ability to draw out her laughter. She had always found a joyous satisfaction in his company. She wanted him to find her in good favor again. But what would be the cost?

She hung onto the hope that he'd changed. That whatever ailed him, he'd rid himself of. How could she throw his remorse back at him without giving him a chance?

"I don't know how to play billiards."

"I'll show you." Anthony kept his gaze level with hers.

Liberty furnished her aunt with a consenting nod. "If my aunt will allow me."

Ophelia clearly objected, yet she did not challenge her niece's choice. She wove another knot in her fingers, then said, her voice chocked full of doubts, "Fielding, if you mean to hoodwink me, I shall do worse to you than boxing your ears."

"Where did you read about coconuts?" Anthony inquired, the baritone of his voice ricocheting across the red billiard table that unintentionally served as a bridge between him and Liberty.

"In a book."

"Which book?"

"A novel on South Seas life."

Anthony drew his brows together. "Interesting choice of literature."

"I didn't choose it, it chose me. I've acquired most all of my books from the Blue Anchor coffeehouse." She purposely brought up that delicate subject, testing for his reaction. When he had no curt response, she went on, not masking the less than ideal facets of her former position. "While performing my cleaning duties, I found many forgotten volumes stashed in the backs of writing drawers or lowboys. Sometimes when I tightened bed ropes, I found publications between the mattresses and the lacings. I have some forty books in my collection. They are quite precious to me."

"I saw them in your bedchamber," Anthony said distantly, as if recalling the morning of his bee stings. He strode to a glass-faced oak cupboard. Pottery and pewter reflected in the silver trim of the cabinet's front as Anthony flicked open one of the doors. He brought down a fluted cruet and a pair of tumblers, then proceeded to pour generous amounts of gold liquid into each cup.

Liberty paled.

Touches of a smile bordered his mouth and eyes. "Apple cider. I do still get thirsty."

"Oh."

He didn't take pleasure in her struggle to capture her composure. Awkwardly, he cleared his throat. "Feathers said I did you grave injustices; no doubt more so than he knows. If you would allow me not to have to discuss that evening, I would be grateful. I cannot tell you how sorry I am it ever happened. It will not be repeated. I've stopped drinking." He would cut himself off of alcohol for six months to show himself he was able. Then he could test the waters again. Ale would not be detrimental in moderation. There would be no need to deprive himself the rest of his born days.

"I think that's admirable of you. If you should need any help not drinking—"

"I don't know how deserving I am of your admiration, and as for help, I won't need any." He grew visibly uncomfortable, prompting Liberty to change the topic.

She ran her palm across the table's edge, feeling the soft, supple material. "You undoubtedly didn't believe me when

I told you I was quite versed on many subjects. The fact that I haven't selected the books in my library firsthand attests to that. There are so many diversified readers these days."

"Indubitably." Anthony left her tumbler on a low table in a corner.

Liberty watched Anthony dangle the cider in one hand while with the other he whipped the ruby cloth off the billiard table. With the experience of a seasoned player, he readied the game without pause. His movements were swift, full of grace and virility as he took off the brass pocket covers, placing them in the cue and stick cabinet at the end of the room.

Liberty stared at the shallow depth of her cider. Lifting the glass, she brought the rim to her lips. Truly cider, as he'd said—not that she dispelled his claim, but in the wake of his . . . Oh, fie, she would not dwell on it now.

She heard Anthony's low chuckle and swung around to face him. Creases of laughter fanned from the outer corners of his eyes; dimples, characteristics she'd never noticed on him before, made themselves known around the fullness of his mouth. "Didn't believe me?"

"I . . no," she mumbled. "Sorry."

"You needn't be." He corrected his grin, thinning his mouth. "I'm not very trustworthy."

Liberty made no comment and replaced the short glass back on the table, primed to play the game Anthony had now assembled.

Anthony rounded the table to stand at her side. He slipped a very long stick in her hands; the touch of his fingers heated her insides, bringing back to life all the feelings she'd locked away for him in his absence. How could she abandon them? She smelled the traces of sweet cider on his breath, the scent of his clean hair. A small strand had worked its way free of the ribbon at the base of his neck; the richly colored skein fell over his temple.

"Hold it thus," he was telling her, but she barely heard him. His warmth suffused her much mended bodice and chemise, filtering through to tap the very skin covering her rapidly beating heart.

"Thus?" she echoed as his fingers curved around her own to show her.

"Aye." Anthony bent his head forward, inching down toward her face. "Balance the middle across your knuckles."

She tried.

"Nay, nay." Anthony moved around her to stand behind her. His body pressed into the curve of her backside and her spine. As he jiggled the stick into the proper position, he flattened himself into the limited gathers of her skirts and undergarments. She felt as if she couldn't breathe and tried to control the vortex of sensations threatening every thread of her equanimity.

"Better?" she whispered.

" 'Tis better if you intend to whack me over the head with the stick. You're holding onto it as if you mean to bat the light fixture."

Liberty kept her chin stiff while raising her eyes toward the ceiling. A small span above them hung a shaded corona light with long tassels and glass-ensconced candles. Keeping a semblance of casualness, she lowered her gaze to her hand. Her fingers curled into a fist over the stick and Anthony's deeply tanned fingers. His thumb ran down the length of her own; dark contrasting with light and the image of all of his skin colored such an opulent shade made her blush right down to her toes.

Trying to nudge her way free, Liberty dropped the cue. "You'd best let me watch you. . . ."

A slow grin spread on Anthony's lips as he backed away. "Sit." The lacy cuff of his white shirt dangled above his wrist as he motioned toward a half circle of chairs.

She sat, barely aware her bottom had nestled into the softness of brown calfskin.

"Watch and listen." Anthony deftly unfastened the two buttons keeping his charcoal waistcoat closed and slid his arms out of the heavyweight vest. He slung the garment over the back of a nearby seat. Loosening the strings that kept his ruffled shirtsleeves in place, he pushed up the fabric, exposing the length of arm between his wrist and elbow.

Her mouth dry, Liberty studied the bronze of his skin and the light dusting of hair that gilded his forearms.

"Cue stick," he said as he picked up the long stick she'd tried to hold properly. "Made of suitable ash, fitted on the end with a leather tip." Pointing the end toward her for her to observe, she mutely nodded that indeed the tip was covered with leather.

"The handle is of lighter wood so you can balance it correctly." Anthony made a show of the precise way to hold the cue in his hand. The length rested effortlessly in his brown fingers as he shifted. Sinewy muscles flexed on his buttocks and down the tightly breeched segment of his long legs.

Liberty blinked.

"Now, the object is to hit all the ivory balls into all the pockets. Understand?"

Not able to trust her voice, Liberty nodded again.

"Watch me."

She could do nothing but.

Anthony took command of the room, moving in all angles. The slap of balls hitting each other echoed distinctly at each turn. He would stop and study his situation before acting, then with the accuracy of an expert, his shot would ring true; another ivory orb fell into its respective pocket.

Two balls remained and for a length, he contemplated his move. Drawing his fingertips to his chin, he stroked the shy growth of dark beard on his jaw. His nostrils flared, then he tugged on the silken end of his cravat. In a snap, the piece of material floated free of his neck and Anthony absently discarded the tie on the floor. He went to his liquor cupboard and poured himself another apple cider, his eyes never leaving the table.

Liberty wasn't sure Anthony even realized she was in the same room with him. His entire concentration focused on the billiards before him. After gulping down his refreshment, he stalked the table, collected his cue and with amazing speed, aimed.

Smack! The ball plummeted into its pouch.

With a slow turn, Anthony faced her. Liberty bit her lower

lip. A fine sheen covered his brow, the lengthy segments of his brown hair hanging in his eyes. With a puff of breath, he blew them from his temple; then he surprised her by removing the top three studs of his lawn shirt; he plunked them on the raised ledge of the table. A mat of hair teased the base of his sun-darkened throat, conflicting with the pristine whiteness of his linen.

"Are you ready for your lesson?" he drawled, his full mouth curving upward.

Liberty couldn't think clearly. Her every fiber was centered on the aura of masculinity he wore without a single hitch. Her heart hammered foolishly, her head felt lighter than a feather. The beats worked their way into her thoughts for they were all a-jumble. "M-my lesson."

"You aren't scared?"

"I am not." Liberty managed to keep her self-control, primly folding her hands together. "It's just that the air in here is stuffy."

"Aye, 'tis hot. All the heat rises to this room in the evening." In a quick stride, Anthony went to the long double doors that opened onto the veranda. With a grunt, he pried open the rusty latch and swung both hinges outward. Immediately a redolent breeze made its way into the billiard hall.

"Better?" Anthony snagged the heavy hem of the drapes over a chair back to further expose the opening for air.

"A trifle," Liberty conceded. She hadn't realized how stifling the third floor room had been until she'd gotten a sample of freshness into her lungs. "I'm ready for my lesson."

Liberty made her way to the table. She could do this. She'd watched Anthony. What he'd done, she was capable of doing. Mayhap not as accurately as he, but how difficult could it be hitting a ball with a stick?

Picking up the cue, Liberty made light conversation, trying to appear relaxed and calm. "I've gotten to know your grandfather. I think he's good-natured."

Anthony lazed at the head of the table, bent at the waist, his elbows grazing the cloth-covered top. The front of his shirt gaped. No matter how hard Liberty persuaded her gaze to settle elsewhere, it roved back to the line of his chest hair that trailed down into the soft white of his shirt and beyond. Beyond her view into the waistband of his gray breeches.

"I never said my grandsire wasn't likeable." Rolling an ivory ball between his thumb and fingers, Anthony let it recoil off the side of the table. "He's a great dueler of wit. Quite strongly presented, I might add."

"I see you in him."

The comment brought a scowl to Anthony's forehead. "Then you, my darling girl, are in need of my spectacles." He gave her no opportunity to reply. Pushing up to his full height, he stood beside her. "Hold the cue, thus."

Liberty seemed to be made of wire. She bent and molded, shaped and held, in whatever position Anthony put her in. At last when he told her to aim at the cluster of balls, she squinted. There seemed to be hundreds of them. Her vision blurred and she blinked.

"Concentrate on the ball in the front," Anthony was telling her.

"I can't seem to keep it clear when I squint." Her words came out in an amateurish rush.

"Just thrust the stick like I did."

Liberty put her meager weight into it and rammed the tip of the stick forward. Nothing happened.

Beside her, she heard Anthony's laughter vibrate through her ears. "You sliced a wedge of air."

Liberty frowned and aimed forward. By her sanity, she would hit one of those balls. But when she made contact with a sphere, her direction grew upward and not straight.

"I hit one!" Liberty's triumphant victory was cut short by Anthony's curse.

"Bloody hell!" Anthony roared as a ball jumped off the table, cleared his head and flew out the open French doors. With a whack and a plop it bounded across the veranda. The overgrown foliage crawling on the balcony outside, cushioned the ball's fall as it rustled downward to the ground.

Liberty wrinkled her nose. "I suppose I shouldn't have struck it so hard."

All she could see of Anthony was the tight shape of his flanks as he bent over the railing to look for the overshot ball. He straightened and turned toward her, his mouth grim. " 'Twould seem the game has come to a crashing halt. Feathers will have to flush out your goof on the morrow."

"Perchance he could go get it now."

"In the dark? Hardly. Even Feathers has his limits." He left the balcony to inspect his billiard table. She'd not only sent a ball to its demise, she'd chipped another as well.

"Well then, whatever shall we do?"

The call of her low voice brought his head up. Taking in her angelic face, he had his ideas. The desire to kiss her had been pulling at him all evening but he hadn't wanted to scare her off. The sweet softness of her mouth, her fragrance, the dark hair twisted atop her head with a lengthy curl falling over her shoulder—he longed to be reminded of how good she felt in his arms. To explore the reasons why she fascinated him so.

"You are perfect." The gentleness in his voice startled him. "I don't know why I've been fighting that."

The color of Liberty's eyes penetrated his mind. A whirling mixture of green and gold limned in enchanting black. The lashes swept down, then up. A dance of slow and naive artfulness. She was a woman of showers, who enlightened, who thundered, who knew every kind of weather. At this moment, she came to him like a tropical storm. Smelling of flowers and sunshine; of balmy breezes.

Anthony bent his head, his lips barely kissing hers. Breath mingled, bodies fused with the lightest of touches. The aura became sensual in the fact that it didn't stem from a heated passion, it came from a place beyond where a loving caress meant more than fulfillment.

Anthony moved his lips against hers, meeting her silent plea, lost on his mouth. The kiss that had been suspended between them grew to a deep need within Anthony. He felt her resist, stiffen, then pull back. He saw the turmoil in her gaze as she fought to keep her distance.

"Don't kiss me." The light that had glistened in her eyes dimmed to sadness. "There isn't an audience to watch the performance and I'm not a good enough actress to play the part with only you."

Anthony let her drift free of him.

Liberty's emotions had taken too fierce a beating to succumb without caution. She had no delusions that he would be cured of this addiction that seemed to consume him at the most inopportune times. She wished she had a physician's learning so that she could be more understanding.

She could not bear his rejection a second time. By keeping a man off, a woman kept him on. She would adhere to Aunt Ophelia's prudent advice about patience being a guiding beacon. She would learn him. Detail by detail.

Liberty wet her lips. "If you please, I'd like to stay in your company for a while longer. Since I've wreaked havoc on your billiard table our entertainments are reduced by one." She gave him a feeble smile. "Do you play cards? I'm adequate at—"

Her sentence was cut short, interrupted by a far-off tolling. The urgent gong of a distress bell cried out, invading the room with ominous warning.

Chapter

9

BY THE LIGHT OF A QUARTER MOON ANTHONY FIELDING'S LAC-quered coach careened over the road into Norfolk, chasing the peels of the town bell. The notes of alarm tapered off, leaving the sounds of the horses' labored breathing and the clinking of tack to split through the night.

Anthony sat forward in his seat, ready to alight the moment his equipage stopped. The cold weight of his pistol lay snugly against his belly, slipped into the band of his breeches. His heartbeat matched the pounding rhythm of the roans' hooves.

Gripping the top of the windowless door, he anticipated what had prompted this midnight call of distress. He hadn't smelled smoke, so he ruled out fire early on. There had been no damning weather to capsize vessels in the harbor and the borough had been coexisting under its British rule without mishap—though tempers had been known to flare and public brawls had occurred.

The carriage rounded the bend at the end of Main Street, hugging close to the land and climbing slightly to higher ground. Whatever the problem, he had not wanted Liberty and her aunt to be part of the solution. He could not be responsible for them in the middle of unrest, no matter how slight. Amid heated protests from Ophelia, he left them at home with his grandsire. She'd blasted him for his mandate, spouting that Thomas's protection was no good at all as he'd previously gone off to bed and had not been roused by the bell. While trekking out the doors of Fielding Manor, Anthony had had to agree with Ophelia on that account. Once Thomas closed his eyes for the night, he slumbered soundly. But knowing that didn't make Anthony change his mind.

Tobias came upon a crowd of people whose torches burned brightly against the backdrop of a black sky. Some had apparently come tumbling out of their houses, sleepy and partly clothed to see the disturbance. They were armed with glinting swords, fowling pieces and percussion pistols.

As Tobias reined the horses to a stop, Anthony jumped down and strode to the group. Raised voices fueled the atmosphere of hostility. Anthony wove his way through to the front.

In the center of the group was a British seaman in his distinctive striped jacket. He wore a three-sided hat and a waistcoat decorated by gold binding. Around his waist dangled a cutlass. He aimed a pistol at the crowd of rumpled civilians. Huddled at his back stood a group of men similarly dressed.

In the middle of the British sailors and the citizenry were tars—Norfolk sailors. They had been blindfolded by their own kerchiefs and brought down onto their petticoat-trousered knees, their wrists bound together. Several had gashes on their heads, as if they'd been subdued by raps on the skull. They appeared to have been treated no better than dogs.

Anthony came upon his friend T. A. Cheswick. The man's fingers rested on the butt of his firearm. Cheswick was a noted captain, Anthony having sold him a schooner three years ago. He piloted it up and down the coast with tobacco, sometimes making runs to the British West Indies.

"Cheswick," Anthony called as he drew up to the tall man's side. They hadn't met since Cheswick's departure on business. "What the devil is going on?"

Cheswick turned his head. An ear string in his left ear

hung to his shoulder-length black hair, ending in an ornamental knot. "'Twould seem the British Captain Lionel Manning took it into his head to steal some of our sailors for his ship. He and his band landed, refreshed themselves with a cheerful glass and marched off to force doors open and drag the tars out. The night watch got wind of things and sounded the alarm. Manning won't surrender his captives."

Anthony regarded the scene. The so-called captives were dead center of the two sides.

"Let them go, in the name of all that is good in this humble port." Paul Price, a member of the Assembly and gentlemen aldermen, stepped out as head of the colonials.

"These men are being summoned by the British Parliament to serve duty for the Crown." Lionel Manning's proclamation brought forth a hum of rebellion from the eyewitnesses.

"Those men have not given themselves to you of their own free will." Price carried the weight of a hunting gun on his arm. "We want no bloodshed, but 'twill spill if you do not heed my warnings."

The hundreds of locals around him followed his lead. The clicking of numerous flintlocks to half cock resounded.

Manning looked to his flock of cohorts, most of whom were blatantly drunk. "We shall fight you for them. Comrades, lift up your weapons."

The paltry group murmured, their weapons haphazardly at their hips. Manning bellowed, "I said draw up your swords and guns!" No response followed. At this time, Manning searched the crowd. Anthony kept up with Lionel's gaze as he appeared to be bent on seeking a certain person in the crowd.

Manning halted his gaze on John Perkins.

The quick exchange lasted only a flash; Manning nodded a fraction and Perkins shook his head. Then he disappeared, swallowed up by the throng.

"I'll not be made to stand alone!" Lionel Manning yelled, lunging for the tar closest to him. Gathering the sailor's collar, he brought him to his feet and pinned the muzzle of his pistol to his temple. "Will anyone among you come forth and claim this man's life?"

Paul Price took a step, but was held back by Anthony. A white-hot rage consumed him. Perkins played into this somehow; the thought of foiling him at any cost had made him come forward. He curbed the alderman and walked to stand before Lionel Manning.

"Let him go." Anthony's deep tone wavered. Inside, his body shook from his recent ailment and the withdrawal he was going through.

"Let him go?" parroted Manning. "Let him go for what? So that I may be tarred and feathered? So that my passel of mates, girlish as they've turned out to be, may be put in irons? I would, sir, surrender them were I so inclined, but alas, I am not." He poked the barrel of his gun at the side of the sailor's head.

Anthony clenched his jaw. "He's not yours to imprison."

"Nay, he's a subject of the Crown and I want him."

"Release him to the colony and the freedom that is his privilege here."

"Release him to the colony? To Norfolk? To the misfits unable to live in the embrace England had to offer?" Manning cocked his pistol. "What's one less flea in a bed of dogs, hmm?"

Anthony rushed Lionel Manning as the explosion of his gun wrecked through the night. The mob took over, weapons primed and chasing after the British sailors who had come ashore with Captain Manning. Anthony pushed his way to the tar Manning had held and grabbed him away, shoving him toward T. A. Cheswick who'd come up behind him. Manning fled, his remaining men rallying around him. Their escape didn't get them far. They were quickly overtaken by the throng and Manning was trampled to the ground by half a dozen business keepers.

In the ensuing contest, eleven men were caught and arrested, then taken to the courthouse. Anthony found Cheswick tidying up the clash by pressing one more British sailor into the group of captives. His long black curls tangled down his back and he brushed at his cuffs. "Gallant this evening, aren't you, Fielding?"

"No more so than you, I see," Anthony scoffed. He cared not how Norfolk viewed him, he wanted to know more about Manning. "Have you ever run across Manning in your journeys up the channels?"

"Nay. But there was an instance similar to this in Carolina week before last. Several tars ended up missing. They haven't turned up. If Manning has been beating the ports, then they very well are in His Majesty's service. Though I can't account for it since the Royal Navy has hotly denied any association with Manning."

Anthony thought about this, wondering where the connection to John Perkins came in. "Perkins is involved."

"I thought so myself," Cheswick agreed. "Did you see the look he shared with Manning?"

"I did."

Cheswick shifted his weight. "Where have you been? I waited for you to come to the Sign of the Mermaid last night."

"I've been . . . ill." Though he and Cheswick were friends, confessing his drinking habit to a drinking friend made him feel less than a man.

"When you didn't show, I left without you and went to Perkins's house." Cheswick rifled through his coat pocket and procured a cigar. He brought the smoke to his lips but didn't light the end. "I caught him sneaking out the back and I followed him to the docks. He met with someone. A sailor-type. Paid him some coin, then left and went home."

"The devil, what is he up to?" Anthony thought aloud.

"We shall find out, my friend, won't we?" Cheswick had agreed to help Anthony trap Perkins. His reckless and daring ways had gotten him ousted from the family's good graces; he was a Lord or some such in England.

As the crowd dispersed, Anthony bid Cheswick to watch himself. His reputation for handling a craft smoothly would make him a target if the kidnapping continued.

Anthony searched for his coach and Tobias in the distance, fatigued and ready for home. The elegant equipage came into view and there at the side of it stood Ophelia, Liberty and Feathers. Ophelia held onto a blunderbuss and Liberty had pilfered the sword he kept hanging on his study wall.

He strode over to them, angry they had defied his orders and ready to pounce on his valet for letting two women petition his service. "What the devil are you doing here?"

"We came to see what was the matter," Ophelia frankly informed him. "This is my country, sir, and I shall defend it to the death."

Anthony glanced at the belled mouth of her firing piece. "I can see that." Then he looked at Liberty. "And you, mistress. Did I not say for you to stay at home?"

"Aye. But they are my people, too."

He gave Feathers a daunting glare. "You are responsible for this."

"Aye, sir. I hitched up the wagon and we came."

"Plague me, no one ever heeds what I say." Anthony walked to his coach.

"Fielding." Ophelia caught up to his side and touched his sleeve with her hand. An uncharacteristic show that left Anthony quite puzzled. "I bore witness to what you did this evening."

"How grand of you."

"I'm not jesting, Fielding. 'Twas more than admirable and full of nerve. You're more of a sentimentalist than you let on. You defended Norfolk."

"Denouncing your preachings, I never said I was untrue to Norfolk when I told you of my devotion to England. 'Tis my duty to be loyal to England, madam. But 'tis my faith in the future I hope for the colonies."

He hoisted himself into his coach. "Come up here," he bade Liberty, then cast his eyes on Ophelia. "Both of you. You needn't be jolted around in that wagon with Feathers."

"Fielding," Ophelia said as he encompassed her hand in his to help her up, "I don't want to find any merit in you."

"Then, madam, I suggest you don't go against your principles."

* * *

Liberty became conscious of the sunny brightness in her room. A shaft of brilliant light stabbed through the part in her drawn curtains, warming her cheek and hitting her smack in her still-closed eyes. Rolling from her side and onto her back, she coaxed her eyelids to open a crack.

The comforts of her linen negligee with red squared pockets six fingers deep cloaked her in sleepy warmth. Not at all the type of sleeping attire worn by a lady of great standing, but she loved its accrued quality.

A knock tapped at her door. Expecting the arrival of Jane, Liberty bade the lady's maid entrance.

The portal stayed shut.

"'Tis Mister Feathers." The valet's monotone voice was muffled through the thick oak.

"Mister Feathers?" Liberty quickly moved for her wrapper. "One moment, please."

She slung her feet over the bed's edge, the coolness of the floor curling her toes. She crossed toward the door to let the manservant in.

Swinging the door open, she stepped back. "Good morning, Mister Feathers. You surprised me."

Feathers was attired in his usual perfect garb; blue coat and breeches. The color contrasted the peculiar orange shade of his cauliflower wig. "I beg your pardon, my dear good lady. But I've been sent to inform you that you've an appointment this morning with Madame Penelon, the dressmaker on the fore part of Main Street. Fielding thought it best you upgrade your wardrobe."

Liberty thought the amount of time Anthony had spent with her this last week wasn't enough to notice if she wore gossamer, thin as a veil with her naked underneath. Since the night of the town alarm, he'd divided his time between the inside of his study, taking lengthy trips to his ship and disappearing in the evenings for long spells before returning home. He'd extended his regrets, but said his work could not be helped. He would rejoin them as soon as possible.

She was sure he hadn't been drinking. In their brief encounters, she'd seen him short-tempered, his hands sometimes jittery and he smelled unusually heavy of cigars—as if he'd traded one habit for the other.

Thinking that perhaps Anthony had found her own clothing lacking, Liberty asked, "He's displeased with the ones I own?"

"'Tis nothing of the sort. They suit you well. But if you are to be a woman of great breeding ." Feathers didn't estimate the smart of his words until he'd spoken them. He certainly didn't mean to imply Liberty wasn't a decent woman. "A woman of social standing has clothing to spare. Changes are made two and three times a day."

"I know that," Liberty recognized with a down tilt of her brows. "I didn't think Anthony expected me to go through with such folly since his grandfather has already been privy to the true nature of my closet."

"All the same, you're to be at Madame Penelon's at eleven. One of the stable boys will be waiting at quarter till the hour to drive you."

"Very well," Liberty absently agreed, then retracted her consent. "Nay. I mean, I'd much rather ride myself." The airing would do her spirits much good. "Does Anthony keep riding horses?"

"Not per se," Feathers reflected. "Fielding doesn't hold horseflesh too highly. There is one gentle nag. Petunia. She hasn't been about in a full moon. But she's fairly cordial."

"Then have her saddled up, please. 'Tis been a long time past since I've ridden. Petunia and I shall both enjoy the freedom."

"Well . . . I don't know what the Lord and Master will think on it."

"Bother to Anthony. 'Tisn't like he's noticed me lately and I'm not doing something out of the ordinary. Women do ride hereabout."

"Aye." Mentally, Feathers added, but with a proper riding habit, boots and escort.

"I'll take full responsibility, Mister Feathers. Don't look so distressed."

"Very good." The valet gave in, Fielding may well never

find out about her capricious excursion. Why worry himself?

Feathers took his leave and Liberty crossed over the floor and began repairing her bed. No sense in making Jane tidy up after her. She knew too well the slovenly character of some people. She vowed to be a different sort of grand lady Even without breeding, she knew proper deportment.

Anthony surveyed the barber with a suspicious eye, trying to detect how many pints Gervase Tankard had already put away this morning. The idea of Gervase holding a honed edge to his throat while inebriated made him exceedingly wary. The barber's eyes were muddy brown, but clear around the edges. Deeming the man fit enough to take a blade to his person, Anthony took a seat in the comb-back Windsor chair.

Anthony knew he should have no complaints about Gervase's drinking. God knew, they both could quaff down their share and remain lucid.

The fact that the barber's shop and the local tavern were one and the same, also helped Anthony to accept his uncertain fate with less apprehension. A few nicks weren't so harrowing when one had a mug of grog in one's hand.

Anthony had fourteen days of sobriety. He needed his hair cut and he'd stood on the shop's steps for a long minute before entering into temptation. He'd reasoned he'd proven to himself he could do it. Why deprive himself for another five and a half months? A single glass of ale could do him no harm, and after that, he'd put the noose on again.

Gervase Tankard had capitalized on his name; a barber by instinct, a drinker by nature, and a name destined to be hung on a wooden trade sign. Tankard's Tankard had an original call to it. It mattered not to Anthony the man was a busy newsmonger, a gratuitous scandal-bearer, generally full of anecdote and wise saws. As long as his flagon remained full, he abided Gervase's long wind.

"What have ye today, Fielding?" Squire Tankard queried. The barber had titled himself squire and would answer to nothing but. Draping a clean square of linen over Anthony's clothes, the man answered his own question. "A cut. And ye look mighty in need of a shave."

Anthony perused the wiry barber. He stood no more than five feet tall, his face pinched and drawn. A single breasted frock coat in brown with vertical pockets fit poorly across his shallow chest. His bibbed white apron buttoned to his waistcoat and tied around his middle. He wore breeches and fine silk stockings with clocks at the sides. The short bob wig on his head had a comb stuck in it.

"Make me feel human," Anthony finally muttered and sank into the hard angle of the chair. He hadn't realized how poorly he felt until he'd woken up.

Gervase gave a hearty laugh. "Ye are looking a crumb red eyed." The barber leaned over Anthony and inspected his face with a forefinger on his stubbled chin, moving first left, then right. "Ye know the only cure for bloodshot eyes, don't ye?"

Anthony shook his head.

"The only remedy known is the abandonment of the vicious habits on which the evil depends!" Gervase chuckled and shoved a chin-fitting soap bowl next to Anthony's neck. "New cravat?" the barber inquired, stuffing the stock inside the linen drape.

One of Anthony's brows rose in idle threat. "Nay, but I'm attached to it. Shall I take the bloody thing off?"

"Not at all." Gervase left Anthony for the other side of the room which made up the tavern half of the establishment. Despite the summer heat, a low fire lay banked in the hearth. A slow boiling pot of water hung on a swinging iron crane.

"Squire Tankard, we be needin' another round," came the cry of one of the ordinary's patrons. Four gentlemen sat at a round gaming table playing loo.

"In good time, Swann. I'll handle ye when I'm getting Fielding his." Gervase retrieved the pot using a hook and a thick broadcloth holder. Without thoughtful care, he brought the kettle to his barbershop.

"What ye be drinking, Fielding, whilst I'm setting out to work on ye?"

"Ale."

"Ale 'tis."

The thin barber walked to the cagelike bar. Planks of two-by-four lumber had been assembled to corral not only the spirits from those who might get ideas about not paying for their drinks, but to protect the barkeep. Fights weren't customary at Tankard's Tankard, but Gervase didn't want to chance breaking any of his glass stock in a flying chair

Anthony recognized three of the four men in the taproom. They were gentlemen aldermen. Their loud talk was scarcely proper; vulgar inanities whisked around the table.

Not really interested in their prattle, for from what he heard, it was nothing but air and the pop of corks, Anthony tuned his thoughts to himself.

Before he'd come to the barber, he'd stopped by Hardress Waller's Billiard Shop to drop off the two balls Liberty had chipped. Feathers had had a devil of a time finding the wayward sphere in the prickly shrubs, blaspheming him in tones he thought low enough to escape Anthony's ears.

"Have you ever felt stripped of your purse and been able to do naught about it?" Anthony asked his barber as the man returned.

"Aye, Every time the tax collector shows his face." He handed Anthony his flagon.

"That weasel-faced merchant Waller wanted five shillings a pair to smooth some gashes from my balls."

Gervase's chest rippled with bottomless laughter. "Good God, Fielding, how the devil did you whittle at your balls?"

"You bloody base-brained lout. I was talking about my billiard balls! *Mine* are exactly where they were the day I was born. And quite intact I might add."

"Pray don't show me." Gervase took up his own pewter tankard that held three pints and swilled down several hearty gulps. "Did I tell ye the physicians have warned me to cut my pints of lime rum punch down to one a day or I'll fall to lethargy?"

"I always said that arrack brew 'twas poison." Anthony took a drink. The ale spread into his belly; comfort from an old friend. He'd missed the taste.

"Bah, I've slashed myself to two pints and I'll be damned about it."

The barber lined up his powder box, pomatum and puffs, then began liberally soaping Anthony's jaw with a musky smelling cake. As he worked, he talked about London, the king and other such nonsense. Periodically he'd stop to take another drink of his rum.

"Did ye hear about Mary Toomoth, James's wife? There's a scourger if there ever was. She was fined, ye know. Beating, battering, cursing, swearing and drunkenness right in front of the candle shop in broad daylight. Too much sack. They gave her a penalty of five shillings." Squire Tankard wiped the end of his razor on his apron, then slanted his slender mouth into a smile. "Now there's something for ye. Five shillings for her indecency and five shillings for yer balls. Where's the connection in that?"

"None that I can see, for I was forced to spend ten shillings to have two new ones turned."

"Ye should have heaved the balls and cursed in the streets and ye would have been five shillings richer."

Anthony let the belittling remark slide, telling himself he was almost finished and he could put up with the keeper's verbal exchanges a scant while longer.

His shave complete, Anthony felt the ribbon around his queue slip free. Gervase took the comb from his wig and ran it through the golden brown strands at the back of Anthony's head.

"Did I tell ye about my friend Colonel Berkeley?" The barber snipped at the ends of Anthony's straight hair.

"If I said aye, would that shorten the story?" Anthony caustically returned.

Gervase overlooked the quip and kept on with his trimming. "Colonel Berkeley had swallowed a large fish bone— no one knows how long before—which he extracted through his natural passages with much difficulty and wounded the parts internally so much so to produce his mortification." *Clip. Clip.* "That would be a mighty pathetic way to depart this green earth. He was a God-fearing man; only once in his life did he run into a morsel of trouble. Had himself a seat on the ducking stool and pelted with rotten eggs and stones for fornication with a cleric's wife."

"Squire Tankard!" The call of the men in the taproom had grown bolder as the men guzzled down more alcohol. "We are in need of more punch."

"Keep yer blooming cock hat on. I'm finishing up." Gervase turned once again to Anthony. "Shall ye be having a bit of powder on these fine looking tresses?"

"Damn your powder, Squire Tankard." Anthony whipped the towel from his shoulders.

"Squire Tankard!" The demand became more brazen.

"Damn aldermen," Gervase griped. "They's all in a celebration because George Abyvon's been made one of them. Made it possible for Booth Smyth to hold status in the court."

At this scrap of news, Anthony froze his ale midmotion to his lips. "What happened to John Perkins?"

"Haven't ye heard? Perkins has been appointed Worshipful Esquire Mayor."

Anthony felt a rush of heat surge through his limbs as he stood from the uncomfortable chair. The blood raced inside him. The thought of that bastard being responsible for the parish's welfare tempered his anger.

He intended to return home immediately, his thoughts speeding ahead of him in pursuit of the avenues he would take toward Perkins's newly gained commission. There were many factors to consider; he and Cheswick had mounting evidence to condemn the man and perhaps get him expelled from his position. Cheswick had found out Lionel Manning didn't have anything to do with the Parliament. He wasn't even a British seaman; he was a fugitive from England who ran the coasts in search of sailors to pilot his smuggled goods. He'd been caught once. Manning had avoided sentencing on those charges—his bond paid for by none other than John Perkins.

But Anthony didn't want to fling his information on the council yet, and run into any kind of snag without further proof of Perkins's involvement. He wanted to catch John Perkins in the act of stealing—Norfolk tars.

Anthony snatched up his ribbon from Squire Tankard and efficiently affixed the trimming in his hair. He paid the gaunt barber his due, then reclaimed his cocked hat from the dressing table and pushed the brim over his brow.

"Ye look like ye've a secret, Fielding," Gervase said in parting. "Shall ye share it with me?"

"Your interest is duly noted, Squire Tankard. But 'twas yourself who told me two may keep a secret only if one of them is dead." Anthony drank the last drops of ale from his flagon and gave it to Gervase. "Good day to you."

Anthony had no sooner executed his exit when he came face-to-face with two ornately dressed gentlemen making their entrance through the taproom doorway. John Perkins sported a braided white periwig with a thick powder masking his face; most notably, around a taint and fading yellow bruise that sullied his right eye. The other man, newly seated Booth Smyth, was a ruddy complexioned, portly man.

John Perkins lifted the nasty arch of his mouth to a snide smile. "Good tithings, Fielding."

Anthony's disdain was measured in his clipped words. "Smyth. Perkins."

"You've heard the news of my appointment. 'Tis cause for a tip of the glass with us."

Anthony flexed the fingers on his hand, absently opening and closing the appendages into a hard fist. The primitive urge to mash the man's dour face threatened to exhaust his control. "The day I tip my glass to you, Perkins, 'twill be over the celebration of your interment."

John Perkins sneered nastily. "Impudence has always been your family's curse."

"Better to be cursed with audacity than smothered with cowardice as your generation has been. Since when does the Crown select murderers to govern our colony?" The insult flowed through Anthony's clenched teeth.

Perkins leaned his face hazardously close to Anthony's. The mayor's eyes sparked venomous fire as he lowered his voice to a deathly tone. "I could have you imprisoned for that sordid remark."

"So you've threatened me before. 'Twould be a waste of the cell." Anthony had been in his own body's prison for the past half score years. The lasting vision of the day on the dueling field and the vile man before him, his arm raised and holding a blood-scarred sword, had jailed his mind with nightmares.

"I shouldn't squander my hospitable efforts on you." Perkins shared a private smile with his companion. "Most say you live in your own hell already. A flesh sinning man who drinks down a guinea worth a day."

"At least the guineas from my pocket are clean."

The implication of Anthony's retort made Perkins's face take on the graveness of a judge.

Smugness filled Anthony at the knowledge his barb had done the man damage. This strike was the first of many he planned on charging the new mayor with at the county courthouse.

"Shall we be off, Booth?" John didn't wait for the other to concur. He strutted to the gaming table of cards and the four gentlemen aldermen whose boisterous voices rose in congratulatory cheer.

Anthony watched his adversary retreat and for the first time in years, he smelled victory.

Liberty had been watching a flock of towheaded children in her path. Boys and girls alike played with toys; a drum, pinwheels, a racket and skittles. At the outskirts, a handful of ragtag scamps pitched pences in a game of huzzlecap. Her merry eyes set on the tykes' activities, she almost missed John Perkins.

He came around the corner of the metal gilder's works in the company of another more rotund man. She hadn't recognized his friend, nor had she any desire to place him. Seeing John Perkins again ignited an undeniable ember of resentment. It had been his depraved conduct that had seen her from her position at the Blue Anchor. Perhaps her chambermaid duties hadn't been the most desirable, but at least they'd earned her honest wages.

She had no reason to skirt him; no logical reason to

decline her rights as a citizen of Norfolk. However, deep down inside, she feared his reaction should she cross him. He'd come after her once before, there was no telling what he would do now that she'd publicly humiliated him in the coffeehouse's lobby.

Holding back, Liberty waited until John Perkins and his fellow had disappeared into an alehouse. She relaxed her shoulders, free to concentrate now on reaching the local livery where she'd left Petunia.

The ride into the bustling borough had been uneventful. True to Feathers's word, the old mare proved a downright good bit of stuff. She had obeyed without undue animation or verve, placidly clopping down the end of the main road from where Anthony's manor nestled in the overgrowth.

Once into the traffic of the town, Petunia held a leisurely gait not at all bothered by the commotion around her. Not having been into the marketplace in over a week, the populated flurry delighted Liberty.

Street vendors of all orders cried their wares. Included in their ranks were oyster men, gingerbread ladies, pie men, hot corn girls, hominy sellers, honeycomb sellers—this peddler made her reminiscent of the days in which, she too, sold her combs for a half pence; cheese men, peanut girls, muffin boys, and the others who hawked flowers, oranges, lavender, buttons and herbs.

After stabling Petunia, Liberty indulged herself with a modest feast—a blueberry muffin and honey. And on a whim, she bought a nosegay of violets to tuck into the band of her Dutch bonnet.

Walking to Madame Penelon's had been a drawn out journey while she finished the crumbs of her treat. Every now and then, a beggar would petition her for a coin. Though tempted to yield each time, she did not; only once did she give a small girl in a much mended but clean smock, a sixpence.

Liberty had known which block the dressmaker's shop was situated on. She'd passed by on occasion. From her glances at the plain shake outside, she hadn't been prepared for the opulent decor on the interior. The greeting room had been papered in burgundy with cherubic angels in flight. Tiny trumpets kissed their rosebud lips as they remained frozen in winged voyage.

Madame herself had been the biggest surprise of all.

Having expected a very refined and elegant Frenchwoman, Liberty hadn't been prepared to meet a stout woman of German descent. The dressmaker had briskly taken her into a mirrored salon and sent a fleet of attendants on her. They measured and prodded, pinned and marked. Bolts of fabric had come out of unseen stores: gauze, bordered cambric, dimity, tabby and moiré. Madame said with Liberty's complexion, pale blue, purple, violet, lilac or dark red would suit her best. And of course, black would be stunning with her hair.

The color gown she wore, her plain blue, Madame had said was quite appropriate. There were specific shades she should avoid so as not to give her a sallowness and assume a sickly, cadaverous or leaden hue to her skin.

Upon her leave, Liberty felt somewhat frumpy and wondered how she'd ever made do with her serviceable wear. The unexpected change in her character peeved her. She'd always considered herself too practical for such blather.

Her near run-in with John Perkins left Liberty wanting to return home. Her excursion need not be extended; she reminded herself of the care she had to use upon her arrival at Fielding Manor. Though Aunt Ophelia had seen no harm in her riding alone on the primary roads to Norfolk, Thomas Fielding would undoubtedly question such conduct.

Liberty lifted one side of her pocket-hoop farthingale to round a rickety stall of potatoes. A cluster of the blue uniformed H. M. Colonial Militia congregated on the stoop of the White Hart under the inspiration of a bowl of punch. Their laughter rang through the cart-laden street and Liberty intended on passing them by without incident.

Her calculations fell short when one of the privates blocked her path. His height barely exceeded hers, but his build was nothing for her to reckon with. Compact, he had the musculature of a man who'd spent his life in a saddle and field training. Though he came far short of Anthony's sound physique, she had no desire to rile the soldier.

As Liberty navigated the far side of the walkway, he reached out a lean hand and pinched her bottom. The squeeze missed the actual curve of her backside, but left her feeling violated just the same. Her pulse raced uncontrollably and she trembled with rage. Unlike the mealymouthed John Perkins, she instinctively knew this man would strike her back should she land a blow on his person. Retreat was her only answer.

Shirking the group who'd goaded the private on, Liberty advanced a few paces forward. The man pinched her again. His gall sent her soaring. In a whirl, she pounced on him, fists raised.

"Watch yourself, Ollie! She's a live one!" someone yelled.

"Sir, you shall take back your blow! I'll not be mauled on a public street without retribution." She tried to jamb a good punch into his eye but he ducked and her efforts glided through thin air.

As his comrades looked on with roaring guffaws at the satirical scene of a woman trying to oust a militia blue, Ollie became visibly rankled over their amusement at his expense. He lunged at Liberty and encircled her waist.

A small crowd of peddlers and fishermen began to gain interest at the spectacle; no one did anything to aid her. This incensed Liberty all the more. The private's hands gripped her like a cooper's rings on a barrel. She was practically helpless to free herself.

Indignation and growing alarm fueled her energy and she struggled to break free. Grabbing tighter around her waist, her captor lifted her off her feet. She kicked and hollered for her freedom. She heard the strain of threads snipping on her bodice sleeve.

"C-can't any of," she huffed, "you crippled wretches h-help me?" Her imploring the crowd brought out a single cry.

"Sweet mercy! 'Tis you, Liberty Rose!"

Hearing the boyish voice of Barlary White, the lad who drove the dairy dray, Liberty halted her tussle slightly.

The young man came through and at once dumped the empty milk vessels he carried. Hollow tin rang out as they landed on the cobblestones.

Gangly and thinner than a maypole, what he lacked in brawn, he made up in excessive height. He clubbed his hands into solid fists. "Unhand her at once!" Barlary demanded taking a step forward.

"This yer baggage 'ere, mate?" For the first time the uniformed man spoke. His voice bore a cockney accent, clipped and heavy in dialect.

"She's no baggage, you sot. Unhand her."

"'Twill be my pleasure t'free my arms so's I can be poundin' the cuff out of yer 'ide."

Without ceremony, Liberty was released. A fence of solid brawn, His Majesty's Militia garbed men guarded her from escape.

"Go on, Ollie, give it to him right," one of the brass-buttoned privates spurred.

"Barlary, nay . . ." Dread colored the youth's name as it slipped free from Liberty's lips.

Too soon, the fisticuffs began. Promptly Barlary sustained a bloody nose. Crimson dribbled from his nostril but he had no chance to swipe at it. Already another blow smacked into his belly. Daze clearly etched his face as he lunged toward his assailant. He managed a clean shot and socked the private's shoulder; the impact did little damage.

Her imprisoners caught up in the brawl, their leash on her relaxed. Seizing the opportunity, Liberty jumped headlong into the skirmish.

What happened next, Liberty couldn't be sure. She remembered making contact with hard flesh—facial, she thought, and quite soundly—before being yanked out. She felt herself being lifted off her slippered feet by powerful arms, her straw bonnet slanting askew on her tumbled curls. Wide-eyed, she watched as Anthony Fielding disengaged Barlary from the hellish private and tossed him next to her.

158

Barlary's raging breath expended his lanky chest, and he doubled over in visible pain, yet he still managed to put a protective arm around Liberty.

Liberty remained rooted to the spot, her gaze never leaving Anthony. For a time, the men shared equal stamina, each putting forth their best efforts to pummel the other. In a break of energy, Anthony took the upper hand. He pounded his opponent mercilessly, bloodying his face. Pressing his advantage, his attack raged on even though the soldier had given up the fight, his arms sluggishly protecting his chest and jaw. Liberty thought Anthony would absolutely kill the man. Then the crack of a flintlock's discharge pierced the air and the harried exploits died.

Liberty turned to see the authoritative Lieutenant and Chief Commander of the County Militia pointing a musket toward Anthony and the regular. The stinging smell of gunpowder drifted across the scene in an eye-tearing cloud.

Swinging around to Anthony, a gasp escaped her mouth. His skirted coat maintained a long rip at the lapel, his left eye reddened from a direct strike. A small cut plagued the corner of his full mouth, blood flowing seriously enough for him to draw out a handkerchief as a blotter. The buff of his snug breeches showed scratches of dirt. His gaze captured hers and she saw the prominent anger in his brown eyes. What bowled her over far more than the events preceding was the realization that his wrath was focused on her!

Liberty broke free of Anthony's condoning glare, too upset to linger over his wounds or any other part of his person.

The chief commander stepped toward the disheveled Ollie and disgustedly spat, "Fighting in a public street. I'll see you written up for insubordination, Private."

Ollie hung his head low, humiliated but not being able to contain a disdainful sneer.

"Gather up your dignity and report to my barrack at once." The chief commander glared at the other colonial militia. "Disband yourselves."

Ollie and the others disbursed, as did the marketplace

crowd. Business resumed, peddling took up and the side-walks and streets once again were inhabited by the mundane.

"I apologize for my lieutenant's actions, er, 'tis Fielding, is it not?"

"Aye," Anthony mumbled deeply, a glower set in the flare of his nostrils.

"I'm Chief Commander Ian Ramsey," he exchanged with Anthony before turning his attention to Liberty. "Madam, I saw naught of the beginning of this ordeal, but were there any improprieties acted on your person, forgive them. The matter will be dealt with quite severely."

Liberty nodded.

"Good tithing to you, then." Ian Ramsey stalked off on the heels of his highly polished black boots.

Barlary still prevailed by Liberty's side, his slender hand wrapped securely about her waist. He gave Anthony no regard even though Fielding had come to his assistance.

"Liberty Rose," Barlary's voice came in a soothing tone. "Are you damaged?"

"Mayhap bruised," she allowed, feeling the ache to her finger joints, "but unbroken save for the cut my dignity took."

"Aye." Barlary smiled, then winced as a fresh trail of blood ran out of his nose. "You are uncommonly sturdy for a dainty wench."

Liberty dug into the deep pocket of her blue dress and yanked out a piece of linen trimmed by cutwork lace. She brought the handkerchief to Barlary's nostril and gently patted the flow of crimson.

"Oh, Barlary, look at what's happened to you because of me. . . ."

Anthony grimaced. Annoyance darkened his already dark mood as he observed the comforting display. The intimate tones of their voices proved they knew each other on a level that went beyond friendship. An image of Liberty returning the stripling's sloppy kiss, goaded him.

"I came by the Running Footman and that old crone, Mrs. McKeand, said you and your aunt had moved out and she wouldn't tell me where you'd gone. Sarah told me you'd been dismissed from your position; she says 'tis flying at the Anchor how unfair you were treated."

Barlary caught Liberty's hand and drew it away from his nose to press at his cheek. "I have missed you, Liberty Rose."

Anthony could stand no more. With both hands clenched at his sides, he interrupted their private folly. "Liberty, it's time to go."

Both heads snapped up, Liberty's hand lowering.

"Who is this man, Liberty Rose?" Barlary sniffed, then sneezed into the soiled crinkles of Liberty's handkerchief.

Anthony wiped off the drying blood on his hand. "Do tell him, Liberty."

How could Liberty explain her relationship with Anthony to Barlary, when she didn't understand it herself? "May I present Barlary White to you, Anthony."

Anthony grunted.

"Anthony Fielding," she said to Barlary, "is my benefactor . . . of sorts."

"What mean you by that?" Barlary wadded the bloodied cloth into the buttoned cuff of his striped jacket. He absently surveyed his damages. His canvas apron had been scuffed and spotted with his blood and one of the lead buckles of his shoes had come off.

"It means," Anthony uninvitedly spoke, "that she is under my protection now and she hasn't the need of your impotent services anymore." Bending at the waist, he scooped up his cocked hat and righted the tricorn on his head. "Let's go, Liberty."

Barlary waited for Liberty to decline Anthony's order. Her refusal never came.

"Barlary, I must go with him." Liberty smiled halfheartedly. "He is my employer."

"Employer for what position?"

"'Tis best left alone, Barlary." Liberty fiddled with the wide sash that kept her straw bonnet in place. "I do hope you have not overextended yourself on my behalf. Seeing your wounds pains me."

Anthony narrowed his eyes to glittering squints. What about *his* pain? The devil! Upon examination of his throbbing knuckles, they appeared to be pulsating to the naked eye. Disgusted, he looked up at an inopportune time; the schoolboy was trying to patch the arm seam of Liberty's gown back together. He touched her ivory skin, the feminine ruffle of her chemise, then lifted the battered edge of her short flounced sleeve to her shoulder.

Swallowing hard, curses tangled in Anthony's mouth. Were he to remain where he was, the next blood on his fist would be that of the lad's.

In a keen sweep of his arm, Anthony wheeled Liberty to his side. "We shall take our leave now, Barley. 'Tis been a most amusing spot we've had."

"Barlary," the youth corrected, a frown set on his glum face. "Liberty Rose, you cannot mean to leave me."

Liberty had no chance to speak; Anthony had grabbed her hand and hauled her past the wharves, flushing a pair of white gulls in his stride.

Liberty twisted forward, trying to ease Anthony's fingers from her own. "I care naught that you saved us when you are being so priggish about it. Ouch!" She'd tripped over a discarded fishing pole that lay over a pier piling and stubbed her toe. "Pray slow down!"

"I don't want to slow down." But he abruptly stopped, taking her shoulders in his large hands and facing her nose to nose. "How do you know this mullethead called Barley White?"

Flabbergasted, Liberty balked. "I don't have to explain my acquaintances to you. And apologize at once for calling him a mullethead. Your referring to him as an elongated fish offends me."

Anthony snarled. "Acquaintance my bum."

For a pulse beat, she squared off with him in silent battle. His eyes sparked golden brown fire.

Liberty moved first. "Unhand me. You may temporarily own the rights to my presence, but you don't own my person."

Dark hesitation marred the removal of Anthony's hold,

then he shook himself off uttering a weak expletive. "God, I can be miserable, can I not?"

"Aye," came Liberty's slow agreement. Her faint smile held a touch of forgiveness.

Mutual surrender filled the void between them, Liberty's watchful expression on Anthony's swelling eye. "Does it hurt?"

"I wouldn't be any kind of man if I said aye."

Liberty suppressed a laugh. "The lobcock should be stripped and boiled for having done this to you."

Anthony gave her a furtive smile. "Then nude yourself up, sweet, and prepare to be drenched in a bubbling tub; *you* were the lobcock who hit me."

Liberty's mouth dropped open. "Oh, dear me! I'm so sorry!"

"No sorrier than I." Anthony stroked the edge of his eye, feeling his damage thoughtfully. He needed the exemplary services of his valet to fix him up. "I'll hire a hackney to see us home. Tobias hit a rut and cracked a wheel hub. 'Tis being repaired."

"We can't commission a coach. I've got Petunia."

"Who the devil is Petunia?"

"She's not a devil," Liberty clarified, this time taking the lead in their walk home. "She's your old mare and quite dulcet in manner."

"'Tis of no mind to me how her conduct is," Anthony said, perusing the swish of Liberty's too-short blue dress and the soft layers of petticoats about her trim ankles. The skin of her shoulder where her sleeve was torn, lay exposed for him and others to view. He didn't like that. "We'll hitch her up to whatever's available."

"Oh, nay. You cannot do that. She's not used to harnesses and tethers."

"Then we'll tow her behind."

"That would never do. I couldn't deprive her of the lead she enjoyed coming to town. 'Twould be humiliating to her to loose her freedom to a rope at the back of a hackney. We'll ride her."

"We'll what?" Anthony stopped in his tracks.

Pausing, Liberty turned. "We'll both ride her home. I'm sure she'll accept us."

"A Fielding does not sit on a horse's ass."

Liberty's greenish eyes widened in surprise. "Why, Anthony, don't tell me you can't ride a horse?"

"Very well," he clipped. "I won't."

Chapter
10

MUCH TO LIBERTY'S JOY, THE DUO SET OUT FOR ANTHONY'S HOME astride Petunia. Liberty's touch on the reins was confident. She straddled her thighs over the mare's flanks in a relaxed hug, her feet firmly in the stiff leather stirrups.

Anthony sat behind her on the horse's rump. There hadn't been room for both of them in the saddle. His long legs awkwardly dangled and bumped hers with Petunia's slow trot.

The snooping gazes of gawkers had chased them while Liberty navigated Petunia down Fore Street and onto the less traveled end of Main toward Town Point. She had felt Anthony increase the pressure of his arms around her waist under the curious stares of ogling innkeepers, the ink-smudged printer of the provincial *Virginia Gazette* and the churchwardens of the parish.

Assessing their combined picture on horseback, Liberty saw them painted in a scandalous image. Her lopsided Dutch bonnet, mussed hair and the most decadent of all, the torn gown bunched up on either side of her stockinged legs. Her eschewal of a sidesaddle courted enough trouble; to enhance the obvious by showing the better part of her legs induced the deplorable. Then there was Anthony's puffy eye and bruised lip to feed the flames of chatter to monumental proportions.

Liberty could only wait and wonder if their exploits would reach Thomas Fielding.

The noisy hubbub of the town streets died as they gained ground; the muted jingle of Petunia's trappings merged with the melodious songs of sparrows and the *chip-chip* of ruby-throated hummingbirds.

A leafy canopy of hickory, poplar and mulberry made shady patches over the country road, lighting up the well-traveled earthen grooves in a latticelike pattern.

"Why don't you ride?" Liberty said over her shoulder quickly taking in the damage Anthony had sustained around his eye from her ill-fated punch. A darkish rim circled the lid and she grimaced but said nothing about his battered appearance.

"Tobias gets me where I want." Fiddling with her hat, Anthony straightened the slant of the brim to rest more soundly on her head. He plucked the nosegay of rumpled violets free.

The deep rumble of his chest when he spoke, met with Liberty's back. "Such a captivating creature you are, Liberty," he said more to himself than to her. "You make no qualms about going the rounds with a bruiser, then at the next turn, you are the softest of females. Posies in your bonnet and a sweet curl to your hair." He caught one of her tresses and toyed with the skeins in his fingers.

Liberty shivered.

"I *have* been on a horse before," Anthony announced without preamble. "Quite a few times actually in my youth. While living on Antigua 'twas the only means of cutting through the tall sugarcane fields. Once my parents resettled here, for a time, I did have a horse. A real dasher . . ." His words drifted off as if remembering. "I recall the hunter's name—Black, but after a while, I no longer rode him and my mother sold him." Bitterness crept into his tone. "The truth of the matter is, I cannot seem to hold liquor and the reins at the same time. 'Tis a fear of mine that I'll fall off and be trampled."

Liberty remained silent, unsure of how he wanted her to answer. She wondered why he drank if he had such fears. Had something terrible happened to him? Perhaps his indulgences were a product of an unhappy childhood. He didn't speak about his parents   Somehow she sensed he didn't want her to answer him with any kind of compassion or a note of sympathy She would broach the subject later "Then 'tis good you've stopped drinking."

A series of Petunia's clops filled the silence between them.

"That boy," Anthony finally spoke, "called you Liberty Rose."

"Barlary," Liberty supplied. "Aye, he did."

"I asked you how you'd come by such an unusual name once and you told me you may tell me one day " Anthony moved against Liberty's body, going with the slow movements of the horse. "Is today a good enough day?"

"If I tell you, I need to tell you everything." Liberty kept her focus on the copse of great cypress along the road. Since Anthony had revealed a little of himself just now, she could do so also. "There are things that involve my aunt that I shouldn't like you to hold against her "

She sensed Anthony's growing pensiveness. "I'll not think any more unkindly of your aunt than I already do."

Liberty shot him a warning stare over her shoulder.

He smiled feebly. " 'Tis the best I can do. You have to admit, she can be quite a thorn."

"Perhaps if you knew more about her, you'd respect her thinking much more than you do."

"Perhaps, but doubtful. Proceed."

"I gained my name from my aunt whilst we were in the middle of the Atlantic Ocean. Though I was only an hour old, I somehow think I can remember it. I know that may sound strange, but 'tis true."

Anthony did not interrupt her and Liberty continued on, thinking that it was good Anthony know about Ophelia. "My aunt, and my mother and father, were indentured."

"Indentured?"

"Aye. Exiled from England on charges of treason. As you know, the colonies were considered hellish by the English and hence, deemed suitable for those not conforming to their society My father stood up for freedom—for his rights as a man to freely oppose the ideals of government. In doing so, he imposed that his opinions were perchance better than theirs, better for England. The courts did not think so. My mother stood by his side. And, of course, Aunt Ophelia was very adamant, too. She is my mother's sister," Liberty added. "Once sentenced, they were put on a leaking frigate that had barely crossed over the channel when an attack of smallpox struck the boat—"

"Vessel," Anthony faintly corrected.

"My father was one of the first to succumb. He died not knowing whether I would be a boy or girl, but he did tell Aunt Ophelia to watch over my mother and me. My mother gave birth to me, only to die from the ordeal and the grief of her husband's death. Aunt Ophelia knew right off what she would name me. Had I been a boy, I would have been Justice; but since I was a girl, I became Liberty For 'tis the law that any child of an indentured servant will be free." She paused reflectively, licking her lips. "I became the freedom my parents would never have. I became Ophelia Fairweather's hope."

"Damn " Anthony breathed in disbelief. "What happened when you anchored?"

"Aunt Ophelia said the boat first lay anchor in Newport. Her indenture was to be bought there, but was reneged since she had a babe to care for The boat cast off for New York, where she was met by the same fate. Then finally Norfolk. She was bought by a chair maker Benjamin Hogg."

"I don't know the name."

"He lived in the country Ten miles past the street leading out of town. He did venture into the city on monthly trips to sell his chairs. Neither myself nor Aunt Ophelia ever went with him."

"Where is he now?"

"Buried in a small apple orchard as of last year "

"And what of Ophelia's indenture?"

"She gained her freedom when I was four years old. Benjamin had married her He loved my aunt very much.

He grew quite fond of her freethinking and quick wit. You see, some do find my aunt charming."

"I never said she lacked charm. She's full of it; that and wry perception that bilks me of all tolerance. Other than that, she is a fine woman."

"Don't make fun."

"I am not." Anthony shifted his weight. "How came you to live in Norfolk? Did this chair maker not bequest you with his properties?"

"Aye, he did, but the rent on the cottage was too expensive, quickly using up a large portion of our savings. We found it necessary to move into town and pay cheaper lodgings."

"Ah, the Blue Anchor."

"Nay. I only worked there. I lived at the Running Footman."

"The devil? I've been to the Footman on several occasions past. I never saw you."

"And I never saw you. My aunt has kept me quite sheltered from the dregs of Norfolk. Not to say you are amongst that rank and file."

"I am and you know it."

This time, Liberty laughed. "Aye, but you are very interesting rabble. My aunt will swoon if she finds out about our scuffle. What shall we tell her happened to your eye?"

"The truth, of course."

Shocked, Liberty threw him another stare across her shoulder.

"That I met with the blow of a madman while defending a lady's honor."

"And the lady in question shall be?"

"I was hoping you might shed some light on that."

"She should be of high standing if you want my aunt's sympathy."

"A respectable woman in the community?"

"Aye, quite."

"Fishmonger's wife?"

"Nay," she scoffed.

"Butcher's wife?"

"I think not."

"Member of council?"

"Better"

"The best I'll do is the recorder's wife and even that is stretching things a bit. Anyone higher and the news would hit the presses."

"I think she'll do. What is her name?"

"The devil if I know Make one up."

"Very well. She'll be Polly"

"Settled."

Liberty enjoyed their repartee and as they neared the beginnings of Anthony's drive, she didn't want things to end.

She maneuvered Petunia down the shabby hedgerow driveway, thinking that her outing with Anthony had been unlike any other they'd shared in the past. There were no overtures of seduction, no kisses to melt her wits. This time, they were two friends exchanging ideas. She found she rather liked him as her friend.

"Anthony," she drew out his name. "What about your own parents? Do they live nearby?"

"They're dead. Both of them."

Then he said no more. From the chilling tone he'd used, Liberty dared not speak on the subject further.

As Liberty steered Petunia to the open doors of the stables, emptiness greeted them. The low nicker of the roans filled the large, straw-scattered room and Petunia's ears prickled. Liberty guided the mare to the entrance of her stall. Before she could dismount, Anthony's hand slid down her waist; a gentle touch, as if to say he was sorry for being so short with her

"And the Rose? How came you by that?"

Her heart caught in her throat from the tenderness in his voice. She slowly faced him. " 'Twas my mother's name."

" 'Tis a grave pity she does not know you, Liberty Rose. A grave pity indeed."

The startling brown of his eyes made her insides quake. Anthony—"

"I was wondering when y'all would be coming back." The

burly voice of Tobias cracked the static air surrounding them, crushing Liberty's next words in one fell swoop.

As soon as she recovered, she was almost glad the servant had come when he had. Were she to tell Anthony of her true feelings, she'd frighten him off. He didn't want any claims of affection from a love struck chambermaid. Things were as he wanted them, with no entanglements or melodramatics.

She had to remind herself she was just as much of an employee as Tobias was. The reality of her position caused her to abandon the small well of hope inside that Anthony could love her in return.

The possibility of a lasting relationship could never be; not with five hundred and five pounds standing between them.

"Something isn't clear to me, Anthony." Thomas reclined on the ruby settee in Anthony's darkish study "Your fiancée and her aunt don't fit the mold of blue bloods. Mind you I find no fault in that, 'tis their story of being old acquaintances that's sketchy"

Anthony leaned back in his chair, the wooden joints creaking like an old woman's bones. He'd wondered when his grandsire would get around to broaching this subject. "We've passed each other in social circles. I took exception to Liberty, but took my time proclaiming myself."

"Feathers proclaimed your intentions." Thomas lit up a pipe from the flint wheel he'd procured from Anthony's desk. He waved his hand, the finely crafted smoking device in his fingers leaving a ribbon of tobacco scent in the air "I want the banns posted at once. I'm staying until you're properly wed."

Anthony's chin shot up. "You needn't hold yourself over on my account. We had planned a quiet church wedding with only Feathers and Ophelia as witnesses."

"I dare say, I wouldn't miss my grandson's wedding. And what kind of attendant would your valet make? Really Anthony, 'tis quite out of the question."

Anthony frowned. Things were not going his way He had thought his grandsire's insatiable quest to see him wed would be quenched by the mere presence of Liberty Rose Courtenay and her aunt. Wrong. Thomas Fielding wanted things legal. And binding. All before he left.

Staring pensively, Anthony contemplated posting the banns. In a way, that meant nothing. It just announced his matrimonial intentions. They could be easily gotten out of should that become necessary But what if he could not wind his way free of the public proposal? Rogue that he was, the first thought that sprang to his mind was to hire a fictitious clergyman to perform a fraudulent ceremony. As easily gained as that could be, he didn't want to take that route unless absolutely pressed into it. He had Liberty to think of now

Before, he may have gone through with it if he didn't have to think of the repercussions of Liberty's hurt feelings. He could not hurt her any further He'd already done worse. The whole mien was becoming most troublesome to him. Now with Perkins in a prime seat to be dunked, Anthony wanted to concentrate his efforts on the man's destruction, not his own.

The devil, things were too complex.

"You haven't heard a word I said." Thomas stood at the edge of the desk, one elegantly dressed thigh boosted on the edge.

Anthony furtively stared. "What?"

"I was speaking of my daughter-in-law—your mother."

Anthony glowered at the impeccably garbed man. Since the subject of his mother was one of his formidable topics, Anthony decided not to add to the conversation.

"When are you going to come see her?"

Anthony looked down on a small stack of bills spread out before him, waiting for the proper vouchers. Absently he flipped through them. Tar. Hemp. Canvas.

"Listen to me!" Thomas's fist slammed down on the desktop, toppling the well of ink on the lid of the writing box.

Righting the ink pot with his own fist, Anthony pounced the container down with as much zeal as his grandfather had shown. "I shall never see her You know that."

"How long are you going to keep up this pretext of hating her?"

"'Tis no pretext," Anthony said unequivocally, keeping a tight hold on his emotions. He would remain undaunted under this man's scrutiny. He had neither the need nor precedence to be cowered at his age. As it was, he'd already bent under the man's thumb enough.

"You are every kind of fool, Anthony"

Anthony's underlying respect for his grandsire made him keep quiet.

Thomas stood and caught up his pipe from the desk which had slipped away from him. Grief painted itself on his face. "Your problems are of your own making. You will never get on with your life unless you confront your past. I don't know how you can tolerate yourself."

Then the elderly man departed on the heels of paternal self-righteousness. The slamming of the door echoed throughout the study.

The study's eerie silence enveloped Anthony. Rather than let his temper blind him by needing a stiff drink to slice through his rage, an odd sort of placidness befell him. Despite his grandsire's tongue-lashing, some of what Thomas said sunk through to him, belting him with truth.

In shock over the death of his father, Anthony had not listened to his mother's defense. She'd said she was sorry; he hadn't wanted to hear her remorse. She'd said to write; he hadn't wanted to sully his pen by writing her name. His hate for Perkins had stamped out all his reason. He'd tossed aside the woman who'd bore him, who'd nurtured him. He hadn't given her a chance. What kind of man was he?

Anthony's spirit had been dead a long time. He lived on a diet of revenge; feeding on another man's mistakes— Perkins's. Perhaps now that he could finally devour his adversary, he would be able to speak civilly to his mother on her betrayal of his father.

The thought of actually seeing her stretched his nerves to the point of pain. What would he say to her? What did one say to one's mother knowing she had an affair with the man who killed his father? I forgive you?

Anthony feared he didn't have the forgiveness in him.

Closing his eyes against the image of his mother's face, Anthony rested his forehead in his hands. He made himself take partial blame. It had been because of his own rage, he'd not heard his mother out. Her cries of reason had gone unheeded.

Maybe now was the time to listen.

"What the devil are *you* doing in here?" Anthony bellowed. He'd been in his bedroom searching for notes on the snow rig's rudder, found they weren't on his chest-on-chest, then came downstairs to probe his study.

Ophelia stood by his desk, the top cleared of his papers and now strewn with cosmetic trinkets, puffs and linens.

"I find the light in this room far superior to that of the parlor."

Frowning, he looked at his opened curtains. Bright sun spilled into the room.

"My ladies and I won't be long."

"The devil!" Anthony looked beyond Ophelia, noticing for the first time, the small huddle of spruced up matrons. Giggling behind their fans, they resembled copies of Ophelia in their garish dress and baubles.

"Fielding, mind your wordage in my presence and my clients. I have warned you numerous times."

The females tittered again.

Anthony stalked to his desk, ignoring the feminine cackles. "Where are my ledgers? My documents? What have you done with them?"

"Safely put down there." Shrugging, Ophelia pointed to the corner of the room by the hearth.

In neat piles, Anthony's accounts lay just as they'd been on his desk. And if he would admit to Ophelia, better organized than he'd left them. He went and bent over the drafts and found what he needed. Standing, he tried his best to glower at Ophelia. She stared at him as if she hadn't done anything wrong, and oddly, he found he couldn't stay mad at her

"Come here, Fielding." Ophelia's gaze seemed to size him up; most notably, the hair on his head.

Anthony looked behind him, as if she weren't addressing him, but some other Fielding in the room.

"What do you want?" he asked suspiciously, inching his way toward her.

"Nothing. Nothing at all."

Stopping short of the wide bell of Ophelia's skirts, he warily eyed her. "What is it, madam?"

Before he knew what hit him, a host of females swarmed him and he was clamped down into the seat of his desk chair.

"What the hell are you—?"

" 'Twill be quite painless, I assure you," Ophelia guaranteed while positioning her ring of friends, like starched military, all around Anthony. "The cone, ladies."

"Cone?" Anthony murmured. "I say! Let me go."

Strong as he was, he'd barely raised himself up when he was pushed back into the chair by Ophelia's army

"Drape him, ladies."

"I don't need *that!*" he protested as a cloth was fitted beneath his chin.

"I need you, Fielding. Your hair color is perfect for my new collection of permanent hair powders. Once applied, you needn't ever worry about wigs and headpieces again."

"I like my hair the way 'tis!" Anthony bellowed, trying once again to free himself from the meddling crones. They stuck to him like leeches, keeping him firmly in place with their perfumed arms. If he wanted to get away from them, he'd have to resort to physical blows.

Ophelia bent low, ruffling her fingers through his hair and assessing its color. "Whimsical White. I'd say that's your shade, Fielding. What say you, ladies?"

"Whimsical White," they said in chorus, nodding their heads in agreement.

"Whimsical White my eye!" Anthony didn't care whose bosom got flattened; he'd never struck a lady in his life, but his own was at stake. He elbowed anything soft, plump and padded from his person and bolted to freedom.

"Madams! Control yourselves!" he yelled. "I'm not my valet. I suggest in the future, you refrain from abduction and practice on willing participants." He tugged the cloth from his neck and threw the drape on the floor with a shudder, then retrieved his scattered documents.

"Fielding, you don't know what you're missing. You could have been the envy of all your peers," Ophelia sniffed.

"If my valet's wig is any indication of what I would have received, I severely doubt that, madam. Clean up all that mess when you're finished." He motioned to her wares as he headed out the door "And close my curtains before you leave— *ladies!*"

The tinkling laughter followed him and he grimaced all the way to the beach. "The devil . . ."

Liberty wore a white muslin dress, closely cut, the skirt indecently narrow and nearly gatherless. No petticoats filled the underside and she'd slipped on men's drawers with cinched ribbons at her ankles to keep the hems from falling open. Though still summer, the lightweight material had long sleeves which had been set in tight, deliberate stitches.

The high-necked frock had been her own invention—a bee dress, she called it. She'd laid a pattern out, cut and sewn the pieces together. Not exactly a work of art, but quite efficient against stings.

Liberty stopped at the kitchen door A veil of netting capped her braided flaxen bonnet and she fastened down the last tail to seal her face off from aggressive intruders. Today, she needed to check the hive's interior to see if the combs and chambers were free of disease; disgruntled outrage usually met her at the entrance.

Shoving the door open, she walked the short span to the kitchen area, going through yet another portal to reach the cooking room. Not since that first morning at Fielding Manor had she presented herself in the cook's domain. On that other occasion, she'd found herself alone, yet admiring the shining tidiness of Quashabee's territory

She'd formed a varying degree of images of the trigger-happy cook. In all the pictures she'd conjured, never once did the woman appear thin as a nail; she'd figured Quashabee to be plump and steely, mayhap with even a faint mustache to fuzz her upper lip.

So when Liberty came face-to-face with Quashabee on this hot August morning, she wasn't quite sure how to react. The cook was stooped over the hearth, an apron sagging around her narrow middle; the gilt handle of a small pistol protruded from the apron's square pocket.

"Good morrow," Liberty said cordially. In spite of her supposed station, she couldn't bring herself to affect a tone of superiority in her greeting.

Quashabee glanced up and Liberty took notice of the cook's face. Gaunt, yet not unduly haggard. Ice blue eyes and a narrow nose with a horizontal mouth, neither elevated nor depressed. No facial hair of any kind.

"You fair gave me an attack of the heart." Quashabee inched her brows up suspiciously. "What you be doin' about when the flamin' sun isn't even up yet?"

Taken aback only marginally, Liberty's gaze never faltered. Not an expert in the regions of accent, she put her best guess that Quashabee's heralded from the darkest streets of London. "I'm going to care for my bees." Then without taking a breath she continued, "I'm Liberty Courtenay." She extended her hand—a hand Quashabee warily eyed before accepting. "And you are certain to be the cook, Quashabee."

" 'Twas the name me mum allotted me."

"Quite an interesting one."

"Quite so." A thread of mistrust still wove itself in the cook's backward enunciation.

"Well, I shan't keep you from your duties." Liberty took one step toward the door leading outside.

"What's with them strides?"

Liberty turned around. "Strides?"

"Them clothes."

Liberty had to remember the snug fit of her hive wear. "I don this to protect myself from stings."

The expression on Quashabee's face said she wasn't entirely convinced by Liberty's explanation. All the same, she shrugged. "Right, luv."

The cook inspected the gears on the smokejack, then sparked up the low fire, sending a hind leg of beef to slowly rotate once the curls of smoke hit the angled blades of a circular fan. Liberty tried to keep her glance from straying on the peppered and skewered slab of meat. Shivering, Liberty once again set off with her bees in mind; Quashabee's guttural voice stopped her short a second time.

"Here. Be takin' yourself off with some tucker." She handed Liberty a roll which she'd neatly wrapped up in a homespun napery. "Bees is an odd turn for a lady like yourself to be dillydallyin' with."

"I don't consider myself any kind of grand lady and bees are the most loyal of all God's subjects. Should you like to watch me with them one day, you have but to ask."

"I don't take kindly to pests," Quashabee said while tightening the bow on her apron. Pushing her pistol farther into the lining of her pocket, her eyes narrowed as if she'd seen an insect hovering in front of her face.

Not waiting to see if the cook would unload her weapon, Liberty shot out the door.

A hazy glow balanced the early sky to the east. The morning air smelled of musty waters, a vague floral fragrance and the distinct sweetness of bee nectar. Liberty took the steps down to the bee gum, slowly approaching her wards. She set down her folded napkin, then put on a pair of gloves and readied her smoker by stuffing it full of dried grass and sumac fruit. As she did so, she watched the steady stream of workers who went back and forth over the alighting board, their hum coming to her in a gratifying melody to mix with the trill of the songbirds.

An hour progressed as Liberty cleaned the hive, finding it free of infection and sanitary. The bees had created a modest hill of dead bees on the grassy ground two feet below the landing plank; death in the hive was not an uncommon occurrence and once the poor drone or worker had perished, it was disposed of immediately. Highly sensitive to offending smells, the hive ejected their deceased mates to an open-air grave.

The sun's heat had begun to radiate down on Liberty's back, managing to pierce through the large mulberry's gnarled branches. The hive would be an oven if it didn't have ventilation on a day like this. She propped open the cypress board, allowing the air to circulate through the top and the opening.

Cleaning up the dried bees that carpeted the earth in front of her shoes, she dumped them into her work pail and put a dented tin plate on the top to keep the scent from disturbing the colony.

Perspiration dotted her high-necked collar and the hollow where her shoulder blades met. She loosened the netting around her face. Sitting down on the bench she ate the sweet bread the cook had given her, idly observing her bees.

Afterward, she climbed the steps of the veranda in search of something cool to drink. She hoped Quashabee wouldn't mind if she invaded her kitchen once more.

As she reached for the elongated glass door leading into the dining area, Hiram Feathers appeared holding a hamper covered by a stretch of light cloth.

"Mister Feathers." Liberty smiled genuinely, her fondness for the valet shining through. Though she'd not had as many occasions to speak with him as she might have wished for, she had come to greatly admire and respect the man for his ideals on life. He got on quite nicely with Aunt Ophelia and she secretly harbored hopes that perhaps more would come of the friendship. Her aunt had gone on too long without a man to pamper her. And Mister Feathers needed a little coddling, too. She wondered if he'd always been a bachelor or if he was a widower?

" 'Tis always a fine spot in my day to see you, Mistress Liberty."

"How kind of you to say." Famished and still quite parched, her gaze inadvertently lingered on the basket Feather held onto.

Stepping out onto the covered porch next to her, Feathers lifted the material a fraction. "A late breakfast for Fielding."

Liberty had assumed Anthony to be in the house, but thinking on it, she grew increasingly aware of the drone of workmen's tools coming from the boat Anthony was constructing.

"He's been about for some time," Feathers supplied. "Once he's near to completing a project, he puts himself full body into it. Would forget to strap on his napkin were it not for me taking an eye to him."

Liberty looked beyond the boughs of the leafy mulberry to the grand boat in scaffolding. Her knowledge of boats was nil, but to look at Anthony's she knew it to be an exceptional one. She'd always wanted a better look at the hull but never managed to get close enough. Possibly her fear of interrupting him had hung in the back of her mind. Knowing how absorbed she became over her own work, she had given Anthony privacy when he'd engrossed himself in his own. Now, a gentle courage sprang to life, telling her that perhaps she should go investigate if the timing was right.

Looking back to Feathers, she impulsively reached for the foodstuffs. "I wouldn't mind bringing that along to Anthony if you don't."

"I don't mind a'tall, Mistress Liberty. In fact, I think 'tis a splendid notion." Adjusting the forehead fitting of his peruke, he sheepishly added, "Ophelia has invited several lady friends over and as we speak, they are ensconced in Fielding's study. She means to unveil a new hair dye to them."

Liberty smiled. "And would this color be called Majestic Marigold?"

"Aye, 'tis so."

"And I suppose you shall model it for the fine gentlewomen?"

"Only because Ophelia asked. Lud, I pray they won't laugh at me." Feathers's face paled in contemplation.

Liberty placed a light peck on the valet's cheek, making him blush deep red—a most glaring contrast to his orange wig. "Should they laugh I'll not let a one step foot into our salon once it's open."

"You are kind and good, Mistress Liberty. I think of you often."

Touched by his endearment, Liberty honestly replied, "And I you, Mister Feathers."

"Hiram!" Ophelia's merry voice winged its way to them through the depths of the house. "Where are you?" The cheerful tone abated to a bothered mumble that was still intelligible even from the distance Liberty and Feathers stood. "Pish! Fielding keeps the man on a chain. The wretched scoundrel has my Hiram dancing a fine tune. Off he's gone to deliver the rogue his breakfast . . ."

"I should go mollify Ophelia before she indulges her guests with fierce tales of the Lord and Master's habits," Feathers suggested with a wink of his gray eye. "Enjoy yourself with Fielding. You're a far sight better to look at than me."

After Feathers left, Liberty headed toward the beach, her mind on Anthony. Ever since their run-in with the militia man, he had distanced himself from everything but his boat and the endless hours walled up in his study. No more billiard lessons. No more displays of false affection. He had been kind and congenial.

By some miraculous good fortune, news to contradict the story they'd fed Aunt Ophelia and Thomas never came to Fielding Manor. The duo of seniors thought Anthony dauntlessly aided a lady in distress. No one was the wiser that the lady was indeed herself.

Halfway down the gravel and sandy beach, she halted. Looking down at her attire, she immediately wondered whether or not she should proceed dressed as she was or go back to the house and change. Her costume was uncommon, but the dress did serve its purpose of business. A sweeping glance at her outlined figure made her wary. Would Anthony find it laughable?

In the end, pride won over. She never meant to hide herself away on simpering legs. If Anthony disapproved, he would have to speak his mind.

Clutching more firmly to the food basket's two handles, Liberty admired the hub of activity on the looming bulk of finely planed timbers. Tall and streamlined, the boat easily matched the height of a three-story dwelling. Though handsome in structure, the craft appeared out of place on the expanse of low-lying waterfront in a spot where nature hadn't intended to put an object of such enormous size.

The cut of a broadax, the grate of a plane and the smooth whir of an adze overpowered the placid birdcalls of the morning. A crosscut saw shredded through dry wood, the noise growing louder in Liberty's ears once she reached the bottom of a very tall straight ladder. She quickly deduced the imposing string of flat rungs were the only means to get aboard the craft.

Liberty brought a shading hand to her brows, trusting she'd find Anthony in plain view. His familiar build didn't come into sight; only a scrubby looking man who hung one leg over the hull's side while working on the railing with a tool foreign to Liberty.

He noticed her and raised his head, smiling weakly as if he wasn't sure to greet her with a hello right off or fetch his employer. Apparently he decided on the latter for he disappeared, returning in a quick jaunt with Anthony behind him.

Still using her palm to shield the sun's blinding glare, Liberty stretched her neck way back to study Anthony who stood in a cutaway on the quarterdeck. Had she thought her own work clothes scandalous, Anthony's were as shocking —at least to her. Close-woven fawn breeches hugged every curve and swell of his long, muscular legs. Knee-high boots of finely tooled brown leather embraced his calves without room to spare. An apricot linen shirt clung to his chest, his body's moisture making the thin fabric a sheer layer of little substance.

"You've seen your way clear to my madness." The rich timbre of Anthony's voice drifted down to Liberty.

He leaned his bare forearms over the richly stained wooden rail. The tan that covered his skin contrasted next to the embroidered ruffle of his cuffs which had been pushed up to his elbows. Strands of sun-hued brown hair tumbled down his brow and he pushed the wayward locks from his eyes.

"I wouldn't call this madness. Glorious is more suitable."

"You like her?"

"Very much."

"In that case"—he swung a booted foot into the top step of the ladder—"come on up."

The muscles of his buttocks barely rippled as he made his descent. He climbed down with an agility born to a maritime man used to seeing his way up and down masts. In a final hop, he landed next to her.

The familiar strands of hair eluded his tie. A healthy tone spread over his cheeks and jaw, the bridge of his nose a burnished bronze. His gaze traveled the length of her dress.

"Interesting frock."

" 'Tis my bee dress."

"And how they must love it." He poked at the wicker basket with a long forefinger. "What's in here?"

"Breakfast," she said, reminding herself to breathe.

"From Feathers, I'm sure."

"You're right."

Anthony took the hamper from Liberty "Can you climb in your . . . dress?"

The narrow skirt of Liberty's bee trappings presented a problem; how could she manage the ladder without splitting the side seams? There seemed to be two answers—one respectable and one not. She could decline his invitation and accept it at a later date when she was more suitably dressed; or, she could cast caution aside and hike up the hem.

Anthony appeared to have come to the same conclusions for he gave her a broad smile. One side of his mouth lifted in a rakish dare. "You wouldn't be thinking about showing me something to make me swoon with shock?"

"I should say!" she countered, her indignant plea only mildly effective. "Is that a challenge?"

"Call it what you like, Liberty." His voice grew husky.

She accepted his invitation without further thought.

Inching up the skirt's muslin hem to her hips, she exposed her homemade white drawers and the pastel ribbons tied around her ankles. "Any subsequent comment on my attire will be beyond the boundaries of good taste. As 'tis, I'm dangerously close to being called a tart."

Anthony's resonant laughter filled the morning air. A tingling warmth seeped through Liberty's limbs and in a quick twirl, she grasped hold of the ladder's edge. Her shoes, sturdy in sole, took the rungs easily. In no time, she'd reached the top. Looking down, she saw Anthony close behind, the food basket effortlessly in his hold.

She quickly pushed down her skirt, keenly aware of the inquiring gazes set upon her by the shipwrights.

Anthony hoisted himself to standing and lazily dumped the hamper onto a half-opened keg of tiny treenails. "Nicely done."

Despite herself, Liberty felt a blush creep over her cheeks. Knowing that she had been privy to his backside upon his decline, surely her bottom had given him an eyeful on her climb. Well, there was no sense in worrying over it.

Perusing the workings around her, she discovered them quite interesting. Most of the men were garbed in Monmouth caps and simply made canvas jackets of old sailcloth, patched and repaired; full, sturdy trousers, ribbed stockings and shoes with simple pewter buckles completed their wardrobe. The man who had brought Anthony to the railing continued on with his task, taking sly, eager peeks at her. His hair had been drawn up and clubbed with a piece of twine. She smiled at him and he rapidly put his concentration back on his labors.

"That's Jacob Miser. A good training carpenter."

Liberty wet her lips, tasting the salt on her mouth. "He wonders about me. Have you not told them of your fiancée?"

The good humor on Anthony's chiseled face faded a tad. "It slipped my mind."

Mildly hurt, she put her emotions in perspective. How could she expect him to tell of their betrothal when they truly were not? What would be the purpose to that? None that she could readily think of. To Anthony, she was just a houseguest, nothing more. In a matter of weeks, or quite possibly less, she would be gone from his home. But until that time, she intended on being cordial and respectful of Anthony's wishes. What he said was his own affair. She would follow his lead.

"Would you show me around?"

"Whether you wanted me to or not." Some of his devil-may-care disposition returned as he politely took her hand in his. He gave her a wide tour from the aft to the stern; from the port to the starboard side. She hadn't known those last factual names, thinking a ship had a front and a back, a left and a right. She felt confident enough in remembering the bow and rear, however port and starboard eluded her until Anthony told her a riddle to keep it straight. The port was the left, as the word *left* had four letters in it like *port*.

Fascinated with the details, she listened as he explained the various points on the vessel which he'd identified as a snow rig. It had two masts, both square-rigged with a spanker on the mizzen as well.

"How did you begin this? With little more than cleats of wood?" Liberty asked him when he'd taken her full circle. He ushered her to the top of the half-deck, the reclaimed hamper set out before him.

"I had a draft—plans, which were made up to my specifications."

"Are all your boats the same?"

"Vessels. I vary the structures, learning and incorporating newer techniques each time." Anthony had removed the cloth and spread out scones and jam. A breeze caught his hair and he absently tucked the willful shocks into his queue.

He ate with relish, as if the river wind enhanced his appetite. Liberty was content with the brief lull in their conversation. She took in the exhausting work around her, still marveling in the finishing details being put to order.

The smell of hemp drifted to them on the current and Anthony pointed out the new coils had been freshly twisted from the ropewalks. She nodded, feeling very proud of him.

He was an extraordinary man, knowledgeable about his trade. She hadn't realized just how educated he was until now. With his periodic lapses of inebriation, she'd thought him almost doltish at times; how wrong she'd been.

The light wind dried her mouth and she was once again reminded of her thirst. "Is there anything to drink?"

Digging into the recesses of the hamper, he produced a clear glass jar of crimson liquid with a lid. Thinly sliced lemons floated on the surface.

Anthony pulled out a single, wide-footed glass. "We'll have to share."

"All right." He gave her a sample first and she savored the cooling punch on her throat. "What is this?"

"Virgin sangaree."

Liberty took one more taste, then handed the glassware back to Anthony. In a few gulps, he'd drained the sangaree and poured more, passing the beverage on to her.

There was something wicked about putting her lips on a glass Anthony had touched with his own. A fine prickling teased her nape. She dismissed it as nothing more than the stiff netting of her veil abrading with her skin. But she knew better. She was sitting with the man she loved. That revelation struck her to the core. She'd always known she'd been infatuated with him and had enjoyed their companionable talk. But things were different now. Inside her heart, she felt wonderful. Joyful. And these feelings only surfaced when she was with Anthony.

Inwardly, she sighed. If only she could have his love in return.

As they breakfasted, Anthony took up his plans, showing her the various notations. The length on deck, length on keel, breadth of beams, depth of the hold and the tonnage.

"Where does it say how you'll get her in the water?" Liberty asked, brushing the crumbs from her lap.

"She's sitting on a type of rail that once the ropes are cut free, she'll slip into the river's edge. The buoyancy of her hull will keep her balanced until the weight sees her to the middle waters where they run deep."

"Hmm." She gazed into the passionate depths of his brownish eyes. "Your perception is very astute."

"The lives and property of men depend on my decisions." Anthony felt Liberty's thigh next to his. He'd hardly taken notice of what he'd eaten. All during their time together, he had barely heard himself talk. So engrossed in Liberty and her nearness, he'd gone through the motions of explanation. The pure enthusiasm he felt about his surroundings was his only saving grace. If it weren't for the fact he could talk about his rig even thoroughly bewitched, he would have babbled on unintelligibly.

Sharing this part of himself had been oddly gratifying. He'd never once had a woman on deck. Not that he held onto the age-old commentary of superstitious seamen. He hadn't ever been inclined to reveal this part of himself to a female. Annoyingly, he thought of Eden Bennet. Her delicate nature wouldn't have afforded her the nerve to climb the ladder.

With a vague smile, he recalled the vision of Liberty mounting the straight ladder. The sight of her legs had made him tense. Legs. Mere legs. Were he to describe the kind of man he was, he'd most likely say it was a wench's bosom, pale skin and coiffure that attracted him. But Liberty's legs, moderately long and extremely well shaped, had sent a fist of craving in his belly. Her rounded derriere, a gentle sway first to the left, then to the right, had unintentionally toyed with his control. It had nearly been more than he could stand. His footing had slipped and with a muted curse, he'd reclaimed his hold.

Strike him blue, he'd become snarled in a plot of his own making. He'd never expected to become attached to her.

He stole a glance at her profile; the saucy tilt of her nose, the fullness of her mouth, the incredible sweep of her black lashes. The silhouette remained uniquely set as she watched an apprentice with a bow-drill. His lower extremities tightened in response. She turned and gave him a smile which dissolved through his body, impacting his soul.

An ebony curl teased her cheek and he had the strongest urge to kiss her. Then he thought of why she was with him.

Maybe if he reminded himself of the reasons she'd accepted Feathers's miserable proposal, he could set himself up for indifference.

"Tell me about this salon you and your aunt want to establish."

She looked at him, surprise clearly marked in her hazel orbs. "The salon is to be a place where women can assemble, speak with a free mind and be administered to by a woman of professional fashion background."

"Blind me, don't say the professional is Ophelia."

"Well, she is," she squarely debated. "You may find her a bit . . . colorful, but her knowledge on cosmetics and the makeup of dyes and perfumes is truly remarkable."

Recalling Ophelia's attack on his person, he begged to differ with Liberty's opinion on her aunt's talents. But he couldn't dispute the fact the woman could whip up perfumes. The sensual fragrance Liberty had worn on their first meeting, had fairly grabbed him by the vitals. "Go on."

"There's not much more to tell. Only that we don't have the funds as of yet to set up business."

"Only fifty pounds," he reminded her. "What happened to the rest?"

She lowered her chin. "I had to pay some . . . debts my aunt incurred."

"They were quite costly."

"Aye, they were."

Anthony moved on to another subject, seeing Liberty was grateful for his turn in conversation.

"Have any of the new dresses arrived?"

"Oh, aye." Her face lit up. "Late yesterday afternoon. I would have mentioned them at dinner, but under the circumstances, your grandfather would have wondered."

"He would have." Anthony took another swallow of the sangaree. "Are the gowns to your liking?"

"They are indeed wonderful; even for day dresses, the cut is exceedingly detailed. Madame Penelon said the rest should be arriving by the week's end."

"Good." Knowing the designs of Helga Penelon as he did, he felt certain she'd outfitted Liberty in the manner in which a lady was accustomed to. "You did order a ball gown."

"Aye. As you instructed." Liberty flattened the brim of her bonnet. "I must tell you honestly, I felt rather awkward about it. The whole idea, actually. It's shameful for you to be outfitting me. I intend to reimburse you once I have the available means."

Anthony grew perturbed. "There won't be any paying me back." She made a move to protest when he cut her off. "As your employer, 'tis my duty to see to your clothing."

The statement had been meant to placate her, but had sounded domineering and vulgar. Once spoken, he wasn't sure how to smooth things over. Like an idiot, he went on from there, trying to think of a diversion and something every woman wanted to hear. "We've been invited to a masked ball and I intend to show you off to Norfolk."

Silence greeted his ears and he wondered if when she sulked, no amount of coaxing would bring her around.

"Does that not please you?" he asked, trying to keep the impatience from his tone.

"It would." Liberty clasped her hands together. "But as you had no use for riding a horse, I've had no use for ballroom dancing. I fear I haven't a clue how to step unless it's on your toes."

"Oh, sweet Liberty," he murmured softly, relieved that was all there was to it. "All you'll need to do is sway your body with the natural rhythm of motion."

"I cannot."

"You can, and you will."

She questioned the veracity of his wisdom by narrowing her lids to distrustful slants. "I shall be laughed at."

"Then we will both cause hysterics, for my dancing has, as of late, consisted of a stein of ale and an arm about the waist of any convenient wench—both holds quite sloppy at that. Since I will be as sober as a judge on this festive event, 'twill be like starting over."

Chapter
11

"WHO IS HE?" ANTHONY ASKED CHESWICK.

From the dark shadows, T.A.'s voice came in a low whisper. "Phillip Hawker. A rather sordid chap. Would sell his mother if he thought he could get a fair price for her."

The man about whom they spoke stood in front of a small tavern called The Spanker.

On their nightly vigils, Anthony and Cheswick had watched Hawker and Perkins have a private meeting in Perkins's warehouse. Cheswick had used his contacts to exact further information on Phillip Hawker. Like Manning, he, too, was a captain of sorts. This was a new link to Perkins and the abducted tars, only Anthony had not been able to catch Perkins in the act.

Hawker appraised the sailors as they came out in pairs; then a lone tar appeared and Hawker grabbed him from behind.

Cheswick made a move, but Anthony held him back. "Not yet. We can't go after him till we see Perkins."

"And what if he doesn't show himself? This poor lad will find himself in the services of a smuggler without the benefits of any of the booty."

"We can't." Anthony felt his friend's frustration, but to

announce their presence to Hawker to save the sailor would ruin everything.

So they waited.

The tar was taken off by two other discreet men. Then Hawker glanced up and down the dimly lit street. Soon, he left toward the docks.

"I'm going after him," Cheswick informed Anthony. "Stay here and wait to see if Perkins shows."

Anthony nodded.

By two in the morning, neither Perkins nor Hawker had returned to The Spanker. Frustrated, Anthony went home, the urge for a drink pulling at him the entire way.

"Mister Feathers, I'm in desperate need of your help." Liberty hastily explained her lack of dancing skills to the attentive valet while a crooked smile defined his narrow mouth.

"I have had happenstance to see how 'tis done—er, rather, how 'tis not." A thoughtful expression befell his face's bony planes. "Fielding has taken me to several functions as his attendant and I was made to watch his painful display." He shook his head as if to clear the pitiful images. "I did take exception to those about him who seemed to enjoy themselves without staggering."

"Could you show me?"

"Lud, I could try."

"Right now," she impatiently suggested.

"My dear lady, now?" Unsure, Feathers glanced at the privacy of their surroundings. They stood in the middle of Liberty's bright yellow bedchamber. He'd brought the young miss an afternoon cup of coffee since Ophelia had been too busy to take scones with them, having shut herself in her room to concoct more hair tonics. Pausing to listen, he heard the tinkerings of his beloved as she jingled jars and potions, lightly scenting this adjoining room with spicy herbal smells.

Feeling the heat of the day lingering in the open-windowed bedroom, Feathers shucked his servant's coat, neatly folded the jacket over Liberty's book stand, and trotted to the open door. He checked the empty length of darkened hall in both directions. Not seeing or hearing the Lord and Master, he closed the door in place.

Fluffing the full, plain ruffles on his sleeves, he raised his arms, extending them to the level of his shoulders, with his palms facing Liberty. "All right, Mistress Liberty. Come, come."

Liberty accepted his fingertips and he did his utmost to smoothly direct his steps, leading hers along with his. "'Tis a flirtatious game, dancing. Don't let Fielding make an idiot of himself, you, or the art."

Concentration marking her face as she followed his lead, Liberty spoke while watching the tips of her slippers. "He said he shall keep up his sobriety."

"He will?" Feathers couldn't contain the astonishment in his voice, the tempo in his movement becoming sloppy. For Fielding to be in a roomful of tippers would be quite the temptation. Feathers crunched Liberty's toe under his heel and instantly begged her pardon. "I told you I wasn't much of a stepper, having observed more than participated."

"I think you're doing splendidly." The green in Liberty's eyes matched the brightness of spring leaves. "Do you know the moves for a minuet?"

"Aye," Feathers moaned. "'Tis what we've been dancing."

"Oh . . ." Arching a delicately shaped brow, Liberty queried, "Do you know the steps to the cotillion?"

"Aye, but 'tis best with two couples."

"We can make do."

Over the course of the next hour, they bowed, balanced, toe pointed and hopped. Toward the end, Liberty succumbed to a fit of giggles, imagining how impossibly bumbling they appeared. Growing more daring, Feathers maneuvered all sorts of intricate steps, some of which she was sure he made up. Her laughing became unstoppable and soon the portal connecting her room to Ophelia's opened and her aunt stood in the doorway.

Hands on her panniered waist, Ophelia Fairweather broke into an infectious grin. "So this is the cause of all the rabble my ears have been subjected to. I dare say, were I not so engrossed in my formulas, I would have put my nose in here sooner. 'Tis a good thing 'tis you in here, Hiram. Had you been Fielding, I would have had to take my blunderbuss to your backside."

"Rest assured, dear Ophelia, my attempts at the quadrille have been most innocent. Wretchedly so."

"You need another partner." Ophelia jumped in, putting her hands in Feathers's. He gallantly bowed and clicked his heels, then set her off in a stilted whirl.

The three laughed and curtsied, humming tunes in off-key notes. In the height of their gaiety, Liberty lost her balance and fell on the throw rug. She sat in a puddle of petticoats and skirts, undying mirth spilling from her throat. Resigned, she leaned back on her elbows, content to finish out the afternoon by watching the attractive pair her aunt and the engaging valet made as they smiled into each other's eyes.

Tromp!

Anthony gazed at the ceiling for the dozenth time, his attention drawn away from his work once again. For most of the day, he'd been hibernating in the sanctity of his darkened study. The morning hours had been spent reading through the sketches of his rig's final details, and these last hours had been used to record John Perkins's activities in his journal. Manning had managed to avoid sentencing; someone saw to his escape. Anthony had no proof it was Perkins, but knew the bastard had paid someone in the courthouse to look the other way.

All Anthony and Cheswick needed to do, was lure Perkins into a trap. And what better bait to use? A captain who could navigate his way through sandbars blindfolded. Cheswick had set out to make himself visible; the plan relied on the fact T.A. had not been noticed by Manning the night of the town alarm. After Cheswick had followed the two men who had taken the tar the other night, Cheswick pretended to be drunk, spouting what a good captain he was—

Thump!

Anthony flinched. The noises aloft had sounded like Liberty had been moving furniture; this freshly muffled stomp causing the unlit brass chandelier above his head to rattle and sway. A second thud went as far as to eject a taper from its holder.

His eyes narrowed suspiciously while appropriating the candle from the ledger books on his desktop. Dried yellow wax crumbled under the pressure of his fingertips and he glared heavenward again.

"The devil, what *is* she doing up there?"

No sooner had he voiced his question, he'd stood from his chair to find out for himself.

Taking the flight of stairs to the second floor, he stalked down the hall and stopped at Liberty's closed door. Silence greeted him. Not trusting the lull, he pressed his ear to the paneled door.

He heard soft laughter. Female laughter. Then—

Jerking his head away as if he'd been scorched, he ground his teeth together.

A man's guffaw.

The distinctively male tenor burned a fire through his entire being.

By the mass! She entertained a bloody swain in her chamber! A scant minute passed as he mentally ran down the list of every male, servant or no, on his property. Save for Feathers, none had free reign of the manor. Judas, had she taken a fancy to one of his shipwrights?

Feeling the blood pulsate in his veins and heat his skin to a deathly blaze, Anthony grasped hold of the knob without any intentions of knocking. This was *his* house and no—

His tirade fell abruptly short, when, through the sliver of a crack he'd created, he spied Ophelia Fairweather and Hiram Feathers doing a beastly imitation of the rigadoon.

Anthony frowned. His anger somewhat repressed, he took notice of Liberty sitting on the floor. Her feet stretched out before her. Her dress's wide skirt flowed around her hips and legs making a fetching picture in light blue. She clapped her hands to a beat lacking any cadence, but apparently no one noticed.

Tormented by confusing emotions, he questioned the rationality for suddenly feeling like a left-in-the-cold by-stander in his own dwelling.

Righting the door back into place, he leaned against the jamb no one the wiser of his unvoiced intrusion. Envy, a strange and new sensation, claimed him with raw disquiet. He called himself every kind of pathetic fool.

He'd been reduced to a spectator in his own home.

Liberty had never seen such frippery.

Not only in the opulent ballroom of Mister and Missus Adam Hunter, but in the guests that filled the illuminated salon. Cavalier cock-robins and showy debutantes vied for equal attention. Pruned, snipped and clipped, their coiffures and costumes had been finely hedged. All wore the requisite facial disguise: a domino. The cut varied from one wearer to the other; frilly to not, somber to gay, beribboned to stark. The colors of their masks fluctuated in all spectrums. Pale lilac, starling green, peacock blue and lemon. Variegated hues clothed their backs and bosoms; silk, satin, cloying velvet.

Far from apropos, snug breeches had been stitched too tightly as if cut by inexperienced tailors; lush and, not so, bosoms ran over the low lace trimmings of bodices. It seemed to Liberty the entire room, though supposedly filled by upstanding citizens, meant to capitulate to debauchery before the eve crested into sunrise.

She stood amid a sea of people, feeling like a lonely gull. Having never attended such a grand soiree—or any soiree for that matter—she hadn't been sure what to expect. Certainly the position of wallflower had not been on the list of probabilities.

Liberty caught sight of Ophelia on the dance floor with Thomas Fielding. Her aunt looked splendid this evening in a moiré gown of watered blue. She danced with a grace no one would know had not been inborn in her. Mister Feathers had seen to the fine-tuning of Ophelia's skills. Unlike Liberty, Ophelia had attended several neighborly functions with her late husband, Benjamin Hogg. She knew enough to tap out the quadrille or a version of the cotillion.

Liberty's own misgivings over her talents in the dancing department had seen her beg off Thomas's request for her hand in the minuet. Instead she thrust her aunt at the gentleman. Anthony had made no comment on her slight, actually smiling over it, and ready to take her into his own arms when a man heavily into his cups had whisked Anthony away from her to the smoky drawing room reserved for the men.

Alas, she held her own place in this room of animated couples as they joyously whirled on by.

Prior to Anthony's exodus she'd been introduced to the host and hostess; Adam Hunter had ogled her with an infinite gleam to his monocled eye while Mary Hunter stirred her fan in front of her powdered face, indifference sketched in the line of her brows and mouth. Mercurially glimpsing a coated man in periwinkle, she had dashed off without a single serving grace. Her husband had muttered his good riddance. Anthony had let the host's unrefined behavior slip.

Recalling the incident made Liberty's mouth sour. If this was what the elite deemed fashionable, then she'd gladly be the lesser in social standings. No wonder Anthony drank as heavily as he did. Everyone around her indulged in liquor. They clustered at the punch bowl and limp-wristedly stole champagne glasses from the circulating butlers' silver platters.

Anthony had done so well with his abstinence, how could he expect to maintain himself with liquor so close at hand?

Liberty became unforeseeably angry. Were there none among them that talked of the political issues that affected them all? Were they so indifferent to the king's laws that they would accede to them without a fight?

While trying to tamp down her temper, Liberty relied on the festoons of the room to distract from her growing perversity. Throughout the grand apartment, the burning stems of candles flickered, reflected in the magnificent silver frames of their oval mirrors. Glowing stalks of orange flames writhed on the walls under drifts of air. Every floor-to-ceiling window had been removed to allow the sweet summer breeze to engulf the dancers.

Standing or seated, the congregation of party goers smiled and chatted, smartened their frocks and hitched their clothing to show off finer features since faces had been hidden behind character facades.

Liberty tried to lend her ear to the music. Strains of a harpsichord, two cellos, a duo of fiddles and a flute drifted through the dance floor; a multitude of colorful dancers whirled to the meter.

Sighing, Liberty clasped her fingers in front of her wondering when Anthony would return. He'd been gone interminably.

She tried to seek his tall frame out above the dancers, looking beyond and into the corner where an elderly man had stationed his portly weight in a Windsor chair. His brown domino had slipped free, his eyes exposed and fluttering closed for the night. A woman who matched his age, tottered to him and with a light tap of her fan, tickled his chin. Her elbow jogged him wide-awake and he stoutly grumbled.

Liberty couldn't help laughing. It was the first sign of normality the entire evening. Caught up in the scene, she wasn't prepared for the clumsy touch on her arm. Startled, she pirouetted to level her stare on a face covered by dandelion yellow papier-mâché. The gentleman stood at her height, garbed in foppish attire adorned by garish gold trim.

"At last . . ." Instantly she smelled the spirits on his breath. ". . . someone worthwhile," he slurred. "Fun is now afoot. I know you, fair mask!"

"Sir, you've confused me with someone else," she formally returned. The crowded room offered little comfort to this man's gregarious presence. She sensed him to be snobbishly sure of himself and not easily put off.

"Then I shall know you now, my angel." He bent his head toward her for a kiss and she jumped back on her heels.

"You take too much liberty, sir!" Her heartbeat plucked out an uneven count and she desperately hoped he'd go away before Anthony returned.

"I've distressed you." His words were spoken in a drowsy tone. "I should render an apology."

"'Tisn't necessary." She hoped her curt dismissal would send him off without further incident.

"You see I've been gone for quite some time. On the sea, in a ship. 'Tis been a long duration since I've feasted my eyes on such a pretty wench as you—" He suppressed a belch.

"A truce, sir," she impatiently broke into his long-windedness. "A truce to your fooling."

"'Tis no fooling. I've been on a hellish ship and now I'm making up for lost time, loaded to the gunwales and," his lengthy excuse rambled on, "I saw you from over there." He turned to point and wobbled. "Well, in any case, from somewhere there. I said to myself—"

"You've said enough." The even baritone of Anthony's deep voice washed over Liberty's shoulders, wrapping her in the protection of his guard.

Her new suitor traveled his gaze up and down over his competitor, tilting his head way up to get a good picture of Anthony's face. Masked in heavy black satin, Anthony Fielding looked like the devil incarnate. His nose came down in a straight line from underneath the bridge of his domino, his nostrils flared by annoyance. The fullness of his mouth as he frowned, left little room for retrospective discourse.

"Ahhhhhh." The sigh escaped from the brazen man's lips in a choked whisper. "I hope you'll find a duel unnecessary, sir. My pistols are incapacitated at the moment."

"Much as your head, I would guess." The scathing bristle netted home and the popinjay lurched forward on unsteady legs. He shook his forefinger in front of Anthony's eyes.

"I should insist on a duel now, sir." A crease of stubbornness etched into his lead-powdered forehead while lowering his finger. "You've insulted the way I hold my liquor."

"You mistake my meaning." Anthony took a step forward, towering over the man by a good head. "I've insulted your manners. I'm sure they're just as vulgar whether you're booze-blind or not."

The ruffled fop took immediate action; he retreated without a backward glance. So much for wounded dignity.

Anthony sneered at the man's fleeing form, a sickening hindsight traveling up his spine. Exchanging snubs with the swell had made him take clear assessment of his own imbibing habits. Did he act as inane under the influence, too soaked to notice what a deplorable scoundrel he was? It was enough to make him give up his alcohol for good.

Anthony gazed at Liberty to find her mildly smiling at him. A mellow warmth seeped through him, more acute than the pleasure a fine glass of cognac could give him, reducing that indulgence to insignificance.

"You cut him down without raising a fist. Your tactics are to be commended."

Anthony laughed. "You think I handle all my disagreeable affairs with my knuckles?" He tucked her fingers into the crook of his arm. "Damn me, but you think I'm some hellion going around putting up fights with whomever will indulge me?"

"Not so," she returned, her chin tilted engagingly up. He saw the brilliance of her eyes behind the slits of her bloodred domino tied with pink ribbons. The winged sides had been trimmed with a garland of tiny roses doubled under a white gauze.

Holding back the breath that filled his lungs, he took a quick minute to assess her. Her raven hair had not been powdered. She wore cosmetics to a purifying degree, drawing out the sweet curves and sensual lines of her face. Her lashes had been dabbed with black, her face dusted lightly with a peachy powder, her lips had been tinted a shade of red—not flamboyant or excessive; the hue matched the tone of a ruby rose. The illusory comparison made him smile, recalling the soft temptation of her lips against his own.

Her breasts were outlined in the square-necked, pale violet bodice of her gown, the swells sublimely teasing into his view. A waterfall of taffeta ruching and single pink camellia lay nestled in the valley of her breasts. He'd recognized the flower as growing on the shrubs outside his study; he could imagine her seeking out the bush and snipping one off to place in her casting bottle, the small vase hidden in the neckline of her dress.

She inclined her head, her study of him as firmly affixed on his person as his was on her. With her movement, he'd been granted the scent of her perfume as it floated in the heavily fragranced room. Once again, the smell of her wildly aroused him. He'd known he desired her from the beginning; an oddity that had thrown him then and still tossed him at a loss. He was beginning to tire of reminding himself he preferred women of wan complexion and hair. He was ready to call a forfeit and give into his capricious cravings.

Liberty boldly met his stare and he dueled with the green-gold of her eyes. Even knowing he'd assessed her in a rakish manner, he could not stop his appreciative gaze. "Impudence always seems to get the better of me."

"I have noticed," she whispered.

Between the ostentatious laughter and snatches of song in the crowded room, Anthony could only wonder if he'd really heard the breathless nature of her voice.

"Shall we dance?"

"Only if you don't mind getting your toes trodden upon. I told you I wasn't much good."

"I know the steps well." Anthony had no reservations in making the vain remark. Damn, but he did know how to do several things which conformed to society. "I am excellent when I'm not drunk and lucky for you, I am not."

Slightly laughing, she arched her neck back. The satin streamers on her mask caressed the naked porcelain column and without thinking, he grazed his fingertips over her flesh to move the ribbons.

"Perhaps I am foxed, but not by any kind of liquor." The poeticlike words slipped free, at first taking him by surprise, then registering into his mind. He had meant exactly what he'd said.

Seeing a petite blush color Liberty's cheeks, he squeezed

her fingers and escorted her to the dance floor in time to dance a reel. She danced far better than she let on. Her ear for the beat made her movements more graceful than a beginner; she talked to herself, keeping count of her steps. Feeling the energetic lilt of her in his hands, he thought it good to dance without the impediment of demon rum. He didn't falter once.

From the sidelines, Ophelia Fairweather took a sip of her punch. With great interest, she watched her niece glide in Anthony Fielding's direction. Somehow Fielding seemed different tonight. She'd observed the change in him as the week had worn on. No longer did their evening meals consist of saucy meats and game; a sudden occurrence of extravagant vegetable dishes were served. And although Anthony appeared preoccupied and locked himself up for endless hours in his library, he had been missing one large trait: his liquored behaviors. True to his word, he'd kept off the evil waters.

She had to admit he looked splendid tonight in his coat of robin blue satin and waistcoat of silver trim. He had turned quite a few heads, but he'd taken no notice of the fancy ladies trying to catch his eye. His eyes were trained on Liberty. Only Liberty.

Could it be that Anthony Fielding was falling in love?

The idea sounded illogical and ridiculous to Ophelia. She wasn't even sure she wanted to think it, much less accept it for truth.

Needing a draft of air to clear her head, she put down her empty glass on a tea table and strolled toward the open window ways.

The gardens were a delight. Aisled bowers, groves, terraces and steps. She followed the footpath leading toward the river, trying to keep her sister's child from her thoughts. Certainly Liberty was safe in a crowded room.

While admiring the cut of the leafy fences, she let her mind drift to Hiram Feathers. He'd accompanied them to the masked ball, but hadn't been allowed to partake in the festivities. He'd been made to stay with the other servants. An abomination to say the least. Her right to attend this gentry occasion had been falsified by her guise as Ophelia Fairweather, grand lady, houseguest of Mister Anthony Fielding.

"Dear lady, I was wondering when you'd scare yourself down my way."

"Hiram!" Ophelia started at the sound of his voice. Her heartbeat thrumming inside her chest, she smiled tenderly at the dapper valet. "Have you been hiding in waiting all this time?"

"Pray not too long, love. But I had hoped you would have been along sooner. I've already had to flush out one amorous couple. My idea of entertainment does not include watching a pair go at the intimacies a man and woman share."

"Good gracious!" Ophelia sighed, sneaking into the arbor Hiram had been shadowed in. She slipped into his embrace, allowing him the freedom of a modest kiss to her lips.

"Are you having a good time?" he asked against the tower of her bright orange hair.

"Not so much without you, Hiram. I've danced with Thomas on several turns and a few lifeless old poops. None to compare to the youth in you."

"You shall swell my head to that of a whale's, my dear Ophelia."

"'Tisn't fair. I've no right to be in there amongst that crowd." She'd since told Hiram Feathers of her marriage to Benjamin Hogg and her humble beginnings; all, including her indenture. Hiram had been lovingly tender and had even become misty-eyed over her plight.

"I don't mind." Feathers drew her to a stone bench and sat her down, bringing her close to his shoulder. "I haven't much liking for these sorts of people. Too many counterfeit beginnings. Believe me when I say, the lot of them are not better bred than we. They just have the pocketbooks to command the proper amount of respect."

Ophelia broached a delicate subject for she knew Hiram to be unfailingly loyal to his employer despite his grumbling to the contrary. "Do you think thus of Fielding?"

Feathers grew reflective a moment. "Fielding is a lost

man, my dear. I don't think he knows which side of the coin he fits on. I assume that is why he drinks so much."

"He hasn't been gratifying his thirst of late."

"Aye. I feared for him that last time he didn't come 'round." Feathers's silence mingled with the far-off melody of music and the whispered laughter of lovers.

"Have you any thoughts as to why he stopped?"

"I think we both know, 'twas due in part to his feelings for your Liberty."

Ophelia laid her head on Hiram's shoulder. "I've doubted he had any room for love."

"Every man does, my dear. I had thought mine nonexistent till I met you."

Ophelia laughed softly. "And now you shall forever be the wiser."

"Do tell."

The couple sat for a while longer listening to the muted notes of dance. Ophelia had no desire to return inside, yet knew she must. Supper would be served shortly and she would be missed. Sighing, she straightened.

"I hope nothing dreadful has happened in my absence," she mused, teasing her hair with her fingertips and shaping the bright curls to a high pile.

"You've not been gone a half hour." Hiram waved his hand at a moth flitting through the air in front of Ophelia. "Nothing dreadful could possibly have happened in such a short span."

Eden Bennet uttered an expletive under her breath that would have made a roomful of clergymen get down on their knees in heavy prayer. The coach had been late in its arrival to their lodgings. The masked ball had commenced some time now and she would have to make an entrance. It wasn't that she minded making a grand appearance; in fact, she rather preferred the opportunity for upstaging.

The only thing that deterred her from that was the fact the soiree was masked. No one would know who she was anyway until the supper, and by then, couples had already paired off.

STEF ANN HOLM

She thought of Anthony Fielding. Despite the horrendous note they'd parted on last time, the stretch of days she'd not seen him had softened her temper. So he didn't want to get married; she'd find other ways to catch him.

Cyril Lamont, the proprietor of the Blue Anchor had already told her upon her arrival late this afternoon, that Anthony had sent his valet in search of her weeks ago. That had to mean something.

The rented barouche finally rolled to a stop and she departed the equipage on her father's arm. Hearing the strings of music renewed her spirits.

The sparks of the town danced and flirted under the inspiration of a bowl of fruited punch. Anthony stood on the sidelines, a tight grip on his glass as he watched Liberty twirl a cotillion in the arms of Booth Smyth. The man's squat build could not be hidden behind a domino. Anthony hadn't been able to dissuade the man from claiming her without giving away his identity. Thus far, he'd gone through the evening without any unpleasantness. He didn't want to start now.

But Anthony did give a minute's thought to where John Perkins was. If the many town officials were here, the mayor could not be far behind.

The taste of citrus fruits lay heavily on his tongue and he dumped his cup's remaining punch into a potted plant. Moving to the terra-cotta terrace, he refilled his glass with water from the crystal fount. The clear liquid cooled his mouth, cleansing away the sourness.

Back inside, heat from the confining room hit him. He would have gone back out on the patio but he wanted to keep watch on Liberty.

The ballroom reeled with merry confusion, everyone not knowing with whom they stepped to the music of spinets and strings. Under the mask, dancers were at ease in the rigadoon and French dances; the false faces gave life, freeing spirits.

Anthony's eyes trained on Liberty as she concentrated on her passes right. Smyth took her up in his arms again, a grin etching its way on the mouth of his covered face. Though attuned to the couple on the polished oak dance floor, Anthony felt another presence enter the room. He turned to see a woman and man enter the salon doors. Even masked, there was no mistaking who they were.

Montgomery Bennet and his daughter, Eden.

Chapter

12

STRIKE HIM BLUE, ANTHONY THOUGHT, OF ALL THE TIMES TO HAVE to have a run-in with *her* He'd known this moment would come, but he'd hoped it would be in the privacy of his own home or in a dark corner of a coffeehouse.

Montgomery made straight for the table of liquor, while Eden strutted through the room in her azalea-colored gown. Anthony noticed her bantering freely with several young men, catching them by the arm and sending them on their way with plenty of jealousy to the one she'd left. A practiced blush washed over her face at what must have been a compliment from an aggressive suitor.

As she gained closer ground, Anthony heard her avowals and declarations, words that, barefaced she never would have breathed. She encouraged the shy, knitting momentary romance and lifting the hopes of those who would never stand a chance for her favors.

Eden's sweeping lashes lifting up, her fair violet orbs clashed with Anthony's hard glare.

Anthony didn't realize the cotillion finished; his stance remained fixed. He looked upon Eden Bennet as if it were the first time he'd seen her—*really* seen her. Her pale hair and face—segmented into halves by the brightly colored red domino, did nothing to stir him. He remained impassive to her charms, if indeed she had any to practice on him.

As she sashayed toward him, she moved in a manner that had been rehearsed and refined; a whole little parody of nods and smiles, dainty rigmarole of listless vapors, a studied preen of pride all the while her gaze never left his.

A randy fellow crossed her path and she gave him a tiny tap of her closed fan, sending him on his way. A space of several feet stood between them and she stopped. Above the humming of the room, Anthony could hear her clearly.

"Are you as happy to see me as I you, Anthony?"

He never got the chance to answer. Liberty returned to his side, an animated flush prettying her cheeks. "I didn't do as well as when I'm with you, but I managed not to tread on the man's toes."

The seductive gleam in Eden's eyes dimmed.

Anthony had no time for introductions. The boisterous call of the host cut through the room after a dramatic spinet introduction interrupted the guests' talking.

"Madames, Mistresses and Sirs!" Adam Hunter's voice demanded attention. "Lend me your ears! 'Tis time for the unmasking. Those of you who have been naughty shall now have the opportunity to see with whom you've been naughty!"

A chorus of laughter chimed.

Anthony rigidly stood next to Liberty. She had no idea what she'd intruded on, her beautiful mouth turned up in an anticipating smile. She was enjoying all of this and once the dominos were removed, a dilemma would be unveiled.

The spinet player made a show of moving his fingers across the keys, playing a silly tune. Then silence droned. The materials of fine gowns and coats fluttered silkily, the stiffness of petticoats rustled softly.

"Unmask yourselves!" came Adam's shout.

In a furor of excitement, the satin masks lifted free.

Liberty unfastened the link of ribbon around the back of her head, letting her domino float down in her hand. Smiling at Anthony she drank in the handsome planes of his face revealed for her view. It took a heartbeat for her to realize he wasn't smiling back. The set of his mouth bore the thinness of a somber line.

A chilling fear inched down her spine. Had he succumbed to temptation and gotten foxed? "Anthony . . . what is it?"

"Not 'what is it,'" a feminine voice answered. "'Tis, 'who is it?'"

Liberty's eyes snapped toward the woman who addressed her. Dazzling in a floral pink gown, her stature resembled Liberty's own. A wig towered on her head, attaining a height of one foot and cascaded with curls and jewels. Her mouth resembled a rosebud with a shorter upper lip; her chin was small. Long, wide eyes shimmered without tranquility; she used her eyes to her advantage, for without saying a word, they conveyed the inner soul of their possessor. At this instant, the violet melded to a pool of fiery arrogance. Her snobbish nose curved in a thin and noble tilt.

Anthony shifted his weight, dropping off his empty cup on a butler's tray as the servant crossed through the ballroom. "Eden Bennet, may I present Liberty Courtenay."

Liberty's good spirits fell. *Eden Bennet.* The woman Anthony had sent Mister Feathers for. The woman Anthony had wanted instead of her. Refined, gracious, wealthy and of a respectable family. All of the things she herself was not.

With a strong hesitancy, Liberty extended her hand to the woman as Aunt Ophelia had told her was a cordial gesture that shouldn't be reserved only for men—then immediately retracted her polite offering. The scathing condemnation in Eden's eyes said she was under the temperament to bite off Liberty's fingers. An undignified, "Well!" escaped Liberty without warning and she mentally scratched "gracious" from her list of Eden's so-called attributes.

Any consternation she had over Anthony's offense at her slip, vanished.

He'd chuckled under his breath.

Eden flicked open her fan. The silken body and ivory struts played over her fingers, then came up to her cheek, fanning out her temper with a quick flicker of her eyelids.

"Well-a-day, indeed!" she sniffed. "You scoundrel. I'd been made to think you sorely missed me and here you are with this hussy."

Liberty cared not for the woman's uncouth manners but had let them sail over her head; only when Eden's treachery reduced Liberty's moral standings did she vow a retaliation. "My good madam—"

"Mistress!" Eden corrected.

"I find your tactics deplorable. You know naught about me to go making vile accusations on my character. I demand an apology."

Eden's fan swished to and fro like a pigeon's wing. With a jerk of her wrist and compression of her lips, she closed the delicate web. "Good gracious, wherever did you find her, Anthony? No wonder you're keeping her company. She's amusing."

When Anthony saw Liberty's fingers tighten to a fist, he interceded, taking a step toward her side. Not caring about Eden's wrath, he put his arm around Liberty's waist. "You had it coming, Eden."

"La!" Eden's face reddened unbecomingly. "For the longest time, I put up with your drunken meandering, agreeing to everything you said, *darling*. I had assumed you liked a woman to be congenial." Vaulting her brows, she looked down the bridge of her nose. "What a fool I was."

"Nay, Eden," Anthony said around the tightness of his jaw. "I was the fool."

Liberty listened, knowing that there was far more to the spat than met the surface. Plain to say, these two had been more than mere acquaintances. The obvious truth wounded her to the core. She'd heard the gossips of Ophelia's customers in the Running Footman reliving tales of spurned mistresses and their devious scorn. Jealousy crept into her heart.

She took a long, drawn-out look at Eden. Surely she had kissed Anthony—and much, much more. The woman had lived out the daydreams she herself had had. Eden Bennet *had* basked in the affections of the man she desperately wanted to shower on herself. Liberty forced herself to loathe Eden, but the emotion came with a bitter edge of pity.

Eden apparently didn't have Anthony's affections anymore and it incensed the beautiful woman to think of his sentiments belonging to another.

The atmosphere around the trio grew heavy. No one moved when the announcement of supper came. It wasn't until Ophelia and Thomas came to them, followed by a man in outlandish garb, that someone said something.

"Father," Eden purred. "I'm so glad you've come to my aid."

"Aid for what?" Without waiting for his daughter to explain, Bennet reached out his hand to Anthony. "Fielding. Damn nuisance I was detained. What should have been a fortnight turned into three weeks of misery on my behalf. I had a business crisis. I trust you got my missive."

"I did."

Liberty eyed the man who wore a gold coat with tight sleeves, deep cuffs and a full skirt with enormous hempockets. His calves had been padded and were covered by strawberry pink stockings.

"'Tis been a while, Thomas," Bennet said congenially greeting Anthony's grandfather.

Introductions flowed in a circle, followed by a brittle silence. Though now known by name, it seemed everyone was apprehensive to comment to one another.

Finally a butler scooted them from the room and they were all seated at a grand table in the dining area. Liberty felt thankful that at least she hadn't been seated next to Eden. Anthony was at her left while Ophelia took up her right; Thomas across from her aunt.

Her face minus its domino, Liberty caused quite a stir at the table settings. Everyone wanted to know who she was and what was she doing with a libertine like Anthony Fielding. The young men in the dining room tripped over themselves to catch her attention and the matrons spilled gossip behind their manicured hands. None of them had ever wanted their daughters close to that rascal Fielding before, but now that it had become apparent he was under the influence of a very beautiful and gracious woman, they plotted how to throw their own female offspring in his path.

Liberty caught snatches of these conversations here and there and thought it all quite comical. How mealymouthed these people were! Had they no scruples over their past treatment of Anthony? She was proud to be with him now and before. It made no difference to her whether he was in their good favor or not.

She tilted her head and gave him one of her most endearing smiles, then looked straight ahead without giving him the chance to respond to her affectionate display.

The softened glow of green sweet myrtle candles burned from their receptacles atop the table. Silver bowls of fruit ran the length of the settings. Vases with three royal roses opening their hearts to the subdued light filled the room with subtle fragrance. Little dishes of bonbons, olives, salted almonds and filberts were on hand for the guests to nibble.

Feeling so wonderful with Anthony by her side, Liberty had forgotten what lay ahead: the meal.

A sedate footman halted by her side and began ladling her soup bowl with highly seasoned oyster stew. Too late to stop him, she could only watch in helpless terror as the delicate china dish brimmed with the milky sauce, reddened by cayenne. Shimmering pieces of fish meat floated in the center, surrounded by green herbal leafs.

She swallowed, carefully taking stock of those around her. Everyone had taken up their cutlery; soup spoons dipped into the stew and were brought to lips with relish. Her throat closed. She couldn't do it. But if she didn't, she would disgrace Anthony in front of his friends. Oh, she knew he didn't think of them as his peers, but she could tell that his social standing fit in and he readily accepted them as his equals.

She couldn't disappoint him.

Grasping hold of the handle to her spoon, she sunk the well of the utensil into the sauce. The first taste hadn't been as jolting as she thought. No overpowering taste of oyster permeated the milky stew. She smiled inwardly. She could eat just the juices and no one would notice.

"Tell me, Miss Courtenay," Eden addressed from her chair across from Liberty's. "How did you meet our Anthony?"

Liberty felt the muscles in Anthony's thigh tighten as he pressed his leg into the folds of her skirt. "We met at a party," she responded vaguely.

Not letting Liberty off easy, Eden continued her nasty interrogation. "Anthony has never made any mention of you to me." Turning her attention to Anthony, she throttled him with her violet eyes. "Is she another daughter of a business acquaintance, darling?"

Ophelia's knife clattered distractingly into the crystal stem of her wineglass and all gazes turned to her. She made no apology for her unmannerly clamor, merely took another sample of her oyster stew, daring anyone to comment.

Thomas who had been seated next to the host, Adam Hunter, clanged on the brim of his own glass. The noise was very intentional and didn't still until all eyes were upon him. When he'd garnered the attention he sought, he cleared his throat.

"Adam, if you'll permit me?" He stood and proudly puffed his chest. He'd adorned himself in a coat of peacock blue stitched in golden threads. He looked quite dandified and at the moment, a wide grin had spread itself across his weathered face. "I'm afraid I cannot keep silent any longer." Pushing a corkscrew white curl from his temple, he raised his glass and paid tribute to Anthony and Liberty. "I must make the announcement now or I'll burst from the news of it! A toast. To my grandson, Anthony, and Liberty Courtenay, his future bride."

The dining room buzzed louder than the drone of bees in Liberty's hive. *Snap. Flick.* Elaborate fans briskly unfolded to cool the flushed bosoms of those hopeful, and now disappointed matrons; their daughters would not catch Fielding tonight. More than a few brows rose. An overstated sigh. A gasp. Eden Bennet sharply drew in her breath, then whimpered dejectedly.

"Isn't anyone going to toast with me?" Thomas still held

his position, feasting his gaze down one end of the table to the other.

Liberty searched Anthony's face. He scowled, then snagged his wineglass. He'd previously ignored the white wine, now, he drained the glass with a toss of his head.

Liberty felt crestfallen.

Gradually, everyone had taken up their stemware and sipped to the up-and-coming nuptials.

No one was more puzzled over the guests' reactions than Liberty. They should have rejoiced because Anthony Fielding had at last found love even though they didn't know the love was a fabrication. Anthony Fielding had been supposedly redeemed by a woman's devotion.

The curious glances in her direction made Liberty think that all these people cared about was feeding gossip. Once Anthony Fielding had domesticated himself, his exploits would be empty fodder for their grapevines. The thought of it all made her so angry, she nearly stood from the table and told them all to take their forced felicitations and keep them.

Instead, she persevered under the stares. She would see the evening through and play along with the game no matter what mood Thomas's announcement had put Anthony in. If she really focused on his reaction, she would be painfully hurt. Even as she tried to vanish the look on his face, the expression wavered in front of her eyes. He'd been shocked; his nostrils had flared, then his jaw had clenched in tight anger over his grandfather's salute. Was the idea of marriage so displeasing to Anthony that he didn't want to bind himself to her, even in a lie? That the thought made him break his resolve and drink his wine?

The main course arrived disabling her to ponder the deep-rooted meaning of his resentment. The object of oohs-and-aahs was a golden suckling pig on a bed of watercress.

"Isn't she magnificent!" Mary Hunter gleefully clasped her hands together in front of the low cut of her gown. "Our new cook is simply wonderful! A true culinary master." She said the latter with a far-off gleam to her eyes as if the chef had not only mastered the kitchen but the madam's bedchamber as well.

Adam Hunter accepted the carving knife held out to him by the dark footman. Wielding the blade as if it were nothing more than a feather, Adam put the keen edge into the flesh of the pig.

Liberty sat up straighter in her chair, taking small panting gasps of air. At the moment, the stays around her middle were her only means of support. She watched as Adam made easy cuts into the roast and lay them on his guests' plates, one by one. Since the host had started on his right and worked his way counterclockwise around the table, the meat would be served first to Anthony, then herself, then Aunt Ophelia. They were the last three.

Adam steadied his grip on the knife's handle, neatly digging the tip into a fleshy joint of the hind leg and pulling the appendage free.

Liberty brought her fingertips to her mouth as Anthony's dish returned in front of him. The smell of cooked hog curled around her nose, wafting down into her stomach where she fought the wave of nausea. She closed her eyes against the sickness.

When she opened her eyelids, she found a dozen gazes lingering on her expectantly.

"Your plate, my dear." Adam held out his hand. Waiting.

No one had taken up their forks. She supposed the rule of thumb meant all had to be served before any could partake in the repast.

She made no move for the bone china in front of her.

"Is something wrong?" Eden Bennet's irritated voice rang through the hall. "You're being quite rude. Do you have some sort of aversion to this meal we should all know about? You break out in a rash from pork? Hmm?" A light smirk dusted Eden's pink lips.

The smart in the other woman's words was just enough to send Liberty's defenses. "As a matter of fact, yes. I cannot eat this." Then looking to her host. "I'm sorry. I do not eat meat."

"Nor I," Ophelia chimed in. "Please accept our apologies."

Mary Hunter frowned disgustedly. "I have never heard of anything so absurd."

"Of course you haven't," Eden added. "It must be a part of some abnormal ritual."

"Eden, mind yourself!" Montgomery Bennet tried to curb his daughter's wayward tongue.

"I am an authority on health, having devoted my life to the beautification of the body. And in my years, I have come to understand that the consumption of flesh is not necessary. In actuality, meat is a hindrance to our fitness. Not to mention the killing of God's creatures is cruel. My niece and I so choose to live without it."

Undaunted, Eden picked up her fork and stabbed a segment of roast pig. "La! Such a passel of drivel." Then she popped the meat into her mouth and chewed with great relish. "There, you see. My body hasn't lost its shape."

Anthony rubbed his jaw, feeling the soft lace of his shirt cuff tickle his chin. His concentration zeroed in on one subject: Eden's rosebud lips and tiny white teeth as she masticated the food in her mouth. He made himself affix his gaze on her, denying himself the opportunity to turn away. He thought of the reasons why he'd fancied her; none came to surface. Any emotion he'd ever felt for her, tangible or no, drowned inside him. A new, crystal clear image came to light; he despised himself.

Ironic if he thought on it. The detest should go to the infuriating woman. But, he couldn't punish Eden for being what she was. A snobbish, boring, stuffy, sniveling little bitch who he'd been too half-cocked and none too caring to see through until now.

In Anthony's quiet revelation, he brought himself to an untroubled decision. The impact of what he was to do grew from a flickering flame to a roaring blaze he had no control over. Yet the more he adjusted himself to the idea, the more pleased he became.

With the stateliness the finest gentryman could offer, Anthony put one extended forefinger on the rim of his plate.

A steady push saw the English china slip into the avenue of the table decorations. He bumped a vase, sending the red petal of a fully opened rose to float down on his slice of roast.

"I'm sure your cook went to a great deal of trouble, madam," he said to Mary who had watched him with mild shock on her pallid face. "But I must stand beside my fiancée's wishes and abstain from the consumption of flesh."

Anthony heard a soft sigh come from Liberty and he took up her hand, closing his fingers around the warmth of her skin. Looking into the depths of her hazel eyes, he found a glimmer of adoration.

Ophelia leaned forward and gave Anthony a smile; the first one he could recall being directed at him without the accompaniment of a snarl. "Well done, Fielding."

A tingle akin to that of a shot of liquor coursed though Anthony, yet he hadn't had enough to get a flea drunk—one glass of wine. His reaction was a purely sober one; a feeling that for once, he'd done something good and thought of another human being. Strike him blue! He never thought he'd do something humanitarian. Especially in front of a room of pompous upper crusts.

Thomas who had kept himself silent eventually spoke. "I should say, as freethinkers, we should respect the beliefs of these women." He paused. "And my grandson."

Adam Hunter shrugged and put down his knife, waving for the footmen to bring on the rest of the meal. "Well, I dare swear. 'Tis been a most riveting prelude to our supper."

The ball guests resumed their dining, light discourse filling the room. No one voiced an objection to Anthony's expulsion of his meat. In fact, while Adam Hunter had dished out his platterful, he'd mumbled there was all the more roast for him.

From across the table, Eden Bennet looked up through the pale fringe of her lashes while absently swirling the tips of her fork tines around her pork; she never took another bite.

Anthony dropped Liberty's hand into her lap, suddenly feeling doubtful over his goodly deed. Did she think him a fickle wretch carrying out a desperate act to win her respect? The devil, it was true enough, but he had executed his plan with good intentions.

Her fingertips brushed his knee in a manner that was no accident. His gaze arched slowly to hers. She faintly blushed pink, but made no move to withdraw her touch.

"You approve?" he asked, despite telling himself he wasn't going to, that he didn't need to hear her say the words.

"You did me the honor of giving your approval and I give you mine as well." Then she removed her hand and took up her glass leaving him to wonder if her declaration was the product of the heroic deed he'd just bestowed on her, or if she approved of the man himself.

As the evening progressed, Liberty thought nothing could spoil the remainder of the night. Anthony had stood up for her! Her heart filled with sunshine, warming her down to the satin roses on the toes of her slippers. He *did* care. In his own way, he'd said to the world he believed in her.

And Anthony seemed happy about his decision to take a stand on her behalf. In all their time together he'd never truly abandoned himself to laughter and lazy amusement. His self-indulgence vanished; his spirit drifted free, in its path was a new man with purpose. Even the way he looked changed. Though the same lines and shapes marked his visage, the expression had softened. Humor shone in his eyes.

Supper had long finished on the heels of silver cups full of cooled, fruited creams. Now, the dancing had begun anew without the guise of masks. Flirtation among the throng became more selective as partners could see each other's faces.

Liberty had danced her share, finding herself at the end of many inquisitive questions about her and Anthony. Most of the talk stemmed on the fact they had never seen her before, and now, here she was promised to Anthony prior to the banns being posted.

Taking a rest from the music, she stood at the open terrace, a refreshing glass of lady's punch in her hand.

Thomas Fielding and her aunt had just finished a minuet and stood by her side.

Ophelia's face was flushed from exertion. "I dare say, I've not danced so much in all my days!"

Thomas drew out his muckender and dabbed the delicate swatch on his temples. "Myself, I like a good minuet or quadrille. 'Tis the reels that leave me gasping." He snatched a goblet brimming with bubbling champagne. He drank several deep swallows. "Where did your fiancé see himself off to?"

"The direction of the smoking room last I saw. He'd been enticed into conversation by Mister Bennet." Liberty sipped her water. "I believe they were discussing Anthony's boat."

"Bah. This is a party. Where are his manners? 'Twill be more than ample time to discuss business tomorrow. Let's go fetch him away, shall we?"

Liberty set down her glass. "If you don't think he'd mind being interrupted."

"I don't care if he minds or not. You're too comely in that dress to be left standing at odds with the assortment of young bucks in this room." Thomas finished his champagne and placed his empty goblet next to Liberty's on the refreshment table. "I'm too old to be defending your honor."

Aunt Ophelia sent Liberty off, leaving Liberty to wonder if her aunt had had a change of heart where Anthony was concerned. In the past, she never would have waved her toward Fielding without a fight. Perhaps Aunt Ophelia was beginning to see the good in Anthony that Liberty had seen all along.

Steering Liberty around the host of celebrants, Thomas would stop now and then to properly introduce her. As they neared the wide doorway out of the grand salon, Eden Bennet collided with them on the arm of a late arriver. Liberty's cool gaze fell on Eden. Too late, she recognized Eden's escort.

Eden kept company with a man of distinguished prominence. The Worshipful John Perkins Esquire Mayor

Liberty couldn't gain her freedom without being seen by the offensive bag of bones who had manhandled her in the Blue Anchor coffeehouse. Looking at him now, she grew still. His ruddy cheeks contrasted sorely with the braided white periwig snugly fit over his head. Her fingers achingly remembered the bruising she'd given his right eye. Would he have the gall to call out her indiscretion in front of Thomas and Eden, or would his composure be cool and calculating? Either way, she felt doomed. Her identity had just fallen into base hands.

"Perkins," Thomas said flatly. "I thought we'd all been spared your insidious presence."

Liberty heard the bite to the words, knowing she hadn't imagined the sting. Apparently Thomas Fielding held the new mayor in high contempt also. Why?

"Ah, another Fielding." John Perkins's snide commentary rang with the same disdain. "I'd wondered if you still resided on this green earth or if you'd been called off to join—"

With an agility that startled Liberty, Thomas had sprinted from her side and sunk his fingers into the sleeve of John's coat. "Don't you dare say it, man," Thomas threatened in a deadly tone that whispered its lethal intent. "Don't you dare utter my son Richard's name. Your barbed tongue would carve it to pieces . . ." Thomas's fist slackened, his face pained by distant memories. ". . . as you did the man."

Liberty, though her own worries were great, digested this news with interest. Had John Perkins killed Anthony's father? Anthony had said his parents were dead . . Good God, what sort of treachery had Perkins descended on the Fielding household?

John Perkins drew up his weak height. "Unhand me before I call a member of His Majesty's Army on you."

A flash of indecision crossed Thomas's face, then he uncurled his fingers and lowered his arm. "Bloody bastard," he cursed under his breath.

Eden Bennet smiled with great satisfaction, as if she'd known precisely what collision these two men would have upon meeting. Liberty took sides with Thomas, pressing her fingertips into his coated forearm. He patted her hand reassuringly, though the equanimity of his normally reserved smile seemed far from even.

John Perkins preened and fluffed the cascading spill of his lawn cravat, fixing and modifying the shape in which it lay. He cast his watery blue eyes on her person, pinpointing her with an eaglelike assessment. "And what have we here?" Fleshy lips turned upward, leering as if she were a treasured bird and he a cunning cat licking his chops at the thought of devouring such a succulent morsel.

He stared interminably.

An uncontrollable shiver racked Liberty's shoulders. If he intended to humiliate her, why didn't he get on with it? Unless . . . he didn't recognize her. She hadn't counted on that. This evening, she looked nothing like the chambermaid John Perkins once accosted. In her finery, she appeared very much the lady of quality.

"Have you a name, fair maid?" Perkins's syrupy question melted sickeningly through Liberty's veins. The last time he'd addressed her, he'd called her an insolent baggage. What a change in his tune!

"You needn't bother yourself over her, your Worship," Eden flippantly chided. "She's already spoken for. By Anthony." She ground out Fielding's name as if it were wheat under a grist stone.

"What is this?" Now Perkins appeared more interested in Liberty than ever. "The drunken buffoon has found himself someone to suffer out his wine soaked days?"

Liberty stiffened. "Poor sir, you've not only insulted my prospective husband, you've insulted me."

Hooking his arm into hers, Thomas tried to appease Liberty's growing outrage. She ignored him. Her gaze zeroed in on Perkins's hands as they smoothed over the satin of his waistcoat. She remembered what his fat belly felt like against her as he'd groped her in the coffeehouse. She relived the day those fingers reached out to abuse her body. It was all she could do not to scream her hatred of him.

With an icy tone, Liberty said, "I shall have an apology from you or you'd best pray against the consequences."

Perkins mildly stared at her, as if he weren't sure he'd heard her right. Then he burst into laughter. "Come fair, come foul, the wench has a mean streak in her." He chuckled deeply, tears gathering in his eyes. "You and Fielding will make an attractive couple. He'll be woofled and you can henpeck him into the ground! I should say, 'twill be quite the happy home!"

"Sir, you say too much." She did her utmost to remain collected and not give her true identity away, but her hands clenched at her sides and her fingers itched to take another swing at him.

John Perkins laughed. Hard. And continuously, making snide comments under his breath. "Fielding Manor will be the epitome of poor taste."

"Good heavens, your Worship," Eden said, glaring anxiously at Liberty's fists. "She looks ready to hit you."

"Watch my eye!" Perkins quickly shot back, covering his face with beringed fingers. "My face 'twas recently the object . . ." When no assault was forthcoming, he slowly lowered his defenses. Then, his jaw dropped open and his whitened brows came thundering down into point. "Mercy!" He sputtered to recover, then gasped, "You're the lunatic wench from the—"

Anthony's voice interrupted the thought. "The only lunatic I can see, Perkins, is you."

ANTHONY'S FACE ENGRAVED IN UNADULTERATED HATRED, HE growled, "You shall beg the lady's forgiveness."

"This *lady*," Perkins spit out, grinding his teeth, "is no lady." The mayor huffed in a tight laugh. "She is a lowly chambermaid—a dram of cider vinegar that I'd thought better left on the ducking stool to dilute her sharpness."

Liberty's heart fluttered like a new-caught bird in a cage. Panic-stricken, terror ran up the length of her spine. Though she'd known Perkins's challenge of her character had been coming, the telltale words threw her without mercy into harm's path.

"Say again! You don't know what you're talking about," Thomas interceded. "Your tawdry yarn is naught but poor stuff. This is Liberty Courtenay, my grandson's betrothed."

"Isn't this *great folly?*" Perkins rumbled in a delectable note, wiggling his fingers. Quite put upon, he wormed his way out of Anthony's loose trap. "I charge you, she's been cramming your ears with sheer farce, Fielding! Believe me when I say, I know the woman." Abruptly his gratified mood soured and he brought his limp hand to the edge of his eye as if remembering the blow he'd attained there. "Aye, indeed I know the saucebox."

Liberty couldn't meet the sloe-colored gleam in John

Perkins's irreverent stare for fear he'd be able to read her alarm. To appear scared in front of him would be her undoing; all their undoing. She had to keep her conduct conforming to that of a highborn lady by putting on airs of indignation and resentment.

She looked down her lightly powdered nose at the mayor "I will not be taken to task by that vulgar epithet."

"I shall make no retraction of it, my dear good *lady,*" he drew out the formal address in an undignified accent, "for I recall your saucy fist."

"Your recollection is off course." Anthony's cool and exact voice poured over Liberty like snow water. Nearly paralyzed by his chilling tone, she glanced at him. A stony expression masked his face, chiseled by intense hatred for the man who had attacked her.

Heedless of the edge in Anthony's voice, Perkins did not digress. "I should say," he refuted hotly, "'tis you, poor Fielding, who has been drawing a herring across the trail, duping all those you cross."

Anthony inclined his head. Liberty knew him well enough to see the challenge in the flare of his nostrils, the tensing of his jaw. He put his arms akimbo, loathing mirrored in his eyes. "Pray what interest would I have in a lowly chambermaid besides bedding her? I am sure I wouldn't parade the baggage around and announce my engagement to her."

Liberty couldn't quell the sharp intake of her breath. She knew in her heart Anthony had to disavow her true position, but to hear the biting words was like a slap in the face.

Eden Bennet spitefully smiled at Liberty. "Why, Goody Courtenay, how evil of you to play our Anthony false with your cunning dress."

Though she hid her emotions well, Liberty smarted at the menial form of address used for women considered of lower social rank. Hearing Eden refer to Anthony as belonging to their higher class made Liberty feel worse. Anthony's words may have been spoken to save the masquerade, yet they were true nonetheless. Anthony Fielding would never marry a chambermaid. She had been a fool to ever dream it. There was no denying what she really was, what she would always be. Someone with no wealth or title; the daughter of indentured servants.

Though feeling as if the fight had just been sapped out of her, Liberty squared her shoulders. For Thomas's sake, and Anthony's, too, she would defend her story. "Worshipful Esquire Mayor," she began, wetting her lips and crushing the despair from her bones. "I don't know why you think we've met. I've only just arrived in Norfolk. As for my being a—a chambermaid, the idea is preposterous and one I find quite offensive. I would never tarnish my hands in such a manner."

As she said the disclaiming promise, Liberty hoped she spoke the words with enough convincing snobbishness. The entire condemnation tasted bitter on her tongue and she prayed this would be the end of it.

Perkins's dark eyes showed signs of uncertainty, as if her performance had swayed him into confusion and perhaps misjudgment. "I know naught of duties other than those of a mistress in leisure. Each morning I awake to the scratch of my maid at the door of whom I enquire about the weather and complain of a frightful night's sleep. She then hands me a cup of chocolate and my slippers. I breakfast on a lacy pastry with honey butter, and on occasion, a light portion of rice pudding. The rest of my day is spent on correspondence, choosing which social function my presence is worthy. No matter what my evening's activities are, my retirement is the same. Upon my request, my bed is turned down a quarter fold and waiting on my dressing table, a half glass of pale Spanish sherry and a single truffle." In conclusion, she snapped, "I know who I am, your Worshipful Esquire Mayor, I may hope now you are convinced as well."

John Perkins grew solemn and reserved. He pulled out a monogrammed piece of linen from his waistcoat and brought the perfume scented cloth under his nose. Sniffing daintily of the musky fragrance, he blinked his stubby lashes. "It behooves me, dear mistress, to beg your pardon. I spoke out of turn and with great inaccuracy."

Eden colored in discouragement, clearly put out by the

mayor's apology. The far-blown excitement apparently done with, she shifted her expression to one of boredom, scanning the crowded dance floor.

Anthony put his arm possessively around Liberty's silk waist applying gentle pressure. She looked up at him. "Say the word, sweeting, and I'll call him out for daring to insult you. I've a room of witnesses that can attest to my provocation for such a match."

No matter the animosity she felt toward the mayor, Liberty couldn't have his blood spilled for accosting her—and for catching her in her lie. "Nay, Anthony. I think his Worship has paid his penitence this eve; his remorse is plain to see." Feeling Anthony's strength, Liberty lost a little of the hold she had on her trembling and fell into his embrace more soundly. "I'd like to go home now."

"As you wish, sweeting."

The endearment washed over her in a golden veil, warming her and setting her pulse to a soothing stride. It made no difference if the word had been staged for the others, she pretended he really meant calling her sweeting.

Thomas grumbled his resentment of Perkins before setting off to fetch Ophelia.

Perkins withdrew himself from their presence on the high heels of stiff dignity. Eden tucked arm-in-arm with the mayor, neither bid a cordial farewell.

Liberty wanted nothing more than to cut free her stays and plead the sanctity of her bedchamber at Fielding Manor to console her wounds.

Tilting her chin upward in the curve of Anthony's long fingers, fascination clouded his eyes. He let her go, trailing his gaze down the slope of her neck. "Your recitation had me believing, too. How did you know what to say to Perkins?"

Keeping her chin high without his gentle support, she tutored, "You forget, I've been serving women like Eden Bennet a cup of chocolate and a half glass of sherry for several months."

She lowered her face, her eyes aching from unshed tears. She would never cry over what she was. Witnessing the toadying ways of these elite people, she embraced her common origin as being the better of the two.

"Divine grace, how I long to put an end to this charade!" Words of woe, so long trapped in her head, were now unleashed at the pair of white herons fishing in the river's shore.

Unmindful of the route she took away from the estate, Liberty had wound up on the stretch of beach backing Anthony's home. With each impatient step, tiny pebbles rained their way into the instep of her leather shoes. The water-smoothed grains hurt the tender flesh on the bottom of her feet. Bothered that she had to interrupt her flight, Liberty sought the help of a poplar.

Once under the quaking boughs, she used the peeling trunk for balance. First came off one top-knotted shoe, shaking out the offending rocks and brushing the soiled heel of her white cotton stockings; the other foot followed suit and was tidied in the same no-nonsense manner.

Off again, she carefully chose her steps lest she be plagued by the ruinous stones again.

She could not attend another soiree such as the one last night. To be beset by the Worshipful John Perkins Esquire Mayor and that boldface, Eden Bennet, had been too much. Such an upbraiding, she didn't deserve.

Her steps growing more sure, the pebbles returned to annoy her.

"Oh, fie." Liberty swore her disgust, flushing a beach sparrow from its roost on a driftwood limb. She twirled around. Spying a small patch of high grass on which to plop down, she headed for the area. The wind-shaped branches of a honey-pod tree became her parasol, shading the midmorning sun from her unbonneted head. In her haste to be gone, she'd left her straw hat in her bedroom.

Dropping to her knees, she dusted off the fallen pods that littered the silky green carpet to make herself a clean circle on which to sit. She removed her shoes and shook out the rocks once more. In a fit she knew to be childish, she threw the slippers a yard away.

Bunching up her homespun undercoats, Liberty smoothed her skirt beneath her and sat.

She plucked at a loose thread in the hem of her frock. The print, a sad-colored calico in a gray-russet, reflected her mood. The dress had come to Fielding Manor in the bottom of her iron-banded trunk, a layer of dried dogwood petals between the folds; the faint scent remained in the weave of the fabric. Looking down on the worn bodice and patched pockets, Liberty accepted the tenfold mends as a sign of reality. The garment befitted one of her station in life.

She thought of the rich gown she'd donned seemingly lifetimes ago for the masked ball; it lay heaped on the floor of her dressing closet. The frills were nothing more than a tag of falsity. She'd never truly own such a piece in all her days. She was destined to marry a boy more to the tune of Barlary White than a well-to-do man of Anthony Fielding's fame. She wished she'd never thought otherwise.

Shifting on her bottom, Liberty lay down on her back and crossed one leg over the other. The cool, shaded air swirled around her stockinged legs and she absently wiggled her toes. She closed her tired eyes.

Her despondency had made a sorry bedfellow. Sleep had come in fitful patches during the night. In the short stretches she'd dozed, she'd had restless dreams of John Perkins looming over her, his right eye rimmed in bruised black, and Eden Bennet by his side cackling and egging the pretentious mayor on. And then there had been Thomas Fielding's words of warning to Perkins as well. The name Richard had clouded her slumber. Richard Fielding. Anthony's father.

Why hadn't Anthony told her about him when she'd asked? She'd opened up to him, relating her childhood, but he'd remained closed and distant. She never should have hoped he would be as honest with her. They were doomed to a bargain. An agreement of five hundred and five pounds. How could she have thought otherwise?

Liberty had awakened in a cold, dewy sweat, her thin night shift damp and clinging between the valley of her breasts. She'd untangled her legs from her bedclothes, kicking the stifling linens over the footboard. For long periods afterward, she'd lain there, her eyes searching the darkness for answers to her troubles. There seemed to be no solution other than leaving Fielding Manor—immediately. She couldn't bear to share the same dwelling as Anthony, knowing what would never be.

By morning's first light, she'd resigned herself to looking pitifully wretched and an imminent headache. As she came to full awareness while reclined on her bed, Jane had knocked upon the door. Liberty had bid her to come in. The maid carried a tray decked out with a cup of shaved hot chocolate and a buttered, fresh apricot pastry.

Liberty had risen on her elbows, a shock of tangled black hair cascading over her shoulder. She had not ordered such a repast and having spoke about a feast like this not several hours past, she could only frown at the spread out tray. It was Anthony's doing. She knew it to be true.

Humiliation had woven a hurtful course through her. Did Anthony think she desired the pampered breakfast service to be like Eden Bennet? Surely, she did not!

Quietly Liberty accepted the tray, not wanting to raise questions to Jane. She'd dismissed the maid and sat up in her bed. She stared at the vanity where Jane had placed the tray she had not requested.

Some time passed before Liberty decided to rise and dress herself in her old clothes. She could not bring herself to lace up in the fancy gowns Anthony Fielding had laid out coin for. She'd put on her age-softened slippers and left the room.

Despite the faint stirring in Liberty's empty stomach, the luscious chocolate and flaky roll were left to grow cold.

In the time Liberty had sat on her bed, she'd thought of her future. For certain, the forecast looked bleak should she stay another day in Anthony's home. She'd fallen hopelessly in love with him and he didn't return the feeling. How could he after what he'd said at the party? Even if most or all had been fabricated, he'd never once said he was fond of her. She couldn't bear to give him all her adoration and receive a cold heart in return.

Knowing her and Aunt Ophelia's departure would stir a passel of questions from Thomas, she'd reasoned Anthony should be left to think of his own story for her leave-taking. It was, after all, his invention of a fiancée that had seen her to play out her part; let him invent her out of being his affianced. As for the remainder of the money . . . she would get it, somehow. The only certain way she knew to have it soon, would be to indenture herself. That option had made her shudder. She could not break the dream of freedom her parents had for her.

She would find another way.

Her decision made, Liberty should have felt better. But she hadn't. She still had to confront Anthony with her news; but first, Aunt Ophelia.

She'd found her aunt in the blue sitting room, seated in the arm chair with her ribbons. Her nimble fingers stretched and looped, knotting away at a brisk pace wrought out by years of practice.

"Good morrow, Aunt," she'd greeted in her most pleasant tone. Recognizing what she would have to say would be upsetting, Liberty strolled toward a Windsor chair.

The hard wood brought no comfort to her backside which without the many layers of rich silk petticoats, was at the chair's unpadded disposal.

"Ah, my lambkin." Ophelia neither looked up nor missed a beat with her knotting. "I am quite melted after last night's merrymaking. I didn't know parties could be such tiresome affairs."

"They are more than tiresome for others," Liberty mentioned offhandedly.

Ophelia pulled a long loop in her ribbon and dropped the double-sided satin tail in her lap. She wound the length of knots onto an enamel spool. "The young Fielding looked rather debonair last night. Don't you think?"

The impromptu remark about Anthony caused Liberty to sit lighter on her chair. "I thought you despised him."

"Tut!" Ophelia's head bobbed, her tower of fuzzy, peach-colored hair threatening to topple. "I may not agree with his opinions, but I've found him—only as of late, mind you—more tolerable. 'Tis due in part that his drinking has stopped."

"It has not ceased—he had wine at the table. Do not let his cunning fool you. He's a black creature and I'm not sure I like him anymore." The rush of words had come out before Liberty thought better of them. She gasped and put a hand to her mouth—now shut closed.

"What is this?" Liberty's affront put a spike in Ophelia's gears and she shut down her knotting in a pinch. "I thought you were quite taken with Fielding."

"As of this moment, I know not how I feel about Anthony." Liberty looked down at the toes of her worn shoes and the twist of black ribbon decorating the tops. "I thought myself in love with him and now I find only sorrow in my heart when I think of him."

"And why is this, pet?" Genuine concern touched Ophelia's voice.

Liberty raised her gaze. "Because he thinks of me as a bossy serving wench temporarily under his employ."

"What did he say to you?" Anger laced through Ophelia's question. Then she paled and bolted upright. Wringing her hands, she bewailed, "Sweet Mary, has he snatched you from under my nose? Taken you to a place of seclusion and—and—I cannot bear to think it much less breathe it! Has he ruined and undone you?" The query hung on a dreadfully high-pitched note. "I shall take him down with my blunderbuss! The rutting peacock!"

"Hold! He did nothing of the kind."

"Gracious, thank the Lord for that blessing." Ophelia eased herself back into her chair, a sheen of light moisture appearing on her face. She shoved her knotting from her lap and grabbed hold of her fan. Waving the gadget in front of her bosom, she sighed. "I fair had an attack of the heart."

"No more so than I last night when I had my run-in with John Perkins," Liberty murmured.

Though Ophelia had not been with Liberty during the mayor's confrontation, she'd been furnished with the entire exchange in the landau on the way home. Her aunt had *tsked* and *tutted* at the abuse her poor pet had been made to suffer by that irascible cretin. Anthony had brooded during the retelling, his arms crossed over his chest. He, of course, could not ask the question that Liberty knew to be scorching the tip of his tongue: What *had* the past encounter been between herself and John Perkins? For Anthony to speak his mind at that moment would have pulled the wool out of the bag. Thomas Fielding thought Liberty a poor, misjudged maiden in the eyes of Perkins.

"Such a man is he, this ruffian mayor." Ophelia forced her words out with the beat of her fan. "He should mind his politics more than his affection for young wenches. 'Tisn't as if he were such a charmer to gaze upon. The man's puff and pride are to be held in highest contempt."

"Anthony wonders how I know him."

"He's asked you?"

"Nay, though 'tis only a matter of seeing him next when we are alone that he will hound me for the answer." Liberty sighed, her sight wandering to the mound of gazettes next to Ophelia's chair. "I suppose it doesn't matter if he knows. He thinks me quite common already. What's one more truth to add to his low opinion?"

"I think he would stand in defense of your honor should he know what that vile rodent Perkins did to your person and what you were forced to do in return."

"Aunt?" Liberty shook her head in wonder. "Such a turnabout for Anthony has me questioning your sanity. Are you the same aunt that said Fielding was a man to be thrown off a roof? I cannot believe what you speak. What has he said to you?"

"Nothing in words, my lamb. His loyalty to you by pushing his plate away at the supper table gave him great merit in my mind."

"Don't think him so noble. He's lied to me."

"What?"

"Not exactly lied," Liberty rephrased. "He's kept the truth from me. I'd asked him about his parents once and he said nothing more than they were deceased. I know his father was killed—by John Perkins. Thomas Fielding said as much."

"Tut! Can that be?"

"I'm quite certain. If Anthony held any affection for me,

231

he would have enlightened me when he had the chance. As 'tis, I've bared myself to him and received not a single consolation."

Ophelia slapped her fan closed and stuffed it between the chair's cushion and arm. "My . . . pet . . . bared yourself?"

"In the mind."

Ophelia sighed, "Thank heaven for that . . . If that 'tis all that's bothering you, I'm sure Fielding will come 'round. Give him time to get used to you. Now, at eleven I'm expecting a selected group of fine madams to try out my new perfume, *Passion and Truth.* I spoke with them last night and they were quite thrilled by my talents. They said they never knew a lady of my breeding to take up an occupation such as beauty consultant. They said," Ophelia rushed on, her enthusiasm stoked, "that all they know how to do is hold a needle and snipping. Snipping! Such a silly passion of snipping colored papers to paste and varnish on their hatboxes and coffers. I mentioned the salon and they were gone with excitement. To actually have a place to rid themselves of their husbands was the icing on the plum cake and they said they shan't rest for anticipation of its opening!"

Liberty looked down at her hands which were folded in her lap. *The salon.* The salon was what was important to Ophelia. Liberty had been ready to give it up because of pride. How could she now with her aunt going on about it so?

"We'll have such fun, we two, at our salon. We'll have a grand room and fine settees the likes of which no one has ever seen. Blue is the color of the season, you know."

"Aye, I know." In a hasty rush, Liberty stood. "If you'll excuse me, Aunt, I must be on my way." She couldn't bear to listen to another word.

It had been that blinding need to seek refuge from her aunt's spirited talk that had led her to the beach behind the house.

A stillness settled over Liberty as she drifted, her memories of the morning slipping away. She eased into a white cloud of sleep. She'd had enough reminiscences to last the day. . . .

Anthony had been looking for Liberty all morning. He found the woebegone mistress asleep under the natural awning of a honey-pod tree. In his pursuit, he'd nearly passed her by but the feminine white of her petticoat pulled his gaze toward the tufted slope where she lay. Treading quietly he went to her.

Flat on her back, one leg bent and crossed over the other, Liberty unconsciously granted him a daring view of opaque stockings and the plain linen ruffle of her undercoat. Eyes closed and ruby lips parted, she slept soundlessly. The long black strands of her hair built a framework of silky tresses around her ivory face.

He allowed himself to think of her sharing his bed and waking every morning to bask in this picture of prettiness. To feel the satin of her ivory skin, the tease of her lips on his own. To know that she would return his passion and surrender to him . . .

Plague him! The image shattered like a thousand pieces of glass, pointed shards that pierced his daydreams. He could not in a score of years ever hope to gain one such as she for himself. If he put the glass back together and looked into it, he would see himself. A vestige of a man whose fame with poetry was pathetic at best. What should have been words of love turned to slurs of ribald suggestion.

He was a blackguard to ever have allowed her to stay with him. He should have sent her off with his blessings and the bloody purse, her not having to do a stitch for the coin. Her integrity and virtue alone were enough to earn out five hundred and five pounds. Plague him again. . . .

Making the minimum of noises, he sat down beside her to await her awakening. He hadn't the heart to jar her to consciousness.

Anthony leaned his back into the trunk of the honey-pod tree. He brought his legs to his chest and sat for a lengthy spell while Liberty slept on. He watched her. He watched her steadily and thought of all the things he would say to her, rehearsing them in his mind over and over. He called himself a smitten pup.

Patience not being his greatest asset, Anthony grew restless for Liberty to wake. He brought his knees down and sat cross-legged, tapping his fingertips on the sole of his boot. It he were left alone with his imprisoned thoughts another minute, he'd forget his resolutions and begin dreaming up a dozen ways to kiss her to wakefulness. Not a bad thought, but one which would make him abandon what he needed to say to her. And at this point, he couldn't afford to lose his head.

He pulled his gaze away from her, foraging the ground around him for a stick to tickle the tempting, bare skin of her inner arm. Seeing the abundance of honey-pods at his disposal, he trapped one between his fingers, raised his hand above Liberty's waist and let the pod plummet to her midriff.

Liberty's thick lashes flew up, her sleepy hazel eyes searching the mesh of branches above her. Apparently not noticing Anthony looming at her side, she let her lids slip closed once more, absently brushing the honey-pod from her middle.

Anthony felt impatience settle in his hand as he stretched his fingers over a cluster of pods. Grabbing one, he pitched it at Liberty's shoulder.

She bolted upright.

"I say . . ." she mumbled, still drowsy and knocking a wave of shimmering black hair from her brow. The lazy sensuality of her gesture made a crooked path to Anthony's lower abdomen, making sitting in the position he was, an uncomfortable feat. He sat more firmly on his buttocks, ignoring the strain in his breeches.

His timely movement caught Liberty's attention and her eyes widened finding Anthony an arm's length away.

"Mistress," he intoned as innocent as a cleric's wife, "it grieves me to have awakened you."

"Anthony " Her voice, husky from sleep, held a smidgen

234

of reprimand. "I thought some rodent bombarding me with honey-pods." She sighed. "I can see I was right."

Anthony folded his hands together in mock atonement. "I'd say you wound me, but I've been called worse."

Liberty swung her gleaming black hair over her shoulder. "You big villain. Coming upon a woman unawares in slumber."

"Would you have allowed me to approach you were you cognizant of my presence?" Anthony gave her no time to answer. "Your avoidance of me since last evening would have me say no."

Liberty bunched her threadbare skirt under her stockinged feet hiding her daintily molded legs from his view. The fact that she'd donned such rags when she had expensive frocks aplenty in her closet, tugged at his ego. He'd thought she'd been pleased by the gowns.

"I have no reason to hide from you." The coolness in Liberty's tone gave her away.

"Were I you, Liberty, I'd be hiding from me, too. Perfidious soul that I am, I took you for granted. May I say, 'twill never happen again."

Liberty picked up a honey-pod and toyed with the stem before crunching the twig in her fingers. "I am sure I don't understand you."

"The cup of chocolate and roll. I ran into your aunt this morning and she told me you were upset over them."

"Perhaps I was. But more so over another matter."

"Which is?"

"Not which, who." Liberty's head shot up. "John Perkins. You've been trying to get me to tell you how I know him, when 'tis the same question I should be asking you."

"There isn't anything to tell about Perkins. He's shown his true colors. He's a bastard."

"A harsh word to call our mayor. Maybe you use the curse because of what he did to your father."

Anthony's blood heated. "How do you know about that?"

"I suspect I'm the only one who didn't." Her fingers trembled and Anthony watched her quiet them in her lap.

"How could you withhold that information from me? After what I told you about Ophelia and my parents. I'd asked you about your own and you give me a short answer."

"My father is dead. Does it matter how he got that way?"

"Aye! To me. I'd thought we were becoming . . . close. That we shared things. Shared our thoughts. How wrong and silly of me to allow myself to . . . never mind." Liberty's lashes lowered. The fringes of black looked like delicate lace against the pure whiteness of her cheekbones.

Anthony reached out his hand and cupped Liberty's chin in his fingers. "You're right. I should have told you." The feel of her skin under his touch was warm and smooth. "John Perkins murdered my father when I was sixteen. I witnessed his death."

"Anthony . . ."

He didn't want her consolation. He wanted to tell her what happened. It was time he faced the images that haunted his dreams; he had to speak them to someone who cared. "My father challenged Perkins to a duel. He was defending my mother's honor. You see, she had an affair with our Worshipful John Perkins Esquire Mayor. I had the bravado of a youth to think I could handle being on the dueling field and watch it all happen. Seeing the blood . . . the death." Anthony shuddered.

"I went after Perkins. I meant to kill him. I waited for him in his home, and when he didn't return, I got drunk. I immersed myself in the unfeelingness of liquor and blinding my belly with numbing fire. I stayed in my pints for a week after it happened, never going out-of-doors."

Liberty met his gaze and he stared at the vast green-gold of her eyes. Luminous and wide, they fixed on him without faltering.

"By the end of the seventh day, I had no feeling left in me. I merely existed because I breathed. I dragged myself home in time to watch my mother flee for Antigua, a refuge from the scandal she'd caused by her affair with Perkins."

"But you said she was dead," Liberty interjected.

"To me, she is," he said unfeelingly. "In the ensuing years,

I decided to kill John Perkins alive. To make him live out his death sentence and be made to suffer the way I did over my father's death. I would publicly ruin the man. That's why I got involved with shipbuilding. I knew Perkins owned a marginally successful shipping line."

Liberty listened quietly as he went on.

Snorting, Anthony sat back on his hands. "I socialized with those who knew John Perkins, attending their parties, drinking their fine wines and rich brandies. Through this, I gleaned information.

"Though Perkins served as a churchwarden from time to time, he made a terrible alderman. He held a position in the Assembly with aspiration of becoming our Worshipful Mayor even back then. He inaugurated folly laws—any servant in town who rode faster than a foot pace, his master would be fined two shillings, six pence. Perkins was tolerated far more than the fops around him due in part to his heavy monetary contributions for Norfolk's growth."

"You know him well," Liberty commented softly.

"Very. He keeps company with numerous well-off whores and women of servitude, but never keeps any of them in favor for very long. He drinks only *premier cru*—the first growth wines of France. He hates the Scottish for their political beliefs."

"If you know him so well, you should know what he did to me."

Anthony's gaze narrowed. "I suspect he's not been a proper gentleman. Tell me, dear girl, he didn't—"

"He tried," Liberty finished. "But I blackened his eye."

Anthony's low laughter filtered around them. "I'd been envious of the man who beat me to that. How ironic 'twas you, sweeting."

"I should have done far worse, but my wits fled me. He got me fired from my position at the Blue Anchor. That's why Mister Feathers found me out of employ." Liberty worried her lower lip. "You've spent so many years chasing the man . . ."

"I had him two years ago." Anthony closed his eyes in

remembrance, then slowly lifted his lids. "But he got away. Not this time, though. This time we'll have him. I'll see him in hell."

"Anthony . . ." Liberty's eyes sparkled. "Is this why you drink? To dispel your past. Anyone would turn to their cups if they'd—"

"But you forget," he said bitterly. "I don't drink anymore."

Deep inside, Anthony hurt. He also felt as if he'd just gotten rid of a heavy burden. He looked at Liberty, read in her eyes a depth of emotion. She'd never been one to mask her feelings for him. Though he'd ignored the gestures, he could deny them no longer—she was in love with him. Anytime in the past, when a female had gazed at him so, she'd feigned the expression with a practiced blink and a coquettish quirk of her mouth. In Liberty, the expression was virginal.

Plague him thrice, she meant it.

For all the wretch that he was, he could not accept her gentle offering without pondering the lasting effect he'd have on her. He'd crush her, of course. Like a flower just bloomed, she'd come into her own and once undone, she'd wilt. She couldn't last, now that she knew the truth about him.

He would have to set her free.

Good God, where had his sudden burst of nobility come from? He had to remind himself his good attributes were virtually nil. He was a rogue, a rake, a drunkard without scruples who'd had scads of lowly women at his heels for pleasure. He bore no fondness for his mother, he feared marriage and he'd spent his adult life destroying himself. What would she see in him and why would he want this one woman when he could have dozens of others?

How could he not want her?

Her face, tempting his sanity, stared into his own. His heartbeat had slackened and speeded up, as if uncertain of the route to take. At one turn, he said be done with it and kiss her to madness; at the other turn, he pushed her away and reminded himself what a cad he was.

He touched her cheek.

Cursing under his breath, Anthony felt as if he had been ignited by peat fires and as he sat and breathed, he burned in Hades.

Before he could change his mind, he removed his hand and practically pounded his fist into his knee. "I'm sorry."

She seemed to understand his hesitation. She tilted her face toward the dappled sky and laughed. Her humor came in a light, gentle bubble of notes. "Isn't this a fine fix? We've both had our share of John Perkins and despite his vile capacity, he's the one who brought us together. You needed my services and I needed your money. Whatever shall we do when it's all over?"

"I don't know."

"Of course you don't." Disappointment creased her temple and she frowned. "We could always tell your grandfather the truth and be done with things now. Once he got over the blow of my being a chambermaid, he may have himself a stiff laugh."

Moving closer to her, Anthony caught the indignant sparks in her eyes. Blast, he'd told Perkins his interest in a chambermaid would never go beyond bedding her; he'd said the words to throw the mayor off track, but only now, sot that he was, did he digest exactly what his comment meant to Liberty. He'd unwittingly insulted her in the worst of ways. And then he'd topped her humiliation off this morning with a prissy cup of chocolate and a bloody roll.

Anthony growled inwardly, now damning his resolve to remain free of liquor. He could use a draught of something sharp to slap him in the gut.

Bringing his eyelids up, he grabbed Liberty by the shoulders, dragging her toward him. Her hair fell over his hands, caressing his splayed fingers. Eyes wide with shock and surprise, her mouth fell open. Her lips, tinted red and ripe as a summer berry, beckoned him, but he held off kissing her. Instead, he tried to think of one line, one single message of prose to make amends.

Grappling, he struggled to recall something to make her see his error by way of an apology conveyed in sweet words.

Being a craftsman of ships, only those passages in reading that paralleled his trade, did he bother to remotely store in his head. In this present emergency, he brought forth a particular line from Shakespeare's *As You Like It* and prayed God he could recite it on memory alone.

"My brain is dry as the last biscuit on a voyage; it has strange places crammed with observations which I vented in mangled form." His tongue tripped over the exchange and his trouble was met by the blank stare in her gaze. "Strike me blue, it goes something like that. I mean to say, my mind was not thinking of your feelings when I spoke as I did to John Perkins."

"You shouldn't worry so, Anthony. You express yourself well enough without prose." She breathed in short gasps. "You meant every word last night. There's no need so spare me now. Let no more lies exist between us."

Frustration made Anthony draw her to him more tightly. "I spoke what had to be said to save us—you, from that swine Perkins. Yet I should have asked your pardon the moment we were alone. I did not. For that, I should forever be in your poor graces."

"Mayhap you never were in my good graces," she challenged, wetting her lips. "Mayhap this role I've been playing has thus far been an amusing diversion you've taken to mean more . . ."

"Such jargon for one so pretty as you." Anthony lessened his hold and rubbed his thumbs into her tender flesh, kneading out any damage he'd done. "You wear your heart on your shoulder, for I have realized it's been there often enough. You're so brave, sweet. So very brave to fray my ego in the hopes of saving your heart."

Gently as fingers would, Anthony traced the fullness of Liberty's mouth. Her lips quivered; her eyelids grew heavy and hooded as she swayed toward him. Cradling the nape of her neck in his hand, he brought her to him. With that first touch of body next to body, Anthony felt fully a man. So trail was she, so delicate in structure, that he nearly overpowered her with his presence.

His willpower had gone far beyond the reaches of his

limits and he no longer fought to suppress his desires. Lowering his head, his mouth claimed hers. When he'd kissed her last, he'd been drunk with bee venom and her bitter tonic. Now, the only poisons in his body were of his own making. Volatile and lethal, the need for her crushed him. A physical aching the likes of which he'd never encountered consumed him.

He slipped his tongue into the sweetness of her mouth, brushing against her straight teeth. She pulled away, frightened by his maneuver. He tried to placate her with soothing strokes of his fingers along the length of her spine. Retreating from his sensual assault, he kissed her softly, coaxingly, regaining her trust in him.

Soon, Liberty returned his kisses, anxious to test the waters once again. She clung to him. Her arms entwined over his back, pulling the breadth of his shoulders into the small swells of her breasts. Her strong grasp excited him, heated him. She'd come into her own, a willing partner.

Anthony tumbled them downward onto the carpet of grass. He smelled the herbal blades crushed beneath their weight. The scent, mingled with passion and the fragrant perfume Liberty wore, combined in his head. The mixture intoxicated him.

His hand at her side, he moved it upward, grazing her hip, her waist, then onto her breast where her pulse beat wildly beneath his palm. Through the thin layers of her clothing, he sought the nipple. His lips remained melded to hers. Blending swift and fervent kisses, he aroused the peak with teasing fingers. That she came to life under his touch, inflamed him.

The hindrance of her frock obstructed his pursuit. He rolled them onto their sides. His arm crooked underneath her, he deftly grabbed for the laces down her back.

The ribbons were threadbare, a fragile reminder of her humble past. Her beginnings did not matter to him.

Pressing a light kiss on the slope of her shoulder, he drew back and looked at her face. He withdrew his hand from her lacings.

A light, passionate moisture misted across her countenance. Her slow gaze caressed his face and she brought her hand to cup the hollow of his cheek. He sucked in his breath as she pushed back his hair and shyly touched his earlobe with her fingertips.

He saw trust mirrored clearly in the depths of her eyes. He saw chastity and honor. Locked into the vision of her heavenly green gaze, the image of an innocent romping vanished and he came to grips with the fact that any tumble with this woman would not be a light affair. It would mean commitment.

Though his logical state of mind had crumbled, even through the rubble, he could not bring himself to pledge forever to Liberty.

The devil take all, he could not ruin her without wedding her. In a church. Legally. Binding for life.

Hell.

Anthony sagged his head back, wishing it had just been chopped from his body by a guillotine. His heart sank into a black pit, his breathing continued to labor within the tight confines of his chest. Principle had consumed him yet again. Like a huge conflagration, scruple burned him to the bone and left him in a pile of ashes, useless for sculduggery and whatever blasphemous deeds he normally lived his life by.

It took him an interminable length of time to get his bearings back and look Liberty in the eyes. She appeared over him; her tangled hair rested on his chest as he lay immobile.

"Are you ill?" she asked so sweetly with concern, his insides turned to jam and he actually did feel afflicted.

"Only in my head when I think of the opportunity I am letting slip me by."

Liberty frowned, her cheeks flushed the most beautiful of pinks.

With a quick and stern shove, he deposited Liberty away from him and sprang to his feet. Clapping the grass from his breeches, he stared down at her as she sat upright, her undercoats spread around her exposed calves.

"I've forgotten an important missive I'm expecting that

needs my immediate reply." His voice cracked like thin ice as he held out his hand to help her stand.

Liberty's shoulders straightened in uncertain comprehension. "A missive?"

"Aye. Get up." His tone was as short as the last grains in an hourglass.

She dejectedly grimaced and he felt run through by a cutlass. "Such a poor memory for someone in the youth of your years, Mister Fielding." If her words were nails, they would have been rusted. She came to her knees herself, then rose without his aid. "I'd have thought your memory still lucid for at least a year or two more."

Anthony could not let her take the blame for his predicament, nor could he stand by and watch her cover her shame in a coat of pretended armor. "Men of drink have poor memories on all accounts. I've not only forgotten my letter, I've forgotten myself."

Anthony's fingers ached to touch her again, but he remained firm in his resolve to let her be.

Liberty turned around and hotly glared at him. Her eyes gave him the cuffing he so deserved. He only wished to feel the physical blow as well to sharpen his good intentions to acceptance.

Without a word, she passed him and descended down the beach toward his home. He was gifted with the sway of her backside, the purpose of her steps.

A honey-pod slipped from the tree and smacked him on his head.

His religious beliefs were almost nil, yet somehow, he took the plummeting piece of tree to be a sign from the Higher Creations. He couldn't be sure what it meant. For all his life, he'd been taking his guidance from the nether regions.

With a shrug, he set off after Liberty, his foul mood tagging along.

Chapter

14

"GLAD TIDINGS TO YOU, REVEREND," THOMAS HEARTILY greeted, after opening the elaborate front door of Fielding Manor. He was elated Feathers had been detained in another part of the house so that he'd been presented with the opportunity to see to the churchman's welfare. "Come in, my good sir."

Reverend William Dresham of the Norfolk Parish Church wearing somber black, stepped over the threshold.

"'Tis been a while since we've seen each other." The cleric, wiry in form and stature, nodded his birdlike face. "Your son and his wife were regular attendants many years back. I must say, 'twas quite a surprise to receive your note. I never thought young Master Fielding would take himself a bride."

"The lad is quite gone over this woman, let me assure you." Thomas led Reverend Dresham into the receiving room.

"I have not had the opportunity to meet the ill-fated—er . . ." the clergyman's blush rose from his neck to the top of his cumbersome wig, "fortunate mistress whom he chose."

"She's a delight, pure and simple." Thomas halted his stride in the middle of the chamber.

Perplexity played over Reverend Dresham's pinched face when his gaze set upon the seven-foot figurehead in the corner, whose wild tresses wrapped around her naked body. He gulped his shock.

"Here now. This is the room I want you to bless, as I said in my letter since I have taken the wedding in hand. You'll perform the marriage ceremony in here."

Reverend Dresham took out his lacy handkerchief and flagged its perfumed scent under his nose. "Forgive my impudence, Mister Fielding, but the room is impious."

"But in your reply, you said that the wedding need not be rendered in the church. I explained my grandson doesn't have a vestry, and his own chapel," Thomas grimaced, "is in disrepair. He's stockpiled it to the rafters with lumber from his ships. But I can assure you, 'tis still a house of the Lord, albeit a house of termites, too."

Reverend Dresham moved closer to the ship's carving, peering down his narrow nose and examining the details. His vision lingered on the ample endowment the statuette boasted. " 'Tis this—this erection of decadence that I find unacceptable."

"That?" Thomas looked upon the object as if seeing it for the first time. "My good sir, it shall be removed if it so offends you." Placing his arm around the reverend's thin middle, Thomas said, "I want nothing to interfere with this wedding. 'Twill go off with all the good graces due a Fielding—with a tidy donation going to the church that I find in my favor on that glorious day."

Dresham's pupils dilated, his thin brows arching. "In that case, 'twould be my honor to officiate the ceremony wherever it pleases you."

"Good, good."

The two men stared at the wooden carving a minute more before going into the study for a glass of port to seal the arrangement.

The wedding was to be the event of all Norfolk, for no one believed Anthony Fielding would actually go through with the nuptials. Hiram Feathers, while briskly walking down the dim, single-windowed hall that led from the kitchen to the dining area, smiled in satisfaction. Some said Fielding had taken himself off the booze and love had given him a new lease on life. The gossip had spread, rising up to the gentry and fueling more hearth-side chats than autumn tinder.

It was Feathers himself who'd started that rumor.

Pushing the revolving door at the hallway's end, Feathers trudged through the empty eating room with the door's squeaking hinges trailing him. He made a note to hunt up some grease to dab on the joints. Ophelia had insisted the house be clean as a new shilling.

A month such as the one just spent, had the braces and rafters of Fielding Manor cracking in confusion. Rooms had been aired, mantels dusted, bedding hung on lines and curtains drawn open to full capacity. Sunlight's gilded rays showered on crevices where only smudges of shadow had fallen for too many years to count.

Thomas Fielding had posted the banns the day after the Hunter soiree and in the process, took the liberty of supplying a wedding date to the *Virginia Gazette*.

Feathers rounded the corner to the welcoming room. The recent household changes put a startled hop in his steps, blurring his mind's reflections. The hip-raised paneling had been polished, the brilliant grains of cherrywood shining under morning's natural light. The olive draperies stood open, swags of golden tassels crimping their folds in perfect pleats. And Fielding's figurehead had all but come alive. The carving of the long-haired nymph looked ready to sail out the front door and take up a post on the prow of Fielding's ship in the mooring.

Remembering his momentum, Feathers passed through the room and regained his speed. He frowned, recalling the events that had caused Fielding to lose his temper. It had been the evening after the ball, when the Lord and Master had returned from a jaunt in town. He'd been keeping company with T. A. Cheswick lately, a curious pair, since to Feathers's knowledge, Fielding hadn't slipped up on his drinking.

Fielding had dashed through the house like a madman with a waded copy of the *Gazette* in his fist having read of his impending marriage ceremony only four short weeks away. He'd been infuriated. He'd cornered his grandfather in the study—literally—waved the crumpled news sheet in the older man's face and demanded an explanation for such bold effrontery. He'd yelled he'd known his grandsire to be a man of strong nerve but he'd never thought him to stoop to a flagrant undermining of his private life.

The last Feathers had been able to hear was Fielding telling his grandfather to keep out of his affairs. Then Thomas broke loose, calmly walked to the study door and slammed it closed. The two were locked up in the oppressive room for the rest of the night.

On the following day, Fielding came out with a scowl on his brow, wrinkles branching across his coat-back, but in surrender to the wedding date.

Feathers knew well enough that Fielding had not been happy about his engagement. Why he'd gone along with things, Hiram couldn't be sure.

Feathers had been dying to know what had transpired, but being a manservant more than that to Fielding, he couldn't very well ask his employer how the old man had twisted him to agreement.

Now with the wedding days away, the house needed dire tidying. Weeks worth of washing had not made so much of a difference that the manor didn't need a little nudge. The layers of grim and dust ran deep into the textures of wood, the rosette carvings of picture frames, and the balustrades of stairs. Even Fielding's study had been ransacked. Freshened and mopped, the floors had been oiled, the heavy red curtains split open in the middle to allow daylight entrance.

At first, Fielding had balked, but Ophelia had snuck up on him gradually. First a dusting, then an airing of pillows. A fastidious arranging of books and ledgers. An accidental spill of his red-hued hurricane lamp to be replaced by clear glass. By the time she'd gotten to the draperies, Fielding had cursed under his breath and said she might as well since she'd already assaulted the room with her spotless attack.

In the end, Anthony had approved with a tight-lipped smile before stalking off to some other part of the house. Mayhap he'd been in search of Mistress Liberty, Feathers couldn't be sure. Since the poor dear lady had heard the news of her nuptials, she'd taken herself off under lock and key to her bedchamber.

A week passed until she came around enough to take meals with the Fieldings and her very own aunt. She'd said she'd had a fit of infirmity. Most likely, a fit of the willies. Scared to death of something, was she, the poor lambkin, as Ophelia had told Feathers. They'd had many a discussion over the two young people.

Ophelia had been aghast that Fielding would actually be made to wed her beloved niece. She'd put up a great argument to Feathers, stating that though she'd found Fielding to be much better in character since he'd ceased downing his pints, there were still too many flaws in him preventing her from accepting him as suitable for Liberty. Feathers sat Ophelia down in the quiet parlor and bade her to please hear his side of things.

"My dear Ophelia," Feathers had said. "Having been in Fielding Manor for so many years and seeing the Lord and Master at his best and worst, I have my own theories on Fielding's behavior. The man sobered to a sober world and its unpleasantness. He's facing what life offers him without the numbing inducements of wine, arrack, brandy and all the other evils he's used to pollute himself and his judgment with. He now has to live his life on sound thinking and rationality."

Ophelia had listened, but gave him her "tut" of doubt.

"The man is floundering like a fish knocked out of a fisherman's bucket—the hook still in his mouth. For I am sure, that hook is pulling at him daily to come take a draught at the tavern and be done with his sobriety once and for all. God praise the man that he hasn't. And why hasn't he? The lout is as in love as they come."

Hard-pressed, Ophelia replied, "It's very gallant of you, Hiram, to take up your employer's side. Still, I cannot be swayed from my opinion."

Then Feathers blabbed. "Fielding has hired a fraudulent man of the cloth to marry him and Liberty."

Ophelia gasped.

"I stumbled upon the news quite by accident a week ago. I'd been in town on an errand when I spied the Lord and Master in a tavern. Imagine the horror I felt to see *him* taking a plunge in his favorite soaking spot. So I went to the window and had a peek and a listen. Fielding hadn't been drinking, but he'd been up to another sort of mischief. He'd been paying a Mister Colin Prentice to pose as a reverend."

"My word . . ." Ophelia had fair swooned. "No wonder Fielding gave in to his grandfather. The rake had no intentions of truly wedding my Liberty!" Reaching for her fan, Ophelia snapped, "I've never heard of such a contemptible man. That he would knowingly set out to defraud my niece by a sham marriage! The entire thought makes me want to get my own good man of the ministry and turn Fielding's ill-deed to rights!"

Feathers, then, had smiled. "That's precisely my thought, too."

"Aye, well despite the ramifications it would have on Fielding, I could never do that to my pet. That is . . ." she'd become engrossed in thought, ". . . until I came upon Liberty at the beach. My dear girl had been holding onto a honey-pod and crying. When I prodded her for an explanation, Liberty said she'd lost herself to Anthony under a honey-pod tree. At the time, I sputtered and coughed my dismay, thinking the absolute worst. I grilled the girl to near sobs, but Liberty claimed her innocent comment meant nothing more than her longing to have Anthony love her."

"And you believed her?"

"Actually, I thought differently. These are the words Liberty herself told me: 'I bared myself to Anthony.' I shuddered to think the worst." Ophelia had shed a tear of apparent revelation. "Hiram! Fielding has apparently deflowered my innocent Liberty!"

On that piece of news, Feathers and Ophelia came to a decision.

* * *

Ophelia and Feathers sat at the cook's scullery table addressing Reverend Joseph Fisher of the Elizabeth River Parish. The man's jowls fleshed out the lower part of his face, the skin on his forehead drooping down to make his brows into a busy ledge of hair that joined at the top of his bulbous nose. A worn copy of the Good Book rested on the scarred table's top; he guarded the Bible with fleshy fingers in between taking bites of Quashabee's apricot comfits.

"Very admirable of you two, I must say." Reverend Fisher chewed while he spoke. His ample lips licked the granules of sugar that dusted his double-jointed thumb. "To have such loyalty in his household, Anthony Fielding is twice blessed with your presence of mind to see him properly wed—especially since you, madam, want things expedited." He dangled his fingers over another sweet, as if in indecision; after a piece, he selected a candied walnut. "This business of a counterfeit marriage is to be scoffed at. If what you say is possible, they should be joined correctly and without falsities." The crunching of nutmeat interrupted his sermon. "I say," he worded around the lump in his mouth, "you are to be praised for your concern. 'Twould be a miscarriage of justice to have your niece undone without a real marriage license."

"I couldn't agree more." Ophelia sat at Feathers's side on the hard beechen bench. She brushed her hand on his gray coat sleeve. "Hiram and I only want what is best for the two."

Feathers looked at his ladylove in agreement. "Aye. Fielding needs our guidance in this delicate matter."

"'Tis plain to see he is under good direction. What will you do with this Mister Prentice?"

"He shall be dealt with," Feathers shot back quickly. "No need to worry over that."

Reverend Fisher washed down his treat with a glass of sherry. Depositing the heavy stemware in front of him, he took up his palmed vigil on his Bible. "Good."

"As for the details"—Ophelia nudged the plate of candies to the far side of the kitchen table, not wanting the clergyman to be tempted to distraction—"we should like you to be here at quarter past eleven on the day of the wedding."

The reverends's hanging scowl nearly obliterated his eyes. "That may pose a bit of a problem. I've a previous nuptial at half till the hour. 'Tis going to be a small affair and short, but travel from my church to here may delay me to half past the hour rather than a quarter past."

Ophelia and Feathers exchanged glances, the valet speaking. "As long as you won't be detained a minute after the half hour, we'll entrust your services."

"Splendid!" Reverend Fisher stood on stubby legs encased by the long robe of his profession. His squat height added to his poundage, filling him out like a ripe pear. "If you'll show me to Mister Fielding's chapel so I may acquaint myself with it."

"I dare say," Feathers broke in, shoving himself to standing, too, "the wedding won't be in the Fielding chapel. The building isn't hospitable for anything but rodents."

"Rodents can be disposed of, Mister Feathers. A few traps would set the place to order."

"'Twould need more than a few traps. Fielding hasn't used it in years." Feathers looked to Ophelia for help.

"We were thinking of the main house," Ophelia suggested. "The receiving room is large enough for a gathering."

"I have fulfilled obligations in homes before, 'tis true." The cleric paused. "Is the chamber close to the kitchen? I become quite parched after a lengthy preaching . . . and famished, too."

"'Tis very close to the kitchen and I might add," Feathers baited, "Quashabee will no doubt outdo herself on the wedding menu."

"Then you can expect me at eleven thirty and not a minute later."

Liberty left the porch's shadow to chase down a drone who'd alighted to inspect every bright colored object in its path. Finally finding a tuft of pollen in the center of a golden yellow pumpkin flower it began collecting its wares.

The fine sand had felt warm under Liberty's toes, but the spiny stickers of the pumpkin vines with their large, spindly green leaves, scratched her ankles and she stepped around the mass.

The plant twisted down a patch of earth on the side of the house. The area was by no means a garden, but must have been at one time, for the vague remnants of a plotted-off section hadn't been taken by the overgrowth yet.

Unseasonably warm October air swirled around her naked ankles and up her ballooning dress. She wore a white cotton shift with a loose-fitted waist and a skirt that gathered yards and yards of material. The short, puffed sleeves had been laced on by ribbons. Underneath, she wore no stays, only a camisole to confine the shape of her breasts. The gown felt wondrously good in the tiny breeze and she raised herself up on tiptoes to waltz under a canopy of crackling oak trees.

As she moved, the shady spots caused by the tree's limbs cascaded over her, cooling her; the sunny splatters of light on the top of her unbound hair warmed her through. The combination of warm and cool made her smile and mellow with discriminating happiness.

There hadn't been too much to be happy about this past month. She was to be married to a man whom she loved with all her heart. Her sad quandary was: He did not return her love.

Perhaps if she was more of the saucebox John Perkins accused her of being, she would wile herself into Anthony Fielding's life and *make* him love her. But she wasn't so bold as to twist his heart to fit her own. If he loved her, he would love her from his soul and nothing less.

It had taken her a week to come to that conclusion. That winning Anthony could only come by honorable motives. To be artful, coquettish and a hussy would not be in her nature. She would have to hope he could love her for herself.

Deception had gotten her into this trouble and she vowed never to resort to lies again. If Anthony could value her for her genuine virtues, so be it. If not . . . Liberty refused to think of if not.

As the drone fluttered off the shimmering petal, Liberty followed it to another flower, watching with great seriousness as the insect packed its legs with puffy orange pollen. The winged creature was healthy and that pleased her. The hive would survive the winter on great stores of aster honey and hopefully remain free of disease.

The drone skimmed away from the lemony petal, hovered in the current on unseen wings, then flew toward Liberty. She smiled as the bee circled her full skirt, then dove under the hem.

"You wicked creature." Liberty stood absolutely still, closing her eyes and meditating. "I dote on you far too much by giving you such liberties. Do not get lost and take out your temper on my thigh."

The crunch of dry fall leaves under advancing footsteps brought Liberty's eyelids up. Her simple game with the bee was forgotten as her heart beat precariously fast seeing Anthony approach. He cut a fine figure in his trimmings and she would have liked to be a hussy at this moment and throw herself into his arms.

Sunlight gleamed off the gilded highlights in his hair. His face bore a deep and golden brown tan. His eyes, the color of rich chocolate, caught her gaze and she swallowed. The light breeze roused the ruffles on his shirt and the wide skirt of his crimson waistcoat. He wore no outer jacket and yet looked every bit the man of wealthy repose without it. Despite the internal conflict raging inside her, she told herself to remain calm and alert.

"Hello, Anthony." Liberty heard the echo of her pulse in her words. The tickle of the bee's fuzzy legs walked down her calf and she kept still. "I would have thought you'd be in your study."

He scowled. "'Tis Friday. I avoid that room like the plague. Ophelia and her troops cackle and drink coffee in there on Tuesdays and Fridays while painting each other up like Rembrandts."

Liberty fought a smile.

Anthony had stopped a fraction away from her, his arms crossing over his chest. He cocked his head and stared at her, assessing her airy dress. He said nothing about her wardrobe though; he snagged his brows upward with a shrug. "'Tis good to see you smiling, Liberty. No matter that 'tis at no one but yourself." The deep timbre of his voice washed over her in a soothing veil. "I've not seen you so in weeks."

She had been her own company in the past weeks. Keeping to her room or occupying her time with her bees and journals. Anthony had not wanted to be with her. The billiard lessons had stopped long ago and it seemed a travesty to sit around and wait for his attention. She'd sought shelter elsewhere, away from the watchful eyes of Thomas Fielding. "I have decided to be happy, Anthony. Perhaps you should be wise and do the same." She bit down on her lower lip. "We are to be wed, I should like to think you're fond enough of me to smile on occasion, too."

Anthony shortened the distance between them with two long strides. She shifted discomfitingly. The drone under her skirt flew off her calf, landed on her shin and promenaded to her knee. The prickling sensation of crawling legs made her mouth crimp upward, holding back a stiff giggle.

Anthony didn't question her battle with laughter. "You do make me smile. You're quite humorous."

Liberty looked down at her bare toes. The laudatory phrase wasn't exactly the romantic kind she sought. "I think your comedy is not all black, either." The bee embarked on its journey and didn't settle back down. "Alas, I would rather you smiled at me not in mockery, but in fondness."

A maddening bit of arrogance overtook him. He put on a self-accusing countenance. "I have smiled fondly at you far too many times to count."

"I do not dispute you on that account, save the show of expression was put on for the sake of another—your grandfather."

Distracted with her thoughts of Anthony, Liberty had overlooked her bee. When its wings pulsated against her thigh, she stiffened. She automatically gathered her full skirts in her fingers and lifted them far more than modesty allowed. Waving her hem across the drone, she shoed the insect free. "Get away, you outlaw. There's no need to sacrifice your life for me."

Looking up, Liberty saw Anthony giving her legs a raking stare. She felt heavy and warm. He swept his gaze to her face, his eyes more heated than the sun. A satisfied light had come into those brown orbs, as if he'd enjoyed himself immensely. Aghast, she broke free of his ensnaring stare.

Trapped in an indecent predicament, she salvaged what she could. Demurely she dropped the curtain of her skirts down past her knees and to her nude ankles. "I was on the verge of being stung. Once a bee looses its stinger, it dies. I couldn't have the poor thing take its life for naught when escape was at my fingertips."

His voice, deep yet crisp and clear, said, "Indeed, you could not." Anthony smiled. "And might I say, 'tis a lucky day I chanced see such a natural exhibition as the one you and your bee gave me. I have never been privy to a fleeing bee."

"You're horrible to make fun." Now able to walk about where she wanted, Liberty trudged past Anthony and headed down the beach. Her gown billowed behind her. Her hair, undone and untamed, streamered around her face and she pushed it aside. Oh, she wasn't angry. Not at Anthony, really. She was embarrassed. To the roots of her hair. How unthinking was she to lift her dress for a man—a rogue such as he—and not think he'd make a comment of it. It was principle for a man like Anthony Fielding to undress women with his words. Even more so to undress them with his eyes. And she'd gone and made it easy for him; she'd done all the work!

"Hold, Liberty!" Anthony caught up with her in no time and encircled her forearm with his nimble fingers. Forced to cease her steps, she cast her eyes on his hand, noting the strength.

"Leave me be."

"I will not." He spun her around to face him. "I've left you alone too long. I won't anymore."

Liberty studied the flare of his nostrils, the hard set of his mouth. He smelled faintly of thyme and the clean scent of honey soap.

"I wanted to talk with you and tell you something very important." Anthony grew sullen. "If I did not care for you, I'd not tell you the truth and let you believe what you wanted. But despite what you think, I do care for you, Liberty Rose, and I wish to enlighten you on the wedding."

Suspicious of his meaning, she could only stare and wait for him to explain.

"On that day, two in coming, a reverend by the name of Colin Prentice will marry us. He is not an ordinary reverend. He is by trade, a barkeeper."

Liberty gasped. "What do you mean?"

"I mean to save us both from a marriage we don't want. There will be a wedding, but it will be fictitious in nature. Colin will go through the motions to make it look legal, but in reality, we will be no more wed than we are now. I've given my grandsire firm orders to stay out of things and let me handle the wedding preparations."

Liberty's heart rose to her mouth and she bit down on her lip. "You mean to deceive everyone!"

"But you," he finished. "I could not go through with it without you knowing the truth."

"I see." Liberty grew pensive. "And what of our wedding night? Have you thought of a fictitious woman to take my place as well?"

Anthony brought her close, his hold tightening. "The devil, nay. But I have given it great thought. For the remainder of my grandsire's visit, I shall sleep in my closet on a pallet and you shall have my bed."

"You have thought of everything." She didn't know why she was becoming so hostile. She should have been grateful not to be marrying the scoundrel. Why then, was she so torn inside?

Wanting nothing more than to flee, she shrugged off his grasp and ran away from him. She was fast, but Anthony was just as agile and soon took hold of her again. This time, he gently scooped her into his arms and held her close.

The strength of his embrace made surrendering to the pain inside her heart all the harder to hang onto. She would not cry over him while he lay witness to her spectacle. But the desire to be enfolded next to the sinewy muscle of his body was too much for her to deny. She lay her cheek on the sleek silk of his shirt, the warmth of his skin seeping through the cloth to heat the side of her face. She heard the desperate rhythm of his heartbeat and wondered why he was so out of sorts when it was she who was dying. Raising her hands to encompass his back, she clung to him all the more.

"Plague me . . . what's this?" The rumble of his voice vibrated through her.

Liberty refused to look up at him.

Bunching up the thick locks of her hair, Anthony cupped the back of her neck and made her tilt her chin toward him. She saw his face through a blur of tears that she still refused to shed.

He lowered his head and brushed his mouth on hers. The kiss was not given in passion or light fancy, but in tender consoling. No sooner had he touched her, he broke the meeting.

"Your lips taste bitter, sweeting. I should have thought you would be overjoyed to hear my plan."

"Then you have thought wrong." Her denouncement put confusion in his eyes.

"You cannot mean to say you would really marry me no matter what the circumstances?"

Her silence was his answer.

Anthony lessened his hold and scraped his fingers through his hair, undoing the mass to fall heavily on his brows. "You have to see that a marriage between us would be utterly wrong. What have we in common?"

"Apparently nothing by birth."

"Strike me down! I did not mean to bring up the difference between us." His face took on a fierce impression. "I was referring to my drink and your lack of it. My roguish ways and your angelic habits. You are, my dear good mistress, a noble wench in your own rights. A man like me would crush you silly."

"You think far to ill of yourself, Anthony. Can you not accept that perchance, a woman could truly love you?"

Anthony Fielding froze, his countenance darkening with dread and pain. His lips thinned to bleakness and his eyes clouded. He'd known she fancied herself in love with him, but she didn't know what she was doing. "No one can ever love me. Not as I am."

"You are wrong. So very wrong." Liberty broke the last link between them, dropping her hands and stepping clear of him. "I wish you could see what you are. You are like a wounded animal. I know that you've been wronged by a man. I, by the same man. But I have gotten on with my life and accepted my fate. You need to live again, Anthony. Before you die in a caustic pool of self-pity."

Liberty's bosom rose and fell. Never had she spoken so harshly to another living soul.

"You are wrong about me." His jaw tensed. "I died a long time ago. And no one can bring me back from the dead. My retaliation with Perkins will play on until I finish him off. And when that time comes, I shall be free."

"I think not, Anthony. You will never be free until you confront the reasons that made you what you are."

Liberty could say no more, chiding herself for already saying too much. Sometimes the truth was the worst way to help someone. She feared she'd just sent Anthony away from her forever.

She turned on her heels and made for the manor house. Her erratic pulse threatened her composure. Only by sheer will did she keep her chin high and her eyesight focused on her destiny.

This time, no footfalls could be heard behind her.

Liberty stared beyond the panes into darkness. The hour had gone past late to untimely late. The last she'd cognizantly heard, the clock on her mantel had struck two.

Endless stretches of black greeted her as she stood at the window of her room and watched for a sign of his return.

Nothing.

Pressing her forehead into the cold glass, the fine mist of

her breath obscured her view. No matter. There was naught to see anyway. Anthony would come home at will, if ever. She'd driven him away with her high-handed lecture.

The cotton of her night rail felt icy against her legs, yet she would not return to bed for her wrapper or the comforts the quilts could offer. Rubbing the moisture from the pane, she looked on, skimming the inky night for signs of life.

Nothing.

Anthony had not returned to the house after she had gone in, nor had his seat been occupied during dinner. He had, in her mind, fled the scene of the crime and the cutting assault she'd landed him.

Pray God, Liberty whispered, he would return home. She would marry him on his grounds, be they false or true. She would tell him of her error in judgment.

Sighing, she gazed on until her eyes became dry from the strain.

She would give him a quarter hour more. Then she would fetch him home.

Chapter
15

THE SMOKE INSIDE THE SIGN OF THE MERMAID TAVERN HAD thinned to a pale blue haze; songs of ribaldry were down to just one inebriated baritone whose pitch sounded pitifully off. The only occupants left at this dreary hour of three twenty-five in the early morning were the proprietor, Daniel Townley, and the two men at the gaming table: Arnold Swinton and Anthony Fielding.

"Mark well what I do say," Anthony sang, crushing his cigar in a chipped bowl. "For tolerably at my finger's end, her stays I will fray. Well-a-day my pretty one, this day you'll be undone."

Anthony's stare wavered on the black hole of his purse and he stuck his fingers inside the velvet pouch. He touched emptiness. No more crowns to be spent. Had he really rid himself of his entire winnings? He'd been doing so well against Swinton . . .

Not particularly disturbed over his findings, Anthony finished off the balance of his bourbon. The devil take it anyway, he doubted he could even play another hand of high-low-jack, for as it was, he'd stretched the limits of his vision. Swinton was but a mere blotch that came into focus on the other side of the round table. A blur of sapphire coat and the halo of a blue-black wig was the extent he could make out of his companion's features.

"Swinton, chap," Anthony muttered over the rim of his tankard, half the deck of playing cards slipping from his fingers, "you're fading. Either that, or I am." Impaired as he was, he couldn't tell which one of them was more glassy-eyed.

Squinting, Anthony barely made out Swinton's eyes dragging closed and the man slithering down the back of his cane chair and onto the sanded floor. Anthony shrugged and declared the other to be more fuddled than he.

Bending at the waist and sticking his head under the table to check his opponent's hand, Anthony smelled the strong vapors of ale permeating from Swinton's cravat. Anthony fought the swell of dizziness that raided his head; with a quick study, he found Swinton's hand to be a losing one.

"'Tis a pity for you, Swinton, but a gain for me."

Straightening and fighting off the sickness inside his head, Anthony examined the shimmering coins in the center of the table. He fingered the silver and counted out twelve pence for a quart of bourbon and six pence needed to pay for fodder—the corn and oats—to get his horse and shay out of hock at the tavern's livery. The devil blind him, he was short three farthings for either the bourbon or the bloody animal.

"Townley, good man," Anthony slurred. "A quart more of bourbon." To hell with the horse and wheels; he couldn't navigate it back home anyway. He'd walk.

Daniel Townley, who never tipped a drop while minding his ordinary, fetched the liquor on steady legs. While sober, Anthony thought the wretch a frightening soul—drunk, Townley conveyed the very image of a monster. He wore his wiry white hair tied up in a filthy bag that dangled between his bony shoulder blades. He had lanky hands, vast jaw-bones and snowy eyebrows that hung over his deep-set icy blue eyes.

Townley stared down at Anthony and the snoozing Swinton without censure on his whiskered face. "There ye be, Fielding. Twelve pence for me trouble."

Anthony readily paid the man, leaning back in his stiff chair. He poured a drink that measured out a quarter of the liquor; in a steady gulp, he tossed it down his throat. His mind paralyzed, but not enough so, he could still hear Liberty.

When he'd calmed enough to think through her words, he'd begrudgingly admitted a lot of what she'd said was right. He hadn't been living his life—he had known that—but he hadn't realized his existence had been tearing him apart piece by piece until he'd turned into a blind mass of flesh and bone.

Revenge had guided him; liquor had obstructed him.

Yet knowing how Liberty felt about him, he'd left the house and turned to the very thing that threatened him, but a comfort for which he knew no substitute. He could have gone to any woman-for-hire for physical release, but hadn't felt like being totally hypocritical.

There was only one woman he wanted.

And he'd been stupid enough to think she wouldn't want him. She had, but he'd pushed her away.

Taking another weighty pull of his bourbon, Anthony rolled the spirits around his tongue. The taste had gone sour in his mouth, but the effects were worth the flavor. He rubbed the bridge of his nose between the pad of his thumb and forefinger, trying to recall the events of the evening. The happenings were difficult to pull together. He'd gone first to the White Hart, then the Crooked Billet, the Red Lion, before ending up at the Mermaid. He usually frequented this establishment last, for Townley was an honest barkeep and no matter what state of mind Anthony was in, Townley would never cheat him out of coin as others had been known to do to their more gone patrons.

The thought of walking home in the gloomy dark didn't appeal to Anthony at all. The evening air had chilled considerably coming off the Elizabeth River and he had left his home without his coat and wearing boots of thin leather. Still clad in only his waistcoat and shirt, he felt half-dressed to be battling the elements under the influence of grog.

Feeling his eyelids grow heavy, Anthony rid his tankard of its contents and fumbled the empty stein on the tabletop. He brought his fingertips to his jaw and scratched at the stubble.

The last thing he recalled was Liberty in her flowing white gown, dancing with bees in his tired garden and looking too beautiful to be real.

"Anthony, pray'thee, get up."

His eyes sealed tight and bathing his brain in black fog, the dispassionate plea made but a slight etching in Anthony's bourbon-painted head. The voice not belonging to Feathers, Anthony's reaction to the trill sluggishly pulled at him. When he figured out the feminine nature of the voice, it was too late; he'd returned to the vapors of his roaring drunk, sleeping off the toxins in his body.

"Oh, Anthony, you've taken on a fine dose. Wake up so I can take you home." The imperturbable tone had changed gears; the unknown wench berated him like a fisherwoman.

"Leave off," Anthony mumbled, attempting to roll to his side. A hard surface dug into his hip, making his change of position quite offensive.

Quickly he took himself back to the void of blackness; a numb world where virtuous women and the contrivances against mayors did not exist.

He hadn't been there long when the sassy wench put her hands on his forearm and gave him a stiff shake; his belly roiled. The fortitude to part his eyelids not within him, he blindly, but impulsively, flailed his hand to swat at the offending agitation. "Back yourself off."

"I will not," she scolded him sadly. "I will not leave you thus. Oh, 'tis all my fault you have gone and done this to yourself!"

The pity in her tone aggravated him out of his despair. The voice became oddly familiar, yet he dared not picture to whom it belonged. Surely *she* would not take herself off to find him in a tavern.

Plague him . . . his slumbers of deep repose had been violated too much to continue without another anesthetizing drop of booze. And in order to rouse himself—if indeed he wanted to—he needed a shot to unlock his eyes. Either way required distilled stamina.

"A drink . . . wench. Fetch my drink." Anthony's head had come to life in a vortex of burning light. He trembled off the frightful illusions, trying in earnest to sit himself up.

"Anthony, you cannot!"

Too late, he understood the woman's plea. He toppled over the edge of some unknown precipice and landed backside down on a cold slab. His head took a beating before he was able to right himself on his elbows. "Judas!" he cussed vilely, his eyes jolting open to a tumbling room. The nausea in his stomach trod up his throat and he choked down his sickness; dewy beads of sweat popped out on his forehead and darts of pain shot down the long length of his bruised spine.

Barely getting his bearings, Anthony realized he'd fallen to the floor of the Mermaid. The sanded planks felt rough and gritty under his palms. "Swinton?" he whispered, recalling Arnold's preceding slip to this nether region of spilled drink and cards. The fellow could not be seen.

Anthony lowered his head, the lengthy strands of his hair obstructing his sight. He must have passed out on the tabletop, slight in circumference as it may have been; this attributed to the fall he'd just taken. "Lud . . ." he said, borrowing Feathers's favorite expletive, "kill me now. I am too miserable to stay alive."

"I won't have you talking such foolishness in front of me, Anthony. I won't."

Straightening his neck, Anthony heard and felt every bone crack and unkink right to the base of his brain. Blowing his hair from his eyes, he tried to see the wench that spoke to him. His eyes watered by his fermented breath and the reminder he was so gone he could barely keep himself conscious. His worst fears met him face on: Liberty Courtenay.

Strike him down a thousand times over.

She lowered herself onto her skirted knees. He unexpectedly felt like weeping in his empty cup over his misfortune.

Her discovery of him in such a pathetic state and having to meet him on this horrid level weighed on him like a slab of marble.

Looking at her strained him, but he couldn't seem to tear his eyes away. Her lacy lashes of inky black blinked in consolation. The precious green in her eyes struck him with reflections of sorrow and worry. The gold spoke of pity and disappointment. Together, the hazel spelled out his failure. Her angelic skin, pure and white, defied the flaming candle-light of a devil's taproom. Her full red lips parted and for a deranged heartbeat, he lost his senses, thinking that if he kissed that mouth, he would be saved.

Snapping himself from the spell, he groaned in internal agony, knowing he was a fool to even think such a thing. He could not bear the pathetic expression her face gave him. He turned his own away.

Anthony heard her quivered sigh, but the courage in her next utterance contradicted her anguish. "Somebody left a bottle of spirits in your way, Anthony. You have been very merry this evening, but now 'tis time to come home."

Her linen petticoats swished as she stood. He lay on his side, entranced by the delicate size of her ribbon-decorated slippers and the fragile bones composing her stockinged ankles.

"Mister Townley. Barlary. You may come hither now and help me load Mister Fielding."

The deafening thump of two pairs of heavy heels walking the floor vibrated Anthony's bottom and sore flank sprawled on the floorboards.

Townley's low-heeled pumps came into Anthony's view with the ugly shape of the tavern-keeper's shins encased by plum hose. Next to Townley rested an unfamiliar set of booted feet nearly as long as arms. The man's right stocking had a tiny run and the pewter knee-buckles under the hems of his red baize breeches were scuffed and ill-tended.

"Be careful with him," Liberty said to the two.

Anthony hotly recoiled. He shoved his annoying hair from his eyes and glared at Townley, then the other man who wore a cone-knitted black felt hat with an edging of white tape. The youthful face sped through his chamber of recollections and the vision hit him swiftly that he had once tangled with this lad.

"You . . ." The single word trailed over Anthony's tongue, then he ground out a name. "Barley White."

"'Tis *Barlary*," the boy amended in his man's voice that had only had two years of practice. "As you well know," he added stubbornly.

"Blame me," Anthony's idiom indulged, "as a thoughtless twit."

Daniel Townley stretched out a gaunt hand, the crescents of his fingernails stained a deep red from the burgundy wines he slovenly poured. "Have to, Fielding. 'Tis time to be off to a proper bed. Swinton's lady-wife came for him some time ago."

Barlary leaned forward, ready to grab at Anthony's sleeve.

Anthony shirked the lad. By the Divine Grace, if Liberty meant to fetch him home, he would get up of his own accord.

"Toddle off, young master *Barlary*." The bent joints in Anthony's arms straightened by his determined will and he crooked his legs one over the other. Turning more on his side, Anthony flexed his knees enough to get onto them. His weight on all fours, he prayed for the vitality to see him to his feet.

"Anthony . . ." Liberty's forlorn cry drifted to his ears. "You need help."

"I need nothing of the sort!" he lashed back too quickly to regulate his harsh tone. A cape of vexation draped over him, pulling him upward. He battled the shadows destroying his sight, grappling for the ale-soiled ledge of the table. A small victory won, once he had the wood in his hold. Pushing himself upward, his elbows snagged the ledge, then his torso. Exhausted, he leaned over the table. The stillness of the taproom urged him on and he shoved away from his crutch.

On wobbly boot heels, he proclaimed himself fit. "You see, I am standing."

Hands pushed at him, then other forces he couldn't name.

A wave of some ocean-born malady roiled inside him, like a vast seasickness he'd never experienced. Moving forward, he saw nothing; he couldn't tolerate the sight of the world. He heard only the dull roar of the illness that worked through his belly and pressured his head. Then he was hoisted into a cart of some kind.

Cold air seeped through him to the bone, clearing his mind a tier or two. Under his back, the musty scent of straw rose up to tickle his nose. A kersey rug smelling of horses and riddled with stiff animal hair, cloaked his thin shirt. Once the wagon rolled into motion, the hollow ring of empty metal urns screamed inside his head.

Mercifully he slipped into an eddy of nothingness.

A time later—it could have been minutes or hours for all he knew—he heard low intonations, disconnected sentences he couldn't comprehend. The dray struck an uneven depression in the road and his belly revolted.

The fingers of a brisk night curled around his drunk. He felt the cart's mildewy bed beneath him, but he viewed himself outside his body. He saw a corpse in his likeness; lifeless and unfeeling. This was the end for him. He supposed this moment came to all those who overindulged. The dark hour when the last sip would be too much. He'd never before promised himself to stop altogether; he thought he could go without, then pick up the habit again in small doses. Wrong.

Now, he imposed his lifelong sentence. He would never again take liquor to his comfort. Never. On this, he swore.

Counting on the pledge to salvage what was left of him, Anthony dozed off.

"We're home, Anthony. Can you get up now?"

Liberty's announcement brought Anthony back to earth. He'd been sitting across a flaming table with the devil, discussing the legalities of leaving purgatory for the purer pastures aboveground. Liberty's call to him had been his token out of Hades. Surely she was his angel sent down to him from heaven.

"I can—" The words stuck in his throat and he swallowed the cotton. His mouth had dried up like a windblown puddle, cracked and parched. He ventured anew, "I can get up."

The corrupt night's shroud came tumbling down around him. He tried to gain his direction but his untied hair kept blocking his way. Disgusted, he yanked the shocks from his temple, wrenching a few roots from his scalp in the process. Slowly he eased himself to the cart's end and dangled his feet over the down-turned gate. By this time, the world had righted and he recognized the courtyard of Fielding Manor. A bloom of hazy light lit the lofty, double entrance doors; a singular wrought iron lantern dangled on a chain beneath the cornice.

Liberty took hold of his elbow and Barlary gripped his wrist. Leering at the youth, Anthony stood on his unsteady legs. What a final plague upon himself to have this school-boy see him in such a debilitated state.

"We've but to get him up three flights of stairs," Liberty instructed her accomplice. "I'd suggest letting him sleep in his study, but I fear his comfort on the settee will be damaging to his limbs."

"He won't know the difference," Barlary ungraciously pointed out.

Anthony jerked his hand from Barlary's weak hold. "I know enough to recognize I don't like you!" The loud timbre in his tone startled even Anthony.

"Anthony, please," Liberty entreated in a tight whisper. "You'll wake the house."

"I don't care."

"Quit being impudent and shush."

Anthony glowered at his pretty-faced savior, but kept his mouth snapped closed.

"Come along," she ordered, bracing his waist with her arm.

His steps clumsy, Anthony bumped into Liberty. She remained steadfast in her grip. The scent of her perfume wafted to his noise. Ah, *Passion and Truth*. Ophelia had unveiled it to the entire bloody hamlet and there was nary a woman who didn't wear the fragrance—but none so well as his Liberty. The subtle essence burned hot in his loins; were he in a better frame of mind, he would have liked to foolishly kiss her.

Barlary collided with Anthony's shoulder on the front steps and Anthony nearly fell. His descent was halted by Barlary's quick action; the lad snagged him around his shoulders with his lanky arm. Anthony looked up into the youth's face. A stripling, no disputing. The top of his hat nearly brushed the base of the lantern.

The bourbon in his brain made Anthony critical of the lad's wear. The pointed tip to Barlary's ridiculous cap had begun to droop in the mist. He looked asinine enough for Anthony to laugh. Softly at first, then loudly.

"Anthony! Henceforth, you will hold your tongue or pay the consequences," Liberty lectured.

The front door gave way to the silent interior and the shadows of the entry decor. Anthony's heels scuffed the newly polished floor and he smiled at the low burning taper on a saucer set atop the receiving table. Feathers. Irreplaceable Feathers had left him a night-light. His valet would never desert him.

The long, imposing sight of the staircase made Anthony rethink his snub of Barlary's suggestion. By the mass, he'd slept more times in his study than he did in his bedchamber. Alone, he could never hope to tackle such foreboding risers.

Liberty increased her pressure around his middle and the muscles climbing up his back tensed. Her unbound hair met with his chin when he turned his head in her direction. He inhaled, gathering in his lungs the floral smell of her hair soap. He grew dizzy in a pleasant way.

"Lead on, sweeting," he murmured, facing away and daring Barlary with a sneer to suggest otherwise. "I believe you are destined to haul me up these stairs. Remember the bee stings? Hmm?"

"Yes, Anthony. I do. His other arm, Barlary," Liberty said. "Grab hold."

"A sweet pickle this is," Barlary sniffed his displeasure, latching onto the object of his disdain. "A dreadful trial, to be sure. Ads bobbers, let's get on with it. I'll be low in pocket if I don't make it back in time to collect the milk from Mister Pedley."

Anthony felt himself being pulled up the stairs. He made an attempt to hold onto the banister, but his fingers wouldn't work. Any grip he had slithered from his reach.

The attainment of the higher levels in his house taxed Anthony considerably. His breath came in large gasps and his chest felt the pressure of his labors. He would have liked an interlude from the torture, but his captors seemed dead set on hauling him to the third floor in record time.

The pungent fragrance of wedding garlands strung through the banisters caught his nose.

When his foot left the last riser and hovered over the landing, he tangled himself in the hem of Liberty's dress. Falling like a stone weight, he took her down with him to the carpeted hallway of the third floor.

Strike him blue, he'd landed between her sprawled legs. The bulk of his torso lay wedged in the abundant folds of her skirts and frilly undercoats.

Before Anthony had a chance to enjoy the indecency of their tumble, Barlary's piteous cry of indignation bewailed in Anthony's ears. The sound spiraled through his throbbing head, seizing him with great pain.

"Shut yourself up!" Anthony shouted.

"Get off her, I say!"

"Oh, pray heaven!" Liberty righted herself onto her elbows, pushing her bodice into Anthony's face. "All this voice raising will stir Mister Fielding."

"Bah." Anthony shifted his position, the soft rounds of Liberty's breasts tempting pillows for his weary head. He stared at her bosom while relating the following facts. "My grandsire sleeps as if he were whacked over the head by a cord of wood. Even a call from the Lord himself would not summon the man from the hereafter. He binds himself with a sleeping mask and closes off his ears with wads of beeswax. Blame me if I cannot hear the man's snores now."

"By the grace of God, Fielding, get off her." The lad's

voice cracked like a china plate meeting its doom on a brick floor.

Liberty thought Barlary would spill tears from the distress in his tone. The hard weight of Anthony on her pelvic region kindled the emotional workings of her heart. His head was but a feather's width from the valley of her breasts. That he'd imbibed so much to clumsy himself in such a manner made her sad and sickened. "For want of grace, Anthony, I do think you should navigate yourself to your feet." Her voice quivering, she added, "I wouldn't want you to get a cramp in your neck."

"Smartly said, sweeting." The lean length of Anthony's hand pressed into her thigh and she jolted under the sensual pressure he imposed. "You do mince logic very prettily."

Anthony rolled free of her and hoisted himself to standing by way of the upper level balustrade. His tall frame teetered precariously; he stumbled into the gilded leg of a console table, tipping the rose-filled vase upon its marble top. Water dribbled over the side in a steady drop. The hall taper's hazy glow reflected off a wet spot growing in the leaf-and-shell pattern of the carpet.

Seeing the stupored expression on Anthony's face, Liberty righted the vase she had seen Aunt Ophelia industriously arrange that morning. Liberty's finger took a sound scratch from a thorn. She mumbled a wincing "ouch," bringing her fingertip to her mouth and biting down on the needlelike prick.

"The tipsy fool." Barlary's whispered remark held a high amount of disparagement.

Anthony grunted his resentment and staggered down the hallway without aid from either of them. His hands groped and fumbled the sills of the wainscoted walls.

"Barlary, please," Liberty implored. "Calling him names won't help." She set off after Anthony, Barlary close on her heels.

"It makes my heart bleed, Liberty Rose, to see you subjected to this insolent creature. Look at him."

Anthony having gained a good three yards ahead of them,

271

Liberty gleaned a view of his broken outline as he stalked under the lone, flickering wall sconce, came into view, then lightly faded into a dim patch. The clumsiness of his step sapped the strength of his legs and he relied more heavily on the wall for support.

She did think him pitiful. She was terribly ashamed that he'd poured his vow down his throat. Perhaps her stern preaching had sent him to the bottle.

"I suspect he doesn't even know which room is his." Barlary's easy footfall pattered over the newly cleaned runner that spread the length of the hall.

The words to renounce Barlary's accusation as a mistake were lost in Liberty. She couldn't be sure where Anthony would take himself.

As if to prove a point, though he could not have heard Barlary's comment, Anthony's bumbling stride halted in front of his chamber door. With a shove, he pushed the sound wood inward and stumbled into the room.

Liberty measured out the remaining steps to the threshold of his bedchamber. She put her hand on the doorjamb and froze upon seeing the low-lit interior vacant of any presence.

Anthony had disappeared.

"Anthony?" she called to him but heard no noise. A perplexing fear seeped through her bones and she took one careful step into the room. "Anthony? Pray come out."

Barlary nudged up to Liberty's back, his face just as curious as her own. "Mayhap he fell out the window."

Liberty shot Barlary a warning glare for his impudence, but just the same, she made a quick glance at the window to see the portiered treatments shut and unmoving from night air.

"For goodness sake, where is he?" Barlary stretched his long neck to inspect the tester of the bed, the folded down leaf of Anthony's work-stormed writing desk, the toiletry strewn across the top of his dressing stand and his easy chair clothed with discarded cravats and shirts. "He's neither above nor below his personals."

As bewilderment claimed Liberty, she heard hoarse

LIBERTY ROSE

breathing coming from Anthony's dressing closet. She strode quickly to the ajar door and whisked the portal open. Meager illumination overflowed from the bedroom into the cubicle. Her eyes unable to see in the near darkness, she could only guess Anthony's direction by his sounds.

"Barlary, bring the taper." She listened to Anthony's slumber as his snores rose to her ears from the floor. Liberty lowered herself onto her knees to find the origin of the raspy sighs.

Her fingers ran over the soft-woven throw rug, then a supple leather pump with its cold buckle. She tossed the shoe from her path and found a brocade waistcoat and silk shirt still warm to the touch. Her skirts bunching up her thighs, at last, the feel of smooth, heated skin met with her exploration. She skimmed her hand over the plane of a tightly muscled chest, the vibration of Anthony's breathing beneath her palm. How he'd gotten in this state of undress so quickly amazed her.

She ventured her fingertips up the slight, but hard slope of his chest and the modest wedge of coarse hair on his breastbone. Indeed, just like the day of his bee stings. She had touched him like this then.

She furthered her exam in this murky world where her sense of touch had been heightened by the loss of her sight.

A frilly tail of material tangled its way in her fingers as she discovered he'd not shed his neck cloth. She tugged on the fancy tie at the pulse point of his neck. Her knuckles felt the uneven rhythm of his heart as it kept poor beat with his breathing. As she tried to strip him of his cravat, a fearful image built in her mind. She recalled reading in the *Virginia Gazette* an incident involving a man left to sleep off his drink in a tavern. His friends hadn't loosened his stock and on the following morning, they found him dead from asphyxiation.

"I need the light!" she called to Barlary who seemed to be taking his time fetching one. Panic darted through her fingers as she toiled on the evasive knot.

Barlary appeared behind her. In his enormous hand, he

bore a brass receptacle whose dying candle was but a sputtering wick of sparse light. He hovered next to Liberty as she frantically tried to undo the linen securely around Anthony's neck.

"Ads bobbers, is he dead?" Barlary's grip on the lamp slackened, tipping the holder. A puddle of wax sloshed over the edge and spattered the outer curve of Anthony's ribs.

Anthony's growl of aggravation didn't revive him. With eyes closed, his arm rose and splayed fingers came down to scrub his injury.

"Apparently not." Barlary answered his own question.

"I find no comfort in your humor, Barlary." Liberty's tone chastened as well as held an urgent edge. "Please fetch yourself down here and show me how to remove this."

Barlary knelt down, deposited his nearly expired candle next to Anthony's head, and dexterously pushed one snowy end of the cravat through the knot. "'Tis a topsy-turvy way to undo it. You were pulling when you should have been pushing." The binding length of linen slackened enough for Barlary to remove it from Anthony's neck.

Immediately, Anthony's ragged breathing lessened to a more subtle note of sleep. Liberty sighed her relief, but felt the stifling walls of the closet moving in on her. She had to get Anthony out and into a proper bed.

As she leaned over his dormant frame, the candle gave off its last spark and the dressing area was once again consumed in pitch.

"Oh fie," Liberty cried, her eyes widening to see even the vaguest outline. Nothing. "Barlary, there's another candle on his desk."

She heard Barlary get to his feet. The homespun of his breeches grazed her arm as she sought Anthony's hand.

"You know his bedchamber intimately." Barlary's croak of astonishment rang through the cubicle.

Liberty had no tolerance for his wounded manner. Briefly, she explained, "I was here but one time previously and the hurricane glass on his desk had been lit so that he might better see his writings."

Liberty made no further issue of Barlary's disapproval at her bold knowledge. He could believe what he liked.

Without another word, he took his leave. In the stillness of his departure, She thought perhaps she'd made a terrible mistake by availing herself of his help. But there had been no one else in town at this abominable hour that she had enough faith in to assist her. She had known precisely where to find Barlary. He'd been hitching up his dray at O'Donnell's Livery, making ready for the collection of milk from the farmers. Once telling him of her plight, he'd reluctantly agreed to aid her, save he said, he'd only be doing it for her and not the drunk-as-a-drowned-rat Mister Anthony Fielding.

Finding Anthony's hand, Liberty cupped the fingers in her own. The ruby signet ring she'd never seen him without, felt heavy behind his knuckle. The pads of his fingertips were smooth to the touch, but his palm suffered traces of calluses. She massaged the lines and natural creases in the joints, wondering it he understood it was she who tended him.

Bright light filled the dressing closet as Barlary stood in the doorway with the hurricane lamp. Seeing Liberty's fingers entwined with Anthony's, his blue gaze went from clear to frosted. "Let us be on with this deed that is by far too humane." His throat stuck out like a walnut had wedged in his Adam's apple.

Liberty slipped her hand from Anthony's, angered at the guilt she felt and certain she'd blushed up to her ears. "Come hither and give me the lamp. I cannot lift him by myself. I think 'twould be better for you to help him and I'll guide your way."

Annoyance muddied young Barlary's visage as he stepped forth. "I will say it again, Liberty Rose. Were it not for you asking me, I would not, by no means of pretty smiles and charming promises, do thus for any other." He shoved the wavering lighted hurricane lamp at Liberty, bent and gripped Anthony under his slackened arms to drag him out of the cubicle. "Mind you," he huffed while lifting

Anthony's broad shoulders off the floor, "not to say you have given me a single smile this evening, or a promise of any kind."

Liberty backed from the tiny room and into the bedchamber without opposing Barlary's heavy dose of sarcasm. It was true, for all the patience she had given Anthony, she had reserved none for Barlary White. He had assisted her under protest and had she a kind word for him? No. She'd sullied and bullied him when he'd goaded Anthony.

She would try and be more civil with him; Barlary had always had kind words for her.

Stowing the lamp's base on the writing desk's open leaf, Liberty tossed the earthen colored pillows from Anthony's headboard. A messy yank saw the tester fly toward the footboard. The bed in such a disorderly manner, her mind recollected the meticulous readying she'd once given the bedding. Crisp corners, neat folds and quarter tucks. To be sure, how quickly forgotten was her chambermaid's deportment.

She met up with Barlary who'd lugged the dead-weighted Anthony to the side of the bedstead. Stooping, she took hold behind Anthony's ankles. The black leather of his knee-high boots pliantly gave under her fingers.

"You'll tax yourself." Barlary's grasp on Anthony remained steadfast.

Liberty paid no attention. "One good hoist and he'd be atop."

"And we'll have our epilogue to this wretched tale, then."

Liberty ignored Barlary's satirical fling. "I can lift him on this end, if you can lift him on yours."

"Aye. On three."

After Barlary counted to the designated number, Liberty put all her energy into propelling Anthony off the carpet. Gasping, she managed to heave him to the edge of the mattress. The hemp ropes complained in a stretching protest, yet held fast.

Anthony muttered something in his sleep, what, Liberty couldn't be sure. His bare chest and the breadth of his shoulders stood out with gooseflesh. She wanted to get him disrobed and the comforter tucked around him as soon as possible.

Without thinking of the implications, she reached for the silver buttons on the side of Anthony's crimson breeches.

Barlary's hand shackled around her wrist, his nails nearly digging into her. Her chin shot up to see the shock in his eyes. "What do you think you're about?"

Liberty stared down at her immobile arm. "I was going to ready him for his bed."

"My Lord, Liberty Rose, you cannot mean to say you're going to strip the man? Summon his valet!"

Liberty's eyes widened. She hadn't thought to call for Mister Feathers. Earlier, upon setting out to find Anthony, she'd caught the unsuspecting manservant sneaking his way down the hall in his stockinged feet. He'd come to Aunt Ophelia's door, lightly knocked in a well-thought-out pattern and was given immediate entrance. Liberty had not been surprised by this; she'd suspected a love affair had been brewing betwixt the two. She would give them her blessing when they asked for it.

But what to say to Barlary now? She couldn't call for Mister Fielding's valet because he was abed with Mistress Courtenay's aunt. Sweet grief, what to say?

She ran her moist palms down the folds of her skirt. "Mister Feathers wasn't feeling well after supper. He said his stomach was kicking up. My aunt gave him a tonic for it and I'm sure he'll be sleeping till dawn without twitching a muscle." Her breathless voice sounded strange in her ears. "So you see, there is no one to do it, save me."

"Or, *me*," Barlary ground out, the corner of his mouth pulled into a tight, dark smile. Without ceremony, he released Liberty's hand.

Heat stole into Liberty's face. She should have thought to ask Barlary, of course. But she'd assumed the responsibility for herself, thinking she was more understanding to his needs.

The graveness of her mistake showed itself in Barlary's

saddened eyes. He hung his head with sorrow for her lack of modesty, making not a single move to divest Anthony of his breeches.

"What's the matter?" she asked when she could stand his silence no more.

"It behooves me that I have to spell it out for you," he explained, his voice dry and bitter. "Turn yourself around."

Feeling like a poor awkward soul, Liberty swallowed her mortification and turned away from the bedside so Barlary could undress her fiancé.

"My decent girl, Liberty Rose, you cannot mean to marry this drenched lout!" Barlary wailed. "I cannot live to see you bind yourself to a man who doesn't know hill from dale when he's in his cups."

Shamed by her deception, Liberty could not divulge the grim reality she knew for truth. In honesty, the wedding would be a sham, a fraudulent lie to see through to the end of Thomas Fielding's visit. All she could do was try and make Barlary understand as if she really would be marrying Anthony—legally. "I—"

"Let me say my peace whilst you are not looking at me so forlornly." His tone, whetted by heartache, cut her to the quick.

Liberty heard the bed moan and groan as Barlary shucked Anthony of his boots. "Mayhap I should have made my feelings for you more clear. I did show you great favor and 'twas my mistake to never act solely on my high regard. To my discredit, I did court your company while courting Amelia Cookson, the scullery girl from the Crooked Key Inn."

Barlary grunted and Liberty could only assume he'd brought down Anthony's breeches. Her mind's picture heightened her embarrassment.

"When you and your aunt left the Running Footman, I came to realize how much you meant to me. And then when I saw you in that tussle with the military, my heart went pitter-pat over such indecencies being played out upon the fair Liberty Courtenay I dashed," he paused to rustle the sheets, "to your rescue, only to have you land in the arms of another. This—this man of riches and pomps. I know you well enough that I dare not mention you are with him for his purse—"

"You have overstepped—"

"'Tis not true, aye. But why you are, eludes me. When I read the banns, my heart broke. I'm loath to think what your life will be like if you go through with this marriage. You cannot be made to suffer his drunk with him, not to mention the censure his people will put upon you."

Liberty could stand no more of his ruminations. Imitation marriage or not, Barlary's injustices went without reason. On her heels, she turned to defend herself, not caring if Anthony lay unclad as a babe.

Her brows rose as she perused Anthony, his beard-shadowed chin tucked snugly under the covers. His face looked pale and lethargic in contrast to the bleached white of the bedclothes. A shock of hair rested on his forehead and she had to stop herself from brushing the strands back.

"Now let me say," she began curtly, then reminded herself that Barlary had always been loyal. Her tone changed to a softer and more patient note. "I am appreciative of your apprehensions for my honor, Barlary. Truly I am. But you must understand, I'm in love with him. Beneath the charade of drink that marks his character, he is an honest and truehearted man. I am not so foolish to think I can show him his better self. I know that I cannot do that, but I can stand by him until the day he finds his way clear."

Barlary's eyes grew bathed in tears.

"I'm sorry if my news is hurtful, but I do love him and I cannot talk myself out of my affections."

"He is a wastrel, a degenerate, a flatterer of wenches. I know this to be correct. I've seen him in the ordinaries with many a mistress."

Liberty grew sad by this retelling. Not that the account of Anthony's indulgences came as a surprise, but that Barlary felt he needed to reduce her feelings in such an ugly manner. "You will not change my mind, Barlary. I'm sorry."

"No sorrier than I, Liberty Rose." His tall, narrow frame slumped in remorse. Adjusting the knitted red cap on his head, he sniffed. "Then there is no more to be said."

Barlary stepped around her and trod quietly to the door.

"I could not have managed without your help," she called to him, holding onto hope they would part as friends. She said as much. "I shall always consider you a true friend, Barlary. Should you ever need anything . . ."

Barlary kept his back to her, the long strings of his apron dangling about his backside. "My dear decent girl, were I to do that, 'twould be a disservice to you, myself and the drunk."

On that, he departed.

The stillness of the bedchamber encompassed Liberty's senses. She felt numb and dragged about, tired and worn beyond her fragile years.

Sinking her bottom onto the bedside, she stared down at Anthony's placid visage, wishing he felt about her the way Barlary did.

She'd lost youthful infatuation when Barlary White walked out the door. Since meeting Anthony, she'd known real love in her heart. She regretted losing her friend while figuring this out.

Anthony appeared better now, his breathing even. Dark shadows smudged the underside of his lashes where they lay in wisps of brown. His lips, painted in paleness, barely resembled the full mouth that had kissed her so blissfully. Such a strong and vigorous man, taken down by a bottle of ale.

Alone, she swept the silky hair from his temple, her fingers massaging the tight skin of his forehead. A tick played at his jaw and she pressed her fingertip along the line of bone that composed his chin.

Her heart pounded an erratic rhythm as she imagined being crushed in his embrace; to feel the soft silk of his shirt next to her cheek, his hand cupping her cheek.

She looked back to the first day she'd seen him; he'd been in this same deadened state, sleeping off his pints, soon to pay dearly for his indulgence.

"Anthony, you promised," she whispered. "You said you wouldn't drink anymore."

He'd done so well. Yes, she had come to understand he inebriated his mind to keep his ghostly spirits at bay. The liquor put his brain into a shell that he'd thought to be protective of his emotions. Instead, the hull had locked his pain inside. If he kept on in his wretched ways, his torment would gobble him up and there'd be nothing left. He had to let his past catch up with him.

"Anthony, you dolt." Closing her eyes, Liberty buried her face in his throat, empathic tears splashing his neck. "You have to risk feeling hurt if you want to feel anything at all." She wet her lips and whispered in his ear. "I would kiss you now for fortitude it you'd know the kiss came from me."

Absorbing his warmth, she tingled and she regretted ever having to move away from him.

The clock's workings ticked off a slow minute; she felt suspended, unable to breath, unable to move from the man she loved.

Without warning, she felt the deep rumble of his hoarse voice. "Sweeting, such charitable words for a drenched lout like me."

Chapter
16

LIBERTY'S EYELASHES, HEAVY FROM DROWSY TEARS, FLEW UP IN surprise. She pushed herself into a sitting position, tossing her unbound hair over her shoulder. Her pulse quickened at the obvious implication—he'd been alert for quite some time. "You're awake?"

"Barely." Anthony's wide, well-cut mouth cultivated a wincing smile.

"You heard what I said?"

"Part of it," he slurred, the liquor fuzzing his speech. "I'm touched by your generosity to a degenerate like myself."

"You should be pickled in saltpeter!" In a flurry of petticoats, Liberty hopped off the bed, sprinted to the middle of the room and turned around. Anthony Fielding's prostrate form and drunken expression snipped short her pity. "You play a very pretty unconscious! I thought surely you were doomed."

"I stumbled and hit my head on the edge of my clothing cabinet. I roused for a minute to young Barley's womanish voice and his opinions of me." Anthony slipped his bronzed arm free of the snowy bedclothes, brought his fingertips to his temple and rubbed. "Bruised, am I?"

"I care not!" Beset with embarrassment, Liberty hid her mask of misery in the palms of her hands, unable to look at

Anthony any longer. He'd heard her sentimental overtures of love. What a grand old snicker he must have had in his sodden head. How she hated his liquor and the state it put him in. She lifted her face from the web of her fingers, unshed tears in her eyes. "'Tis no wonder you sought a woman to pretend affections for you. More to your grief you met me. Someone who would offer her devotion to you genuinely. I would have been your wife in earnest. But what have you done with my heart?"

Liberty left him then to think of his own answer.

Calling out to her, he struggled to sit up, but collapsed back, exhausted. Dazed and too drunk to go after her fiery contempt, Anthony slept.

He slept for short spells and woke, dripping with cold sweat and despair He had failed. Failed himself. Failed Liberty He wasn't a man; he was a delinquent.

After these brief fits of self-loathing, he tumbled into his nightmares again. Dark memories.

John Perkins running his father through with his sword. Blood. A week of liquor as his comfort and the budded craving that had taken seed in him. His mother coolly asking him to listen to her. Endless hours of plotting against John Perkins only to have the man get away. A look of accomplice in Lionel Manning's eyes as he sought the mayor in the crowd.

All these pictures swirled in his head; like a tornado whipping him about until he became so dizzy in his sleep, he couldn't stand the pain. His walls of emotional torment bent and threatened to cave in. In this swirling vortex came one image. A face. Pure and good. Black hair, hazel eyes and ruby lips. When he looked further, a flowing white gown with laced-on sleeves made her dance on a cloud.

Liberty Rose.

She called to him. She spoke his name. He heard pieces of conversations he'd had with her, reliving them, hearing them again only differently. The voice was hers, yet it wasn't. It was a frightening mixture of Feathers, Ophelia Fairweather, his grandsire, Cheswick and even Gervase Tankard. "*'Tis only a blind man's eyes that see naught in a world of light." "The only remedy known is the abandonment of the vicious habits on which the evil depends." "Face and rectify your errors and you will grow from the experience." "Your problems are of your own making." "You will never get on with your life unless you confront your past." "What have you done with my heart?" "What have you done with my heart?" "What have you done with my heart?"*

The question echoed inside him until he thought he'd go mad. He yelled for her to stop. He reached into the golden aura surrounding her, grabbing for what he could, wanting to hang onto the gathers of her gown. He felt nothing. Air. Thin and cold.

Then she vanished.

He called for her but she would not return.

Anthony's eyes flew open and he bolted upright, his sheets soaked from his perspiration. Wet hair clung to his forehead and lay plastered to the column of his neck. His uneven breath racked his chest and he pulled in deep gulps to calm himself.

When he'd quieted enough to get his bearings, he saw where he was. His bedroom was dark, but not black. Dawn would come soon.

"Judas . . ." He could barely speak the oath as he sunk backward into his downy pillow. A pinfeather poked its shaft out of the linens and stuck his shoulder.

As he came to full consciousness, he made himself recall his insufferable dreams. Perkins. Always Perkins. But this time, a new feeling washed away his hatred. Despite the chaos of his dreams, something tangible overshadowed the horror: truth and a willingness to embrace it.

For nearly half his life, he had feared John Perkins. That boy who had gone to kill him, hadn't the courage. He'd stayed in that man's home and as each hour had turned off the clock and Perkins's hadn't returned, Anthony had been more and more relieved. He had wanted to be a man and avenge his father's death as a man would. But he had only been a boy. A broken, grieving boy.

Why this revelation came to him in this manner, he had no answer. Not being one who held God close to his bosom, he couldn't understand why he'd been given this message so spiritually.

He closed his eyes and looked for the walls of pain. They had crumpled. Light streamed into his soul and he wasn't trapped and helpless anymore. He was free. Free from anger, free from fear.

Once he'd acknowledged this change within himself, he waited. Waited for it to disappear like some foul hoax. It did not. A placidness flowed through him as he slowly opened his eyes again to stare at the faint outline of his ceiling.

This startling discovery of inner acceptance made him weep. The hot sting of tears was foreign to his eyes as he cried for the first time over the death of his father. Over the loss of his mother. Over the years he'd wasted on drink.

He was finally ready to view himself from the outside.

Ever since his tortured age of sixteen, he'd been living on the wrong side of the hedge. Upon his father's death, Anthony had been a traveler on a journey of destruction, meeting with cup brims at slipshod inns along the way. He'd never thought of pursuing a proper home and owning up to sobriety and morality.

His revenge had guided him, his images of felling the man who had slain his sire had been his quest.

Anthony rolled onto his side, tucking his arms tightly to him. A heat spread itself through the marrow of his bones, melting into his muscles and scorching his skin. The intensity of fire inside him, made him break out in a fresh sweat. He'd deceived himself into thinking his hatred of Perkins had destroyed him.

In cold fact, Anthony Fielding had destroyed himself. He'd poisoned his life with alcohol.

No one made him drink as perhaps he'd always thought. He'd often enough claimed to Feathers he'd been forced a glass of sack by someone naming his good health. Or he'd drink to worthy company. Then there were those toasts saluted to brother rakes. Each drop, each bumperful had deluded him to thinking it was all because of Perkins. When in actuality, John Perkins had won the first time Anthony had been too drunk to stop. The mayor no doubt gloated over this point, sneering down his powdered nose and tilting his venerable white locks in disgust. Poor Fielding had become a regular piece of clockwork. Soused day in and day out; a skeleton of a man who'd been too weak to accept his fate in this world of injustices.

Anthony's head throbbed dully. The medicinal tonic Cook made could no more clear his thoughts than they already were. He finally understood the method of his madness. He hadn't succeeded in staying sober because he had never left it. In the back of his mind, had been the steady thought of the day when he could drink again.

But he had had the privilege of other drinkers, only he had abused it so frightfully that now it was withdrawn from him. Forever. On a shaky breath, he accepted this.

To get back at Perkins, he would get well. He would rid himself of this affliction that struck his palate and wooed him to the gutters of gin.

He could no more drink again, than he could give up Liberty Rose Courtenay.

Oddly this came as no surprise to him. There could be no other woman that he thought of as his partner. His schemes to lure Eden Bennet were but a dusty illusion that soured his stomach. He could never be satisfied with a boldface like Eden when he had a dearest love like Liberty.

She was his sunbeam in the dark and musty dungeon of his drunk. She had cleared the cobwebs and vermin from his soul.

When had he fallen in love with her and why had he denied himself his feelings? Because there had been no good in him.

Anthony uncurled his arms and rolled onto his back. He wouldn't let her go. He'd changed. She would know it, wouldn't she? Thus far, all she'd seen in him was the worst and she'd found favor in that. He couldn't descend lower than he already was—at least not in her present esteem of him.

But could she love him again? Not the Anthony Fielding she'd known, but the person behind the shroud of alcohol. Did he know who he was? Did his former self still exist?

Anthony tossed his covers aside, the chill creeping over his bare torso. The person he was before sixteen had to have survived! Somewhere deep in the core of his being, there grew a spark of life.

And the flame was Liberty

On the day of her wedding, Liberty wore a brocaded white silk gown patterned with a network of small, light pink flowers. Spangles ornamented her high-heeled shoes with straps of brocade pulled through the square buckles. Around her neck, a close-fitting necklace Aunt Ophelia had loaned her. The triple row of false pearls tied with a narrow white satin ribbon in back. Anthony had paid a mercer a small fortune for the material and then had Madame Penelon whip it up in no time; why he had gone to the trouble, she couldn't guess.

Aunt Ophelia nervously fussed and preened over the tight sleeves that snugly fit down to Liberty's elbows where three point lace ruffles hung in great depths.

Feebly smiling her satisfaction, Ophelia adjusted the handkerchief of the same lace that covered her niece's shoulders, fastened in front with a large bow of white satin ribbon and a small cluster of ivy.

Liberty looked down on the sprig of green. It had been tradition in her family for the bride to plant the ivy on the night of her wedding so that she may later admire the plant on her yearly anniversary. Ophelia had gotten her the vine and she hadn't wanted to shock her aunt by blurting out the tragic truth. She would no more be married tonight than she was now.

"I am beside myself with pride. I never thought the day would arrive and here 'tis too soon for me." Tears shimmered in Ophelia's eyes. "If only your dear, dear parents could be here to witness this day, though more joyous a one I wish it could be. Fielding has taken—"

Liberty didn't want to hear her aunt belittle Anthony Aunt Ophelia had been battering and "Tut"ing Anthony's name since she'd found Liberty on the beach that day with the honey-pod in her hand. She'd tried to quell her aunt's flighty nerves over her feelings for Anthony, but Ophelia had not listened. "I am afraid my parents would be disappointed."

"Pish, my lamb." Ophelia drew out her silk fan and grazed the web in front of her face. "They would be pleased as punch."

"I think not." Liberty hesitated, almost telling her aunt the truth. She'd always been honest with Aunt Ophelia, thinking of her more as a mother than an aunt. But now, the disgrace of the day seduced Liberty to secrecy. The humiliation was too much to bare at this late notice.

"Your gloves, lambkin. Hurry."

Liberty accepted the long, fingerless gloves and wove the ends of her fingertips through the lacy holes. She took a step toward the door, not wanting to mull over what she was about to do.

Ophelia didn't readily follow. "Oh, pish! Not yet. I've forgotten one thing, pet." She reached into the deep folds of her pocket and produced a gold box. She handed the beribboned gift to Liberty.

Liberty accepted her aunt's offering with reservation. She dared not open the gift. Whatever was inside, she could not accept it on good conscience. "Aunt . . ." Oh, she could no more delude her beloved aunt. The truth had to be told. "There really isn't going to be—"

"Tut, pet," Ophelia silenced. "There *is* going to be a wedding, but not if we are late to it! And we cannot be late."

Gingerly, Liberty unwrapped the present. Inside lay a small vial of perfume on a linked gold chain with a plain ring.

"'Twas your father's wedding band. He gave it to me the day of his death. I was not able to obtain your mother's before she was buried. I'm sorry. They took her away from me after I'd gone to give her linens to another."

Tears burned Liberty's eyes as she thought of her beloved parents, both in graves at sea. The image haunted her vision and she wished, as she often had, they were nestled in some patch of ground where she could pay them tribute.

"Now, now," Ophelia chided. "Pray don't wet your face with tears. 'Twill run like rain." Sniffing into her kerchief, she pointed to the perfume. "'Tis all I made of that batch. When 'tis gone, there will never be more. The base is a tincture of lily-of-the-valley. I've named it, *Forever*"

Liberty raised the vial from its bed of satin. She lifted the stopper and inhaled the subtle, sweet fragrance.

"It isn't for smelling, my dear. Make use of it on your wrists."

Vacillating over whether or not she wanted to smell so wondrous on such a hideous day, Liberty gave in to her aunt's wishes.

"There now." Ophelia took the perfume and box, setting them on the dressing table. "I think we're ready to make your appearance. Never was there a more lovely bride."

Liberty allowed her aunt to guide her from the bedroom. The dry rustle of her fine undercoats swished at her ankles. Her steps were numb, each one bringing her closer and closer to a destiny of nothingness.

Hiram Feathers came running down the hallway, up from the first floor servants' entrance below. Blushing down to his starched collar and quite out of breath, he waylaid Ophelia. "My dear, I must have a word with you."

"Hiram?"

Liberty turned with her aunt, distressed over the valet's obvious upset. "Mister Feathers, what's amiss?"

He feigned a calmness for Liberty's sake, his gray eyes smiling reassuringly. "Nothing, my good lady. 'Tis a matter with the, er . . . cook and the wedding supper. I must confide with your aunt for one moment." Putting his arm around Ophelia, he began dragging her away. "One moment, Mistress Liberty."

Ophelia allowed Feathers to propel her a good distance down the hall, out of Liberty's hearing. "Hiram, whatever are you doing!"

"Shh!" Feathers insisted in a clipped whisper. "She cannot hear. Lud, my gracious, 'tis all a'foul and I don't know what to do!"

"Hiram, please, slow down. What has happened?"

"'Tis Reverend Fisher. He's not here yet."

"What?"

"Shh!" Feathers implored her and took her off several paces farther. "'Tis worse than that. Another reverend has shown up. I know not who he is, though he claims Fielding summoned him. I don't know why since Fielding planned on Colin Prentice to pretend to be a man of the church. And I left that fraudulent barkeep, Prentice, on his way to a good drunk at the White Hart, just like we planned. He couldn't possibly make it here on time—even if he's still standing."

"This new man, did he say who he was?"

"Aye. Said he was Reverend George Moss from the Town Borough Parish."

"Where is he now?"

Feathers's flush deepened to crimson. "I showed him to the study and said I would fetch Fielding. Unbeknownst to Reverend Moss, I've locked him inside."

"I say!"

"Aye, and it gets worse. There is something, my dear, that we did not count on."

"Pray save me," Ophelia whispered, leaning into Feathers for support.

"Thomas Fielding hired on his own reverend. William Dresham of the Norfolk Parish." Feathers took out his muckender and swabbed the moisture on his long brow. "I fear 'tis my fault. I should have suspected he would gain his own man of the ministry. Lud . . . whatever shall we do?"

Ophelia gazed at Liberty who stared at them nonplussed and with worry on her face. Then Ophelia looked at Feathers. "We do naught. If this Dresham is a real reverend, we haven't a worry. Liberty and Fielding will be wed legally"

"I dare swear, madam! 'Tis right you are."

"Go now, Hiram." Ophelia shooed him. "Keep watch over the study and don't let the Reverend Moss escape."

"As you say, my love."

Feathers ran down the stairs.

Ophelia strode to Liberty and gave her a great smile. "Sorry for the delay, lambkin. 'Twas naught important. Let's go on now."

Confused and bewildered by her aunt's strange behavior, Liberty was barely aware of her slow descent down the flower-garlanded staircase.

A tiny host of well-wishers came flooding into her view as they stood in the vestibule. Decked out with finery and frippery, she felt stifled by the forest of feathers and cocked hats. She knew none of these guests intimately. A few faces were familiar from the masked ball, but even those garnered no importance. There was only one she sought, and when she found him, she refused to be taken in by his captivating presence.

Anthony stood at the landing, clearly uneasy. He shifted nervously and made no effort to hide his discomfort. He wore a formal suit of green velvet with marcasite studs. His hands went in and out of the large pocket flaps and he'd left his waistcoat open; then he'd button it, then he'd unbutton it. His shirt linen spilled ruffles between the part in his coat. When he turned his head to stare at the double entry doors, she saw his neatly coiffured tie wig whose lengthy braid of brown lay secured at his neck by a black ribbon. The snugness of his breeches was almost indecent. Silk stockings of white with tinseled clocks encased his well-defined calves.

Liberty refused to be undone by his beauty. His nervousness attested to the fact he did not want to be here. Why should he be so tense when he wasn't really getting married?

Anthony Fielding took one more short glance at the front doors of his home. Where the devil was Reverend Moss? He'd secured the man yesterday; short notice to perform a wedding ceremony, but the parson had graciously accepted.

Unsure, yet wanting to discuss his spiritual awakening with a man of God, Anthony had gone to a little church at the outskirts of town, the Town Borough Parish. He confessed his addiction to liquor and his dream about Liberty. He asked Reverend Moss why it had come to him. Moss has not mocked or scoffed at his illusion, rather, admitted it was not that uncommon to have a vision in one's sleep and awake to recall the details. It was the spirit's way of telling the soul to put the prophecy into reality.

They talked for several hours in the rectory. Anthony felt great hope in the noncondescending mannerisms of this parson. Moss had done him the honor of granting his officiating presence. When Anthony left the church, he headed straight for Colin Prentice's tavern to tell the barkeeper his services were no longer needed.

Prentice was not in. His wife claimed he'd gone off into the woods hunting and he wasn't expected to return until after dark. Not having time to wait, Anthony gave the woman a note and ten pounds to pass along to Prentice for his trouble.

Now as his house had filled with guests, Anthony had neither a real nor false cleric to marry him. What would he say when he reached the receiving room and there was no one standing at the pulpit?

And there was no time to prepare Liberty.

He had decided against telling her his switch in plans. She'd been so angry with him that he feared she wouldn't want to marry him now. He couldn't risk losing her. Not when he'd finally understood he could love her and have her love him in return. Once they were legally wed, he would tell her.

Liberty passed Anthony by to meet Thomas Fielding who broadly smiled at her.

Wanting to put Anthony from her thoughts, Liberty concentrated on Thomas. He'd donned himself to great lengths in robin blue with a black crepe neck cloth that looked to be squelching his airway. He came up the last stair, putting himself on Anthony's level, then he proceeded to go around his grandson. He proffered the crook of his arm and led her past her anxious groom.

Liberty was taken to the decorated receiving room—minus Anthony's figurehead—where a flock of chairs had been set up; the guests had left the foyer and were now seated in them. Thomas guided her to the front of the rows. At the end, stood a wiry man whose wig looked two sizes too large. For a barkeeper, Liberty thought the man looked more suited to the cloth than a taproom. His ceremonial robe lent him great credibility.

Refusing to gaze at Anthony, she heard him come into the room. He took his place by her side and she couldn't help but notice him. Rather than looking as if a tightening noose were on his neck, a dark frown of confusion lit his handsome face. He stared beyond her to his grandfather and in a low tone asked, "Who is this man?"

Thomas returned in a hushed voice, "'Tis Reverend William Dresham of the Norfolk Parish."

Dresham arched his bland brows, but remained stoic.

"I thought I told you not to intervene in this matter. That I would secure my own clergyman."

"Aye, you did," Thomas hissed softly, "and I know the reason why."

"Meaning what?"

Liberty felt as if she were a spectator; the heated words soared right over her head as if she didn't stand between the two. What was going on, indeed? Why was Anthony so perturbed? Hadn't he set this up himself?

"I think you know precisely what I mean," Thomas protested. "Trying to deceive an old man."

Ophelia and Hiram Feathers appeared to join the quiet commotion induced by Anthony. Ophelia tried to remain inconspicuous when she murmured, "There is no problem here, Fielding. This man—Reverend, er—?"

"Dresham," he replied in a muted tone that blended with the growing buzz of guests's voices. "Reverend William Dresham of the Norfolk Parish Church."

"Is a true man of God," Ophelia finished.

"I don't care who he is. I will not be married by him," Anthony exclaimed softly.

Liberty's heart sunk. Somehow, something had gone wrong with Anthony's plan. Thomas Fielding had gained his own clergy and Anthony was desperate for a way out. The utter humiliation that ran through her made her weak and faint.

The room grew suddenly unbearably hot and she prayed

for prudence not to crumple. As warmth spread across her face, a frightful pounding came from where she gathered, Anthony's study door.

"Open up, I say!" A muffled call pleaded. "Fielding! Are you there? I say, I've been locked in."

"Lud . . ." Feathers backed away, but was stopped by Anthony's bristling command.

"Hold yourself, Feathers." Anthony's brown eyes narrowed. "Is that Reverend Moss I hear?"

"Reverend, who, sir?"

"Moss!"

A gasp rose from the room.

"Aye, sir," Feathers meekly confessed.

Thomas glared in turn to Feathers, Anthony, Ophelia, Dresham, and lastly, rather weakly at Liberty. Then he wheeled around and addressed the well-wishers. "There has been, ladies and gentlemen, a slight delay. Allow us if you will, a minute of privacy."

He stalked from the receiving room and headed directly toward the knocking sounds which still persisted. The wedding party followed.

Once at the study door, Thomas grabbed hold of the knob and jiggled it; it held fast. "Anthony, kindly unlock this door."

"I don't have the key on me."

Feathers pushed his way forward. "I do."

"Feathers!" Anthony blared. "What has gotten into you, man? Have you gone daft?"

"Nay, sir."

"But I may think it!"

Thomas rammed the key home in the brass plate, unlatched the knob and pushed inward.

Reverend George Moss's mouth fell agape as the group descended upon him. He jumped as Thomas closed the portal.

Liberty was beyond wondering. This new man—this Reverend Moss—who was he really? His height was pleasing, his face not too full of characteristic flaws. He seemed devout without falsity A genuine leader of a flock.

"Anthony, would you care to enlighten me on what is transpiring here?" Moss's black cassock reached his ankles and buttoned down the front with tight long sleeves. He joined Anthony by the desk.

"My grandsire has interfered in my plans."

"I should say I have," Thomas exploded. "I—"

The drumming of heavy feet crossed over the veranda outside the window. Two men in black flashed by the panes. No sooner had they passed, they returned. Wide-eyed, they peeked inside the full study.

Ophelia announced, "Oh, my! 'Tis Reverend Fisher at last. And—oh my!"

With lethal quietness, Thomas moved to the window and lifted the sash. The duo climbed in and stumbled over the padded seat. The first, his fleshy face reddened as if he'd just ridden up to the house, gasped for breath. The second, plainly swayed from drink. The garment he wore could not have been his, for the hem dragged about his booted ankles in great waves. He hitched up the cloth and made his way toward Anthony.

"Hyar I be, Fieldin'. Like ye said. Wouldn' haf made it weren' for this man hyar. Found me and m'horse—me not on the damn animal—in the middle a the road."

Fisher smelled of lathered horse. Quite disturbed, he faced Ophelia and Hiram Feathers. "I beg your forgiveness. My horse and chaise were stolen and I had no way of getting here," he gasped, his portly weight hindering his wind. "I say, I'd walked halfway here, when there in the lane, this man dressed as a clergy lay facedown drunk. I charged him to give me loan of his mare," he huffed, crooking his fingers into the stiff linen collar around his fat neck, "and would have left him in the gutters, save I am a man of the Lord, and could not do that. Imagine my surprise when he said he was on his way to this very house!"

Prentice nearly toppled into Thomas. Disgusted, the older Fielding shoved him away. "See here. Who are you?"

"I be the Reveren' Colin Prentice."

"Prentice, you idiot!" Anthony hollered. "I gave your wife ten pounds to keep you at home!"

"Me wife?" He screwed up his ruddy face. "The slut didn' give me ten pounds."

"Sir!" Thomas crossly said, "remind yourself you are in the company of God's disciples."

Liberty stumbled into the armchair behind Anthony's desk. Whatever she'd thought her wedding day would be, a great farce had not been among the list of possibilities. Anthony appeared ready to kill Colin Prentice; her aunt and Mister Feathers stared guiltily at Reverend Fisher who battled to get hold of his breath; Reverend Dresham stayed impassive and rather miffed; Thomas looked wise and able to get to the bottom of the situation. She sagged into her seat, helpless to do anything but.

"Someone need start at the beginning," Thomas declared, and since no one seems to know what is going on, I shall be the one to start." Facing Anthony, he began, "Nearly a fortnight ago, I came down for one of Quashabee's comfits and there stuffing himself on them was this parson"—he pointed to Fisher—"of whom I have never laid eyes on. He sat with your valet and your intended's aunt. Not wanting to impose myself on their conversation, I readied to turn back the way I'd come, undetected. I stopped short, hit with shock when I heard Anthony planned to dupe me by hiring, apparently"—he singled out Prentice—"this invented clergyman to marry him. I could not and would not let anything happen to misrepresent this marriage. Why then, did Feathers and Madame Fairweather want Fisher? I could not guess and wondered if this Fisher was indeed a fraud, too. He said he was from the Elizabeth River Parish and would be performing nuptials at quarter past the hour. I made sure Reverend Fisher would not get here on time."

Reverend Joseph Fisher snorted. "You, poor sir, what have you done with my horse and coach? You must have known my parish reached to the borders of town and I could not gain another in its place without taking half an hour to do so!"

"Your chaise and horse are in the stables."

"Stealing is an illegal offense!"

"I'll give them back to you. I merely borrowed them."

Anthony unbuttoned his coat, which had been fastened and unfastened a half-dozen times. "Why would you do this, Grandsire?"

"Fieldings have always associated themselves with the Norfolk Parish. I wanted to see you wed properly. My question to you, is: Why would you not?"

Anthony raked his hands through his wig, accidentally pulling several neatly combed strands from his braid. "I *do* want to marry this woman." He gazed directly at Liberty who squeaked her surprise. She was recovering from the surprise of knowing Aunt Ophelia had found out about Anthony's plans to fake the wedding. "But with my own reverend. I have found Mister Moss quite to my liking."

"I need a glass of wine to restore me," Fisher lamented.

"That sounds like a ripe idea," Prentice seconded, pursing his lips. "An' drain it so's I can hit that slut o' mine o'er the head wi' it!"

"Gentlemen!" Thomas barked.

"Feathers, get them out of here—discreetly." Lashing down the button of his coat, Anthony opened the door. "And tell the guests, we will be out shortly."

"Aye, sir."

Feathers ushered the two men under the jamb and quickly steered them down the hall and toward the dining room.

An artificial quiet settled over the study. The two prevailing clergy surveyed each other.

"Are you a fraud, sir?" Thomas asked George Moss.

"Nay, I am not."

Thomas said to Anthony, "You claim to want to marry this woman. Then you shall. I don't care which one of these men you choose, but choose one and let us be done with this."

"Reverend Moss."

"Done."

A short time later, Liberty was saying, "I take you for my husband," barely hearing Anthony's reply of, "I swear by all I hold sacred and Holy never to have another wife than you."

At the close of the liturgy, a ring was placed on her fourth finger. A golden band without adornment. The circlet suited her fine as she was not at all convinced they were really wed.

"If you would like to add any words of your own, now 'tis the time to make them known." Reverend Moss looked expectantly at Liberty.

"I have none . . ."

Ophelia rushed to her side and shoved a tiny piece of paper into her hand. She whispered, "I took the freedom, my dear, knowing how you felt about Fielding."

Opening the parchment, Liberty tentatively read the written words. "Oh thou, whose very existence my reasoning mind denies and rejects, but whom my heart craves and longs to adore, accept my homage and be mine forever." She looked up at Ophelia.

Her aunt nodded, tears swimming in her eyes. "Forever 'Tis the perfume.

Feathers slipped up to his employer's side and shoved him a note of his own. Whispering, he said, "Knowing your ill-favor to writing, I took the liberty myself, too, sir."

Anthony perused his valet's words, his mouth turning in a one-sided smile as he finally read, "I was not overreached into this match by art, nor hurried into it by passion, but from long experience of her sense and worth, I reasoned myself into it. I found I had so engaged her affections that no other man could make her happy; and so dallied her character, that only myself could repair it." He laughed softly. "Well penned, Feathers."

"If that 'tis all?" Reverend Moss inquired. When no other voices spoke, he concluded. "Then I pronounce them husband and wife."

Anthony pulled Liberty into his embrace and chastely kissed her mouth.

For better, for worse—the deed was done.

Silence enveloped Anthony as he sat in the darkened alcove of his newly polished study. The only light came from a fire sparkling gilded flames over the grate in his hearth. A pleasant warmth met with his feet which were propped on an ottoman. He wiggled his stockinged toes, thinking of the hours he used to sit this way with a glass of brandy to round out the picture.

In his hand tonight—nothing but the strength of his convictions. He hadn't much thought of drinking the entire day. Too many other reasons to keep his mind from straying. Liberty for one.

By all accounts, he should have felt the irons upon him. He was, after all, a married man now. He'd been wed for half a day and no unseen shackle had clamped about his ankle to drag down his steps. If anything, he felt lighter on his feet.

He had himself a wife.

Rising from his settee, he strode to the door on quiet heels.

The house was silent as all had gone home after the wedding supper some three hours past. He'd danced with his bride and made a merry evening, counting the time until he would be alone with Liberty. Once opportunity had presented itself, he'd been issued orders from Ophelia to leave his bedchamber and return at ten o'clock. The devil, the crone was giving him mandates already. But he'd accepted this nonsense on good terms, retiring for a spell in his study to meditate on his future.

With a wife and no liquor, he couldn't have asked for a more different life than he'd already lived.

As Anthony took the risers to his apartment on the second floor, he thought of what he would tell Liberty to quell her fears over marrying a drunk. He would never drink again, but a drunk he would always be—if that could make any sense to her. She may have wanted him sober, but would she love the man underneath what the drink had concealed?

He'd had all his booze tossed in the bins, not trusting himself yet to be in the same household with it. His resolve was strong, but so was the calling to drink. He *could* do this, he swore.

Reaching the landing, he trekked his way down the hall and stopped at his closed portal. It seemed odd to knock on his own door, but he reminded himself of his lady's privilege.

His light tap of knuckles bid him a quick entry by way of Liberty's voice.

"Come in," she said to him through the oaken grains.

He twisted the knob and entered.

The bronzed room came into focus. There were no traces of a female, save for the satin wrapper at the foot of his bedstead—and the woman in his bed. Of all the women he'd had, none had ever slept in this apartment.

Liberty lay on his mattress, the testers covering her up to her chin. Her long black hair flowed down her shoulders and over the puff of pillows behind her back. She had the face of an angel; porcelain and too fragile to be real. Her eyes glowed under the candlelight; a delicate green-gold fused by wariness.

"Wife, you look quite fetching." Anthony strode to her while loosening the tie of his cravat. He'd left his coat, shoes and wig in his study.

Liberty shrunk into the soft gathers of the bedclothes. "Aunt Ophelia fixed me."

"How could the woman fix something that didn't need fixing?"

"You are too kind," she said stiffly.

He arched his brow, wondering over this polite conversation. Were all their talks from now on to be spoken with only the highest esteem toward each other? He rather liked her witty tongue and hoped it hadn't been left at the altar.

Sitting on the edge of the bed, he rested his elbows on his knees. She skittered toward the opposite side.

Rather than undressing himself, he lay down next to her, on top of the covers, and stretched out his legs before him. Perhaps if they talked awhile.

He'd always relied on inebriants to see him through awkward situations. Now he had to make a go of it dry.

Liberty bit her lip, thinking Anthony too casual, too handsome for his own good. This intimate way of sharing the bed, though she under the bedclothes and he on top, sent tremors down her spine. His informal air as he'd entered the bedroom had played havoc on her emotions. His sunny brown hair had been combed free of any ties and rested over his shoulders—currently just one shoulder as he'd moved to lie on his side. The gathers of his expensive shirt lay in a soft cascade down his middle, trimly tucked into his breeches.

"We can look back at this day when we are decrepit and laugh over our four reverends, or shall I say three as Prentice didn't count."

"I should say our wedding was very much out of the ordinary," she replied. Liberty shifted her weight and Anthony smelled the scent of her perfume, a heady concoction that aroused him to wayward intentions. He nipped his bawdy thoughts.

"You looked lovely."

"As you've told me a dozen times."

Anthony smiled. So he had. But she was. He rolled onto his side, resting his head in the palm of his hand. Liberty froze, staring straight ahead. "What's wrong, sweeting?"

"Are we really married?"

"Of course." When she said nothing, he brought his finger to her chin and turned her face to him. " 'Tis true! Today was the first day of my real sobriety and I had to have control of it. *I* requested George Moss because I needed to make that choice. Not my grandsire. 'Twas wrong of me to have believed I owed him his happiness."

"Are you happy?"

"Quite. Aren't you?" Worry ran through him.

"I would be if only I could be sure . . ." There had been too many duplicities for Liberty to truly believe anything without sound proof.

"Be sure of this, sweeting." Anthony drew her face close and put his lips on her mouth. He kissed her, cherished her, coaxed her to give herself up to him. She tasted like sunshine, sweet and warm. So good, he shuddered. He felt her resistance and deepened his kiss, wanting to melt away her doubts and fears.

He tried to lower the comforter she protectively clutched. She held fast and he broke the kiss. "Let go." The simple words brought hesitation to her green eyes, but she loosened her hold.

"I don't know what to believe."

"Believe in us," Anthony said, then slowly, peeled the heavy bedding away to view her loveliness. Her gossamer nightgown was nothing more than a delicate web that exposed more than it concealed. The frail outline of her figure was defined by the shimmering cloth, the tips of her breasts a dusky pink beneath the sheer white. A ribbon so narrow it could have been thread, was tied in a celestial bow in the valley of her bosom.

Anthony lowered himself onto his back, taking Liberty with him. The strain of her breasts burned through the thinness of his shirt. The feel of her gown was silky under his fingertips. The warmth of her skin as he splayed his hands up the slope of her back, came through the diaphanous material. The nightrail was so flimsy, he could tear it from her without even trying.

She'd made fists of her hands and they rested on his shoulders like two heavy blocks of uncertainty. He would not have her fear him on their wedding night. She would know that she was loved.

Anthony slanted his kiss and opened her mouth with his tongue. He teased her, persuaded her, until she met him. Her fingers opened, her palms flattened.

"That's the way, sweeting," he breathed against her red lips. He kissed her this way for a long time.

Liberty thought that she would die from what Anthony was doing to her. He'd never kissed her like this before. So long, so torturous. Her nipples had hardened against the solid wall of his chest. She had wanted this, but reservations kept her from surrender. They still persisted, though weakened by Anthony's kisses, his artful advance.

Without breaking the kiss again, he pressed her into the mattress. Her breasts ached for his touch. Twice before they had started something and both times she'd been denied what followed. This mysterious need to have him explore every inch of her returned. To have him touch her secret places and make them his own.

When Anthony reached out and pulled at the single satin ribbon at the front of her nightrail, she shivered. With a tug, he freed the bow and parted the fabric.

No matter the strong desire for him consuming her, her doubts persisted. He'd never said he loved her. Did he fear his grandfather so much he'd settled on a "sham" marriage —real perhaps in its outward form, but still false at its heart? Did he not understand that she loved him, that though she surely would have married him, it was not the ceremony she wanted, but him? His heart, his love, the true essence of a genuine marriage.

His rough fingers brushed the column of her neck, searing her and she was almost ashamed that she wanted him so, even with her uncertainties. Quivering, she was incapable of doing anything but urging him on.

His fingertips grazed an idle path over her collarbone, the fullness of her breast and finally, her sensitive nipple. He circled the crest, never taking the slight mound into his palm. She shivered from the desire pouring through her, the torture of his lazy caress. Her back arched and she wanted more than this slow touch, this dizzy torment.

Anthony's fingers grew less than steady and he took her offering with a husky groan. The heat of his tongue wrapped around the puckered bud. She writhed beneath this exquisite torment. A quickening started deep inside her; the intimate place between her legs grew heavy and thick.

Twisting, she brought herself closer to him. His hand reached out and cupped her other breast, giving equal attention to both. The combination of stroking fingertips and mouth drove her senseless.

Her womanhood ached and she shifted, wanting to ease the tension. Anthony broke his mouth free and got off the bed. His warmth vanished in a cold current of unoccupied space. Complete turmoil raced through her heart, until she saw what he was doing.

Anthony yanked the tails of his shirt from his breeches and ripped the closures free; he tossed the frilly garment on the floor. Bare-chested and bronze, powerfully muscled, he was perfect. Made like no other. The sight of him was both pleasure and pain. He unfastened his breeches at the side and shucked them free. Bending, he removed his garters and hose.

Naked, he came to her.

She sucked in her breath, his virile arousal registering in her head. The male display did not terrify her, nor did she think it offensive. His weight as he lay down again, dipped the bed; she rocked toward his sleek and taut frame. Her exposed breasts met and abraded against the light wedge of curls on his chest. Drawing her hands across the breadth of his shoulders and down the length of his back, she reveled in his satin-tight skin.

He kissed her again. This time with an urgency that came without warning. Her lips felt bruised and swollen, wet and passionate. He touched the pulse that beat at the base of her throat. Then with quick light strokes, he played his fingers over her neck, her earlobes, her breasts. His hand explored every inch of her; down her waist, over her nightgown and finally to the hem that had bunched up her thigh. He reached underneath, dragging his fingernails up her bare leg.

Tingles ran down to her toes. She was devastated that he would evoke her total surrender when she was unsure of his feelings.

The place where her thighs joined, strained for his hand —for something. For release from the pressure. She couldn't stop moving, kissing him, panting. He stroked her, then his fingers were inside her. She jolted, her heart quaking and beating rapidly. Rhythmically, he massaged her, his thumb circling over a tiny part of her womanhood. This new awareness, this response, was forged with liquid heat. It consumed her, made her lose control. She was on the edge. The edge of something wonderful and she couldn't stop it. She didn't want to stop. She thrust against his hand, the magic it offered and then, suddenly, she felt the cord inside her snap.

Before she could breathe, Anthony had taken himself away. He stripped her of her nightgown. She looked at him, into his eyes. The golden brown glittered with passion and she pressed a quick, breathless kiss on his wide lips. A silent thank you, a shared intimacy. He lowered himself on top of her and entered the place his hand had just been.

Her moistness enveloped him, making the small, sharp

pain that cut her, more bearable. He filled her, stretched her farther than his fingers had. Raising his torso up by putting his weight on his hands, he pushed himself deeper. Then pulled back. Each time he returned, he buried himself farther. The movements became quicker, shorter, harder.

Liberty met his thrusts, straining and drawing her pelvis upward. Her nails dug into his shoulders and she rocked. So soon after her first release, the second was longer in coming. When she thought she could bear no more, pleasure showered her with white light and she savored the fulfillment he left in her.

Anthony thrust a final time, moaning and collapsing on her damp cushions of breasts. She clutched him, feeling him throb inside her, wrapping her legs around his hair-roughened thighs and holding him close.

"I love you, Anthony." She couldn't help saying it, hoping he would repeat her vow in their dreamy world of contentment.

He did not.

For many heartbeats, they lay unmoving, joined together.

Spent and damp, Anthony nuzzled her nape and pressed a feathery kiss on her earlobe. She shivered, dismayed and yet loving him so much, she ached.

Then he pulled away from her and sat up on his heels. He looked much different now. His own body had changed, sated by their lovemaking. Relaxed, he was still magnificent. Locks of brown hair tumbled over his brow. His tanned chest glistened.

"Don't go away." His voice, hoarse and deep, made her smile.

She shook her head. There was no place else she wanted to be.

The bed ropes creaked as he stood and walked to his chest-on-chest. She delighted in the defined cords of muscle on his bare buttocks; the long, sturdy shape of his legs. He opened the top drawer, collected something, and came back to the bedstead with a long velvet box.

Sitting on the edge of the bed, he presented the gift to her. "I want you to know how I feel about you."

Liberty gazed at his offering, dismayed that she hadn't a gift for him in return and also perplexed over its meaning. From the start, she had known he was a man to buy what he wanted. Did he want her so badly? He had never once said he loved her; her qualms returned.

She cautiously lifted the lid. In a nest of blue silk rested a diamond necklace. The gems had been cut in squares and set in gold. They caught the candlelight, sparkling off the walls and shimmering in her hand. She lifted her lashes to see him expectantly staring at her, waiting for her response to such a luxurious token.

Words stuck in her throat. Was this his way of gratifying her without saying he loved her? Her voice distant, she said, "Thank you, Anthony. 'Tis beautiful."

He kissed her, not knowing the necklace had just sent her doubts soaring.

Chapter
17

THE NEXT MORNING, LIBERTY AND ANTHONY SAT ON THE FLOOR of Anthony's bedchamber—their bedchamber—sharing a private breakfast that Quashabee had fixed for them. Anthony spread out linen clothes and made a picnic of sorts.

Liberty in her wrapper and Anthony in his blue silk banyon, he poured her coffee and tea for himself. His long hair disheveled and his expression serious, he said, "I've abandoned my former pursuits. I vow never to drink again and this time I will not. 'Twill be hard for me and I may become short-tempered, but I swear to you I will be sober until my dying day." He nervously tapped his fingernail on the edge of his china saucer. "Having never been in trouble with the bottle yourself, I'm sure you won't understand my moods."

She tried to say she would but he silenced her.

"I won't burden you with my efforts, for you cannot be my crutch anymore than Feathers has been for the past ten years. I have to do this on my own."

His severe tone didn't allow her room to dispute him.

Anthony reached for Liberty's hand. "When you left me in my bed the other night, I had a dream. A series of dreams. You were in them. So was Feathers, your aunt and my grandsire. My barber's voice came to me, too. Perkins's also. But it was you, Liberty. You who came to me with such clarity, you made me realize my life has been nothing but an illusion."

She squeezed his fingers.

"No one person or incident made me drink as I've always thought. 'Twas my own weakness that reached for the bottle. My own way of blinding what had happened to my father."

"And your mother? Do you still think of her as dead?"

"Nay. A gross injustice on my part. I should write her, but don't know what to say. I've so recently come to know myself, how can I know what she expects of me?"

"I think she'd want you to be yourself. Her son." Liberty brushed her thumb across Anthony's. "And John Perkins. You said you dreamed about him."

"Aye. He's known all along about my weakness. He's spit my incompetency in my face enough. All these years, he was no doubt laughing over my addiction. But there's still time. He hasn't won. Not yet."

"Anthony, can't you be done with him? Let things rest as they are? What difference will it make if you go after him?"

"'Tis been in my blood for too long. I will ruin him, Liberty. And when I walk away, I'll have complete freedom."

"You have me, Anthony." She pressed her cheek to his shoulder and he held her close. The old problems that led him to drink were still with him. His intentions to destroy John Perkins could get him into trouble and she prayed he would mind his shipbuilding more than his revenge.

Going into Anthony's study the next day to borrow some ink, Liberty found Anthony working at his desk. She'd seen his hands tremble as he examined a document. The paper rustled. Frustrated, he dropped the parchment and cursed, pulling his glasses down the bridge of his nose and tossing them on a stack of ledgers. She'd opened her mouth to say something, but he growled at her to leave him be.

She collected a spare inkwell and left him. A mixture of hurt and resentment poured into her heart. His need to alienate her was unreasonable and she'd wanted to criticize, then she remembered how much he must be hurting, too.

Quiet patience, tolerance and understanding would be better than words of sympathy.

Liberty stood on the veranda at the rear of Fielding Manor watching the gathering of laborers on the flat river beach. Anthony had completed his snow rig and earlier this morning his band of shipwrights and carpenters had set her afloat. It had been a grand sight and the men who'd toiled over her made a big celebration over the launching.

The autumn day was glorious for such an occasion. A light wind ruffled the small waves lapping at the shoreline. Tankards of ale were passed around and everyone toasted. She had been down there when Anthony was offered a foaming cup; he'd refused, immediately occupying himself with chores.

Among those who'd come to wish the ship well were Thomas Fielding, Aunt Ophelia, Mister Feathers, the handful of servants Anthony employed—including Tobias, and the reed-thin Quashabee whose apron fluttered in the breeze. In her shallow pocket, the handle of a pistol caught the daylight and glinted.

Montgomery Bennet and his daughter, Eden, had arrived to watch the festivities. They brought with them a captain to sail the rig to Williamsburg. The Bennets would return home by coach.

Eden had worn a gown of bold crimson with a deep stomacher. Her cosmetic white complexion and dusted hair set the red off as if the frock were made of fire. Liberty thought the woman, though short on good nature, undeniably pretty.

She and Eden had exchanged no words, but when Liberty had been close enough to her, she'd smelled narcissus on Eden. A jeweled coffer dangled on her wrist by a gold chain. It had been strongly impregnated by perfume paste.

She had been on her own to enjoy the show, Anthony being too busy to be by her side. She'd stopped to chat with her aunt when she caught Eden gazing at her. The look in the other woman's eyes didn't carry nearly the venom it had at the masked ball. Only a vague spark of harmless jealousy was reflected in her face. The snub didn't disturb Liberty Anthony may not have made infinite vows of love to her, but she knew he did not love Eden Bennet.

Wearing a new gown of her own, dimnity-looped emerald chintz, Liberty had strolled up to the back porch to fetch her fan.

It had been a week since her wedding and things at Fielding Manor had gone on much as they had in the past. With small catastrophes and contrary inhabitants.

Anthony had given Liberty another billiard lesson and the ball she'd struck flew through the window and broke a pane. The cook shot a hole in the flour bin—weevils. Aunt Ophelia and Mister Feathers had a secret of some kind, but wouldn't breathe a word of whatever it was. Thomas and Anthony had quarreled one night after supper over a woman named Elizabeth—Liberty later found out from Mister Feathers that Elizabeth was Anthony's mother's name. Thomas seemed quite content and full of himself, up to something that had him riding off to town each day. He would not divulge his purposes to anyone.

After Liberty's bridal night, Aunt Ophelia had had a heartfelt discussion with her. She confessed to having arranged for Reverend Fisher to take Colin Prentice's place and her reasons for doing so. According to Aunt Ophelia, Anthony loved her very much and he wasn't that bad of a fellow after all. He'd proved himself by little margins. His abandonment of liquor—Aunt Ophelia had not known about Anthony's falling out and Liberty didn't disclose it—his brave confrontation with Captain Lionel Manning, his devotion to Liberty, and his variety of garden edibles at the dining table. And just yesterday afternoon during dinner, he'd asked her aunt her opinion on patriot ideology and the Townshend duties.

Of course, Fielding wasn't perfect to Aunt Ophelia, but he'd become more human.

Liberty picked up her tortoiseshell fan from where she'd left it on a wickerwork table. She sat down in the shade to watch her husband. His height and confident stride set him apart from the rest of the men. Since he'd stopped drinking, he spent more time outside and the tan on his face had deepened. His windblown brown hair was gilded with highlights from the sun. The full sleeves of his snowy shirt blew around his arms as he coiled a line of rope. He wore no coat or waistcoat, his buff breeches molding his backside and thighs, tapering down into the black leather of his jackboots.

She no longer doubted the legality of her wifely status. Each night when Anthony made love to her, her misgivings had broken apart until they'd faded. He could not have fooled her with a sham marriage and then made her his so completely. Anthony did feel something for her, but it still didn't change the fact that he had wed her under duress.

She leaned her head against the chair's back. Looking at Anthony now, he seemed to be at ease with the world. Sunbeams lent him a fervent glow of generosity as he laughed at something Jacob Miser said to him. The kind distinction gave her a pleasant view as he jaunted toward the foppishly clothed Montgomery Bennet and his daughter. The two men spoke, Anthony pointing to the snow rig whose crisp sails had just been unfurled.

Liberty found the common picture of her husband very satisfying. From the start, she'd known he was not an ideal man. She'd fallen in love with his face, then learned of his vast temperament, his addiction and his tortured past.

They shared a certain strange combination of spirits. Like Liberty, Anthony lived by his own rules. He had the heart of a builder and his passion was not for fame or position, but like her with her bees, a true love of creation and the harmony that can be found beneath bustling confusion.

Anthony may have thought himself the Crown's most loyal subject, but beneath that facade, was the best kind of rebel.

Even flawed, he was far more gratifying to watch than her bees.

Anthony shook Montgomery's hand, sealing their transaction. The musty scent of the Elizabeth River filled his lungs and he swore it smelled better sober. After the initial few days of feeling sick to his stomach, his senses had cleared. Everything seemed enhanced. Food tasted finer, his home looked brighter, his eyesight appeared keener.

His wife couldn't have been more beautiful. He caught her staring at him from the porch and he waved. She returned the gesture and he smiled.

Eden dejectedly sniffed, drawing her wrist to her nose to appreciate the delicate fragrance—and to mask her hot tears. She had never cried over a man in all her life and she would not blubber in front of Anthony.

Her father questioned her. "Are you catching ill again, Eden?"

"Certainly not," she replied primly, blinking her lashes.

Accepting her word, Montgomery shrugged his daffodil-coated shoulders. "Fielding, I'll see you in the spring. I've designs for a frigate."

"I'll look forward to it."

"Congratulations on your new wife."

Eden felt like slithering to the sand. How could her father have rubbed salt in her wounds? They'd been invited to attend the wedding, but she had pleaded serious illness and begged him not to leave her alone in their apartment at the Running Footman. She'd gone on so about her pains his face had paled with fear. He immediately employed a physician to tend her.

They missed the wedding, but it cost her a nasty dose of quinine.

"Shall we go, Eden?" Montgomery queried. "I've given Mister Lamont instructions to have us loaded and ready to depart by three. I shouldn't want to get a late start and have your mother worry."

Eden bit her lip. "In a minute, Father. I would like a private word with Anthony."

Montgomery gave her a placating nod and left them.

A wired curl skimmed against Eden's vermilion-tinted cheek and she pushed the kinky tendril away. "I suppose you wonder what I could have to say to you when I have already said so much."

"That thought has crossed my mind." Anthony folded his arms across his chest and the pit of her stomach churned. She had always thought him the most handsome man she'd ever run across. Though drunk and clumsy, she'd over-looked these facets of his person because he'd been so attractive—and wealthy.

"I know something that would be of great interest to you."

His eyebrows raised inquiringly.

"Two nights ago, John Perkins saw you at the wharves spying on him."

The honey brown of his eyes darkened to molasses. "Explain."

"He said it wasn't the first time he'd caught you. Once before, you were with a tall man who had dark hair. He couldn't make out who he was but he recognized you right off. He said," Eden continued hastily, "he was going to foil you and do you great damage."

Anthony's mouth took on an unpleasant twist. "Why would he tell you this?"

"Because he knows how out of favor I was with you. He thought I would take great delight in his news."

He regarded her with a speculative gaze. "Why are you telling me?"

"You may have rejected me and for that I was spiteful, but you and my father do business. For that reason, I would not have you harmed. I've the power to inform you, and I have."

A cold and calculating expression settled over his face. He took a deep breath and lowered his arms, stretching the tendons on his fingers. She'd just given him monumental information and he looked through her as if she weren't even there.

To her annoyance, she started to blush. "I have to go to my father."

He touched her crimson sleeve, halting her. "Eden, thank you."

His strong fingers on her made her tremble and suddenly she couldn't trust her voice. She answered him with an impersonal nod, then turned quickly and walked away from him as fast as her legs could carry her.

A branch of red candles gave light to Anthony's study. The hour was late, the house quiet. He'd told Liberty he would be up shortly. That had been—he glanced to the mantel clock—blame him, three hours ago.

An ebbing fire cracked and popped. Leaning his elbows on his desktop, warmth spilled from the hearth to heat his right side; in contrast, his left side felt cold. He should put more fuel on the hissing embers, but he felt tired and did not want to waste the effort.

He sipped a cup of weak tea. The brew had turned tepid and disagreeable. A glass of brandy would have been far more soothing to his belly. It was hard being alone and thinking of alcohol. He hadn't intended to pine for his headstrong appetites.

After Eden and her father had left this afternoon, Anthony scribbled a note to T A. Cheswick telling him their plans would have to change and be expedited. If Perkins was onto them, too many lives hung in the balance.

Anthony had given the dispatch to his valet to deliver.

Feathers returned shortly after six to say he'd been unable to find Cheswick in any of the seaman's usual ordinaries. The undelivered note which Feathers returned, lay under Anthony's fist. He picked at the unbroken wax seal, thoughts of his friend's safety coming to mind. Cheswick could certainly watch out for himself, but if the mayor had gotten wind of their scheme, it would change things dramatically

Anthony had spent the better part of the night, going over in his head, the fine details of putting the elaborate game he and Cheswick were playing on Perkins to work.

"I shouldn't have wondered where I would find you." Liberty's voice carried to him and Anthony lifted his chin.

His wife walked into the room, her flowing night coat swirling around her ankles. Her feet were bare and she headed directly to the ottoman in front of the fire grate. She sat, stretched out her legs and smiled at him.

"I lost track of time." He guiltily organized the drafts and compasses spreading over his desk.

"I was worried. I fell asleep and when I woke, I saw you hadn't come to bed." Her black hair drifted past her waist, the tresses hanging in a sleek curtain.

Anthony stacked several vouchers and stuffed them in his glutted top drawer. A newly penned contract captured his attention and he pulled it out before shoving the compartment closed.

Feeling the rough growth of beard on his chin, he met Liberty's gaze. Her eyelids lowered in a sleepy sweep of her thick lashes. Without getting up, he turned his chair to face her "My lateness is a gross error of judgment on my part." He scooted closer "It should never happen again."

Her doubtful face didn chide; she gave him an appealing grin that said he would contradict himself sooner or later. Seeing her now her nearness lifted his spirits.

"What have you been doing?"

He sighed heavily. "Thinking about John Perkins."

"A dangerous subject."

"To be sure, but I've a way to crush him."

"Care to share it with me?"

"I'd rather not." Hurt sprung into her eyes and he hurried to correct his offense with what he hoped would give her great happiness. "I will tell you, just not now. I've something far more important than the mayor to discuss with you."

The green in her eyes brightened. "And that is?"

"This." He held out the slip of vellum for her to take. She did and read the remarks.

"Anthony, what does this mean?"

"I've been commissioned to build a sloop for Quentin Clark. He's given me one thousand pounds in collateral to start it. I've put in the necessary orders for pitch, tar, rosin, turpentine, planks and timber for hulls, masts and yards. While the ship is under construction, though Quentin has secured it for himself, 'tis in my name." Anthony leaned forward and ran his finger down the page. "There. That

315

article says you now own the sloop and will glean all the proceeds. I'm giving her to you, Liberty."

The fireside grew unbearably hot. "This is very generous of you," was all she could manage. Another gift. Like the necklace, it had no value to her. The one true present she'd wanted to receive from Anthony, he'd not given her. Every day, her love deepened and intensified for him. Every day, her insecurities grew. He'd never said that he loved her. He'd been a kind and generous husband, but each of these gifts meant nothing to her without his vow. Were they just another form of deception? A tender facade to cover the void in his heart?

The document slipped from her fingers as he took it from her hand and filed it in his writing box. "I think you'll like being part of the ship's beginning."

"I'm sure I will," she absently agreed, thinking she'd give a fleet of ships if that's what it would take for his declaration. Maybe Aunt Ophelia had been wrong—Anthony didn't love her. He was only fond of her. Why then, did he look at her with so much emotion in his eyes? He openly appraised her, his mouth tilting upward in a fine smile. His open examination made her shiver.

"When I look at you, I feel like I'm drunk—a good drunk."

The odd endearment could only have come from Anthony. "Do you miss it much?" she dared ask. They hadn't discussed his resolution and she saw he was having a rough go of things.

He pushed a shock of brown hair behind his ear. "Only when I'm left to think about it. When I keep busy, I can do tolerably well."

"Then you shouldn't be in here alone with your thoughts. Come to bed."

She stood and lifted her hand for him to take. Without warning, Anthony brought her down on his lap. His chest bumped into her shoulder and she automatically put her arm around his neck. He smelled of musk and wind and wood, the scents she'd come to equate him with. Her pulse lurched and she nuzzled the warm curve between his shoulder and neck. He was so different from her; rigid and compact.

"I can keep your mind off drinking . . ." She whispered the brazen suggestion in his ear, brushing her lips across his earlobe. She felt him quake.

"That you can, sweeting. Quite easily."

Anthony drew her chin up with the tip of his forefinger, then cradled the column of her neck in his wide hand and brought her face to his. He kissed her with a startling hunger, his mouth slanting over hers. The bottom of her stomach reeled in a pleasant way, tightening her muscles.

She opened her mouth to his, glorying in the passion he instilled in her. Her hands slid down the silky back of his shirt, pulling him closer. She loved the feel of his hard chest against her breasts.

Dragging her fingertips up to his hair, she curled them in the soft locks. He groaned and parted the front of her robe. Then he tugged at the dainty bow of her nightgown.

Cool air teased her nipples to hardness. He pulled her more soundly on his lap. She felt his ready maleness straining against the close cut of his breeches, pressing into the soft round of her bottom. His hand found the bare breast she offered him. The calloused pads of his fingers circled the dusky crests. Shafts of drowsy heat shot through her.

She could hardly breathe. Breaking her mouth from his, she gasped, "Let's go upstairs."

"We don't have to." Anthony's raspy voice interrupted her thoughts of running to the secluded bedchamber they shared. He slipped his muscular arm under her legs; the other arm circled her waist tighter and hefted her closely to his chest. He stood and carried her a step to the carpet. He sat her down in front of the hearth, the red-gold lights of fire dancing on her thin wrapper.

To Anthony, she looked like a goddess. A beautiful angel cast in heavenly shades. Her ebony hair clouded around her face, her cheeks flushed. The moist red of her lips called him and he kneeled to kiss her.

She clung to him, raptly and completely. His wife was a sweet torment in his arms. She was a gift to him. A heaven-sent creature who'd saved him from the devil. God knew he loved her more than anything. He'd been trying to tell her, but he hadn't found the words. He'd never told anyone he'd loved them. He couldn't be sure of the right way to say it. He wanted her to know, by little measures, so he gave her gifts. Small treasures to say he cared.

He worshiped her with his hands, running them up the curve of her slender waist and the perky tilt of her breasts. He bent and ran the tip of his tongue around her nipple. He teased the top, drawing her to him by entwining his fingers in her hair. She shook with tiny tremors as she arched her back to give herself to him. He moved to the other nipple and glided his teeth over the puckered offering.

"Anthony . . . please."

The seductive plea burned through him and he tore himself away. He stood and divested himself of his boots. As he striped down, he was entirely aware of the woman watching him. Her gaze danced as it lit on his bare chest and followed his hands as he unfastened the buttons of his breeches and peeled them down his thighs and calves. His desire for her throbbed proudly. He felt a shock of pleasure, knowing his wife didn't find him lacking.

He went to her, the firelight bathing him in hues of bronze.

His eyes captured hers as he dropped to his knees beside her. Slowly he lowered the sleeves to her robe, watching as she bit her lip. The garment fell behind her in a cloud. She was left in the sheer nightrail, the low neckline already sagging and open. The untied ribbons trailed down in a gentle wave, resting on top of each perfect breast.

Liberty reached up and touched his jaw. She slid her fingers over his chin feeling the coarse stubs of his evening beard. He enjoyed her touch, firm and persuasive, as she felt his face. He closed his eyes, and leaned his head back. She mapped a trail from his collarbone, into the mat of hair on his chest, down to the slabs of his rib cage. She took her course lower, his insides clamping and the fiery knot igniting his loins to a nearly painful ache. She outlined his navel, then moved to his erection.

His eyes flew open. His heart and lungs jolted as her fingers embraced him. The heat of her hand and the unsure pressure she applied made a loud moan pass over his lips. "Oh, I'm sorry," she rushed, quickly releasing him.

"No!" He grabbed her retreating hand and put it back. "It feels so good."

She held him gently, as if she were afraid she'd hurt him. He put his fingers around hers and squeezed. "I won't break." He showed her how he liked to be touched.

When Liberty learned the motion, he let her go to stroke her breasts. He teased them mercilessly, abrading the pads of his thumbs over the crowns. He watched as Liberty broke out in a light film of moisture that brought out the fragrance of her perfume; sensual and erotic.

As he increased his assault, so did she. The rhythm of their stroking became a passionate duel. The blood in his veins raged through his heart, pumping and beating until he heard the echo in his ears. Finally, he gave in to the fierceness of their hunger and broke free of her.

He pushed her down into the carpet, lifted the hem of her gown and plunged himself inside the hotness of her. She spread her legs wide, then locked them around his thighs and clutched him close. She matched his driving need, thrusting her pelvis into his.

Their lovemaking was frantic and urgent. Only when he felt the tension inside her snap and she cried out his name, did he seek his release. It came in a hot, blinding river that racked his body with a final thrust.

In the aftermath, he lay on top of her, damp and spent. His breathing raw and hoarse, he kissed her dewy lips. "Much better than a glass of brandy," he raggedly said against her mouth.

Pushing himself onto one elbow, he caught one of her black curls between his fingers.

"Fielding!" The muted call came from the curtained study window, then a tap sounded on the panes.

Anthony swore at the ill-timing of the visitor, his heart frantically beating. "The devil," he grated in a whisper, " 'tis Cheswick."

A look of bewilderment flashed in her fulfilled eyes.

"Fielding, are you in there? The light is on." He rapped on the glass again. "The devil take all, Fielding. Open up. 'Tis to be tonight. Manning wants me to have my ship ready. He said he's got some new recruits. Perkins is to be there. We've got him, Fielding."

Anthony's pulse, still rapid from the exertion he'd just undertaken, soared anew. *Perkins!* They would have him.

"I've called in Ramsey," Cheswick continued. "He's putting his men in place."

"Forgive me, sweeting." Regretfully he pulled away from her, sorely missing the pulsating warmth of her womanhood. "I've got to go." Stalking naked to the window, Anthony pushed the heavy red drape aside. He used the bulk of it to skirt his lower extremities. "Cheswick, quit knocking."

"Lift the sash and let me in."

"Nay. Wait out there and I'll be with you in a minute."

"What are you doing?" The man's gruff voice filled with curiosity. "Why are you bare-assed in your study?"

"Shut your mouth." Anthony dropped the portiere into place, closing off Cheswick's deep laughter.

Anthony strode to the heap of his clothes and snatched up his breeches.

"Anthony, where are you going?" Liberty sat up, her face full of concern, lovely and disheveled in her mussed nightgown.

He stepped into the legs of his pants, buttoning the bottom two fasteners, then grew distracted by reaching for his shirt. He shrugged into the garment, not bothering to button it, nor finish with his trousers. They were tight enough to stay up without the last closures affixed. "I have to go out for a while. I want you to stay here and be a good girl."

"I'm not your pet, Anthony. You may admonish your dog like that, but not me."

"I don't have a dog."

" 'Tis no wonder. Now, pray tell me what you are up to."

Liberty pouted so prettily he could only think of placing

his mouth on those luscious red lips. With great restraint and will, he returned to his task at hand and stuffed his bare feet into the soft leather of his jackboot. "I've waited ten years to destroy John Perkins. Tonight will be my victory."

"Oh, Anthony, I know how much you think you need to, but you don't. Not now."

"I'm sorry." He hopped on one foot while forcing his heel into the snug fit of his other boot. He took purposeful steps to his desk. Lifting the false compartment of his slanted writing box, he recovered a flintlock dueling pistol.

He heard Liberty's intake of breath as she scrambled to her feet. He felt her hand on his forearm.

"Don't do it! Don't kill him."

Checking the priming on the weapon, he assured her evenly, "I don't intend to. This is just insurance. He'll rot in the hell of his own making." The trigger and hammer in a ready position, he shoved the piece into his waistband. Forgetting that he hadn't secured his clothing, the pistol slipped down. He let out a miserable howl.

Liberty circled to his front. "Have you hurt yourself?"

"Plague me, nay!" He wrenched the flintlock out and tossed the offending iron on the top of his desk. "The blasted thing is as cold as the Arctic Sea. I've just frozen my privates."

"Oh, fie! Is that all? I thought—"

"Madam, a man is very sensitive in that region to extreme temperature—as you know."

Liberty blushed.

Anthony made haste to button his breeches and shirt. He withdrew his coat from the settee and pushed his arms inside. "I want you to go to bed. Don't wait for me."

"I will wait for you, Anthony." She circled his neck with her arms and pressed a hard kiss on his mouth. She undid him with that generous symbol of affection. Before he lost his mind, he got away, putting a good foot in between them.

"Do as I say." Snagging his cocked hat from the globe of his cold hurricane lamp, he fit it on his head. Her forlorn look followed him out of the room, melting over his back and confusing him out of sorts. He had to put the memory of her behind him. He would share all his tomorrows with her. But for tonight—

He'd waited a lifetime for tonight.

The night's blanket closed around Anthony and Cheswick as they huddled on Boush's Wharf. Out of sight behind crates and casks, they waited. Water lapped softly against the pilings. The creaks and moans of timbers from ship's hulls rising and falling on gentle waves, stretched out into the darkness. Anchored not ten paces away, the ducking stool. In the light wind, it swung as far as the rope-lashed axis would allow, then squeaked back again.

"They should be coming out soon." Cheswick's wild mane blew in front of his glittering black eyes. "Ramsey said he couldn't leave the men in too long or they'd really be soaked."

"Aye." Anthony's gaze narrowed on the tavern up from the wharf.

The Spanker—the favorite spot of the roving Norfolk tars. The sailors that drank there were usually hearty types. Men without families who put into port for honest work. It took special sailors to navigate the perilous waters of the Perquimans River or the mouth of the Chowan, from there to Albemarle Sound and Powell's Point, risking running aground on one of the islands of Currituck Sound or stick on the sandbars passing through the inlet. Not just any lackey could do it. In his investigation of John Perkins, Anthony found out it was these men that the mayor had singled out. They were skilled and they were harder to trace as rarely anyone inquired about their disappearances.

Last night, Perkins and Phillip Hawker had a meeting in Perkins's warehouse. Then, six men stocked a large rowboat with goods, and rowed it late at night to Hawker's cutter, the *Tabitha*. Hawker in turn, called on one T. A. Cheswick to captain the ship north when the time came.

When Anthony had first seen this sly expedition, he couldn't believe Perkins would run such a foolhardy risk by showing himself to the handful of miscreants handling the loading and oars. The man had to be stupid beyond measure. Either that or he didn't trust Hawker and was forced to keep watch on him.

Cheswick and Anthony had looked on from afar as the belly of the *Tabitha* sank deeper and deeper into the Elizabeth River. By the week's end, the ship's hold was ready to burst.

As Anthony now watched, he thought of the dozen militiamen inside the sleepy tavern disguised in filthy sailor's garb and pretending to be drunk as fowls. They would stumble out into the foreboding night and be targets for Perkins and his ensemble of men.

As Anthony ran over the plan in his mind, he checked off its components. Lieutenant and Chief Commander Ian Ramsey had gone along with this plot, wanting to flush out Perkins and see him caught once Anthony had relayed his information. He'd thought of everything. This time, there would be only success. Years of waiting and now . . . at last . . . the trap had been set. All they needed was a foot to step in it and snap it closed.

Like a beacon, the door to The Spanker opened. A dim wedge of light spilled out in a silent signal as the group of spurious tars swayed and wobbled. Disguised in knitted Monmouth caps that hung low over their brows and the baggy petticoat trousers of the trade, they looked genuine and unrecognizable for who they really were.

All except for Ramsey.

His military walk had not escaped him and though he put on a good drunk, he carried himself with precision. He began singing an obscene tune, his deep-timbred voice engulfing the staggering group.

Anthony felt for the pistol tucked safely in his breeches, then he nodded to Cheswick. They left their hiding spot and crept over the crate ridden wharf. Slowly, stealthily they bore down on the group, ready to spring on their foe.

Without warning, a half-dozen swarthy clothed sailors descended upon the lone tars. Anthony dug his heels into the ground and charged ahead. His heart thundering inside his chest, he looked for one man alone. *Perkins*. He knew he'd not find him in the center of things. The fighting had broken out right away and Perkins, who'd eluded this moment for so many years, was bound to slip out the instant the militia unveiled their arms and began the swift, systematic overpowering of the company of kidnappers.

Sprinting toward the edge of the crowd, Anthony heard Cheswick behind him, his boots pounding the earth. Cheswick veered and Anthony stole a quick glance over his shoulder to see his earringed friend catch hold of the fleeing Phillip Hawker and tumble him down.

Ignoring the clash behind him, Anthony ran into the maze of dockside buildings, his cocked hat sailing from his head. Perkins was near. Anthony sensed it, felt it. For ten years this man had haunted him, hounded his dreams. It was Perkins's face at the bottom of every cup he'd drained. Blood surged through Anthony, exciting him and fueling his muscles with energy.

Ahead, a scrap of material. Blue. The hem of a flared coat whipped around the corner of a storehouse.

"Perkins!" Anthony roared the name, vengeance propelling his legs.

He rounded the corner and clutched hold of the building's edge to stop himself from overrunning into the river. Nothing. No sight of Perkins.

Anthony's labored breath rasped in his ears, obscuring his sense of hearing. A noise to the right? He jerked his flintlock free and swiveled, his left hand steadying the gun. Only the water lapping at pier.

Dry heat burned his throat. He took a cautious step forward. The weathered boards beneath his boots groaned and he froze. A dim-glowing lantern swung above his head, the wire hanger rattling against the building. He'd barely given it a glance when he caught the glint of a blade in his outer field of vision.

Perkins lunged at him, putting his squat weight into thrusting his knife. Anthony had just enough time to dodge the pointed weapon and slam the short barrel of his pistol on the side of Perkins's forehead. Though the force of the blow hadn't been lethal, the impact knocked the man's tricorn and periwig off. Stunned, Perkins fell onto his knees, the knife slipping from his grasp.

Perkins lifted his hand above his ear. Blood oozed from a gash, slicking his hair and spreading over his fingertips. Seeing the crimson stain on his fingers, he reeled. "Come fair, come foul . . . Fielding, you have maimed me."

Anthony's chest heaved from the efforts to quell his racing heartbeat. "I have spared your life," he managed in a tone clogged with emotional scars. Blind temptation coursed through him and slowly, slowly Anthony raised the pistol until he aimed the flintlock directly at Perkins's head.

A sob escaped from John Perkins's throat and his blood-smeared hand crashed over the lace at his neck. "Divine Grace, Fielding, don't dally with me!"

Without his proper curly white wig, the mayor's prim appearance had been reduced to that of a sniveling common man. His thin hair bore streaks of gray, balding at his crown.

"Dammit." Anthony's knuckles had whitened on the trigger. His arm shook and his breath stilled in his lungs. With all the will he could muster, he lowered the gun to his side. He sucked in air, struggling to calm the rage that rocked him. "I needed to see if I could stop myself."

"You poor wretch, *what if you hadn't?*" Perkins's lips quivered and he clutched the side of his head. "Mercy, I'm in great pain! The devil take you, Fielding. Let me go so I can seek my physician. Godamercy, I demand it. I am the Worshipful John Perkins Esquire Mayor!"

"You are nothing." Anthony's tone was edged with steel and was without a single vestige of sympathy. The fury in his eyes must have frightened Perkins. He moved for the discarded knife at his knee. Anthony ground the heel of his boot into Perkins's outstretched hand.

Perkins yelped.

"I think not," Anthony said, then he kicked the knife out of Perkins's reach. With a forlorn clatter, the blade fell over the wharf's edge and dropped into the water.

Pocketing the flintlock, Anthony studied the mayor. In his weakened condition, Perkins couldn't possibly overtake him. If the mayor had had another weapon on him, he would have gone for a pistol and shot him dead rather than take a chance on regaining his knife. "Lieutenant Ramsey will be here soon. Before he gets here, I need to know some things."

"I have nothing to say to you, Fielding. This matter is all a mistake. I will walk away from it. You cannot prove anything."

Anthony ignored him. "Two years ago, I almost had you. All I needed to show was a full warehouse. How did you know I would have it checked?"

Perkins's laugh was strained and he groped for his missing wig. Finding the hairpiece he latched it atop his head and did his best to rearrange it; his attempts left the wig askew. Under the lamp's muted cast, blotches of crimson smudged his false hair. "Ah, that. I made a friend of His Majesty's Exchequer. He took half of what I had."

Anthony shook his head. " 'Tis no wonder the man left his post shortly after."

"Why wouldn't he? He'd been soundly paid for his troubles. But I dare say, Fielding," Perkins winced as he tended his wound, "you cost me."

"I stopped you for a time."

"Perhaps. But I've made up for it."

"You are caught now, Perkins."

"Caught at what?" He smirked, furtively dabbing the cut on his head causing his periwig to slip farther.

"Smuggling. Kidnapping. Treason. 'Tis a lengthy list."

"I dare swear, you can't prove any of it."

"I couldn't prove it before. Manning never talked and the ones arrested with him didn't know you were involved."

"A pity." Perkins blotted his wound with the cuff of his sleeve. "My handkerchief . . ." Wiggling his fingers inside his outer pocket, he produced a linen square and put it to the side of his head. "I am in pain, Fielding. You shall pay for it."

"I doubt that. You've been seen by six scurvy seamen, Perkins. How daft do you think me or them? They will talk to the militia and say who you are."

"Ha, they cannot speak." His laughter wavered. "Don't look at me as if I'm mad. You think I would show myself to men who could utter my name? Those six cretins have all had their tongues cut out by pirates. Why do you think I abided them?"

Anthony felt a tick in his jaw. He would not be fooled. "They will write your name—"

"They cannot read nor write—"

"They will point," Anthony returned, jabbing his own finger at Perkins, "to you. And if they will not, Hawker is as good as exiled. As we speak, the Royal Navy has boarded his cutter and in the hold they will find a gallery of goods meant to be shipped without the proper duties. And you, sir, will go down with him."

For the first time, panic rioted over the mayor's pale face and his soiled handkerchief limply dangled from his fingers. "I shall not."

"You shall pay dearly for your disloyalty to England and your dishonor to this provincial town."

John Perkins's head slumped forward and his shoulders shook. "Fielding, I am in pain. Allow me to . . ." His hand moved for the inside of his coat.

"Hold!" Anthony roared, taking a step closer. He hadn't thought Perkins further armed, perhaps he'd been saving one final move in this veritable game.

Perkins lifted his chin. "'Tis a drop of comfort to alleviate the pain. The pain, Fielding. I cannot stand it." He fit his fingers through the lining pocket and pulled out a flattened crystal flask trimmed with thin silver. "Fine claret. 'Tis a favorite of yours. Remember how you used to drink it while watching my house?" He uncorked the elegant holder and brought the rim to his lips. Taking a slow and steady pull he sighed. "Ah, 'tis like a whore it pleasures me so." He lifted a blood-crusted brow. "Take some, Fielding. You know you want to. Drink it. Let the claret fill your belly with warmth and that comforting feeling you crave. Take it . . ."

Perkins lifted his hand and fit the flask into Anthony's palm.

Reflexively, Anthony's fingers curled around the flat receptacle. The vapors of claret climbed into his nostrils, wooing him, seducing him. The instinct to take a drink was so strong he moved his hand a fraction toward his mouth.

"Take it," Perkins cunningly prodded, the whites of his eyes wild and flashing.

As the rays of the lantern flickered above Anthony, they caught the clear flask. The amber liquor inside shimmered and beckoned. He could see his past in that liquid, the laughter, the good times, the seductive illusion that he could drown out his pain.

Something inside Anthony snapped. He hurled the flask at the planked ground. The delicate holder splintered, a thousand shards of glass glittered around his boots. Each piece was a sharp reminder of the days, the hours, the minutes wasted on the container's lure. It had all come to this. The simplest of powers. The power to simply turn down temptation. Anthony stiffly muttered, "Go to hell."

"With your father," Perkins called, measuring the words slowly. "Your mother wasn't worth dying for. She serviced me poorly, resisting so I forced—"

Anthony dove, clamping his hands around Perkins's sagging neck. Violence tore through him and he strangled and squeezed, choking the life from Perkins. He could kill him. He knew that he could. The man had just confessed to raping his mother! Years of thinking she'd entered into an affair with him. The bastard had raped her!

Rough hands grabbed at Anthony behind his back, digging into the collar of his coat and pulling him off the wheezing Mayor Esquire.

"Don't do it, Fielding," Cheswick's words came out of the darkness. " 'Tisn't worth soiling your hands with his blood."

Ramsey descended on them with several men. He ordered two of them to pull the coughing John Perkins to his feet and shackle his wrists. The icy cold sound of metal links meshed with Perkins's choking snarl, "You will not chain me like an animal!"

He tried to bolt, but Anthony checked him, steadying Perkins's forearms so that the militia could bond him. "You are caught." He inched his knee up into the mayor's groin. "This is for my mother." Anthony dug his knee in deeper.

"Godamercy!" Perkins screamed. "Get him off me!"

"And this is for my wife." He rammed his leg up with a hard shove.

Perkins slumped to a near faint. He panted in great gasps, his face turning red. It took him long seconds to get his voice back. A look of recognition swept across his pallid face. Weeping his anguish, he tilted his head at Anthony. "It *was* her! The slut from the Running Footman."

Anthony backed away, not trusting himself in the man's presence. He nodded to Ramsey, passed him by and moved to the railing of the wharf. Gripping his fingers around the slivered wood, he gulped intense drafts of night air. His lungs needed to be cleansed; he needed to cool his temper.

Cheswick walked up to him. "Ramsey will need us to sign depositions."

"Aye." He stared out at the inky river, waiting. His breathing slowed, the anger draining in increments until the soft sigh of his breath matched the song of the river. He wanted relief. He'd spent ten years of his life plotting this moment. Surely there must be release.

Beneath him, glass ground under his heels; the wooden pier creaked, its pilings rumbling in anguish or laughter. Above him, the vague moon glinted, passing slivers of light on the river's small wavelets. And within him, nothing. No joy, no sorrow, no blessed slap of emotion.

He waited for relief to hit him.

It never came.

Chapter
18

ANTHONY CAME HOME TO THE FIRST CROW OF THE ROOSTER. THE entry doors to Fielding Manor burst open before he'd reached them. Liberty ran into his arms and kissed him, worried tears glistened on her cheeks.

She led him into the house, gently taking his hand and climbing the stairs with him. Once in their bedchamber, she undressed him and put him to bed. He fell into an exhausted sleep and didn't wake until the late afternoon. Liberty brought him a tray of vegetable pie, hot tea and shortbread which he ravenously ate while retelling her the events of Perkins's capture. She kissed him repeatedly, saying how glad and proud she was.

Anthony rang for his valet to bring out the metal tub. Feathers filled it with steaming water, got towels and a cake of soap. He dutifully asked his master if he requested his services. Anthony declined. The manservant bowed with a starched smile and left them alone.

Liberty disrobed and joined Anthony in the bath. She massaged and soaped his shoulders and neck with a cloth; she washed his untamed hair. They touched and comforted each other. The smallness of the tub didn't prevent them from satisfying one another until the water had grown cold.

As sunset burnished the western sky in streaks of blue and orange, they walked hand in hand into the parlor.

Ophelia sat in the reading chair, her spry fingers fast looping her knots. She inclined her head, the colossal tower of her fuzzy apricot hair growing lopsided. "If I may speak freely, 'tis long past the waking hour."

"That it is, madam." Anthony allowed her quip with a grin. "And so freely spoken."

"Quit toying with me, Fielding. You may have the lawful right to trifle with my niece, but not me. Watch yourself."

"I shall take your warning to great task."

Liberty liked the harmless banter between her aunt and her husband far more than their heated debates which had considerably subsided. Everything had fallen into place so perfectly. All except Anthony not telling her he loved her. Happiness claimed her so completely, she would have gone on without his pledge of devotion. But she sensed there was a place in his heart for her. Or had his heart been empty for so long, he would let no one in?

"Ophelia, I have been wondering about your salon." Anthony sat down in the window seat and crossed his legs at his ankles. His damp hair curled on the short collar of his navy brocade coat.

"What about it?"

"I've been thinking 'tis time you open up shop."

Ophelia's pale brows rose in question.

"Aye. 'Tis not just for your own delight, but mine as well. Mind you, I have grown fond of you, but your lady friends invading this house and my study with their shrill chatter is getting on my nerves. The smells of perfumes and hair tonics overwhelm me. And your use of my valet as a headpiece to show your latest colors is ludicrous. 'Tis just not to be born any longer. Therefore, I've seen to your shop."

"What?" Ophelia's painted lips pursed.

"'Tis a building right on Main Street where the country road leads out of town. The corner is heavily trafficked and I'm sure you'll be in constant demand. You needn't ever worry about rent. The shop is paid for. You own it, madam."

Liberty was too startled by his proposal to offer any objection. Anthony's generosity was too much. Aunt Ophelia would never accept such a suggestion. It had been her dream, her goal to earn the money to start her own business, to work her way to success.

"'Tis very kind of you, Fielding." Ophelia dropped her knots, her blue eyes brimming with tears. She dug through her endless yards of ribbon. Satin trimmings spilled around her as she sought her dainty handkerchief in the folds of her bolstered hips. The enamel spool on her lap rolled to the floor. She found the linen and blew her nose. "I knew you were the type of man to be thrown off a roof. What are you trying to do to me?"

"Naught, madam," Anthony returned quickly, apparently alarmed he'd upset her.

Sniffing, Ophelia blinked her lashes. "I'm not easily reduced to crying. I shouldn't like you to make me again. At least not until I hear of your upcoming firstborn." She brushed her tangled hobby from her voluptuous purple skirts and stood. Walking to Anthony, she patted his sleeve with curbed affection.

His rugged face softened by degrees and Liberty thought she saw an awkward flush creep up his neck.

"I accept, Fielding. Thank you."

Amazed by her aunt's consent, Liberty began to wonder if there was anything Anthony couldn't do. He'd just created a miracle.

Liberty silently recognized the undeniable and dreadful facts. Another gift, another way to say he cared without having to say it. His maddening method of going around those three words wore on her. She would surely go crazy if she didn't know. And she was tired of waiting. She would just have to ask him right out how he felt about her. Did he love her? Aye or nay?

About to ask him to accompany her for a private walk, she heard a coach rattle up on the drive. It came closer and circled into the courtyard. Liberty went to the window behind Anthony to stand next to her aunt who peered out with the same interest as her husband.

The hooded equipage belonged to Anthony. The one he'd used to kidnap her in. Tobias was at the reins, looping them around the brake lever. He hopped from the driver's box and advanced to the lacquered door to undo the latch and pull down the steps. Thomas emerged, the corners of his eyes creased by a thoughtful smile. Once on the ground, he turned to help another passenger out.

A stunningly beautiful and statuesque woman who appeared to be in her middle forties, put her hand in his. She wore a full ruched cap, tied under her chin by a wide pink ribbon. She had rich brown hair that cascaded in taped curly rings. Her complexion was not pale as the fashion, but had a rather unconventional tan to it. She gripped a funny pink walking stick. It looked to be made of oiled muslin, full at one end and narrowing to a gathered point at the other.

Liberty surveyed the woman kindly. "Do you know her, Anthony?"

"Aye," he answered, long seconds passing. "She's my mother."

Elizabeth Fielding swept her gaze over the imposing manor that had once been her home. It looked the same, and yet it didn't. The structure had fallen into disrepair, though it appeared someone had made a recent effort to clean it up.

Vines and shrubs were overgrown and in poor care. The trees had gotten bigger than she remembered, their spread branches dark in the growing twilight. She looked to the house once again, taking in the eaves and woodwork in sore need of paint. Around the windows, there—she abruptly held her thought, her heartbeat skipping. Had it been him behind the pane? Or had her mind played a trick on her? He'd be so different. Would she know him?

Of course. A mother would always know her son. He was a part of her.

Thomas guided her up the marble stairs.

She suddenly had great reservations about her unannounced trip. Her father-in-law had written her that Anthony was to be married. She decided to break her silence and come see him take a bride. But her ship had been caught at sea in a storm, detaining her by several days; in fair weather, she would have reached Norfolk in four weeks. She'd only just landed this afternoon, finding out Thomas had been coming each day expecting her arrival.

Now that the moment had come to actually face her son, a shiver of panic twisted around her limbs. Would he push her away? Could she suffer his dismissal? She seemed to be more afraid of herself than him. The house aroused old fears and uncertainties. It was time she told Anthony the truth whether he wanted to listen or not. John Perkins could no longer harm them.

An immaculately dressed manservant opened one of the double doors. She recognized him as Mister Feathers, the valet Anthony had engaged a year before her departure. Even at the tender age of fifteen, her son had said he no longer required the services of his tutor and insisted on his own man to tend him. Willful, then. Would he be spiteful now?

"Mister Feathers." She nodded at him and he cracked an infectious grin.

"Lud! 'Tis you, good Mrs. Fielding!" He bent at the waist quite severely, then stiffened up straightaway. "Forgive my poor language, madam! 'Tis quite a shock!"

"I'm sure I am, Mister Feathers."

"Feathers, see to her baggage." Thomas crossed under the oak doorjamb.

"Very good, sir!" Feathers rushed out of the house, passing Elizabeth in a dash of his coattails. "Very good, indeed, sir!"

Elizabeth entered the vestibule, the ghosts of her past looming up before her. Nothing had changed. The walls were papered in the same pattern she'd chosen nearly fifteen years ago. The diamond design had dulled and faded some with age. A vase of meadow flowers decorated the table at the base of the stairs. A woman's touch.

How many times had she walked over these floorboards

with Richard by her side? It seemed so strange to be here without him. She'd gone on these ten years missing her husband, but not searching for a replacement. She could never love anyone as she had her beloved Richard. She was destined to live out her days without remarrying. It didn't sadden her that she would be alone. She'd found her peace on the island of Antigua. Richard was there with her in spirit and she visited his grave site faithfully. He'd sailed home with her on the ship in his coffin; he'd been laid to rest in his family churchyard.

Seeing this entryway as it stretched in many directions to lead her to the receiving room, the hallway, the parlor . . . and the study, Elizabeth was filled with more than a sense of nostalgia. She'd not only come home to her son, she returned to a frightening part of her past. John Perkins. He was in this home.

It had taken her a long time to stop grieving over Richard's death, but even longer to stop the nightmares of what John Perkins had done to her.

"Anthony, come here." Thomas flung open the parlor door and Elizabeth felt as if her breath had been cut off. Her pulse shot through her body, darting into her fingers and toes. The hold she had on her quitasol faltered and she almost dropped the Eastern umbrella.

The tension that had been building all day rendered her motionless. There he was, by the window. He slowly rose to his feet, tall and fully a man. Silence loomed between them. She ignored everything about him except his face. She studied the smooth planes and sculpted bones. The skin browned by sun and weather, aged to an adult face. Gone was the son she'd remembered. This man's visage was lined with grief and torment. Had she done this to him?

Anthony's honey brown eyes judged her much in the same way she did him. His eyes told all—engraved with pride and endurance; he was his father's son. He had Richard's nose and mouth, but his eyes were hers. They shared the same painful emotions.

Her eyesight blurred and she felt dizzy· The long anticipa-

tion of this meeting made her faint and breathless. She
hadn't found her land bearings yet. The close walls seemed
to be whirling around her head.

"Elizabeth!" It sounded like Thomas's voice came to her
from the end of a tunnel.

"Thomas?" Blackness. A firm arm fit around her waist
and she was helped to a chair. A large, comfortable armchair. She'd closed her eyes against the nausea, but now
opened them. She saw color. Everywhere. Ribbons. Dozens
of them.

She brought her chin up. Surprisingly, it was Anthony
who had caught her. She stared into his eyes again. Those
brown and dauntless orbs that challenged her to speak. She
dared not. What could she say that she hadn't rehearsed a
dozen times? What his answers would be? It had all come
down to this moment and like a petrified child, she'd put up
her barriers.

He must have seen them spring to life in her gaze, for his
pupils narrowed with confused turmoil. He rose from the
knee he'd been on and stood, placing his back to her. His
shoulders, wide and full, quaked as he ran his hand through
his untied hair.

Her mind burned with unbidden memories. She had
come to the point where their relationship had to be
resolved. She couldn't postpone it another minute. Whatever he would say, she would endure. "I'm sorry if my coming
has angered you." Her voice was shakier than she would
have liked. "I didn't want this to be unpleasant."

He abruptly wheeled back to her and kneeled down. An
almost imperceptible note of pleading played across his
face. "Unpleasant? I'm the one who put you through
unpleasantness for years by my refusal to hear you out.
Divine Grace, Mother, 'tis me who's sorry! Sorry for every
cruel and unjust thing I've ever done and said to you."

"You were young, Anthony. I should have—"

"If you had tied me down to a chair, I would not have
given you your due respect." Anthony captured her hands
and kissed them. "I thought you had entered into an affair
with *him*. That your being together was your own choice."

Elizabeth squeezed his fingers. "If we can go on, it doesn't matter what happened. 'Tis finished."

"But it *does* matter! I wronged you. I turned you away, not finding compassion in my heart to forgive you. When it was *you*, Mother, who should have demanded my forgiveness by not hearing you out. Will you accept my apology?"

She nodded, not trusting herself to speak. Hot, rejoicing tears trickled down her cheeks. Her son embraced her. He consoled her.

Anthony whispered, "I didn't know how to see beyond my anger. I hid my grief inside and it nearly killed me."

"I should have come sooner. I'd wanted to a hundred times, but I wasn't sure what to say."

"If you had come any sooner, I may not have given us a chance." Anthony sighed. "I missed you. More than I realized."

Together they mourned their separation and Elizabeth knew she'd truly come home.

Later, after supper, Anthony and Elizabeth sat by a fire in the very same room. The tension between them receded with each hour of the clock. Reacquainting themselves would take time.

"She's engaging, your wife," Elizabeth said, sipping the coffee Ophelia had recommended she try. "So is her aunt. I wish I had been here for your wedding."

Anthony rested his forearm on the mantel, absently poking the fire in the hearth. "I agree on all accounts, save the one about Ophelia. Engaging is not the word for Ophelia; impudent 'tis more to the tune."

Elizabeth set her cup on the tea table, not particularly liking the bitter coffee. She watched her son jab at the burning logs. Though they had gotten through an emotional reuniting, they had avoided one subject all evening. During supper, they had been polite and careful to watch what they said to one another. Too many skeletons had lain between them. If they were to be mother and son again, it would take time. "It won't come back to us easily, Anthony."

"I know that." He stabled the poker and faced her. In this light, he reminded her so of Richard, it was painful. "I'm still unsure of myself. I've stopped drinking; it was ruling my life."

"Thomas didn't tell me you drank."

"He's never acknowledged I had a problem. He thought I handled my liquor like anyone else. I don't." Anthony restlessly tapped his thumb on the mantel. "You have no idea how difficult this is for me to admit."

"I'm glad you think you can to me." If Anthony had had difficulty with drink, then the root of that addiction had to stem from one thing—one man. "Thomas and I know about your involvement with John Perkins's capture. When my ship landed, your grandfather told me the news he'd just found out. The town crier is heralding his arrest all through the town, and your part in it. Being a Christian woman, I shouldn't be glad for what they did to him, but I cannot help myself.

"They tied him to the tail of a cart and marched him to the country wharf. There they tarred and feathered him and set him on the ducking stool and pelted him with rotten eggs and stones. Then they marched him through every street in the town with two drums beating, returning finally to the market house. The Assembly deliberated his fate and ended up throwing him headlong over the wharf. A passing boat pulled him out of the water more dead than alive or he would have drowned. Now he's to face the Justices. Thomas wanted to speak to you about it right away. I wouldn't allow him to, knowing what you thought of him and me."

"But I do know what happened."

"Not from me. Would you like me to tell you?"

Anthony nodded. "I would. If it's not too painful for you." He didn't sit down; he slowly paced the room.

"The day before your father's death, I'd visited the Assembly to incite interest in building a school. On my walk home, John Perkins asked if he could be of assistance driving me to Fielding Manor. Since your father knew him, I saw no harm. Once we arrived, he insisted on escorting me inside. He followed before I could shut him out. He knew your father was not at home. That day, Richard had been in town with some merchant friends of his." Her voice grew vague. "Richard had always forbidden me to go to the Assembly. He said it wasn't a place for women. I suppose I should have listened to him, but . . . I thought I would be safe from . . ."

"Mother, you don't have to," Anthony blurted, his voice shaking faintly. To see the anguish etched on his mother's face killed him. Not only was John Perkins to blame for this, he was, too. Perhaps more so. He'd let her sail away without giving her a chance. He didn't think he wanted to know what happened now; he felt a wretchedness of mind he'd never known, even when giving up his pints. "Please, don't say any more."

"I *have* to say it, Anthony." She gazed at him with tears in her eyes. "Not only for you, but for myself. This house needs to hear the truth." She bent her head and stared at her folded hands. "John Perkins made me go into Richard's study. I'd become quite frightened then and dashed for the bell to ring for my maid. He grabbed it from me and I screamed. He covered my mouth," her voice quivered, "and then he—"

"Enough!" Anthony fell at her feet, cupping her weeping face in his hands. "I won't have you go through this. Not for me. I don't want to hear any more."

"'Twasn't my fault." She bit her lip to control the sobs. "It took me a long time to realize that. 'Twasn't my fault."

Anthony seethed with anger; he felt her humiliation in his fingertips. Clenching his teeth, he swallowed hard. His rage singed the corners of his control and his thoughts raced dangerously to the man who'd done this to his mother. He should have killed Perkins when he had the chance. "It was *not* your fault."

"When Richard returned, he saw my clothing torn and he asked me what had happened. He barely listened once he found out I'd been at the Assembly. He left me then to challenge John Perkins to the duel." She yielded to the compulsive sobs that shook her. "He never came back home to me. I was informed by one of the Assembly of his death and John Perkins told the story in his own way. He said we'd been intimate many times."

Anthony brushed his thumb at the tears on her damp face; he stroked her hair and tried to comfort her. He felt awkward and lacking. He'd dealt with his own misery for so long, he didn't think he knew how to help someone else. If it was enough for him to be with her, touch her, console her and tell her how sorry he was, he would. He'd been grossly unfair and it sickened and revolted him that he'd not gone after her. "I should have given you a chance. Why didn't you make me listen?"

"I didn't want to make you listen. I would rather have had you hate me thinking I'd been unfaithful to your father. I couldn't bear to lose another man I loved over the defense of honor. I would not let you finish the duel that took your father's life."

"You should have let me," he stubbornly whispered. "We could have had ten years together instead of wasted ones spent apart."

"I couldn't take the risk he'd kill you, too." She gulped hard, capturing his eyes with her. "We still have time, Anthony. We *have* another chance. We won't let John Perkins win."

A sense of reliance came to him that this tragedy had not broken their bond. "From where he sits now, the only thing he can win is the hangman's noose."

A week later, Anthony and Liberty, Elizabeth, Feathers and Ophelia congregated at Town Point Wharf to see Thomas Fielding off. He'd made arrangements to sail home to Antigua. Elizabeth was staying on, indefinitely. Liberty admired the fragile relationship that had grown and developed between mother and son.

Thomas held his grandson, clapping him on the back. "I will miss you, Anthony. Take care of Elizabeth. You have many years to make up for."

"I will, Grandsire."

"Elizabeth," he called to his daughter-in-law. She shaded her face with her umbrella, the ribbons on her collar fluttering in the breeze. "Don't worry, I shall have your things sent over as soon as I return."

"Thank you, Thomas." She kissed him on his weathered cheek. "Thank you for making me come."

"Of course. I always get what I want. 'Tis the Fielding nature." He squeezed her hand. "Now you, Madam Liberty, come hither."

Liberty walked to the esteemed old man and smiled at him. "Aye, Mister Fielding?"

"Bah, with that blather. 'Tis simply Grandfather." His debonair mouth curved in a smile. "My grandson—I leave him in your hands, dear woman."

"I shall endeavor to keep him out of trouble."

"Of course you will. Someone with your sensible background will keep him in line. You know, Anthony," he addressed his grandson with a frown, "I'm appalled you kept this dear girl's true identity from me. I've given you ample opportunity to tell me."

A wave of panic washed through Liberty; Anthony said nothing.

"Aye," Thomas gruffed. "I've had my suspicions about her from the start, but only yesterday was I enlightened."

"How did you find out?" Anthony asked.

"You cannot fool someone as sharp as me. I may be old, but I am not blind. When I first saw you," he looked at Liberty, "you were without your bonnet—a cultivated lady would never forget such a thing. A minor point, but one that piqued my curiosity right away. I couldn't frown upon it, for as you see, my own daughter-in-law prefers this contraption. Insists on this great toothpick of hers. A quita— something."

"Quitasol." Elizabeth laughed. "And you gave it to me from your Eastern shipment."

"A dire mistake. I've nearly been stabbed by that thing."

"How else did you know," Ophelia inquired, Hiram at her side.

"Actually, 'twas yourself, Madame Fairweather, that per- plexed me most. You had yourself accepting a servant's favors—no offense intended, Feathers."

"Very good, sir." Though a sneer of doubt lingered on Hiram's lips.

"I wondered to myself, why on earth would a woman of great breeding, or so she says, fawn over a valet? And then there was the matter of Liberty's gowns. Mind you I found favor in your humble attire, but 'twas not adding up to who you claimed to be. I inquired at Madame Penelon's and she said you hadn't a stitch of decent underclothing."

"Grandsire! You didn't!"

Liberty giggled.

"I did," he hotly conceded without embarrassment. "And then out of the blue, the dear girl was outfitted in fine frocks—most becomingly, I might add. 'Twas all sort of peculiar. I may never have fully guessed what was amiss, that is, until yesterday. A knock sounded on the door and not for the first time, I'd been reduced to answering it. Anthony, you must employ yourself a butler," he admonished. "There at the threshold was a woman who likely frightened the bones out of me. She said her name was Mrs. McKeand and she thought I was the butler. She came in spouting let bygones be bygones. She claimed she missed Liberty and Ophelia terribly and said she couldn't live without Ophelia's cucumber paste. I dared not hear more and I shooed her from the house, telling her I would relay the message. I assume you didn't tell this brash woman your stations in this household, for she thought you were maids. She went as far as saying Cyril Lamont had had a change of heart since the mayor had been carted off and he wanted Mistress Liberty back. According to Mrs. McKeand, Lamont said Liberty was the best chambermaid he'd ever had."

"Tut! That McKeand," Ophelia snorted, "'tis just like her to run off at the mouth."

"Then since Mister Fielding knows," Feathers said ignoring Ophelia's outburst, "I've kept mine shut long enough. Sir," he addressed Anthony, "may I present my bride."

"Strike me down, Feathers!" Anthony blazed. "You've tied the knot?"

"Quite tightly," he confirmed.

"When did this happen, Aunt?" Liberty's mouth fell open with pleasing surprise.

"On the very day of your own wedding, lambkin. We couldn't let poor Reverend Fisher go to waste. Not after all he'd been through. I'm repudiating the adage that a woman of my age dedicates her later years to the church. I've far too many good ones left in me."

"Well, well, isn't this all news!" Thomas chuckled. "Feathers, you rascal."

An oarsman docked a small craft by the wharf's edge. "'Tis time to set sail, sir."

"Ah," Thomas reflected with a sigh, "I shall miss you all. But do not despair. I will return in nine months time to hold my first grandchild."

"Grandsire, you expect too much," Anthony warned.

Stepping into the rowboat, Thomas sat down and waved. "I expect it to be a boy. Good-bye, all!"

Liberty squinted, trying to keep her line of vision trained on the formation of billiard balls. The cue stick in her fingers felt much lighter, but it didn't help her game at all. Anthony had had someone named Waller carve it specially. She thrust forward, the smack of balls rolling in all directions.

"Ah-ha," she declared, straightening. "I hit some."

"Bravo, sweeting. May I close the doors now? 'Tis drafty in here."

"You think you're funny, but I don't." In fact, she'd had about enough of Anthony Fielding's good humor and free spirit. His casual mannerisms where her heart was concerned. The moment of reckoning had come. She'd had to put it off because of his mother's visit, then his grandfather's departure. She had to know right this minute if he loved her or not. Great fondness was not enough.

After closing the tall doors, he shifted his weight on those confident legs of his. His molded black breeches made her concentration hard to hold.

This was it. She swallowed. "Anthony, why haven't you said you loved me?"

"What?"

His surprise cut her to the quick. Hadn't he thought she'd

want to hear it? "I've told you I loved you . . . I can't help it when you kiss me like you do. You've never said you loved me back. Do you or don't you?"

He grew uneasy and headed toward his cabinet. The old habits were still with him as he opened the door to the decanters. They were all filled with other beverages now—all but one. He'd had claret put into a blue bottle, just for Liberty or anyone else to enjoy while they played billiards. Anthony would not touch the spirits. "I've never said it to anyone. I don't know how to say it."

"You simply say, 'I love you.'"

" 'Tisn't enough. There has to be more to go with it."

"You're wrong, Anthony." She walked over to him and put her hand on his shoulder. "You keep giving me gifts. They're lovely, but I'd much rather have those three important words. That is . . . unless you don't think you do love me."

"I do."

She smiled, feeling warm and cozy inside. It was a start. "Thank you. You can tell me whenever you're ready. I know you do so I shan't bother you further on it. And stop giving me presents. They aren't necessary."

"Then disregard the one you'll find in our bedchamber tonight."

She groaned. "Please don't think me ungrateful, but what is it?"

"If anyone is to blame, 'tis your aunt." He grimaced. "I sought her advice—a grave mistake. She called me a lobcock and told me to give you something from the heart." He gazed at her. "I planted your bridal ivy. Cook said it was ready. She'd put it in a glass jar of water to get roots to come out on it. May I warn you, madam, 'tis the first time I've ever planted anything. If you care for its life, you'd best tend it yourself."

"Oh, Anthony! 'Tis the best thing you've ever given me. It almost makes up for you not saying you love me."

"Thank you for your unfailing faith," he sarcastically said. "I will say it, then."

"Nay!" She put her hands on his mouth. "I don't want you to say it now."

"Why not?" he asked, his voice muffled by her palm.

"You'd be saying it because I asked you to."

"By my faith!" he growled, putting his hand on her wrist and removing her fingers from his lips. "You are the most confounding creature I've ever known."

"Anthony, do be quiet and kiss me."

His brows rose, then furrowed. He paused, as if in indecision over whether or not to let her boss him around. The idea of kissing her was too much to pass up. He could kiss her if he wanted to. She didn't have to suggest it. And he'd been dying to all night. She'd angled herself so temptingly over that billiard table, he'd wondered if she was purposefully trying to seduce him. Vixen!

He ground his lips over hers and kissed her mercilessly. Her arms went up around his neck. He felt the familiar stirring in him that only she could arouse.

"You know, Anthony . . . I've been thinking," she said on his lips, giving him quick kisses. "My billiard game is hopeless and I doubt it will ever improve enough for me to be a challenging partner. Well, I can't see any reason why the table should go to waste . . . I've been thinking about using it in another way . . ."

He caught her meaning, the fire in his loins blazing out of control. He hoisted her onto the tall red table and climbed up with her. He laid her down and pressed himself on top of her. He kissed her, wanting to feel her naked and yielding beneath him. He loved her most like this, when they were close and made one.

Kissing her temple, he whispered, "I've made such mistakes in the past. My revenge against Perkins didn't give me the release I thought it would. Something was missing inside me—here." He pressed her fingertips to his chest so she could feel the beats of his heart beneath her palm. "I love you, Liberty Rose." He looked into her eyes filled with tears. "It was you, beloved, who gave me my freedom."

Author's Note

Thank you for reading *Liberty Rose*. I hope the subject matter of this book was presented and dealt with in a realistic manner.

A big thank you to all of you who've taken the time to write me and pass on your comments about *Seasons of Gold*. I appreciate them.

It's always nice to hear from my readers. If you have a minute, please drop me a note and you can be assured I'll answer I've recently moved to the Boise, Idaho, area, so my address is different from the one in the back of *Seasons of Gold*. A self-addressed, stamped envelope would be helpful.

Stef Ann Holm
P.O. Box 121
Meridian, Idaho 83680-0121